# LINEAGE

## C. VONZALE LEWIS

BOOK ONE
BLOOD & SACRIFICE CHRONICLES

Midnight Tide
PUBLISHING

# Also By C. Vonzale Lewis

*Blood & Sacrifice Chronicles*
Lineage
Zealot
Tribe

*Novellas:*
Descendants of the Big House

*Short Fiction:*
The Recipe for Cornbread (Link by Link)
The Soulless Ones (Beyond the Cogs)
An Ax for the Storm (Emporium of Superstition)
Harbinger (This Fresh Hell)
When You Hear Them Scream (The Darkest Lullaby)

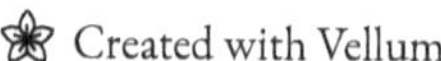 Created with Vellum

*The history of man is shrouded in mystery, magick, and blood.*

*Looking for bright, responsible, career-oriented, self-motivated individuals who have excellent people skills and are able to take high volumes of calls while maintaining a positive attitude. Ability to work with others is a must.*

I glanced down at the advertisement in my hand. I had none of those qualifications according to my last employer—and pretty much all my other previous ones as well. I was, however, a "foul-mouthed, bad-tempered, under-performing"— still didn't understand that one—"sarcastic, waste of space." Although, to be fair, only one of the previous employers actually called me a waste of space, and that was because I had stopped sleeping with him.

This unfortunate lack of options was the reason I stood in the parking lot of Tribec Insurance, smoking the last of my apple-flavored cigars—a habit I learned from my father—wearing a cream-colored dress suit and a pair of matching pumps. I couldn't afford either of them, and I really hated pumps. But I needed the job, so I dressed the part of the career-oriented, self-motivated candidate the ad was searching for.

Most of the jobs in the area required a college degree, or at least several years of experience. I had no college degree, and the longest I'd ever been employed at one job was six months. Thank-fully, Tribec Insurance was always hiring and had no such requirements—a rarity in the uptight community of Alice where Tribec was located.

Through a ring of cigar smoke, I took in the phallic structure that was Tribec Insurance. My eyes landed on the small, stone, pyramid-like shape at the top of the building. It reminded me of an Egyptian Obelisk—a symbol to the god Ra. The Egyptian word for it, "Tejen," meant "protection" or "defense."

Why would the occupants of Tribec Insurance erect a symbol of protection or defense on top of the building?

A slight breeze blew over my bare arms, carrying the salty scent of the ocean and stirring the beads of sweat that had formed on them. My new blouse had molded to my back, and my feet had started to sweat. I was generally used to Tulare Island's oppressive heat, but the anxious jitters in my stomach had caused my skin to flush.

I tried to dispel the nervousness in my stomach. Despite the obvious, I didn't want to show that I was desperate. My best friend Kara spent most of last night trying to prep me for the interview. She advised me to not ask annoying questions, make sarcastic comments, or let my disgruntled attitude show.

Essentially, she advised me to not be myself. There was a message in there somewhere, but I was choosing to ignore it.

Out of our original group in high school, Kara was the only one who was still in my life. The only one who actually gave a damn about me. Marta and I hadn't spoken in years, and as for Steve... Well, it was a long time ago.

I glanced at my watch. Damn. I guess I had procrastinated long enough. I put out my cigar, grabbed my blazer from the front seat of my car, shoved the advertisement back in my overly large purse, and headed for the building. As I walked, I attempted to wrap my head around the fact that I was essentially *asking* Tribec Insurance to let me spend my days chained to a desk, listening to complaints from strangers.

Maybe I should look into prostitution. At least I'd enjoy the job.

Kara also told me to smile a lot, so I pasted one on, pulled open the glass door, and stepped inside. Only to stop dead in my tracks at the entrance.

The walls—painted a burnt gold color that reminded me of the sunset—were lined with Egyptian art. Four glass displays, filled with half-head replicas of deities and artifacts, sat in each corner of the room. Green foliage hung from black ceramic pots near the entrance and the elevator. Something was off about the elevator. It wasn't stainless-steel. No, more like marble. Black marble with gold striations that, at first glance, appeared to be moving. Odd.

And everything, including the guard station—which sat sunken into the foundation in the middle of the floor—was set up in a spherical configuration. Directly behind the guard station was a set of mahogany double doors, with gold Egyptian hieroglyphs carved around the frame. They were also etched around the guard station.

Most people on Tulare Island either practiced one of the four principles of magick or knew someone who did. There was, however, a small group of people who, despite the evidence, still refused to believe in magick. They usually carried picket signs outside of herbal and occult shops, telling people they were going to burn in hell, not realizing they were actually practicing faith magick every time they went to church.

Judging from the set-up of the room, and even the obelisk on the top of the building outside, I could hazard a guess—more like an assumption—that the occupants of Tribec Insurance practiced magick.

Despite my assumption, I couldn't figure out which of the four principles—earth, elemental, mind, or faith—the people at Tribec used. There was, however, a fifth principle—blood—that to my knowledge, no one practiced anymore. And sadly, I didn't know enough about it to recognize any symbols associated with its practice. Yet, symbols from the other four were etched all over the walls. Odd. Especially since people only had the ability to practice one. Not all four.

If it was a job requirement for me to use magick, I was running the hell out of here. I would live in a cardboard box before I got involved with magick. And if I didn't get a job soon, that was exactly where I'd be living. Especially since I refused to move back in with my parents. I had to grow the hell up sometime.

I moved farther into the lobby; the scent of desert sand wafted around me. It had that baked-on smell that emanated off the ground when the sun was at its peak. It was unusual, but the décor could explain the smell. Especially if they added sand to some of the displays for authenticity. The odor that was definitely out of place was the one directly underneath it.

*Blood.* It was faint. I could almost chalk it up to imagination. Almost. If it wasn't so overpowering.

I moved forward cautiously, my heels clicking on the white-tiled floor, as I tried to pinpoint where the scent was coming from. But the farther away from the door I got, the less I smelled it. I turned and started back toward where I'd first detected the smell. A chair creaked, stopping me in my tracks. The space between my shoulder blades started to itch. I turned.

The guard behind the desk was watching me.

I stood there, debating whether or not I should just leave. Yes, I was desperate, but the smell of blood? Was I imagining it? I pulled in a deep breath, trying to find the scent again. Nothing.

*Get it together, Nicole.*

After a short pause, I shook myself mentally and continued toward the guard station with the guard's black eyes boring into me. Sizing me up.

"Can I help you, miss?" He rose to his feet and crossed his arms across his chest.

I placed him in his late twenties. He had a solid frame, close-cropped black hair, deep-set black eyes, and no facial hair. The dark brown suit he wore looked as if it had been poured onto him. Had to be ex-military.

The gold tag on his shirt read "Oliver Strong." It suited him.

"Yes, my name is Nicole Fontane, and I'm here for an interview with..." I set my purse on the counter, ignoring his pointed glare, and pulled out my tattered notebook. "...a Francine Delaporte at eleven."

"Have a seat. I will call someone down to escort you." He inclined his head in the direction of the red leather couch on the right.

"Okay, thanks," I said as I mentally extended my middle finger. Everything about him rubbed me the wrong damn way.

I sat and placed my purse beside me on the couch—the damn thing weighed a ton—and picked up one of the brochures for Tribec Insurance. While I sat there leafing through it, another security guard walked up and blocked my view of the sun. Well, he would have if there had been one inside the building. This burly bastard had tree trunks for arms and a head that resembled a boulder. Did they chisel him from a mountain?

"Ms. Fontane?" the guard grumbled. It sounded as if his voice came from a gut full of rocks.

I stood, which put me at eye level to his massive chest and the name tag pinned to his shirt that read "Duncan Glass."

Maybe when they hired their guards, they assigned them names as well.

"Yes." I tried to push myself up a few inches more. I was already wearing three-inch heels, bringing my total height to five nine, yet this massive behemoth still towered over me.

"Follow me." He spun around abruptly and led the way to the elevator.

I was tempted to salute him or give him the finger—the damn bossy bastard.

*Calm down, Nicole. You need this job.*

Duncan pulled a card from his pocket and inserted it into a slot located on the right side. I guess that answered my question about the oddity of the elevator. Besides the strange composition, they didn't have a call button. They sure did have a high level of security for an insurance company. Maybe they denied more claims than they approved. Greedy bastards.

When the doors slid open, Duncan extended his arm out. "Ms. Fontane."

I stepped inside.

Once the doors were closed, he inserted his card into another slot, and a display lit up with a list of floors.

The number thirteen was among them.

I had once read somewhere that all older buildings either omitted the thirteenth floor or renamed it. It all stemmed from a superstition that the thirteenth floor was unlucky. I wasn't super-stitious, but I did find it interesting they chose to include it.

"They have a thirteenth floor," I said.

"It comes after twelve."

While I was no stranger to snide comments, I really didn't like others using them on me. Bastard.

A few moments later, the elevator doors opened and, thank-fully, deposited us on the seventeenth floor. I followed Duncan to a set of offices in the center of the floor. He stopped at the first door in a row of three that faced the elevators. The silver name plate affixed to it read: Francine Delaporte. After he rapped on it three times, he planted his feet a few inches apart and placed his hands behind his back.

Maybe Duncan thought he was still in the military.

I took in the room while I waited. Cameras inside small black orbs dotted the ceiling. A hazy gray tint covered the windows, allowing minimal light to filter into the room. Industrial gray walls sported a few framed "vonspirational" quotes that referred to "teamwork" and "having a positive attitude." They even had the stupid "Hang in There" poster with a cat hanging off a wire.

Even the partitions that divided the employees' desks were gray. The only break up in the ashen color were the fake wood desks.

It reminded me of a mental asylum.

The majority of the people in the office were women, with a few men thrown in here and there. Did they believe women were more suited to talking on the phone? Either way, everyone in the room was pasty, their eyes sunken in, wearing expressions that suggested they had given up on life. I wouldn't have been surprised if they were all former tenants of the asylum, dressed up in over-sized clothes and forced into the role of "employee."

The fact that no one looked up when Duncan and I got off the elevator supported my theory. They just sat there in their little black chairs, talking into their headsets, all repeating what sounded like the same practiced spiel in monotonous tones, a few minutes behind one another. Like a rolling set of waves crashing against the most boring shore imaginable.

I turned back to Duncan. He still stood at ease in front of Francine Delaporte's door. What the hell was taking this woman so long? My feet were killing me. Like an idiot, instead of breaking the shoes in after Kara left last night, I had curled up on the couch with a bottle of Samuel Adams, contemplating my limited options. My little pity party of one ended at midnight when I realized my only option was one I wasn't willing to entertain.

As I switched my purse from my right shoulder to my left, I caught sight of a faint circular line drawn around the cubicles. I stared at the ground, unsure if I was seeing things, or if there really was a line drawn on the floor. I straightened and moved to the left, trying to follow it. As I stood there transfixed, someone brushed their frigid hand across my exposed neck.

Coldness raced down my spine, and the scent of sand filled my nostrils.

I whipped around.

Duncan was gone.

In his place stood a woman wearing a red pantsuit. Given that she was at least five feet away from me with her hands down at her sides... Who the hell had touched my neck?

Francine extended her hand and smiled. "Hello. Ms. Fontane?"

I stepped forward, my legs suddenly weak, and took her hand. "Hi." I cleared my throat. "Yes, I'm Nicole Fontane."

"I'm Francine Delaporte. Let's get started." She let go of my hand and walked into her office.

I rubbed the back of my neck, trying to warm the sudden chill that had settled there. I glanced around the room. The employees remained at their desks, staring rapt at their computer screens.

A cool breeze circled the room, pulling my gaze toward the ceiling. An air vent sat directly above me.

Before I entered Francine's office, I glanced down at the floor. The markings were gone. Maybe I had imagined them. And maybe the air-conditioning explained the feeling of someone brushing their fingers across my neck.

Yes—for sanity's sake, I was going to go with that.

Just my overactive imagination.

Francine's office was a huge step up from the cold gray of the call center. Bright yellow walls with photographs of what I assumed were family and friends surrounded a large cherry-wood desk that took up most of the small office space.

Burying the unease still brewing in my gut, I sat down, set my purse on the chair next to me, and focused on Francine. She smiled at me again. It was phony, but at least she was trying. I returned a fake grin of my own as Francine shuffled through a stack of folders on her desk.

She was a short woman, battling her body's desire to expand by stuffing a large amount of girth into her red pantsuit that was on the verge of bursting at the seams. I figured she had some African ancestry somewhere by the caramel color of her skin and the curls in her hair, which meant we had something in common —my father was Creole, and my mother, French. We also had the hair in common, although hers was much more controlled. Mine had a mind of its own, and no amount of hair product was going to change it. Believe me, I had tried them all.

Finally, she brought her head up, made eye contact, and launched into her spiel about the company. I kept the smile painted on my face as I learned that Tribec Insurance was founded by the Stewart family in the early eighteen-hundreds. They had grown since then, and now rivaled some of the biggest names in existence today.

She continued, but I tuned most of it out. It was when she stated they only carried medical and life insurance that I actually started to pay attention. As limited as my knowledge was, I still understood that those two things did not go together. Not to mention they were leaving out a number of options that people would need, such as dental and disability.

"Why is that?" I asked.

"Why is what?"

The confused expression on her face had me swallowing hard. I must have thrown her off when I asked a question.

"Why do they carry medical and life insurance instead of just medical and dental or life and disability?"

Francine leaned forward. "That's an interesting question. I can't say anyone has ever asked that since I've been here."

We sat there, staring at each other. I was waiting for the answer, and she was obviously trying to remember where she had left off, if the faraway expression on her face was any indication. She gave up after a few minutes, opened one of the folders on her desk, reviewed it, and then focused on me.

"Well now, what made you decide on Tribec Insurance, Nicole?"

That I needed to pay for the apartment I'd just rented was obviously not a good response, so I went with the answer I'd practiced several times with Kara.

"I feel that Tribec Insurance would be a good place to work, and I'm searching for a stable company in which I can have a bright, productive future." It was all bullshit, but it was nice-sounding bullshit.

Francine tried to hide her eye-roll. A clear indication that she wasn't buying what I was selling. "Well, that's a really good answer," she said, surprising me that she hadn't stopped the interview. "And I see here that, while you've had a vast number of jobs, you have had absolutely no call center experience."

"Yes, that's true."

"So why not choose something more in line with your work history?"

"I wanted to try something that had more of a future in it." She liked my bullshit answer before, maybe she wouldn't mind hearing it again. Besides, Kara and I hadn't worked on this particular question. And I had no idea how to respond.

"Well, I believe you are just the type of candidate we are hoping to hire, and you are still relatively young—only twenty-eight." She pulled a sheet of paper out of a folder with my name written on it. "Can you start today?"

They must have been desperate if she wanted me to begin immediately. I knew damn well that I wasn't the type of candidate they were looking for. And it was written all over Francine's face.

"Sure, no problem."

"Are both your parents living?" she asked.

"Excuse me?" I shifted forward on my seat, ignoring the fact that the movement appeared threatening, and focused on the single drop of sweat that suddenly slid down the side of her face.

"Are both parents still alive?" she repeated much slower as she lifted one eyebrow.

I didn't appreciate the condescending tone. "No, I understood your question. I'm just curious what that has to do with my job interview?" I failed to keep the ire out of my voice.

She studied the paper in front of her. "Oh, well, we need to know whom we contact in case of emergency."

"Yes, they live in New Orleans," I said, lying.

The question bothered me. Asking, "Are your parents still alive?" didn't in any way translate to, "Who do we contact in case of emergency?" I wanted to believe it was just a simple error in wording, but I wasn't convinced that it was.

"And could you provide me their address?" She still had her head down, pen poised above the paper, ready to write.

I had no intention of giving her my parents' real address. And yes, I was being a bit paranoid. "2 Bayou Way in New Orleans." I'd let her figure out the zip code.

She looked up. "Are there any other living relatives or friends that you could list?"

"Do I need more than one emergency contact?"

Her eyes narrowed and her mouth turned down in a slight frown as she regarded me with a contemplative look. After a few minutes of this, she shook her head and scribbled something on the sheet of paper. The chair groaned as she scooted back and heaved up from it. "Now, let me first show you around the call center, and then you can sit with one of the employees to listen to a few calls." She picked up a thick red binder, a headset, a notepad, and a pen.

I sighed as I followed her out of the office. For a moment there, it seemed as if Francine was going to ask me to leave. I tried not to think about the elation I felt at the prospect of her doing that. If I was going to make it here, I really needed to work on my attitude. And my paranoia.

After a brief tour, we stopped next to a man who was a complete contrast to the other semi-dead looking employees.

"Vincent, this is Nicole. I would like her to sit with you for a few calls."

Vincent was a husky man in his late twenties with a mop of dark brown hair, a short unkempt beard, dark brown eyes, and tanned skin. He wasn't wearing a suit like the rest of the drones. Instead, he wore a pair of loose-fitting tan slacks and a white button-down shirt.

He frowned as his gaze went from Francine to me. "Okay," he said finally.

Francine nodded and walked to an empty desk and grabbed a chair.

"Now, sit down here." She positioned the chair next to Vincent. "Vincent can answer any questions about what kinds of calls you will be taking." She handed me the binder, along with the pad and pen. "This is your employee manual. You can read it when you leave."

As I sat down in the chair and placed the heavy binder in my lap, I spotted the gold embossed glyph on the front. It depicted a man standing next to a table, writing on a piece of parchment, with a body laying at his feet. I couldn't make out the various objects in the background, so I pulled the binder closer. The short lines reminded me of people for some reason, all lined up, staring at the man as he concentrated on his writing, seeming oblivious to the body at his feet.

When I looked up at Francine, I caught her scrutinizing me with a mixture of scorn and distaste written all over her face. I narrowed my eyes.

"Yes, Nicole?" She tried to work her face back into the friendly mask she wore a few minutes ago. She failed.

"What does this symbol mean?"

She gave the binder a quick glance. "Well, it's just something the family... Honestly, I never asked." She plugged the headset into the back of Vincent's phone. "Once you've had an opportunity to listen to some calls, we will complete your new hire paperwork." She straightened up and smiled down at me. "Any questions?"

Since she seemed so averse to answer the few questions I'd already asked thus far, asking any more at this point would be a waste of both of our times.

"No, thank you."

She turned and walked away. As I watched her, I entertained thoughts of her too-tight pantsuit suddenly coming apart at the seams. Fucking bitch.

"So, how long have you worked here?" I swiveled my chair around so that I was facing Vincent.

"Almost two years," he said. "I have an anniversary coming up." He picked up an empty family-sized bag of Ruffles. "I hate these things." He balled up the bag and threw it in the trash.

"Why do you eat them?"

Vincent squinted at me with a quizzical expression on his face. As if he was trying to decipher what I'd just asked. Was asking why he ate chips he hated too personal? He turned from me, reached into his side drawer, and pulled out a large wallet. "This was me when I started." He handed me his driver's license.

I studied the picture, my eyes narrowed in on the photograph. The two-hundred-pound man sitting beside me was not the same hundred and forty-pound man featured on the driver's license photo. I looked at Vincent, his driver's license picture, and then the rest of the employees in the call center. Suddenly, that song from Sesame Street that I learned in my youth popped into my head: *One of these things is not like the others.*

I handed him his ID back, and he placed it on the desk in front of us. "I need to keep my strength up, so I have to eat a lot." He put his headphones back on. "I've worked here a long time, Nicole. You should find something better."

"Why would you..."

The phone rang, cutting me off.

"Thank you for calling Tribec Insurance. This is Vincent. May I have your policy number please?" His voice took on a high-pitched sound that in no way resembled his normal bass tone.

I inwardly groaned. They would no doubt require me to sound like a phony-ass as well.

"I don't have a policy number," the guy said.

"Well, sir, let me help you locate it. Do you have your policy paperwork or ID card handy?"

"No."

"Well, let's start with your name." Vincent pushed the mute button. "If you're staying, I have to train you." He peered over my shoulder briefly, and then focused back on me. "You will get a lot of these calls where people don't have their policy number. The best way to locate them is the search field on the side of the screen. If they provide you their name, address, and the last four of their social security number, you should be able to locate them."

I smiled and said nothing.

He unmuted the call. "Thank you, sir. Let me get your address and the last four digits of your social security number, please." Vincent typed in the guy's information.

"Now, I need to place you on hold for a moment while I pull up your account." Vincent glanced at me. "Now, they don't like us using this feature. The company would prefer to have us get the policy number. So, if you can encourage them to locate it, then that would be better."

I nodded. Maybe I should be taking notes.

"Okay, sir. I found you. Thank you for holding. What can I help you with today?"

"It says here on my ID card..."

Vincent pushed the mute button. "I hate it when they do that! Fuck! You heard me ask him if he had his ID, didn't you?"

Again, I nodded. I was getting the impression that Vincent really didn't like his job. Would I end up like him, overweight and angry? Or, even worse, I could end up like the rest of the employees—an undernourished ghost of myself. I scanned the room to see if anyone else heard his outburst. No one was paying any attention. Creepy.

Vincent reached into his desk drawer, which turned out to be a small grocery store, and retrieved another family-sized bag of chips—Doritos this time. His meaty hands shook slightly while he tore into the bag.

The guy on the phone was an idiot. Vincent was becoming more agitated by the minute. Maybe the food was his coping mechanism. I was sure that there were a few alcoholics sprinkled throughout as well.

"Nicole?"

"Yes," I started. "Sorry, I agree, that was a horrible call."

He jerked his chin up, signaling for me to look at his co-workers. "No. Do you see?"

"What?"

The phone rang, cutting off his reply.

"Thank you for calling Tribec Insurance. This is Vincent. May I have your policy number please?" he asked, agitated.

"You people took my wife!"

Vincent grabbed a pen and paper and scribbled down the number that appeared on the display. After he wrote it down, he disconnected the call.

"What's going on?" I asked.

After he tore the paper from the tablet he'd written the number on and folded it, he placed a finger over his lips as his eyes shot up to the ceiling. Before I could follow his gesture, he placed his hand over mine. Something in the way he was staring at me stopped me from pulling away. Desperation filled his dark green eyes. He reminded me of a small, frightened animal who'd been cornered by a much larger animal with no way out.

"They watch us," he whispered.

Okay, so maybe Vincent was a bit of a nut. But then again, there were cameras all over the call center.

"Why do they do that?"

"You'll learn why." He turned away from me and took another call.

I listened to ten more calls after that. Vincent was trying to tell me something about the company, but I couldn't figure out what. No doubt it involved them watching the employees. But in most jobs that was a possibility. So why did he fear them watching him? Was he doing something illegal? Even though he'd *said* I should find another job, I got the impression that's not what he was trying to say to me. Then again, I could be peppering a strange encounter with my own misgivings.

Francine came back an hour later to retrieve me.

As we walked away, I glanced back at Vincent. He was watching me with sadness in his eyes. When he caught me staring, he put his headphones back on and turned away.

What was he trying to tell me? I studied his back for a minute, pondering, until Francine decided to place her unwelcome hand on my arm. I almost lost it. Almost.

"This way please, Nicole."

Reluctantly, I followed the swishy sound of Francine's suit into her office, cursing the stupidity of my life decisions.

Francine had me fill out a mountain of useless paperwork, which included: a W2, employee benefits form, and confirmation I would read the employee handbook. I had no plans to read it, but I signed that I would anyway. And as I went from one form to another, she sat watching me as if I was going to steal her damn pen. When I'd had enough, I glanced up.

"Am I doing something wrong?"

Her head jerked as if I'd slapped her. "No, of course not."

We continued to stare at one another until finally, she looked away. It was a small, petty victory that I relished. And the fact that she didn't escort me out confirmed my assumption about their desperation in filling job positions. Strange, but at least it worked in my favor.

Once the last form was signed, she stuffed them in my folder and handed me a lab slip. "Now you need to go get your physical." She took the pen from me and stood up.

I scanned the form. There were several boxes checked. The urine was understandable. However, the box checked "blood" was not. Not to mention the note scribbled at the bottom to perform a complete physical.

"Ms. Delaporte—"

"It's *Mrs.* Delaporte," she said with crisp pronunciation.

I briefly entertained the thought of telling her to take the job and stuff it in her too-tight pantsuit. After all, the indications of magick practice and Vincent's warning were all the incentives I needed to get up and walk out. But I desperately needed a job—any job. Which meant I would have to reign in my temper. Besides, there might be a reasonable explanation for both scenarios.

I took a deep breath. "Sorry, Mrs. Delaporte. Is this for a drug screening?"

"It was in the paperwork you signed." She put my folder in

her desk drawer. "You will be submitted for a physical, as well as a drug screening, since we are providing insurance."

I suddenly got the impression she didn't want me to see the forms I signed.

"Right, I'm sorry. I thought it would only be a urine test. This slip says blood needs to be drawn." I held the slip out to her.

She didn't even look at it. "Well, yes, blood and urine will be collected," she said with finality.

Now I was fully aware of everything I signed. There was nothing in the documents that stated I had to get a physical.

"Can I see the documents?" I asked, looking pointedly at her desk drawer.

She bristled. "We will provide you a copy tomorrow."

Unfortunately, I had only two choices; I could argue, demand to see them and lose the job before I even got started, or I could accept that she was right. I inwardly sighed and nodded.

"Wait by the elevator," *Mrs.* Delaporte instructed me after providing me my schedule and two additional binders of training material for tomorrow.

As I made my way to the elevator, I turned back to where Vincent was sitting. He was now hidden by the massive number of gray cubicles. I was worried about him, and worried about myself, as well. I really wished I could take his advice, but the choices I'd made in my life left me with very few options.

*Welcome to rock bottom, Nicole.*

The elevator arrived. Another G-man stepped out and zeroed in on me. Wearing the same snug suit as the other guards, he had sandy blond hair, deep-set brown eyes, and minimal facial hair. Though not as large as Duncan Glass, he was definitely trying to catch up. His badge read "George Merced."

"Are you Nicole Fontaine?" he asked.

*Who else would I be?* "Yes, I'm Nicole Fontane."

He nodded once—a simple downward thrust of his chin—and handed me a yellow badge with the word "temporary" stamped across the top. Below the wording was the company logo, and underneath that, my name stenciled in black lettering.

"Your badge is to be worn at all times. You will only have access to the lobby and the training room. If you need to go anywhere else in the building, you will need to be escorted," he said in a clipped tone. "After your physical, we will order you a permanent badge with an additional allocation to enter the call center. If you lose your badge, you will be charged one hundred dollars for its replacement."

"Okay, why would you order another badge after the physical? I thought I was hired. And don't you think a hundred dollars is a little too much to charge for a replacement badge?"

Silence. What the hell was up with these people not answering questions?

I could admit he was probably the wrong person to ask, but he was the only one around. Mrs. Delaporte had disappeared, and I was not going to go find her. Besides, she probably wouldn't answer my question anyway.

George guided me to the elevator, and once we were inside, he inserted his badge into the reader and pressed the basement floor. My heart pounded in my chest—and my internal warning bells starting going off. What was so important about this physical that my future employment depended on it?

Vincent's words popped into my head.

*"I need to keep my strength up, so I have to eat a lot."*

My mind screamed, *Fuck this job*. "Can you let me off in the..."

"Sorry for the confusion," he said, interrupting me. "We only hand out temporary badges until we have a chance to order your permanent badge. They are encoded, so it's expensive to order them."

The elevator door opened.

A chill ran down my back. The smell of antiseptic assaulted my nose. All that was missing was the constant noise and someone being paged over the loudspeaker.

Why would an insurance company have a hospital in the basement?

P anic wormed its way inside of me, twisting my gut into knots. I stepped off the elevator and took in the six rows of padded, pink-covered chairs that sat on both sides of the elevator. A ding sounded and I flinched. I turned around. George stood in the middle of the elevator—expressionless, his eyes trained on me, as the door slid closed.

I was on my own.

I shifted the heavy load in my arms. It felt as if the sterile off-white walls—covered with the company's propaganda, along with a few framed photographs of pyramids and Egyptian Pharaohs—were closing in on me. Again with the Egyptian décor.

Directly across from the elevator was a nurses' station.

A woman wearing light pink scrubs and no makeup, with her blonde hair pulled back in a bun so tight it stretched the corners of her face, sat behind the desk watching me. She had that bright-eyed look seen on either extremely happy people, or those who hadn't been diagnosed as criminally insane yet. I was hoping it was happiness.

Of course, there was a third option... drugs.

Denial wasn't working any longer. Something wasn't right here. The hospital was the last crazy straw. Sweat rolled down between my breasts as I dropped my employee manual and training material on the highly-polished floor, fell to my knees—ignoring the sudden flare of pain—and searched frantically in my purse for my badge. Of course, it had conveniently gotten lost at the bottom. Yanking it from my purse, I jumped up and jammed it into the slot on the side of the elevator.

Nothing happened.

"Oh, that badge won't call the elevator," the nurse said sweetly.

"Why is there a hospital in the basement of an insurance company?"

She didn't answer. Instead, she cocked her head to the side and regarded me. Her eyes glazed over. The expression on her face suggested she might have been consulting her internal computer.

"Well, it's for the employees, of course," she said, sounding as if I was crazy for asking the question.

Okay, so it was option two with an option three chaser. I picked up my binders, walked over to her desk, and set them down hard. I dismissed her shocked expression. I was so past caring about my attitude at this point. I thrust my lab slip at her with so much force that I barely missed smashing it into her face.

"They sent me down here to get a physical."

She reluctantly took my slip and stared at it. Several minutes passed before she lifted her head and refocused on me. That deranged look was still firmly plastered in place.

"Can you call the damn elevator back down so I can leave?" I gritted out.

Most people would have flinched at my acerbic tone, but not her, confirming that she was in fact on something. Well, good for her. As long as she could follow my directions, I didn't care. I wanted to get the hell out of here.

"You don't want the job anymore?"

Movement on my left drew my attention. A tall, attractive man dressed in a white lab coat covering a dark green suit stood there watching us. Possible late thirties with dark brown, medium-length, curly hair and a clean-shaven face that showed off the strong set of his jaw. He wore gold wire-rimmed glasses, and his dark blue eyes reminded me of blue sapphires. His skin was pale, as if he spent too much time indoors or was terminally ill. Since his eyes were so vibrant, I'd go with too much time indoors.

He walked over, extended his hand, and smiled. "I'm Dr. Ronald Stewart. You must be Nicole."

"Yes." I ignored his outstretched hand. Stewart? Was he a member of the family that owned Tribec Insurance? "I need someone to call the elevator back down so I can leave. Now."

He observed me with a mixture of confusion and weariness. Sometimes I had that effect on people and, honestly, it couldn't be helped. I didn't hold my tongue when something bothered me. Dealing with Francine took a great deal of mental gymnastics. Unfortunately for Dr. Stewart, my restraint had just snapped. I wasn't planning on staying, so I saw no reason why I should continue to show decorum.

"Has there been some problem with your hiring process?" he asked.

Were these people stupid? "The problem, Dr. Stewart, is that I don't understand why an insurance company has a hospital set up in the basement, and why I need to give blood for employment. And why my employment is based on my getting a physical?"

He nodded. "Yes, I can see where that might be alarming." He took off his glasses and rubbed the bridge of his nose. When he put them back on, he continued. "The reason we do our physicals on site is because of the cost. But if you are unhappy with the situation, I will be more than happy to have someone come down and escort you back to the lobby." He stared at me, not even attempting to hide the disappointment in his eyes.

He could be disappointed all he wanted.

Dr. Stewart looked at the binders on the desk. If he expected me to pick them up, he was going to be even more disappointed. He spared me a glance before he turned to the nurse. She still had that creepy smile on her face. Was she even aware of what was going on around her?

"Lacy, can you please call George back down to escort Ms. Fontane out of the building?"

"Sure thing, Dr. Stewart." Lacy picked up the phone.

Wow! I was getting escorted not just to the lobby, but out of the whole damn building.

So not a problem at this point.

"Ms. Fontane."

I jerked at the sound of Dr. Stewart's voice.

"Please take a seat while you wait."

"Um... sure."

As much as I didn't want to sit, Dr. Stewart's tone implied I really didn't have a choice.

Once I did sit down, it gave me the opportunity to focus. And I had to admit, I hadn't started this whole process in the right frame of mind. Desperation did that to me. Didn't allow me to really analyze what was going on around me. Hatred for having to accept any form of employment at this point in my life had put me in bad mood.

Given that, it was possible that I was reading too much into the situation. So what if it didn't make sense to me that Tribec Insurance had a hospital in their basement. What did it matter, really, that they decorated their entire building like an Egyptian museum? The more I thought about it, the possibility of it having to do with earth magick made sense. And that might explain the power circle. It wouldn't, however, explain the references to the other principles. But again, what difference did it make? Not once did Francine mention that I had to use or work with magick during the interview process.

Yet, there was still the matter of Vincent. His fear was real; I believed that. So why was he still here? He could be one of those conspiracy nuts that believed everyone was watching him, finding treachery wherever he went. It was the only explanation I could come up with that would explain his odd behavior.

That left the caller. Another conspiracy nut, maybe?

I ran my fingers over the ankh on my charm bracelet my father had given me for my birthday when I was nine. I always wore it for comfort. Sadly, today, it wasn't doing a good job.

*You are such an idiot, Nicole.*

My head pounded. The cloying smell of antiseptic was getting to me. And reality had just reared its ugly head. I wasn't in a position to be picky. I had less than two-hundred dollars in my bank account and rent due in two weeks. Why did I even rent that apartment? I did this to myself—going from one job to the next, making irrational decisions. My father never understood why I didn't want to work with him. I didn't have the heart to tell him the truth that, along with my inability to infuse a basic magick spell, every time I tried working magick, it made me physically ill.

One thing was for sure—I needed to salvage this if I could, uncomfortable or not. If someone would only answer my questions, maybe it would put my mind at ease.

And honestly... I was a little curious.

"You have an entire hospital in the basement just for physicals?" I asked, hoping Dr. Stewart would take that as a sign I wanted to stay.

The elevator doors opened, and George stepped out and stood there waiting, his eyes trained on Dr. Stewart like a good little soldier.

"Would you give us a moment, George?" Dr. Stewart turned to me. "Would you like to discuss this in my office?"

I stood up. "Sure."

"This way." He extended his arm to the right.

I followed him into a small office at the end of a short hallway and took a seat in one of the plush red leather chairs in front of a large oak wood desk. A matching breakfront sat on the left, and a fake fern tree occupied the corner near the door. The walls were painted a cream color that had a slight yellow tinge. His medical degree, framed in gold, was the only thing that hung on the wall directly behind his office chair.

Dr. Stewart shut his door and perched on the edge of his desk, facing me. He took off his glasses and rubbed the bridge of his nose. "I hate wearing these." He slid them back on. "Unfortunately, I don't have a choice."

Why was he telling me this? "Why don't you wear contacts?"

"I keep losing them." He smiled at me. There was a little more than friendliness behind that smile. "Nicole... I'm sorry. May I call you Nicole?"

"Yes, that's fine."

"You obviously seem unnerved by something here. Do you mind telling me what it is?"

It was a fair question, and since he appeared to be genuinely interested, I decided to tell him.

He listened attentively to me as I recounted the many strange things I'd noticed since entering the building. His face remained passive and his eyes never left mine. I paused when I got to Vincent, though. For some strange reason, I got the impression it might not be wise to give him too much information. Besides, I didn't want to get the big guy in trouble.

"Nicole, I actually have no real answer that would provide you with the security you seem to need. I can offer the truth, but would that be enough?"

"Well, at least it would be an answer."

He stood and walked over to the bureau and pulled out a decanter filled with dark liquid. "Would you like a drink?" He looked over his shoulder at me.

"What?"

He sighed. "Sorry, I'm not good at this." After pouring himself one, he sat down beside me. "I don't usually drink on the job but today has been rather stressful." He took a large sip and shifted his eyes to me. "You are the first person who has ever asked about the medical clinic in the basement. You are also the first to mention the art décor. Most of the pieces are from a Pre-dynastic time period. I believe that's a few thousand years before the pharaohs of Egypt. It is very rare. Of course, there are some zero dynasty pieces in there, too."

"What?" Wow. I thought the décor in the lobby was fake.

He finished the contents of his glass and grabbed the decanter for a refill. Apparently, we were going to take the long road toward the answer to my question. I might as well get comfortable.

"I think I'll have one of those drinks."

He smiled. After pouring me a glass, he extended it to me, but pulled back before I could grasp it. "You have to keep this between us," he said in a conspiratorial tone.

"Um... okay."

He handed it to me, and I took a sip. The warm liquid went down like melted chocolate. Brandy—and not the cheap stuff, either. I resisted the urge to smack my lips.

"This is good." I held the glass up in a mock toast.

"The art is from the Gerzean culture." He took off his glasses again and set them on the desk. After rubbing the bridge of his nose, he continued. "I believe their civilization thrived from 3500 to 3200 BC. I'm not as much of an enthusiast as my siblings. My real passion lies in medicine. I do know that the art they collect is rare and expensive." He glanced at me. "Which is why we have the high level of security in the building. I have asked my family repeatedly why they leave the exhibits open with so much exposure, but they insist they like it that way. I had suggested they move the more expensive pieces back to our farmhouse, but they refused, so I have let the matter drop. So now your concern about the smell of blood." He raised his arms in a gesture that said look around.

Well, that answered one of my questions. He was a member of the family that owned Tribec. And I'd come to the same conclusion about the blood on my own when I stepped off the elevator. If they had a hospital in the basement, chances were, the building might occasionally smell like blood.

He reached over, retrieved his glasses, and slid them back on. "The thirteenth floor is considered unlucky to people who are superstitious." He smiled at me. "My family is not, so we saw no need to eliminate the floor. As for the lines on the carpet, that does sound a bit strange. The only thing that comes to mind is that we probably need to change cleaning services."

Okay. If he wanted to blame the power circle on the cleaning crew, I'd let him. I wasn't going to debate the issue with him. Especially since I was pretty damn sure he thought I sounded like a lunatic already. Besides, he'd been so forth-coming thus far, I doubted he would omit they practiced magick. At least, I hoped he wouldn't.

He stood and took his empty glass back to the bureau. "Now, let me ask you a question?" He poured another drink.

"Alright."

He leaned against the bureau. "Why stay? I mean, it's obvious something here unnerves you. I know I provided you some explanation to the concerns you have, but the mere fact that you observed these things and still stayed is somewhat puzzling to me." He emptied his glass and poured another one.

I sighed because what he said was true. Anyone else would have run, but I continued along the process even when I had an out. "I need the job." I sounded stupid. Of course, he would already know I needed a job. Why else would I be here?

"I'm sure there are other jobs out there that you can get."

"I'm not college educated." Why was I telling him this? "So, I'm not going to find a job with decent pay unless I go back to school." I left off the fact that I'd worked at every worthless job on the island already. It would sound too pathetic.

"You don't want to go to college?"

Dr. Stewart's phone rang, saving me from having to answer his question.

"Excuse me." He straightened his tie and picked up the phone. He listened for a short while and then hung up. Once again, he removed his glasses and rubbed the bridge of his nose. He really needed to get some contacts.

First Vincent with his obsessive eating, now Dr. Stewart with his alcohol, and I was pretty damn sure Lacy was on something. I placed my still-full glass on the desk, which was too bad

—the stuff was good. Not my usual drink, but it did hit the spot. Then it suddenly dawned on me that I was sitting in a doctor's office, at the place I was just hired to work, drinking alcohol.

*Bad move, Nicole.*

"I apologize for my unprofessional behavior." He opened a small refrigerator next to his desk and retrieved a bottle of water. "Did you want some?"

"No, thank you."

He drained the entire bottle and continued. "The reason we have a medical clinic here is because of the convenience to our employees." He got up and moved to the chair behind his desk. "The cost we save from having to pay outside people to do what we could do allows us to pay you a better wage than most places. It also gives us an opportunity to ensure our employees are healthy. Less sick days and all." He smiled. "Does that answer your question?"

"It's a better answer than I've received to any of my other questions," I said truthfully. It was also long-winded. But I didn't say that. I got the impression Dr. Stewart needed someone to talk to. And honestly, I really didn't mind doing it. While it was a little troubling he was one of the proprietors, his at-ease mannerism really helped calm my nerves. It might not be a bad idea to have such a high-ranking person on my side. Especially since I was bound to fuck up eventually.

He stood up. "I hope you will reconsider a position with us. And please forgive me for my behavior. As I've said, it's been a very stressful morning. We have six new-hires, and the process is—"

I waved my hand to silence his apology. "I'm the one who owes you an apology. I shouldn't have behaved the way I did. Honestly, I'm surprised you haven't tossed me out."

"You speak up when something concerns you; there is nothing wrong with that. And I'm not in charge of the hiring and firing. That would be my brother Thomas's department."

"Yeah, well, my mouth has gotten me into a lot of trouble over the years."

His eyes zeroed in on my mouth. "Is that so?"

I stood up. "Okay, Dr. Stewart. I've already tried dating my boss." More like sleeping with the boss. "It never works out."

The conversation had taken a strange turn. Now, I wasn't opposed to a little harmless flirting, but given how our meeting first started off, it didn't make much sense for him to suddenly start making advances toward me. Yet, he didn't seem to mind drinking on the job. So, I guess flirting with the female employees wasn't completely out of the question for him.

"I won't be your boss," he said.

"But you will be my doctor."

"So I guess asking you out to dinner would be out of the question?" His eyes had that hopeful look men get when they know a woman isn't interested but can't help but try anyway.

"Exactly." I picked up my purse.

"That appears to be very heavy."

"It is. Should we get started?"

He stared at me for a moment, probably waiting to see if I would change my mind. I had to admit, he was handsome. In any other circumstance, I would have allowed him to buy me a drink. I looked at the glass of brandy I'd set on his desk. Or, rather, another drink.

"Well, let me show you to an exam room," he said.

I followed him out and down another hallway that sat adjacent to his office. I had to walk fast to keep up. When he stopped, I almost ran into the back of him.

"Sorry," I said, giving him a sheepish smile.

"Oh, no, I'm sorry; I have to remind myself constantly that not everyone walks as fast as I do." He stood to the side and waited for me to enter the room.

The room was small. A red-colored exam table sat flush up against the far wall. The opposite side of the room held a chair and a tall table with a laptop sitting on top. The sink was next to the door, with cabinets directly above it. A pink gown lay on top of the exam table. The gown was unsettling, because not more than ten minutes ago, I was ready to bolt.

"You assumed I was staying?" I set my things down on the exam table and picked up the gown.

"I hoped you were." He winked at me.

Despite my resolution not to sleep with anyone I work with again, I was definitely on the fence about going out with him. Besides, he did say he wouldn't be my boss.

"We need to do a full examination, so I need you to change. My nurse will be in momentarily." He grabbed a clipboard and a few sheets of paper from the stack on the desk and handed them to me. "I need you to fill these out while you wait. Normally, we would have had you do that in the waiting room, but—"

"It's okay, I understand."

"I will let you get changed." He opened the door.

"Thanks, Dr. Stewart." I stared at him. He was definitely my type.

"It was my pleasure, Nicole... and you can call me Ronald."

"Okay, Ronald, I have to take my clothes off now."

"Now you're flirting with me," he said, arching his eyebrow.

"Sorry, couldn't help it." Yes, I could. "It won't happen again." It probably would.

"That's too bad," he said, and then walked out the door.

It was too bad.

"Not gonna go there again," I said, knowing full well that I was lying to myself.

fter I changed into the gown, I sat on the table and filled
out the medical questionnaire. What was it with all
these damn forms? Were they trying to write a book
about me? Once finished, I sat back to wait for the nurse. I didn't
have to wait long.

A woman entered the room, smile first. "Hello, I'm Emilia.
You must be Ms. Fontane," she said in a sing-song voice.

Emilia, a short, four-foot-eight blonde woman, might have
weighed a hundred pounds. With her waifish features and green
eyes, she could've easily been mistaken for a pixie. Her pink
hospital scrubs had to have been specially made to fit her small
size, along with her pair of doll-sized white Reeboks. How
adorable.

"Yes, and please call me Nicole." I handed her my clipboard.

After scanning the forms, she eyed me up and down, assessing
me. Like she could tell what ailments I had by simply staring. I
shifted, and she smiled. "What principle do you practice?"

"Excuse me?"

"Never mind. I need you to step on the scale, please."

"Is that a job requirement?" I climbed down and did as she
asked.

"Your weight?" She played with the sliding bar.

"No, using magick."

She laughed. "Of course not. I was only curious. Most people on Tulare practice, so..." She shook her head. "Forget I said anything." She adjusted the height bar. "Okay, five-foot-six, and a hundred and forty-seven pounds."

I hated the scale. It was a constant reminder that I ate and drank too much, and since I was already aware of that, I saw no point in the scale reminding me of it. Besides, I couldn't help it; there was something about a big, juicy cheeseburger, a mound of salty fries, and a cold Sam Adams that called to me.

"Damn, I need to lose seven pounds."

"No, you don't." She set her clipboard on the exam table. I doubted she could reach the long table with the laptop on it unless she had a stool. "Try weighing ninety pounds and looking like a boy."

I laughed. "You don't resemble a boy. A pixie maybe, but not a boy."

"Yeah, I guess I can see that." Her cheeks flushed. "It's embarrassing when I go out with friends. Guys always assume that they brought along their kid sister." She shook her head. "You can climb back up on the exam table." She surveyed the room. "I'll be right back."

"Okay."

While it wasn't *completely* unheard of for people to ask about someone's magick abilities, it wasn't commonplace for them to do so. In some circles, it was even considered rude. She said it wasn't important, so why did she bring it up?

Emilia returned, carrying a metal stool. I covered my mouth to suppress my laugh; the thing was almost bigger than she was.

"Sorry, they forgot to put this in here for me." She set it down in front of the long table. "Go ahead and laugh," she said, smiling.

I shook my head and smiled. "How long have you worked here?"

She took her clipboard off the exam table. "Here? About two and a half years. But I've been working with the Stewart family for over seven years. And I've been a nurse for eight."

"You're kidding. How old are you? Sorry, don't answer that."

"I don't mind. I'm thirty-two."

I cocked my head to the side. "I don't see it." I would have guessed twenty at the most.

She shook her head, smiling. "Now, when was your last Pap smear and breast exam?"

"Do they really need to know that information for my employment?" That was just a little too personal. Besides, I'd already filled out all their damn forms. That should be enough.

"For your physical portion, yes."

I went through my mental rolodex. "Well, I believe it was last year some time."

"Do you have an exact date?"

"No, I'm afraid I don't, but I can get the information for you from my doctor." Truthfully, I didn't have a regular doctor, since I'd never been sick a day in my life. The last time I was even seen by a doctor was when I went to my gynecologist for a pregnancy scare. She prescribed birth control; I would need to check when it ran out.

"I'll ask Dr. Stewart if he still wants to give you one today." She jotted down a note on her clipboard.

I could answer that question for her.

Emilia put her stool in front of the exam table and climbed up to take my blood pressure and pulse. She smelled like licorice and wildflowers.

"Is the medical clinic hiring?" I asked.

"Why do you ask?" She walked over to the door.

"Just curious."

"It's Mrs. Delaporte, huh?"

"Um..." I was not going to answer that. I'd just managed to dislodge my foot from my mouth. I wasn't going to stick it in there again.

"It's okay; we get complaints about her all the time. She's bipolar." She laughed. "Don't tell anyone I said that." She walked to the door.

"Okay. Do you have to deal with her on a regular basis?"

"I don't really have to, but since the company wants everyone to stay healthy, I have to see her at least once a month since the other nurse, Judith, refuses to see her." She opened the door. "I will get Dr. Stewart. You can lie back if you like."

She shut the door before I could respond. That was the second time I'd heard they wanted to keep everyone healthy. On the surface, that sounded okay. I mean, no one would want their employees to be sick. For some reason, though, I got the impression it meant something entirely different here. Besides, if that was the case, why was Vincent so overweight? And the rest of the employees sallow and sickly looking? Before I could ponder this further, the door opened, and Dr. Stewart came back in.

"You're still here?"

"Very funny, R—" Emilia followed him in, so I corrected my familiarity. "Dr. Stewart."

He caught my stumble and winked. Okay, so maybe a harmless dinner date wouldn't be too bad.

He set my chart on the long table and opened it. "So, Emilia says that you don't remember the date of your last Pap smear or mammogram."

"No, but I can get that information. I'm certain it's been in the last year."

"That sounds fine. If you are unable to locate the information, we can always schedule you for one." He pulled his stethoscope from around his neck and put the earpieces in his ears. "This is going to be a little cold." He moved the front of my gown to the side and placed the cold stethoscope on my chest.

My libido kicked into overdrive as his fingers touched my bare skin.

"You have a strong heart. Can you turn slightly? I want to listen to your lungs." He moved closer. "I understand you smoke."

"Yes." I cleared my throat. "I'm trying to quit." I inhaled the spicy scent of his cologne and licked my lips.

He stared at my mouth for a moment before stepping back.

He turned to Emilia. "Nurse, can you get the blood collection cart? I will draw Ms. Fontane's blood. They have sent Vincent down again. I need you to examine him."

"Yes, Doctor." She cut her eyes toward me. There was a faint question in that look, one that said, '*Will you be comfortable if I leave?*'

I smiled at her.

Once Emilia shut the door, Ronald moved back toward the exam table. "You appear to be healthy."

"We agreed, no flirting." I leaned slightly forward.

"I didn't agree to that." His eyes dipped down to my mouth. "Um... you smell like apples and my favorite brandy." He was flush up against me now, heat radiating off his body, and his lips were a hair's breadth away from mine. I was so tempted to close the distance; except he beat me to it. He brushed his lips over mine, and I reluctantly eased back.

"Stop, Ronald." My voice sounded a little breathy.

The door opened and Emilia came back in, carrying a red tray with needles, bandages, and a tourniquet. "Are you sure you don't want me to draw Nicole's blood?" She set the kit next to me on the exam table.

Ronald moved back some. "Yes, I'm fine, Nurse Emilia." There was a touch of anger in his voice. "That will be all."

"Yes, of course, Doctor." After a brief hesitation, she left.

Ronald cleared his throat.

"Are you two dating?" I asked as he tied the tourniquet on my arm.

He smiled. "No, she likes to keep an eye on me." He pulled a tube and butterfly needle out of the kit. "Are you scared of having your blood drawn?'

"No," I said. "Hey, I almost forgot. What about the brandy I drank? Won't that show up on your tests?"

"We don't check for alcohol." He wiped the spot on my inner elbow. "Just a little poke."

I averted my gaze as he drew my blood. Why would they not

be concerned about alcohol? For a company obsessed with keeping everyone healthy, it was a little strange. And why was Emilia keeping an eye on him? Was it the excessive drinking, or something else? "Do you flirt with all the female patients?"

He smiled. "Only the pretty ones."

Well, that excluded the group of women upstairs. Besides, I seriously doubted they would be able to register any type of flirtation from Dr. Stewart. They all looked as if they barely had pulses.

Ronald bandaged the area and set the vials of my blood in a little tray. "After Ryan takes you to get a chest x-ray, I will have you go to the bathroom and leave a sample of urine. And then we're all done." He put the tray on the cabinet near the sink and moved back over to me. "Unless you will allow me to talk you into going to dinner with me." He moved in close again with his eyes on my mouth.

I smiled. "You're persistent, I will give you that." I licked my lips. "Why don't you give me your card?"

He reached into the inner pocket of his suit. "Is that a yes?" He flipped the card over and scribbled something on the back.

"It's a maybe," I said, taking the card from him. "Now, I need to get dressed."

He stared at me for a minute. "I guess that's going to have to be good enough." He opened the door and turned back to me. "The restroom is at the end of the hall. Make sure you write your name on the cup." He smiled. "I hope I hear from you."

"Bad move, Nicole," I said after he shut the door.

I didn't have to wait long for Ryan. Once my x-ray was done, I left a urine sample, got dressed, and went back to the waiting room.

"Lacy, can you call someone down to escort me to the lobby?"

She smiled, stretching the sides of her mouth into a comical mask, and picked up the phone.

While I waited, my mind drifted to Emilia. The look she gave me when she left the blood tray in the room concerned me. It was a little more than the average worry for a patient's comfort.

There was genuine fear in her eyes. Yet, I couldn't figure out what she would be afraid of. Ronald said they weren't dating, and except for a little over-indulgence with the alcohol and some very forward flirting, he seemed harmless. Woman scorned, perhaps?

George arrived to escort me to the lobby. I picked up the heavy manuals and followed him into the elevator. Bastard didn't even offer to help me carry them.

When we reached the lobby, I breathed a sigh of relief. I couldn't believe how badly I'd fucked up today. I also couldn't believe I'd managed to get the job. My strides were quick as I crossed the lobby on my way to the front doors.

"Did you need some help?"

I came to an abrupt stop. A man, early thirties, six-foot-one with sandy brown hair and dark brown eyes, was standing a few feet away from me.

"No, thanks. Are you here for an interview?"

"Yes." He extended his hands. "Are you sure you don't need help carrying those binders out?"

I smiled. "No, I got them. Good luck on your interview."

He dipped his head in acknowledgement and made his way back to the red couch. A short woman of mixed Asian descent was sitting there watching him. She glanced at me and then back at him. After exchanging a few words, she turned back to me. There wasn't any anger or jealousy in her eyes. Only curiosity. I was tempted to walk over and find out why she was staring, but I'd had enough of Tribec Insurance for one day, so I turned and left.

When I reached my car, I chucked the manuals in the backseat along with my blazer and climbed in. As I dug in my purse for my leftover cigar, a feeling of dread settled over me and a shiver ran up my spine. Something was wrong.

Regardless of what Dr. Stewart said, I was still unsettled about something I couldn't readily put my finger on. I pulled my notebook out of my purse along with a pen. I opened it up to a clean sheet and wrote down "Gerzean culture." I also wrote down the things that were bothering me, including what Vincent said.

I had developed the habit of writing things down when I was a teenager. Sometimes my mind would become overloaded, and the only way for me to figure something out was to write it down. I had over fifteen journals filled with random thoughts and observations. Funny thing was, despite my obsessive writing, I was still trying to figure out my life.

Once I'd smoked the rest of the cigar, I started my car. As I was backing out of my spot, a stray wind blew into the open window... carrying the scent of blood.

I pulled into the parking lot of my apartment complex located in Brunswood and parked near the building. Unfortunately, parking was on a first-come, first-serve basis, which left me more often than not having to park my car near the dumpster.

My apartment was on the first floor of a three-story building that used to be a mental hospital in the early 1900s. Rumors of patient abuse had caused the hospital to be closed down. But it didn't remain closed for long. Two years after the last man—Abel Sanders—was arrested for raping and mutilating seven female patients, a former patient—Lemuel Oren—bought the place and started a faith magick cult called His Holy Need.

Five years after the cult had started, someone had alerted the authorities to a strange smell coming from the building. When they raided the place, they found all thirty-nine followers in the basement, dead from mass suicide.

Lemuel Oren was never heard from again.

The outside of the building was never changed—red brick with white wood trim around the windows. A green awning with the name *Rose Garden Apartments*, stenciled in white, replaced the hospital sign. Cypress trees and a small garden were located in the back of the building. I had access to the garden from my sliding glass door, along with two other tenants.

I entered the building and stopped at the wall of mailboxes outside the manager's office. The smell of shrimp fried rice and beef drifted from under the door, and my stomach growled. Mr. Wan, a sixty-year-old widower, had invited me to dinner a few times since I moved in two weeks ago. He was a nice old man who loved to cook.

Every time I ran into him, he was wearing the same outfit: khaki pants and a white muscle shirt. Laugh lines surrounded both his eyes and mouth, and he always wore his dark hair combed back from his face.

Most of the mail I received was for the previous tenant— Jeremy Wright, a fifty-five-year-old mailman who, after twenty years, was fired for drug use. His drug of choice had been marijuana, and since he had suddenly found himself broke and unemployed, he thought it would be a good idea to grow his own for both personal and business use. He never did get a chance to get that lucrative business off the ground since the Gardner Mr. Wan hired always pulled up the plants. Jeremy, who I figured wasn't too bright to begin with, decided to complain to Mr. Wan, who then complained to the police.

After writing "Return to Sender" on the envelopes, I stuffed them in the out box and continued down the hall to my apartment. My arms were shaking by the time I got the door open.

I dropped my purse and the manuals on the floor and shut the door. I stripped down to my bra and panties, balled up the yellow itchy polyester suit, and draped it over the arm of the couch. I would hang it up later.

I've always hated wearing clothes around the house. Something that my mother said stemmed from childhood. She told me once she had the hardest time keeping clothes on me. I even went so far as to hide them. Even in the winter, I wear only panties when I'm indoors. Of course, I have the heater cranked up full blast to keep me warm. I think it's the confinement that bothers me. All those layers piled on, restricting me. Maybe I'm claustrophobic.

I stood in the middle of the living-room, surveying the place. My apartment was decent enough, with a small living-room just inside the front door that also doubled as a dining-room. Directly across from the front door was a sliding glass door with a tiny alcove-style kitchen to the left of it. It had barely enough space to fit two people cozily. A short hallway sat off the kitchen, leading to a small bathroom and a medium-sized bedroom. A decent-sized linen closet sat next to a built-in washer and dryer space that was hidden by two French doors.

Boxes were scattered all over, and I still had more at my parents' house to pick up. I seriously needed to buy furniture. The dark brown loveseat I'd picked up at the Goodwill was on its last leg, along with the small, round coffee table that doubled as a dining-room table. I had a complete bedroom set that had somehow survived my constant moving. Maybe I will replace it as well. The wear and tear on it was becoming noticeable. The wood was scuffed up, and a few of the dresser knobs were missing.

I sighed and picked up the manuals off the floor, along with my purse, and set them on the table. After a brief search of the apartment, I managed to find my emergency cigar and, with trembling fingers, lit it. Mr. Wan didn't want me to smoke indoors, so I opened the sliding glass door and stood just inside the frame. As I bared myself for all to see, something rustled to my left.

"Hi, Wade," I said.

Wade Johnson—an attractive man in his early forties with long dark brown hair, a goatee that surrounded thin lips, and pretty hazel eyes—stood in the middle of the small garden, staring at me. He was twice divorced and not at all good in bed. Well, I have to rephrase that. He might actually be good in bed, but sadly, we never got past the foreplay. We both had gotten too drunk, and Wade fell asleep.

He was also a pompous jerk, which I later learned when he tried to proposition me for another chance at sleeping together. He told me the reason he had such a difficult time getting it up was not the alcohol, but my unwillingness to apply myself. I told him that they made pills for his problem and slammed the door in his face.

I was surprised he kept trying.

"Nicole." He set his hose on the grass and walked over to me. "How have you been?" His eyes wandered down to my chest and remained there.

"Fine." I blew smoke in his face. It was rude and childish, but I really wanted him to go away.

I'd tried to be patient with Wade. Tried to keep my inner bitch from showing her thorny head. I'd just moved here and had no plans of leaving any time soon. But after the day I had, patience was the last thing I was going to practice.

"What are you doing later?" he asked as he fanned away the smoke.

"Laundry." I moved back to shut the sliding glass door.

He looked up from my breasts. "Did you want me to come over after?"

"Did you get those pills?"

"What?"

I slid the door closed and let the curtain fall back in place. Maybe he would get the hint.

After bundling all my laundry, I went back into the living-room and retrieved my purse. I dumped the contents on my bed and pulled my wallet out of the pile, along with my cell phone. I spotted Ronald's business card and picked it up. He'd scribbled *please call* on the back.

"Well, Ronald, I might just do that." After storing his number in my contacts under "Sexy Doctor," I headed out to my parents' house.

I ARRIVED AT MY PARENTS' house in Pleasanton twenty minutes later. A few mom-and-pop stores, an island police branch, one lone supermarket, and a large ballpark made up the majority of the settlement. The rest was covered in middle-class neighborhoods.

As I pulled into the driveway, Fi'—my mother's white Bolognese dog—popped her head up and yapped in delight. Originally, they had a regular mesh screen in place, but Fi' had chewed through it in her mission to get outside. They had to replace it with one that had a solid bottom. It didn't, however, stop her efforts to gain her freedom.

I suspected she was trying to escape my mother and her obsession with dressing her up in little doggy outfits. Even if she did get out, she wouldn't get far. They'd tied a tiny bell to her collar.

I walked up to the door. "Hey, Fi'."

She stared at me while her tail twitched in delight. I opened the screen door and scooped her up. She had on a pink doggy tutu with a little pink ribbon tied around her head. As I rubbed her back, she bathed my chin with kisses.

I scratched her head. "Don't worry, Fi'; when Mom gets older, we'll dress her up in ridiculous outfits and tie a bell around her neck, too."

She yapped her consent.

I carried her off the porch with me to my car, belatedly realizing there was no way I could hold her and get my things out of the car too, so I sat her down beside me. She, of course, took this as an invitation to run off. I smiled and shook my head as she made a mad dash toward the neighbor's yard.

I peeked across the street at Cherry Miller's house. She sat in her usual spot, holding a glass of her favorite drink—gin-flavored lemonade. It was the only thing she drank besides water.

"Hi, Cherry," I said.

Cherry waved, took a long swallow of her lemonade, sat back in her rocking chair, and started humming to herself.

On nights when I couldn't sleep, and the snippets of my suppressed memories became too much, I would venture across the street and sit with Cherry. She was always outside, sitting, watching the neighborhood, drinking her spiked lemonade.

Sometimes she would share stories of her life with me, and other times she would just sit there, humming to herself.

On one such night, she shared with me the reason she had killed her husband, Jack.

In December of 1974, while attending a neighborhood Christmas party, she learned from one of her husband's employees that while on his two-hour lunches, he routinely made house calls to all the married women in the neighborhood.

When she confronted him, he pleaded his innocence. Cherry said she believed him, and later—when she learned he was lying—she decided to catch him in the act. She said men like Jack don't change overnight, and sometimes, you need to teach them a lesson.

That lesson came in the form of fire.

Cherry practiced elemental magick.

She used her magick to burn down the house of her husband's mistress while both of them were still inside. The police found her sitting outside in a lawn chair, drinking a glass of lemonade while flames danced around her.

She was found criminally insane and sentenced to twenty years in Pike Forrest mental institution. When she got out, she moved right back into her old home.

There's even a drink on the menu at Jordin Cisco's named after her. Cherry Falls Lemonade.

I hauled my purse and laundry basket out of the car and started back up the steps. I glanced over my shoulder at Fi'. She sat at the end of the yard, watching me, tail wagging, her bell tinkling.

"Come on, Fi'."

She didn't budge.

I set down my bag, and she sprinted to the neighbors' yard. I was not going to chase her. "Come on Fi'. It's hot."

She yapped in reply.

I should have never sat her down. It would be hell to try to get her to come back to the house.

"Nicole, what... Fi'! Get back in this house right now!" My

mother, Anne, emerged from the house, holding a green-coated paintbrush in her hand. Her long black hair was pulled up on top of her head, and she was covered in both sweat and paint.

"Why on earth did you let her out?" she said, her French accent sounding more pronounced.

"Sorry." I hugged her and breathed in her familiar vanilla scent.

She scrutinized me, her dark eyes assessing. She kissed me on my cheek. "What is wrong?"

"Nothing, Mom."

The creak in the floorboards announced my father's approach. He pushed open the screen door.

"You moving back in?" he asked.

My father—Henri—fifty years old and still in good shape. A few laugh lines around his mouth and a touch of gray running through his curly hair were the only hints of his age. He had café latte-colored skin—a result of his mixed heritage—and a thin goatee surrounding his mouth. I got my hazel eyes from him.

"No, Daddy." I wrapped my arms around him. He smelled like apples, paint, and sweat. "I'm only here to do laundry and eat your food." I plucked at his stained white t-shirt. "What are you two painting?

"Your room." He kissed my forehead. "So, I hope you like sea foam green."

"I'm not moving back in," I insisted, my voice slightly elevated.

"Stop yelling, Nicole. She let Fi' out," my mother said, as she handed my father the paint brush and pulled her hair out of the knot.

He watched her with a barely contained lust as she re-twisted it.

My parents met when my mother, at eighteen, had come to New Orleans on holiday with a group of her friends during Mardi Gras. My father was nineteen and spent his nights throwing beads out at the women who exposed their breasts. He said when he saw my mother, it was love at first sight. Knowing what the "at first sight" included, I tried really hard not to picture it.

"Fi'!" my father bellowed.

After one last defiant sniff of the neighbor's roses, she trotted her way back to the house, and I swore if dogs could talk, she would have muttered the whole way.

"Mom, that outfit is ridiculous."

"She looks so adorable," she said.

My father and I shared an eye roll as he picked up my laundry basket.

Fi' climbed the steps, peered up at me with accusation in her eyes, and went inside the house. We followed her, laughing.

The front door opened up to a large family room on the right with a formal dining room on the left. Since the house was built before the emergence of open floor plans, a long wall separated the two rooms. A short hallway connected the kitchen to the dining-room.

There was a guest bedroom next to the kitchen that my mother had converted into a small studio for her clay pot-making. She sold the pots in my father's apothecary shop.

The laundry room was situated off the kitchen. It used to be a storage area. My mother, tired of doing laundry in the kitchen, decided to convert it. Unfortunately, the room didn't have an air-duct for the air or heat. By the time I got my clothes sorted and one load in the machine, I was drenched in sweat.

"Cherry Miller asked me to lunch yesterday," my mother said, joining me in the kitchen. She pulled her wet hair back and tied it with a green scarf.

"What did Daddy say?"

My father didn't like Cherry. On numerous occasions, he'd referred to her as a cankerous, bitter old woman. He also warned her not to talk to me about magick. Told her it was his job to teach me. Unfortunately, his teachings never yielded any results, and I remained unable to access my magick.

I opened the refrigerator and pulled out the sweet tea. Standard southern fare. I preferred no sugar in both my tea and coffee. Since it would take a while to make, I opted to drink what was available.

"He laughed," she said, coming up behind me.

I stepped to the side so she could get into the refrigerator. "Just laughed?" I retrieved a tall glass from the cupboard and filled it with half tea and half water.

"You are the only child I know who does not like sugar."

"I'm not a child, Mom." I gulped down the watery tea.

She smiled. "You will always be my child." She set a plate of seasoned chicken breast on the counter and moved to the sink to wash her hands.

"So, did you go?" I filled my glass again.

"Yes." She turned and leaned against the counter. "Your father told me not to get any ideas." She laughed, her voice sounding husky. "I told him, 'You satisfy me too much, Henri, for me to burn down the house with you in it.'"

"I don't want to hear about your love life, Mom. Remember, we agreed, no sharing," I said, recalling the time my mother, in one of her sharing moods, told me that out of all the lovers she'd had, my father was the best. I told her she wasn't allowed to share anymore.

I set my cup down on the counter and put the pitcher of tea back in the refrigerator.

My mother swatted me on the ass. "Are you going to help me cook?" She moved toward the radio she kept on top of the refrigerator.

"I can't cook, Mom."

"Then go help your father." She turned on the radio. Smokey Robinson's 'Tears of a Clown' filled the kitchen.

When I entered my father's workroom in the back of the house, the smell of ginger root, jasmine, patchouli, and vervain tickled my nose. After winding my way through some of the free-standing plants, I found him standing at his worktable, sorting the herbs he had pulled from his drying rack above the table. He'd changed into a clean t-shirt and a pair of worn jeans. An ankh—an Egyptian symbol for life—hung around his neck, dangling from a braided brown leather cord. It lay against the black apron he wore when he was working.

He glanced up from what he was doing. "You come to help, baby girl?" He picked up one of the dark glass containers he used to store his herbs.

"Yeah, Mom kicked me out of the kitchen." I walked over to the worktable and reached underneath to take out the extra pair of gloves he kept there.

He laughed. My father's voice always reminded me of a large oak tree—one that had been on earth for thousands of years. He exuded calmness and wisdom, but also strength.

"You should learn how to cook, baby girl."

"I'll learn one day." I pulled on gloves.

He watched me. "What's wrong?"

My father wore the love and concern he had for me and my mother all over his face and, at times, I found it really hard to glance away. I took so much comfort in those looks. I hated it when my mother referred to me as her child. It made me want to prove that I was an adult capable of making decisions. However, when my father referred to me as his baby girl, all I could do was smile and allow myself the relief of knowing he would always protect me.

I moved toward him. He put the container down and wrapped his arms around me.

"Oh, baby girl, I wish you would get settled." He rubbed my back.

"I'm working on it," I mumbled into his chest.

After a few moments, I moved back to avoid crying and pulled some verbena down from the drying rack. Without asking, my father handed me the masking tape and a black sharpie. I wrote "Tears of Isis" on a strip of tape and placed it on the side of the glass container.

We worked in silence for a while, sorting the different herbs into containers and labeling them. It was the only part of earth magick practice that I was comfortable with. Activating the spells using the magick that should have been coursing through my blood was where I fell short. My father never said anything about it; never tried to push me. He remained calm and supportive, waiting for me to figure it out on my own.

Once most of the herbs had been packed, I turned to him. "Daddy, have you ever heard of any pre-Egyptian civilizations?"

"From what era?" He picked up the last container and stacked it on the floor.

I took off my gloves and put them back under the table. "Gerzean." I reached for his cigar pack.

He gave me a look—not condemning, just asking. My father was the one that got me started on the cigars as a way to stop me from doing drugs. It was a backwards way of tackling the issue, but he and my mother had already tried everything else. I was really messed up after my best friend, Steve, died, and especially after watching my boyfriend, Frank, get killed. Instead of stopping my drug habit, I spiraled out of control, trying anything I could get my hands on. The cigars had worked, and now they were my go-to whenever my life started to spiral again.

"Get the door," he said as he picked up a few of the containers.

I walked over to the screen and opened it. Fi' stood there waiting.

"Move back, Fi'," I said.

She peered up at my father.

"Move back, Fi'," he said, giving her a stern look. The half-smile on his face took some of the bite out of it.

She ran around the corner.

"She is really scared of you," I said.

He placed the container on the grass. "She'll be back in a minute." He went back inside for more containers.

Sure enough, he was right. Her little bell tinkled as she rounded the corner, carrying her little toy doll in her mouth. I crouched down while still holding the door, and she sat the doll in front of me.

My dad passed by us and chuckled. "That dog thinks you're her sister." He squatted down beside me. "Come here, Fi'."

She swiveled her head toward him, but didn't move.

My father reached over and pulled her to him. "Fi' knows I love her." He rubbed her belly.

She turned and lapped at his hand to show how much she loved him, too.

"Gerzean was the second phase in the Naqada culture," he said as he continued to rub Fi's belly. "Amratian was the first, and the Semainean period was the third and final phase. Each one of them was bloodier than the last." He studied me for a minute. "Why do you ask?" He put Fi' down.

"I saw some artwork at Tribec Insurance that I thought was old Egyptian, but they told me it was Gerzean. I had never heard of that culture before."

My father sat down and stretched out his legs. "You wouldn't. The Council of Principles erased their existence from most books on magick." He reached into his pocket and handed me his lighter.

I remembered Luisah—the owner of a rare book library in Coeur d' Alene—telling me about The Council of Principles. She never elaborated on them or why they suddenly disappeared. She only said they had existed at one time to govern over magick users.

I glanced down at the cigar in my hand. I'd completely forgotten it was there.

"How did you learn about them, then? And why did The Council of Principles erase them from existence?" I asked, lighting it.

My father reached out, and I handed him the cigar.

"Luisah." Smoke lazily trailed out of his mouth. "She had mentioned it one day when I commented on a pot she had in her library. And no one knows why The Council did." He glanced away.

My father was lying. I couldn't prove it, but I got the feeling he knew more than what he was saying.

"I owe her money," I said, giving him an out.

He laughed. "Better not step foot in her library without it."

"Why were they bloody?"

"They practiced blood magick, which eventually led to their downfall." He got up. "Better finish up before your mother calls us for dinner."

The tone of his voice suggested he wasn't going to discuss it any further. My father never talked about blood magick, and he barely mentioned the other three. He made sure I was aware there were five principles and left it at that, focusing all his attention on our own principle—earth.

Because of this, I would need to do more research to better understand what I'd seen, which meant going to see Luisah. Paying her was seriously going to cut into my limited funds. Either way, I was more than a little curious about the way all of the principles of magick had been represented in the glyphs on the walls at Tribec. My choosing to not work with magick never stopped my curiosity about it. And from what my father just said, they also had a representation of blood magick in the artwork on their walls.

Emilia did say working with magick was not part of the job. And they could be just what Dr. Stewart said they were—collectors.

At least, I was hoping that was all it was.

Four of the six settlements on Tulare were divided by small mountain ranges. Because of this, a single road was built to get from one settlement to the next. It circled the entire island and was supposed to make traveling easier. Unfortunately, since it was the main road, it was also one of the most used by commuters to get to work.

It didn't take long for me to join in with the chorus of horn blasts and obscene hand gestures while I crept along with the windows down, sweating in one of my new outfits. My air-conditioning had quit weeks ago, and I couldn't afford to get it fixed.

Thirty minutes later, I pulled into the parking lot of Tribec Insurance with curse words flying out of my mouth. I was running late. Well, late for me. I would have preferred to get here early so I could psych myself up for the day. Smoke a cigar. Or just contemplate life in general. Sadly, my miscalculation about the traffic had me pulling into the parking lot with only a few minutes to spare. After navigating my car into the first parking spot I found, I got out and stormed toward the building.

One day down and so many more to go.

I didn't smell blood when I entered the building this time, but that faint scent of sand was still there, along with the same guard—Oliver Strong.

"Good morning," I said as I set the manuals down on the counter.

"You're not wearing your badge." He stared at my chest a little longer than necessary.

Fucking pervert.

I pulled my temporary badge out of my purse and clipped it to my blouse. "Can you tell me where the training—"

"Nicole!"

I recognized that voice. My pulse raced as trepidation and excitement warred inside of me. I slowly turned around. "Marta," I said as I stared at my estranged friend.

It had been three years since I last saw her, but it felt like a lifetime. She still looked the same. Shorter than me by at least two inches, with long, thick black hair that ran down the length of her back, and smooth, dark skin that accentuated her Mexican heritage. Her bright hazel eyes were full of joyful, unshed tears.

I wanted to go to her, grab her, and say I was sorry, but I stood there, rooted in place.

"Still too stubborn." She swiped at a tear trailing down her cheek.

Yes, I was still stubborn. I expected there to be judgment in her eyes, but there wasn't any; only sadness and longing. She held perfectly still as she studied me, waiting for my response. Marta, even as a child, was always quiet and reserved. I never understood how we had become such good friends; we were polar opposites. Even Kara, who sported rainbow-colored hair and piercings all over the place during high school, was different. And our other friend, Steve Callahan, was a nerd.

The four of us were inseparable. Until Steve died. Then everything changed.

"You still haven't cut your hair," I said, at a loss as to what to say.

A small smile creased her face. "And yours is still all over the place."

I smoothed down my hair. "I'm..."

Marta moved forward. "Shut up, Nicole." She threw her

manuals on the guard counter next to mine and pulled me into a constrictive hug.

"Okay," I said, my voice muffled from the raw emotion stuck in my throat.

She pulled back and stared at me. Then seized my face in her hands and kissed me hard on the lips. "Oh, *mija*, I have missed you so much. The kids miss you." She smiled, and her eyes lit up. "You working here, too?"

"Yes, I had my interview yesterday."

"I did too." She picked up her manuals off the counter.

I was so wrapped up in seeing my friend that I didn't notice Oliver had come around the counter. He cleared his throat. I turned to find him looming over us. He was taller than me by at least five inches, making me look up into his cold black eyes. I'd never seen anyone with completely black eyes before.

He grabbed my arm.

I pulled out of his grasp and moved back.

He stepped forward as if he was going to follow me, but at the last minute, stopped himself. Anger rolled off him like heat. Hatred filled his eyes. If my assumption about him being ex-military was correct, I would bet my entire life savings—all one hundred and sixty dollars of it—that Oliver was dishonorably discharged. Or a trained killer whom, after they had no further use for him, they set free on the unsuspecting public.

Either way, I wasn't going to let him put his damn hands on me again.

"Did you two need me to show you to the training room, Ms. Fontane?" he asked through gritted teeth.

I almost told him to fuck off—had my mouth opened and ready—but Marta intervened.

"Yes, please."

I always admired her restraint. Marta could apply reason and calm to any volatile situation. Maybe it came from being a mother. I, unfortunately, had no such quality, and Marta was very aware of that.

"You will need to put your badge on," he said to Marta as he focused his anger on her.

What the hell was his problem?

She rolled her eyes as she clipped the badge to her blouse. "Bastard," she whispered.

Oliver went over to a set of double doors directly across from the elevator, his shoes soundless on the white-tiled floor.

"Ladies," he said as he opened the doors.

I let Marta walk a few paces ahead of me. "Don't you ever fucking touch me again, Oliver," I said, stopping in front of him.

He leered down at me. "Have a nice day… Nicole." He let the door swing shut in my face.

"What the hell was his problem?" Marta asked.

"I don't know. But something is definitely wrong with him. Maybe he could get some of the mind-altering crap they give Nurse Lacy. She was real happy about her job. Or, at least real docile and compliant."

Marta laughed. "I was scared you were going to hit him."

I linked my arm with hers. "I was very close. Luckily, you were here to stop me."

"Kara would have kicked his ass."

I nodded. "So true… so damn true."

We continued down the hall and entered the first open door we came to. Four other people were already inside, seated at long tables that were set up in a spherical configuration.

It resembled a power circle, minus the lines on the floor.

Power circles were used to channel energy. Candles would be placed on the four points of energy—north, earth; south, fire; east, air; and west, water—and the remaining lines in the circle would be occupied by people or objects that directed the energy to the person in the center. This was used in earth magick rituals for the sick. From my limited knowledge of the other principles—faith, mind, and elemental—they didn't use power circles. Of course, faith practitioners did use prayer circles. But that wouldn't fit with what I was seeing.

I started running scenarios through my mind, trying to come up with a plausible reason why they had the tables set up that way that didn't involve magick. I wasn't having any luck. That worried me a little. If it wasn't part of the job, why would they have so many references to magick? Everything about Tribec screamed they were practicing it. Maybe they found the rituals and symbols used in magick intriguing. Similar to their fascination with Gerzean artifacts.

Besides the power circle, the room had only a few additional items. A white board covered the right wall near the door. On the opposite side of the room was a coffee buffet that offered coffee, tea, doughnuts and assorted pastries, and a water cooler. There were cabinets directly above it. The walls were painted the same burnt yellow color, only lighter, and had a few inspirational posters on them. The wall directly across from the door was covered with them.

"Maybe we should sit down," Marta said, and sat in the first available spot.

The chairs were spaced out evenly so that each person was the same distance from one another and sitting on one of the four energy points along with two additional points. Again, more evidence of magick, and if that was the case, I had no intention of closing their power circle for them. I moved the last available chair—located on the west energy point—right next to Marta and sat.

"I'm surprised you want to work here," Marta said. She pulled a notebook out of her bag.

"I don't." Maybe I shouldn't have said that out loud.

She regarded me with a questioning look on her face. Yep, definitely should have kept that little nugget to myself.

"Then why are you here?" Marta asked.

"I ran out of options." I smiled. "How are the kids?" I asked, changing the subject.

Marta's face lit up as she reached into her bag and pulled out her phone. "They are good." She handed it to me. A little girl, who was the spitting image of Marta when she was young, appeared on the screen, holding a doll just as big as she was.

"Is this Maria?"

Marta nodded. She had filled her phone with images of the bright blue-eyed little girl.

When Maria was born four years ago, Kara and I had teased Marta senselessly about cheating on Manuel with a white boy. Maria was lighter than her siblings and had blue eyes. Marta told us she took after a grandmother on her father's side. But that didn't stop the teasing.

It was at Maria's first birthday party that Manuel cornered me in the bathroom of their home and tried to grab my breast. After I fought off his advances, he went after Kara. It was the years of friendship with Marta that stopped Kara from hurting Manuel. He was drunk, like he always was, but that didn't excuse what he'd done.

We told Marta a few days later; she didn't believe us. And she accused me of coming on to him, bringing up my lifestyle, which, up to that point, she had never mentioned. The argument inadvertently ended our fifteen-year friendship.

"Yes, she just finished preschool," Marta said, her voice full of love and pride.

Maria was my goddaughter, and so was her older sister, Isabel, who Marta had before we finished high school. Kara was godmother to her other two children, José and Juan.

I continued to survey the photos. Isabel's serious face appeared on-screen. While she had the same mouth and hazel eyes as Marta, she favored her dad more. Her hair was pulled back in a ponytail, while dark-framed glasses rested on her nose. She had a scowl on her face.

"How old are they all now?" I asked.

"Maria will be five next week. Isabel is twelve, going on thirty." She laughed. "I swear, sometimes she acts as if she's the mother. José is ten. He's playing soccer and has a game this Saturday." She slapped my arm. "You and Kara should come."

"Okay." Was it really this easy for Marta to set aside her anger? I'd expected yelling and accusations. Instead, we'd settled into our familiar bond with ease. Realization that I'd wasted three years missing my friend when I could have just called hurt me deeply.

"Good... and Juan is eight. He loves to draw. But I worry about him."

"Why?" I asked, my voice catching.

"He misses his father. More than the other three."

Marta turned away. It didn't escape me that she didn't mention her own sadness over Manuel's death. Maybe she finally realized what an asshole he was.

Before I could continue looking through the remaining pictures, the hairs on the back of my neck rose. I turned around.

A tall, blonde woman with cold gray eyes stood in the doorway, staring at us. She wore a form-fitting gray skirt that was eight inches above her knee, displaying her long tan legs, and a silk white blouse that showed off the black lace bra underneath.

A man followed closely behind her who was an older replica of Dr. Stewart. He wore an expensive, tailored dark blue suit with a pale-yellow shirt underneath. His hair—although the same color as Doc's—was much more conservative. He had the same dark blue eyes and strong jaw. If not for the few strands of gray around his temple, they could have been twins.

They both wore anticipatory smiles on their faces as they entered the room. Like meeting us was going to be the highlight of their week.

The woman stopped next to me, bent down, and placed a cool hand on my arm. "Would you please move your seat back to where it was so we can begin?"

There was a barely-veiled threatening tone in her voice that, if I hadn't already been concerned about Tribec, I would have missed it. Since telling her no wasn't an option—especially if I didn't want to be asked to leave on my first day here—I picked up my chair and moved it back to its original location. I, of course, shifted it slightly to the left to avoid completing the circle. I still had no solid proof it was a power circle, but I would trust my instincts.

The woman watched my actions with a slight frown on her face. Her eyes circled the entire table and landed back on me.

I smiled.

She didn't smile back.

"Good morning, everyone. I'm Thomas Stewart—the CEO of Tribec Insurance; and this is my sister, Lisa Stewart—our public relations officer." He observed everyone. "Andrew Snow, who will be joining us shortly, will be your instructor for the next six weeks." He clapped his hands together. "But before you get started learning, Lisa and I wanted to welcome you to the Tribec family. We are both extremely excited to see such a vast group of intelligent people who will take this company into the future. Unfortunately, Dr. Stewart could not make it here to welcome you. During the course of your employment, you will discover that my brother is somewhat shy, and quite reserved."

I bit my lip to keep myself from laughing. Shy and reserved in no way described Ronald. He was an alcoholic. Something I was sure his siblings were aware of and would better explain his absence from the meeting. Either that, or he really didn't give a damn about welcoming the new recruits. Yeah, that sounded about right.

"Now, we have many exciting things that you all will be fortunate to take part in." He nodded to his sister. "Lisa, would you like to take it from here?"

Lisa smiled and turned to the group. "Welcome, everyone." She paused, waiting for everyone to respond.

After a brief hesitation, we all said hello.

"Tribec has always been a small, family-run insurance company, and while we could remain small and profitable for years to come, we have decided to expand the business and open new avenues for growth." She smiled as she looked around the room at each of us. "That is where all of you come in. Our growth would require highly-skilled people."

I tuned out the rest of Lisa's happy welcome speech. To be honest, I was somewhat disappointed. There was nothing nefarious about them. They were a cheer squad in suits, rallying the new employees on their first day. But what did I expect them to do? Walk in here wearing ceremonial robes, chanting while the village virgin followed behind them, waiting to be sacrificed for the good of the people?

Instead of listening to any more bullshit, I regarded the rest of the group.

There were six of us total—two men and four women. Marta sat to the right of me—on a focal point in the circle—and next to her was a young African-American girl who looked to be in her early twenties, with long black hair, caramel-colored skin, dark brown eyes, and a small, round face. She was sitting on the north energy point.

I recognized the man I'd seen yesterday, along with the woman he was with. The woman—of Asian descent, with soft, milky skin, pitch-black hair that was cut to frame her face, and dark hazel eyes—sat directly across from me on the east energy point. She appeared irritated, as she tapped her pencil on her notebook. She caught me staring and smiled; as I smiled back, she rolled her eyes, the universal sign we were both listening to an idiot.

The man—early thirties, short light-brown hair, gray eyes, and a really nice build—sat to her immediate right and directly across from Marta on the second focal point. He watched me as I openly stared at him. I smiled and shook my head as I studied the man on his right, who sat on the south energy point.

He was a lot younger than everyone else in the room and wasn't too bad-looking with his dark brown hair that looked as if it had been cut by his mother, and his bright blue eyes. I could see remnants of pockmarks on his cheeks, probably from a recent outbreak of acne. Once that cleared up and he grew a little more, he might turn out okay. Of course, he would also have to stop letting his mother cut his hair.

"Are we boring you, Ms. Fontane?"

I flinched. Damn, I'd been caught.

I turned back to Lisa. Her eyes were hard and brimming with hostility. Looked like someone did not like being ignored. Oh fucking well.

*Yes.* "No," I said.

"You need to pay attention while I'm speaking."

Thomas touched her arm. She turned to him and nodded.

"Excuse me," the man across from Marta said.

Lisa jerked her attention to him and frowned. "Yes, Mr. Carter."

He raised his hands in placation. "Sorry, had something in my throat and wanted to make sure it was alright for me to get up and get some water."

Lisa looked as if she wanted to argue, but after a while, she simply nodded. "Well, if you would like some, I can wait."

She tried smiling, but no one was buying it at this point; even her brother appeared somewhat disappointed.

I decided I could use a drink myself and got up.

The man, who'd saved me from Lisa, stood by the coffeepot, adding the entire box of sugar to his coffee. I inwardly cringed.

"Thanks for the save back there." I walked up and poured myself a cup of coffee. "My name's Nicole."

"Not a problem. She was a little too intense. And I'm Daniel."

I took a sip of coffee. "Um, she was."

I studied him while he assessed the room as if he was watching for an unseen threat. Interesting. The only people I've ever seen do that were cops or military personnel. Was Daniel ex-military? I scrutinized his stance. Body held alert while his free hand hung down at his side. Like a tightly coiled snake that stood ready to pounce at the first sign of trouble.

Yes, he definitely had some combat training. Only, it couldn't have been the military. Most of the men I'd met who'd been in the military lacked any sort of character. Almost as if it had been bled out of them. Even though he came across as being ready for action, he still had a personality. I doubted he was the most outgoing person, ready to shake it up when his favorite song came on the radio, but he was personable and very attractive.

So, what the hell was he doing here?

"If you don't mind me saying, you and your girlfriend look a little out of place here." I took another sip of coffee.

He averted his attention back to me. "I could say the same thing about you." He took a sip of his syrup and continued. "Especially on Wednesday. You appeared spooked. And today, you paused inside the door." He moved a little closer, a slight shift, so that his back was partially to the room. "Do you mind me asking what gave you pause?"

"The configuration of the room." I picked up a buttery croissant, took a bite, and closed my eyes while I savored it.

"You mean the power circle?"

My eyes shot open and relief flooded me. I wasn't the only one who noticed the damn power circle.

He leaned in a little more. "Don't worry; prior to you coming into the room, Rachel and I had already moved our chairs. So, there was no need for you to move yours."

"What?"

"Can everyone please sit back down? I have more to cover before your instructor arrives," Lisa said, interrupting. She looked pointedly at Daniel. "I trust there will be no more interruptions." It was a statement, not a question.

We both returned to our seats.

As Lisa continued with her spiel about the exciting changes to the company, a pasty, round, bald man with bad skin and clear blue eyes walked into the room. He wore a tan suit that he'd obviously bought many years ago, along with a crisp white shirt and dark brown tie. He scanned the room briefly and then settled his gaze back on Lisa.

Lisa acknowledged him with a nod.

"I see your instructor has arrived," Thomas said, interrupting Lisa. "Now, we will turn you over to Andrew, who will get you started on your journey with Tribec." He scanned the room. "Are there any questions?"

Everyone shook their heads no.

Lisa and Thomas walked out of the center of the room, and Andrew walked in. The way they traded places looked choreographed. Neither one of them touched the center at the same time. That was a little peculiar.

Once Lisa and Thomas left, we went around the room introducing ourselves; and then Andrew went into a long dictation about his life at Tribec Insurance. He tried to make it sound as if Tribec was the best place to work on the whole island, which I wasn't buying. Because for a company that paid as well as Tribec, they had too high of a turnover. But then again, maybe they were increasing their staff because of the *exciting changes* that were coming up.

"I won't make it through two weeks of that," I said to Marta as we walked out of the building. I breathed in a lungful of fresh air.

"You are still the same." Marta smiled and shook her head. "But I know what you mean." She peeked over her shoulder at the building. "I don't like this place too much."

"We should both quit." I pulled my keys out of my purse. "I'm sure we could find something else." Well, at least Marta could.

Marta set her manuals and purse on my car as I opened the driver's side door. After throwing my manuals on the back seat, I set my purse down and pulled out a cigar and lit it.

"I've been looking for a while now," Marta said. "There's not much on the island that pays well."

I took a pull on my cigar and leaned back against the car. "I know." I shook my head, blew out the smoke, and surveyed the building. "I have a bad feeling about this place, Marta." I took another pull.

Marta looked at her watch. "I have to get going. You are still coming Saturday to José's game."

I smiled at her. "Of course!" I pushed off the car. "What time?"

"You can come to my house before the game if you want. It starts at ten in the morning."

"I will pick up Kara, and we can ride over together." I dug into my purse for my notebook. "Let me get your address."

Marta took the notebook and pen from me. "Okay, don't be alarmed, but I live in Perry now." She raised her hand to stop my protest. "I understand that you don't like to go into Perry, but trust me, I live in a decent enough area."

"How far are you from Greenwood Apartments? And define 'decent enough.'"

"I can afford it."

"I'm sure there are other affordable areas," I countered.

"Not everyone can pick up and move when they like to, Nicole. I have four kids I have to worry about. They are my priority."

Her bringing attention to my restless nature stung. It wasn't like I set out to constantly move. And I was trying to get my life together. That should count for something. Marta smiled and touched my hand. I fought the urge to pull away.

"Maybe we can meet you at the park," I said, putting some extra cheer in my voice to help put her at ease.

Marta handed me back my notebook. "You better come, Nicole." She grabbed her things off my car.

I took a deep breath. "Fine, I will borrow my father's gun."

We both laughed.

After giving her one last hug, I climbed in my car and started the engine. I waited until Marta pulled off, then I eased my car out of the parking space and followed her out of the parking lot.

As I drove, the space between my shoulder blades began to itch, and a creepy sensation crawled up my spine. I glanced in the rearview mirror, and a sudden feeling of being watched came over me.

The next morning, I spent a great deal of time in the shower. Contemplating, once again, my options. I had none. Something about Tribec worried me. That concern was now overpowering my need for a paycheck. My father would love it if I finally agreed to work with him. But I hated showing my inadequacies when it came to magick. However, knowing my father, he probably already knew. And was just waiting for me to admit it out loud. Sadly, I was too damn stubborn to do that.

After getting out of the shower, I pulled on a dark green skirt and blouse, resenting the fact that I couldn't wear something more comfortable. I didn't understand how people wore restrictive clothes every day. Dressing up to sit behind a desk and talking on the phone with only your co-workers seeing you was stupid.

And knowing myself, I would eventually tell them so. Thus, ending my career in customer service. I sighed, grabbed my purse, and left.

Thankfully, Wade wasn't in the hallway to greet me. If he had been, I might have slugged him in the jaw.

I HAD this obsessive need to be early to work. Not on time. On time meant I'd have to rush in and try to orient myself. But early gave me the much-needed time to collect my thoughts and psych myself up for the day. Sometimes I'd use the time to really focus on a problem. Not that I solved many of them. But I did think about them often. Yesterday, I didn't get the opportunity to do this, which might explain my trying to create problems where there were none by taking their use of magick symbolism and turning it into something nefarious. So today I left an hour early.

The rumble of a car engine pulled me out of my thoughts. I turned toward the sound. A dark blue Buick LeSabre backed into an empty space a few cars down. The driver glanced over at me, and my heart skipped a beat.

Smooth bronze skin, a goatee my fingers itched to trace, and long curly black hair pulled together with string—he couldn't be any more gorgeous if he tried. I started to walk over, then stopped when Rachel climbed out of the car. She waved at me and I smiled. Was he her boyfriend? He winked at me. Okay, maybe not. But I still wasn't going over there. Despite my hormones' sudden need to make a play date.

He continued to stare, and my body took an involuntary step forward. Seriously?

Rachel smiled again. There was a message in that smile. It said, "Yes, he's available." Well, maybe not exactly. I could have been projecting my own desires. Again, seriously, Nicole?

A few seconds later, a black Escalade pulled in beside the Buick, and Daniel got out and glanced in my direction. I had a sudden urge to fix my clothes. He continued to assess me as the Buick pulled out and drove away. Damn. I missed my opportunity.

When they walked by, I noticed that both Rachel and Daniel were wearing jeans. What the hell? I looked down at my dark green skirt and jacket and sighed. I had to have missed something. Was I supposed to wear jeans today?

While they continued to make their way toward the building,

I stood there like an idiot, trying to recall what I could have missed. Yes, I'd tuned most of yesterday out. Besides, Andrew had spent most of the day waxing on poetically about all of his accomplishments and how Andrew was a great this, that, or the fucking other. And I doubted his love affair with himself was important.

Either way, it was too late to go home and change now. After a brief, curse-filled pep talk to get my feet moving, I made my way toward the building.

WHEN I STEPPED into the lobby, a sudden case of déjà vu swept over me. I sniffed the air, expecting to detect the scent of blood. It wasn't there. Just a cloying sort of earthy smell that had my nose twitching. Like they were burning incense. I took in the wards and symbols. Expectant. Like staring at them would reveal what type of magick the Stewart family was practicing.

Oliver stood up, pulling my gaze toward him. He crossed his massive arms over his chest. Fucking bastard. Everything about him made my hackles rise. He smiled at me. Or, rather, leered at me. What the hell was his problem? From day one, he'd had this barely restrained resentment toward me. Almost like I'd come in here and pissed in his coffee. There was a genius idea I wanted to entertain. If I didn't have the training manuals weighing me down, I would have given him the finger. Instead, I rolled my eyes and made my way toward the training room.

Marta stood at the door—wearing jeans and a T-shirt—holding her manuals, with a huge smile on her face. "I didn't think you'd show up," she said, scrutinizing me. "Why are you all dressed up?"

"Aren't we supposed to be?" I asked.

"It's casual Friday."

Of course, it was. "Nobody told me." I should have paid more attention yesterday. I could have avoided being uncomfortable all day wearing this damn scratchy suit.

She shook her head. "It's in the employee manual."

Well, that solved that mystery. Like I said before, there was no way in hell I was going to read that large monstrosity.

When we entered the training room, I stopped dead in my tracks. The walls were covered in white poster boards with our names scribbled on the top. That toxic magic marker smell filled the room to the point of discomfort. I shuddered at the sight of the five large bowls of candy strategically placed all over the room. Were they going to ply us with candy? Seriously? Like we were kids on some damn field trip?

A group of four men and two women stood in the middle of the room. Each of them had this unnatural sheen on them that made them look as if they were glowing. Complete with glassy-eyed smiles, they looked around the room—taking everyone in as if they were trying to evaluate us. They each wore red polo shirts and hats with the company logo on them and large buttons that said: Ask for the sale. Damn.

Doc stood by the coffee machine, talking with his brother, Thomas. Both were wearing red polo shirts as well and a pair of jeans. Doc was a sight to see. Those jeans fit him real nice. His brother turned and gave me a curious look, almost like he was seeing me for the first time. Doc took in my entire body and licked his lips. Bold bastard.

"Hi, Doc," I said, and immediately regretted it. Even I could hear the inappropriate familiarity in my greeting.

He chuckled. "Nicole. You must like wearing business suits?"

"Not really." I took a seat next to Marta. "But they do make me look sexy."

Thomas cleared his throat, and I ignored him.

The rest of the room had gone quiet. Doc continued to smile at me while his brother stared at him with a new level of hatred brewing in his eyes. Definitely had some sibling rivalry going on there. And, although petty of me, I was happy to help stir it up.

"There's going to be a lot of physical exertion today." Doc said 'exertion' like it was a dirty word used in seedy brothels found off the beaten path.

"Are you handing out red shirts?" I asked.

"Yes." He stared at my chest. "You can change before we get started."

I turned away from him and smiled. In my opinion, you always have to try and find joy where you can. And, right now, I really needed some. They had a fucking sales team in here to teach us how to ask for the sale.

"Um... Nicole, I believe you're on my team," Jesse Rollins said as he pointed at one of the posters on the wall. "So maybe we should sit together." There was just way too much excitement in his voice.

"You have got to be kidding me." I stared at my name written at the top along with Mama's Boy. Well, they didn't write "Mama's Boy," but if I had to be on his damn team, I was sure as hell going to.

I leaned over toward Marta and whispered, "What did I miss?"

She shook her head. "We're getting sales training today."

I pulled magic marker-tainted air into my lungs and let it out slowly. Is it possible to hate a job on the second day?

Veronica Lockwood walked in the room and looked around. She had her long black hair pulled back into a ponytail and wore a pair of jeans and a light-yellow t-shirt—setting off her light-brown skin tone. After a brief hesitation, she made her way toward us. "Can we change seats so I can sit next to my partner?" she asked.

"Maybe we can change partners instead," I said.

"Is there a problem, Ms. Fontane?" Thomas asked.

I smiled at him. He flinched. "No, no problem; just want to change partners."

"Yes, well, we have paired each of you up based on your strengths and weaknesses. You'll be working with Mr. Rollins every Friday for the next six weeks."

The hell I would. And when did they assess my strengths and weaknesses?

I shook my head and looked back up at Veronica. She glanced at Thomas, and I waited.

Yes, in the back of my mind, I realized I was being petty. But honestly, I didn't see a way out of the situation that didn't cause me some measure of embarrassment. And besides, I was committed now, and I refused to back down. *Stupid, Nicole.*

"Nicole," Marta whispered. "Are you trying to get fired?"

Was I? I glanced around at the other people in the room. Yes, they were all looking at me. Daniel had a look of disappointment on his face, while Rachel looked amused. I believed Rachel and I were going to get along just fine. Daniel, however, might be just a tad too judgmental for me. Fuck his disappointment.

I looked back over at Thomas. He was glaring at me. I glanced at Doc. His shoulders were shaking like he was quietly laughing.

"Thomas, why don't we let them choose who they want to work with?" Doc said as he continued to stare at me.

Thomas straightened his tie. "Fine," he gritted out.

Veronica hesitated, then moved to the empty seat next to Jesse. As soon as she sat down, Lisa walked in, wearing a polo shirt and tight black jeans. She had her hair up in a playful ponytail and a strained smile on her face. I got the impression she had been standing outside, practicing that look for a while. Andrew walked in behind her and didn't even bother to hide his disdain. Good for him. No need to pretend to be something you're not.

Lisa clapped. "Hello, everyone! Welcome to our pilot training program."

Thomas flinched, Doc shook his head and smirked, everyone else's eyes tried to pop out of their heads, and I tried to smother a laugh. I wasn't successful.

Her eyes tracked to mine. Damn. She glanced up at the posters on the wall and then looked back at me. Here we go again.

"Thomas," she said.

Doc moved toward her. She turned her head slowly in his

direction as if it hurt her to look at him. He leaned down and whispered in her ear. She shook her head and clinched her fists. If she went into a full-blown tantrum, I was going to lose it.

"Absolutely not," she hissed.

She was gearing up.

"Lisa," Thomas said, his voice strained. "Let it go."

She stared icy daggers at him. My guess, Lisa was a spoiled brat and was used to getting her way. Maybe that's why they put her in the position she was in. Because, in my opinion, she shouldn't be allowed to be in any position that required her to interact with people.

After a few more heated words back and forth, Lisa walked away from Doc and put her happy mask back on for the group. Doc resumed his position near the coffee table and winked at me. I suppressed a smile and diverted my attention toward the center of the room.

As soon as Lisa stepped into the middle of the tables, a slight tug pulled at me. All the air left my lungs. It was as if someone was trying to pull my soul out of my body. I gripped the edge of the table and fought like crazy. My vision blurred. Someone was talking. But they sounded as if they were underwater.

When Veronica let out a gasp, the sensation stopped.

What the hell just happened?

I blinked a few times, trying to clear my vision. My head pounded. Marta laid her cool hand on my arm.

"You okay?" she whispered.

I shook my head and pulled in a deep breath.

Magick? It had to be. I glanced around the room. Everyone's attention was still on Lisa as she droned on and on. So, the only people who'd been affected by whatever the hell that was, were me and Veronica. I leaned back and studied Lisa, trying to see if she would give herself away. And although she was speaking to the entire group, her eyes never left mine. There was challenge brewing in those icy depths. That's okay; I wasn't one to back down from a challenge, either.

Game on, bitch. Game on.

"Nicole, are you crazy?" Marta asked as we made our way to our cars.

"Probably," I said. I'd made an ass of myself today. Sad thing was, while I regretted my actions, I was also secretly elated by them.

"You and Dr. Stewart seem close."

There was a slight hint of judgement in her tone that I chose to ignore.

I glanced over at the building, getting a strange sense of déjà vu.

"Didn't we stand by my car yesterday after work?" I asked. Was this going to be my life now? One mindless day after another. Doing the same thing repeatedly. Like I was insane.

"Yes." Marta stared at me like I was crazy.

"How about we stand by your car on Monday after work. Change things up a bit."

She laughed and looked down at my skirt. "You look like a Christmas tree."

I groaned. Red shirt and dark green skirt—yeah, I looked like a damn Christmas tree.

"Hey, why don't you come to Jordin Cisco's tonight with me and Kara?" I needed several drinks. Not to mention, I had an itch that really needed scratching.

Marta shook her head. "I can't. I promised the kids I'd take them to the movies."

"Okay. Well, I will definitely see you tomorrow at José's game." I smiled at her. Worry lines creased her forehead. "What's wrong?"

She looked back over at Tribec. "I don't know, Nicole. I can't help but feel you messed up pretty bad in there."

I set my manuals on her car and pulled her into an awkward hug. "Why don't you let me worry about that?"

She stepped out of my embrace. "I'll see you tomorrow. Okay?"

"Yes. But I'm not going anywhere near your neighborhood."

She laughed, and the tension dropped. I let out a sigh of relief. The last thing I wanted was to mess up our reconciliation. I'd missed Marta and her motherly ways. I would never tell her that, though. She might just give up on passive-aggressive comments and come right out and call me a fuck up.

After Marta drove off, I got in my car and started it. Once I lit a cigar, I glanced at the building once again.

Even though I couldn't prove it, something inside of me was screaming that the Stewarts were using magick on their employees. Unfortunately, I had no idea what kind of spell Lisa had used on me. But I sure as hell was going to find out.

After changing clothes, I stepped outside into the warm, damp air. I was going to meet Kara at our favorite bar, Jordin Cisco's, for drinks—I really needed one—and a juicy burger. Sex with Jordin, the owner, was an option I was entertaining as well.

Dark gray clouds hovered in the sky, waiting to drop a bucketful of rain. Due to the infrequency and short duration of our rain, no one ever carried an umbrella. I just hoped I was inside before it started.

The gray brick building was a block from my apartment and had blacked-over windows and a single reddish steel door left by the previous tenant. The neon sign hanging above the door was missing most of its letters, so instead of "Jordin Cisco's," it said, "din o's." There was an ongoing game we all played where we tried to come up with phrases for the remaining letters. My last attempt was "din of sin." It wasn't funny, but it fit the place.

A row of bushes—watered with mostly beer and piss—ran along each side of the door. The fact that they were still alive was somewhat of a mystery to all of us. But it was the bushes and the neon sign that kept people from believing the place was closed. I guess they figured if someone was still pissing on the bushes, then Jordin was still in business. Only locals dared go inside.

A billow of smoke wafted out as I pulled open the metal door and entered the dimly lit bar. The smell of beer, cigarettes, and cooked meat saturated the air. The place was packed already. Loud voices competed with the song playing on the jukebox. The entire bar was no bigger than a large studio apartment.

Similar to the outside of the building, the inside was left somewhat in the same condition as before. Padded red walls, recessed lighting sprinkled throughout, stone flooring that had mystery stains near the restroom and the front door—probably someone's failed attempt to make it either to the bathroom or outside in time—and a mix-match of new and old, red and black Formica tables.

Like always, women wearing some degree of cloth barely covering their privates packed the front of the bar, all vying for Jordin's attention. One day, one of them would be bold enough to show up in only heels.

But honestly, I didn't blame them. Between his deep bronze skin color, long, curly, dark hair, bright green eyes, and sculpted body, if I weren't already sleeping with him, I would've been the one to come in wearing only heels.

Only two other people worked at the bar with him. Night Hawk—a Cherokee man with long, dark hair and a love of leather vests and tight blue jeans who tended bar when Jordin was gone; and Renee—a beautiful African American woman in her late thirties with a slim build and large breasts.

They took turns serving food and drinks. While Jordin and Night Hawk subjected themselves to being leered at by the women on the front bar stools, Renee had to break a few hands when men got overly friendly. I once saw her snap a man's wrist and serve his food at the same time. The guy even tipped her after he finished eating.

Kara and Paul sat at the end of the bar, talking. Paul—a recent addition to our Friday night rituals—met Kara two months ago while waiting in line at the bank. Slim build, unkempt medium-length brown hair, and dark blue eyes, he'd have been a perfect rebound. Only, Kara didn't do rebounds. What she did do was latch onto unavailable men until they decided to leave.

When she invited him to our Friday ritual the same day they met, I knew something had to be off about him, so I interrogated him.

*Who the hell are you?*
*What do you do for a living?*
*What are your intentions with my friend?*
*Are you married?*
*Are you a serial killer?*

Kara wasn't pleased with my badgering. Paul smiled and said he was an investment banker and worked from home. I wasn't satisfied, and when I started to point out that he failed to answer all my questions, Kara threatened me with bodily harm, so I relented. She could take care of herself, but it didn't stop my worry. It was when Jordin had served us drinks that I learned what Paul's issue was going to be. While Kara made moon-eyes at Paul, Paul made them at Jordin.

I started toward them.

"Nicole." Jordin beckoned me over with a quick head gesture.

"Hey, Jordin."

His usual black, skin-tight muscle shirt clung to his abs, and his jeans rode low on his hips, cupping his ass real nice. The musical notes tattooed on his chest spread out down his arms, adding a sexiness that made me want to lick every inch of him. He told me once they were his harmony and then proceeded to treat my body like an all-you-can eat buffet.

He took a slow perusal down the length of my body and smiled. My nipples hardened and heat pooled in my stomach.

"Want the usual?" He had a slight accent that I could never place.

"Most definitely."

"Nicole!"

I turned to my right.

"I saved you a seat," Kara said.

I refocused on Jordin. "Yes, on the burger and beer." I leaned forward, pushing my cleavage to the brink.

He moved in closer so I could whisper in his ear.

"And yes on the other as well." I resisted the urge to lick the side of his face.

His lips brushed mine. "Come back at closing."

"Oh, I plan on doing just that."

As I walked away, the hussy committee groaned, one of the girls extending it out to include a long, seductive sigh.

Sorry, ladies, not tonight.

Kara smiled as I came sauntering up. She had her long red hair pulled back into her signature ponytail. Kara, like me, chose not to wear too much make-up; only mascara—which made her dark green eyes stand out—and lip gloss. Of course, she did use concealer every once in a while to cover up the small patch of freckles that spread across her aquiline nose.

We met when we were eight years old. I'd been sent to the principal's office for fighting a bully who'd kept picking on me. As I was sitting there, swinging my feet back and forth with my arms crossed across my chest, in came Kara, escorted by a teacher.

She had climbed on the bench next to me and huffed out a breath. "David is a stupid face and so is Peter, so I punched him."

David was the bully I'd beat up, and Peter was the boy laughing as I was dragged to the office.

We'd been best friends ever since.

"So, we know how your night is going to end," she said.

I shook my head and climbed on the bar stool. "You know me so well."

"I really hate you, Nicole," Paul said.

"No, you don't." I snagged a few chips and dipped them in the bowl of salsa. "Besides, you know Jordin is not gay. You and Kara should make out again." I smiled at them as I chewed my salsa-covered chip.

On a dare one Friday, Paul and Kara shared a drunken kiss. The whole bar cheered them on while the two of them made out for thirty seconds. We could be a little juvenile sometimes, but it was fun. The mixture of emotions that played across Paul's face for those thirty seconds would forever go down in history... because we'd all taken pictures of the event. One of which hung on the Wall of Shame behind the bar.

Paul glanced at the picture while Kara smacked my arm, spilling the salsa on my chip. I laughed and scooped up some more.

"So, how did it feel seeing Marta again?" Kara asked, changing the subject.

"Good. She wants us to go to José's game on Saturday. I'll pick you up, and you can drive. That way I can keep my hands free in case there's trouble."

"Funny, Nicole. Marta doesn't live in a bad neighborhood."

"Who's Marta?" Paul asked.

Kara told him about Marta while I watched Jordin make his way to us. He set a Samuel Adams down in front of me and placed a margarita in front of Kara.

Paul perked up. "Can I have another rum and Coke?"

Jordin glanced at him and nodded.

When he walked away, Paul sighed. "What am I doing wrong?"

I looked over at him, bottle of beer halfway to my mouth. "Seriously?"

"Be nice, Nicole," Kara warned.

Paul stared at me intently. "I can take it."

"He's not gay, Paul."

He shrugged as if that was something insignificant that he could overcome. I wished him well.

Kara put her hand on his arm. "It's okay, Paul. We will find someone for you."

What she really meant was "one day you'll see that I'm perfect for you." And when did *we* get elected to find Paul a date? I stared at Kara, who stared back at me. She lifted her eyebrows in an obvious silent gesture that said, "*Yes, we.*"

So, I guess I was included in this matchmaking adventure as well.

"Did you two order yet?" I took another swig of my beer.

"Yeah," Kara said, "and you owe Paul an apology."

Apologize for being honest? Damn. "Hey, Paul, I'm sorry Jordin isn't gay."

He stared down at the table, refusing to meet anyone's eyes. "I know I'm pathetic. It's just so hard picking up men. It's much easier with women."

Jordin brought over Paul's rum and Coke. "I should stick with women." He downed the entire glass.

"Why don't you?" I asked.

"Because, I have always wanted to sleep with a man... at least once in my life before I let my parents convince me to get married and have kids."

"You've never slept with one?"

He shook his head and held up his finger to signal for another drink. When it arrived, he emptied the glass again. Paul was well on his way to drowning his sorrows in alcohol; no sense in him going at it alone.

"Slow down a bit, man," Jordin said after he delivered the fourth glass of rum and Coke, which Paul promptly consumed.

"Sleep with me!" Paul slammed down his glass.

The entire room grew silent, and I lost it. I laughed so hard, beer came out of my nose.

"Nicole!" Kara yelled.

I coughed. "Sorry... sorry." I turned to Paul and cleared my throat. "Sorry."

Paul slid off the bar stool and left out the front door without a backwards glance.

Damn, I could be such an ass. I jumped off the stool and ran after him, chiding myself the whole way. I found him outside, leaning against the building and lighting a cigarette. His gaze remained fixed on the ground in front of him as he took a deep pull.

"Sorry."

"I can't believe I did that." He exhaled.

I bumped my shoulder against his arm. "Hey, we all put our foot in our mouths every once in a while." I looked up at him. "You shocked the hell out of me in there. Pretty bold move. Made me really proud."

He thumped his head lightly on the side of the building and glanced toward me. "I can't go back in there."

"Sure, you can. If you like, I can go in there and flash everyone. It will take their minds off you." It probably wouldn't. I'd flashed everyone before; as I've said, we could be a little juvenile sometimes.

He smiled. "You'd do that?"

"Sure," I said, tugging him toward the door. He didn't budge, so I leaned back against the wall. "Let me have one of your cigarettes."

He pulled the pack out of his pocket. "I thought you only smoked cigars." He shook one out for me.

I took his cigarette, used it to light mine, and then handed it back. "Yeah. But if I go back in there without you, Kara will kick my ass. So, I'm stuck smoking this nasty Newport."

He blew smoke into the chilly air. "You're not seriously afraid of her?"

I glanced up at the sky. The fat rain clouds still hung heavy while the full moon peeked out between the gaps. I rubbed my arms to ward off the chill.

"Have you ever seen her fight?"

"No." He paused. "But Kara is in love with me."

I smiled. "I'm glad you figured that out."

Paul laughed. "Yeah, well, it was pretty obvious when we kissed that it was a lot more than a dare."

I glanced over at him as he gazed up at the sky. Paul was really handsome. Almost pretty.

He glanced at me again. "How do you do it?"

"Do what?"

"Sleep around so much?" He held up his hands. "No judgment, I'm only... curious."

I would never fit into society's mold of how a woman should behave. I'd tried that once.

The one thing I learned from that experience was that I didn't want to settle down. I liked what my parents had—it worked for them—but me, I'd much rather enjoy the freedom of not being tied down to one man.

"I like sex," I said eventually. I dropped the cigarette on the concrete and ground it out with the heel of my shoe.

"You could always have it with just one man."

"I could, but then I would get too bored and start searching for something more exciting." I regarded the sky as if it had the answers to all my problems. "No, Paul, I know myself well enough to know that I need variety." I thumped my body against the wall.

"I'm in love with Kara, too."

I didn't react.

He bumped my shoulder. "Did you hear me?"

"Oh... I knew you were."

He stared at me, aghast. "How?"

"It was in one of those many faces you made while you two were kissing. I never said anything because I figured you'd work things out. I just don't understand why you're so damn fixated on Jordin."

The metal door opened, and laughter from inside spilled out. I glanced around the corner. A group of women moved off down the street.

"I've always wanted to be with a man." He lit another cigarette. "My family always dismissed my feelings and told me that if I prayed hard enough, they would go away. But no matter how much I prayed, they didn't."

I couldn't figure out why Paul was telling me all of this. After our initial meeting, we kept the talk between us to a minimum. He always focused his attention on either Kara or Jordin. Something that really didn't bother me. So why now? Damn. That would make twice this week that someone had felt the need to confide in me. I seriously hoped this wouldn't become a habit. I had problems of my own.

"I hate that fucking metaphorical closet that society has created."

"Yeah, well, society has a closet for you, too," he said.

"No, promiscuous women don't have closets. We have cages."

"What do your parents think about your lifestyle?"

I pushed off the wall and stretched. "My mother's French; they invented promiscuity." That wasn't the real reason I slept around so much, but I wasn't in the mood to examine my life choices now.

"That's what my parents hated the most. I never was *in the closet*." He laughed without humor.

I really wanted to go back inside, but I didn't want to kick Paul in the guts twice by leaving. Besides, this was the perfect opportunity for me to ask him a few questions without Kara around to stop me.

"So, do you live with them here in Brunswood?" I asked.

He pushed off the wall. "Please don't tell Kara what I told you."

It appeared as if I had hit on something he *didn't* want to talk about. Strange that where he lived was viewed as more personal than his non-existent sex life. What the hell was up with this guy?

"Your secret is safe with me. Now, let's go get that fifth glass of liquid courage."

He laughed. "You don't need liquid courage."

"True, but I do need liquid."

9

W hen we entered the bar, a few people decided it was a good idea to start clapping.

"Cut it out!" Jordin yelled.

I smiled at him and mouthed, "thank you." He winked and went back to making drinks. Damn, that man was sexy.

I grabbed Paul's arm—I was a little afraid he might decide to leave—and we made our way to Kara. She had found a table in the center of the bar next to a group of drunks.

Renee set our food down at the same time we sat, and I wasted no time digging in. The next few minutes were, thankfully, spent in blissful silence while I devoured my burger and trough of extra-crispy fries.

As I ate, I could sense the men behind me shifting and gearing up for a confrontation.

"Are you going to tell us about your second day at Tribec?" Kara said as she shoved away her empty basket.

I sat back and rubbed my belly. "It was okay. I might quit." I couldn't tell Kara how I'd made an ass of myself; she'd get that look on her face. It always made me feel small. So, while Marta preached, Kara had mastered the art of preachy-filled looks. I hated it. I caught Jordin's eye and signaled for another drink.

Paul snorted, and I gave him a pointed stare. He shrugged and went back to picking at his fries.

Jordin came over and set another Samuel Adams down in

front of me. He glanced over at Paul, who was trying really hard to turn invisible. It wasn't working.

"Next drink is on me, man," Jordin said.

Paul glanced up. "Thanks."

Jordin rapped his knuckles on the table and walked away.

"What do you mean, you might quit?" Kara said.

Jordin returned with another rum and Coke for Paul. I took a long pull of my Samuel Adams before answering.

"Something is a little peculiar about the place." I blew out a breath.

"Peculiar how?" Kara asked.

Both Paul and Kara were familiar with magick. Kara a little more so, since she was an earth practitioner. Well, at least, she used to be. She never told anyone why she stopped. But I always believed it had something to do with her evil grandmother. And Paul only indicated he had a working knowledge of the principles. He never stated whether he practiced or not.

"When I went for my interview on Wednesday, I could have sworn they had a power circle drawn on the call-center floor. Then, yesterday, as I'm walking in the training room, I notice that the tables are set up like a power circle, too." I omitted that Lisa might have used a spell on me. I wanted to find out more about it first and confirm my suspicions.

"Did you ask them about it?" Kara asked.

"A lot of companies hire faith practitioners." Paul took a bite of his burger and started chewing. "But they don't use power circles. Maybe a prayer circle." He shrugged.

"That's the same thing I thought. But it doesn't fit. The configuration is not right. Besides, doesn't a prayer circle only involve people?"

Paul shrugged again.

Kara studied me for a few minutes. "You're imagining things."

I finished my beer. "Maybe you're right. But what's really bad is they expect us to sell insurance."

"Don't you need a cheery disposition to do that?" Paul asked.

Kara laughed. I ignored them both. He was right, of course. I wasn't cut out for sales. I was too much of a cynical bitch to ever be able to talk someone into buying anything. Hell, I might even try and talk them out of it.

I smiled at Paul. "Hey, why don't we go to Shasm?"

"What... no, we can stay here," he said.

"I can see your purple thong," the man behind me slurred.

Well, what do you know; one of the drunks had built up the courage to speak.

"Oh, look, he knows his colors," Kara said.

We both laughed loudly.

His chair creaked, and the smell of unwashed ass and too much alcohol assaulted my nose.

"Hey." A dirty hand landed on my shoulder. "I'm talking to you."

I craned my neck and stared at him. Did this guy ever hear of soap? A razor?

"Why?" I asked.

Paul and Kara chuckled.

"Huh?" he asked, as confusion creased his brow.

"Why are you talking to me?"

That seemed to puzzle him even further. He stared back at his friends for the answer.

"Go away," I said when he had turned back around.

His face scrunched up. Oh shit, the confusion must have cleared.

"You think you're better me?"

Well, maybe it hadn't cleared completely. "Better *than* you?" I corrected.

Okay, now I was just poking the bear.

"Leave her alone," Paul said.

He cut his eyes to Paul. "I'm not talking to you, faggot!"

Kara jumped up, and I scooted back out of the line of fire.

"What the F did you call him?"

"You should go ahead and use the word 'fuck,' Kara. It will

get your point across more effectively," I said, and then took a pull on my beer.

She gave me the finger.

"What, no index finger instead?"

She laughed. The drunk stood there through the whole exchange, listing to the side with a confused look on his face. If I looked up at him and laughed, it would only make him more agitated, so I kept my eyes on Kara. Of course, I still laughed.

"Hey!" the guy yelled while alcohol-laced spittle flew everywhere. I guess he was tired of being ignored.

"Go the *fuck* away," I said.

Before he could respond, Jordin came over and grabbed him by the back of his neck. "It's time for you to leave."

The guy tried to turn around, but Jordin only squeezed harder. His friends jumped up as if to come to his rescue, but one look from Jordin had them moving toward the door instead. Jordin let go, and the guy rubbed his neck. He took one drunken step toward me, glanced at Jordin, and then turned around and followed his friends out the door. Of course, he called out a few brave-man words before slamming the door to emphasize his point.

"You guys cool?" Jordin asked.

"Yeah, we're fine. If you hadn't come over, Kara would have kicked his ass," I said.

Jordin regarded Kara, dipped his head in acknowledgement, and focused on me. I smiled and wrapped my lips suggestively around my bottle. He smiled and walked away.

"You are so bad, Nicole," Paul said.

I glanced at him and winked.

He turned to Kara. "Thanks for having my back, even though you really didn't need to."

She put her hand on his arm and smiled. "I always fight for my friends."

That was true.

After Paul had a few more drinks—I really didn't know how

he was still functional—we cajoled him into going to Shasm. Since it was the only gay nightclub on the island, I was really surprised he'd never been. His parents must have really fucked him up.

We all piled into Kara's car, and ten minutes later, we arrived at Shasm. The place was packed. We all climbed out of the car— Paul trying to hide a stumble—and started for the line outside the door.

They let us in fifteen minutes later, and after making a brief circuit around the club, I got approached by Barry, who used to be Belinda. He bought me a drink and convinced me to dance with him for the rest of the night. He kept his hand on my ass the entire time. I broke his heart when I told him I had to leave.

Kara stopped me as I was leaving. "Don't you need a ride?"

"No, I'll catch a cab." I glanced over her shoulder. "Where's Paul?"

She looked around. "I haven't seen him."

I smiled. "Hey, maybe he got lucky."

"Bye, Nicole." She turned and walked away.

I shook my head and left. I really hoped she would get over him soon. Paul's life was too damn complicated.

THE CAB DRIVER—A family man with four kids, two dogs, and an ungrateful wife—dropped me off at Jordin's after two in the morning.

"I hope everything works out," I said, and handed him a large tip that I couldn't afford.

Filled with an abundance of need, I made my way to the rear of the bar where Jordin's apartment was. He was locking up when I strolled up and pressed my body against his.

"Um... hello," I said as I inhaled his sandalwood and citrus scent.

He shifted, wrapped his arms around me, leaned down, and nipped my neck. A shiver ran down my spine as warmth spread inside my stomach.

"Hello yourself," he rumbled, the warmth in his voice washing over me.

He stood in the dark recess of the doorway, the moonlight barely touching him. But I could still make out the strong line of his jaw.

"I've had Barry's hands on my ass all night, and I couldn't stop thinking about you."

He slid his hands inside my jeans and cupped me from behind. "Who's Barry?" He bent down and ran his warm tongue over my lips.

"Who Belinda was destined to be," I breathed as I opened my mouth to his kiss.

Jordin consumed my mouth like a man who'd been starved to death as his rough hands ran over my ass, the friction causing both pain and pleasure. He eased my pants down in the process, and when the cool air touched my bare skin, I pulled away.

"Maybe we should take this upstairs." I kissed his chin.

He shifted to whisper in my ear. "Or maybe you should let me take your pants off so that I can taste you."

My stomach quivered, and I found it really hard to formulate any coherent thoughts for a moment, which apparently Jordin took as consent. He was on his knees in front of me, working my zipper down, before I even had time to register it. I made a half-assed effort to push away but eventually relented as he pinned my bare bottom against the door. If it was cold, it didn't register; my skin was too overheated.

"I really like this purple thong," he said as he slid it down my legs.

I stared down at him as he looked up at me.

"Spread your legs," he said.

I did as I was told and arched back when his mouth found that sweet spot; my fingernails dug into the door as Jordin bit down lightly on me. When he lifted my right leg and put it over his shoulder, I moaned.

He reached up and pulled down my shirt to expose my breast as his tongue worked feverishly. Bringing me so close I thought I would die if I didn't come. It was when he stuck two fingers inside me that I finally lost control. It was also when the cloud that I had noticed earlier decided to finally release the rain it had been holding all day.

I stood there, my legs shaking and my body convulsing while the rain beat down on my overheated skin. I was barely aware of Jordin scooping me and my clothes up and carrying me upstairs to his apartment. When we got inside, he placed me down inside the doorway. I shoved my wet hair back from my face and blinked a few times.

Jordin stood directly in front of me, panting with so much heat in his gaze, I thought he might combust. He kept his eyes on me as he peeled off his clothes and dropped them on the floor; they landed next to my discarded pants and thong. I pulled my top and bra off and stood there waiting.

In one fluid motion, Jordin lifted me up, pushed me against the wall, and entered me. One second, we were panting at each other, and the next, he was filling me completely. I'd lost track of the many times and places that we had sex, but I did know that by the time we actually made it to his bed, my body felt as if it were vibrating, and my legs had gone completely numb.

My gaze landed on Jordin. He was covered in a light sheen of sweat. His left arm was thrown over his face, and his breathing was even and steady. I didn't know how he managed that; I could barely catch my breath.

He turned toward me as if he could sense me staring at him. He kept his arm over his eyes as he reached out and touched my arm.

"I'm spent," I said. I shifted so I could be closer to him and the heat that radiated off him.

"Your body is pulsating. I like the way it feels." He lifted his arm and stared at me. "What are you thinking?"

I shook my head and shivered. His place was always so damn cold. He wrapped his arm around me and pulled me closer.

"Better?" he asked.

The heat from his body suppressed the chill, as his desire to continue pressed against my back.

I reached back and wrapped my hand around him. "I find it real hard to believe that you're in your thirties," I said, stroking him.

"I'm older than you think." He ran his tongue on the ridge of my ear.

"Yeah, well, I don't care how old you are; you can't seriously be ready to go again."

"I'm always ready."

"I'm not up for another round, Coach; you might have to bench me this inning."

He chuckled then rubbed his erection against my hand to emphasize how ready he was.

"Nice, but I can't feel my legs or any damn thing else."

He rose up over me and pushed my legs apart. I had doubts about my ability to go another round, but somehow, with his persistent urgings, I was able to find the strength. We both fell asleep an hour later, still intertwined.

"Did you want coffee?"

I cracked my eyes open. Jordin stood next to the bed, holding a cup of coffee, wearing only his black silk boxers. My mouth watered. And not just for coffee.

"Um… Yeah, thanks." I sat up, took the cup from him, and sipped.

Black. Just like I liked it. But of course, he would know that. We did this song and dance almost every Friday, and on occasion, during the week. I tried not to occupy too much of his time. He did have what amounted to as a harem of women. And I had other men I saw as well. Well, I did have other men. I was going through a bit of a dry spell that could explain my recent bout of moodiness.

Jordin's eyes dropped to my exposed breasts.

I smiled as I took another sip of coffee. Damn, I needed that.

I looked around the tousled studio apartment. His living room comprised of a red futon, purple recliner, a battered wooden coffee table, and two large lamps with mix-matched shades. The kitchen was sparse, with only the essentials.

"Damn, where didn't we have sex?"

He sat down, and I handed him the coffee. "Are you staying?" He stared at me over the rim of the mug.

I glanced at the clock on his nightstand. It was too damn early! If I hadn't promised Marta I'd go to José's baseball game, I would.

"Not today. I have to pick up Kara in an hour."

He set the mug on his nightstand and pulled me up. "We didn't have sex in the bathroom." He kissed my neck. "We can take care of that now."

I followed him into the bathroom without hesitation.

After he washed both of us, he bent me over the sink and reminded me why I was so damn addicted to him.

I ARRIVED HOME AN HOUR LATER, feeling as satisfied as a Cheshire cat with a bowl of cream and some catnip. I plugged in my phone to charge and walked into the bedroom to dig out something to wear to José's baseball game.

When I bent down to rummage through my clothes basket, my eyes were drawn to my notebook that had somehow ended up on the floor. I reached down to pick it up. A single scrap of paper along with an ID stuck out from under the bed. As I picked both of them up, my cell phone rang.

"Hello," I said, still staring at the contents in my hand.

"Nicole, this is Ronald Stewart."

I took the phone away from my ear and stared at the display. Sexy Doc. How the hell did he get my number? As soon as I thought it, I realized that he probably obtained it from my medical forms.

"Hi." I turned over the scrap of paper in my hand. I was so transfixed about what was on it that I missed what he had said to me. "Sorry, what did you say?"

"Is it a bad time?"

"No, it's fine; I was trying to find something to wear." What should I wear to a baseball game? What were the team colors? I should have asked.

He cleared his throat, and I visualized him removing his glasses and rubbing the bridge of his nose. "I was calling to invite you to dinner tonight. I've made reservations at Lucina's."

I absentmindedly agreed and then rattled off my address. I didn't hear what time he was going to pick me up because I was too busy staring at the card in my hand and wondering how the hell I ended up with Vincent's ID.

K ara lived in Brunswood, close to the Cherokee Nation border in a neighborhood that reminded me of the bayou. A small pond separated the settlement from the border, along with two medium-sized hills. Large cypress trees covered in Spanish moss loomed up between the houses, and small collections of water from last night's rain shower lined the unpaved streets.

Kara's small, blue house sat nestled at the end of the block, near the pond. Aideen Flynn—Kara's grandmother—had left her the house when she moved off the island six years ago. It was an abrupt departure that we celebrated with copious amounts of alcohol and fried foods.

I parked my car in front of her house and got out. Two cars, which I didn't recognize, sat in the driveway along with Kara's. One, a small red Corvette, the other a beige, four-door Honda Civic. A mosquito landed on my arm as I trekked through the small puddle of water that always sat at the end of her driveway. I swatted the blood-sucking insect, killing it instantly, as I glanced inside the Corvette and tried to figure out who the car could possibly belong to.

The inside of the vehicle was a study in red and black. Sleek lines, a navigation system, and a shamrock air freshener hanging from the rearview mirror were the only items inside. Nothing personal to give away the owner's identity.

Before I could move on to the Honda, Kara's front door slammed open, and I jumped. Kara came rushing down the porch steps; Paul—carrying a blue cooler—followed close behind her.

"Let's go," Kara said.

The urgency in her voice immediately put me on guard. "What's wrong?"

"Hi, Nicole," Paul said as he made his way to Kara's car.

That explained one car. And the sudden appearance of Aideen Flynn in Kara's doorway explained the other one.

"Hi, Paul." I tried to keep the petty jealously out of my voice. The glance from Kara told me I didn't do a good job of it.

Why the hell did she invite him?

"Nicole..." Kara started. She opened the trunk for Paul, and he set the cooler inside. I seriously hoped he wasn't coming with us.

"Henri Fontane's daughter," Aideen said. "Get away from my vehicle."

Kara's grandmother was a cold-hearted bitch. Her hair—red streaked with steel—was pulled back into a tight bun. She wore her usual attire of black jeans and a black turtleneck. A silver chain lay on her chest, a Celtic cross dangling from it. Her appearance, cold and devoid of sensation as it was, was not the most disturbing thing about her. Her eyes, gray and full of ice, bothered me the most. She never called me by name, always "Henri Fontane's daughter," despite her never having met my father.

"Don't talk to her." Kara turned around and faced her grandmother.

Paul placed his hand on my arm, and I resisted the urge to smack him. "We should probably stay out of it."

I ignored him.

"Watch how you speak to me, Kara Flynn. Remember what I can do to you."

A malignant power rolled off of her, engulfing me in a chilly fog. I glanced down at myself, convinced I would actually see fog rolling over my skin. Except for the hairs on my arm standing up, there was no evidence of what she was doing. I looked over at Kara. She stood there, ridged, as if she was fighting some unseen current.

Aideen was letting her anger show by lashing out with her magick. Using it to prompt a reaction from me or Kara. My father could do that. Could let the power inside of him out in small bursts. I asked once how he did it, but sadly, he never told me. However, I didn't need it. If Aideen wanted a confrontation, I didn't need magick to deal with her. I might feel bad afterwards about fighting Kara's grandmother. Might. But it wouldn't stop me from attacking her if I needed to. I would protect Kara, always.

"I'm not a little girl anymore, Maimeó. I won't kowtow to your threats," Kara said.

Aideen stepped forward, and Kara lifted a foot to step back, stopping herself at the last minute. It didn't matter that she did. The reaction had already been seen. Kara was afraid of her grandmother. And from the looks of it, she always would be.

I moved in front of Kara. Aideen watched me out of those icy eyes. A small smile creased her lips.

Kara laid her hand on my arm. "Don't bother, Nicole. Let's just go."

I kept my eyes locked on Aideen's. I didn't like the menace in hers and refused to back down from her unveiled threat.

"Are you challenging me, Henri Fontane's daughter?"

"Yes. If you don't stop messing with Kara, then I will make you stop."

She laughed—a big, throaty sound pulled from deep inside of her—and turned and went back in the house. It didn't matter that she laughed. All that mattered was she had turned away first.

For the first five minutes of our journey to the ballpark, Kara didn't speak. Paul, thankfully, had decided not to come with us. Selfishly, I wanted it to be just me, Kara, Marta, and the kids, and I wasn't going to apologize for it. Besides, something about him was suddenly making me uncomfortable. Until I could put my finger on exactly what it was, I wouldn't mention it to Kara.

"I'm sorry you had to get in the middle of that," Kara said eventually.

"Why did she come back?"

Kara glanced at me. "You shouldn't threaten her, Nicole. It's not…"

"I can handle Aideen."

"No, you can't. And let's drop it, okay?" She reached out and squeezed my hand.

It pissed me off that hers was shaking.

"Please. Let's just focus on today." She smiled, her mask slipping back in place. The one she wore all the time. The one that told the world that she was eternally happy.

I had learned early in our friendship that it was a lie, but I never called her on it. Besides, I had a mask as well, one that I worked really hard at holding in place. I was surprised it hadn't affected our friendship. Maybe one day, we could be honest with not only ourselves, but each other.

"Are you nervous about seeing the kids?" she asked, adding joy in her voice.

I rubbed my hot, clammy hands on my thighs. "Yes. I should have gotten them some toys or something." My nerves were on edge. I had essentially abandoned them when Marta and I had stopped speaking. What should I say? Should I apologize? "Yeah, I should have gotten them something."

She laughed. "You can't bribe them, Nicole. Besides, they will be really happy to see you—especially Maria."

I smiled. I would be happy to see them, too—more than happy. But it didn't stop my hands from shaking, nor the sudden ache in my heart.

I glanced over at Kara. Despite the levity that she had, the fear was still there, along with a chilling amount of anger. I didn't say anything. Not yet. But I did plan on talking with her grandmother again. She wouldn't cause my best friend any more pain if I could help it.

WE ARRIVED at the ballpark located in the middle of Pleasanton, a mile from my parents' house, twenty minutes later. The ballpark took up a five-mile radius and had seven fields available for games. All the schools—five high schools and seven middle-grade schools, there were no junior highs—used the same field for softball games. We had to circle the site several times before we were able to locate a spot.

"Does every school on the island have a game today?" I asked as I climbed out of the car.

The parking lot was packed with kids and adults all milling around. A couple stood by an old, beat-up red truck, arguing, while their kids danced around them—screaming at the top of their lungs. A group of teenage girls wearing matching white shorts and blue tank tops played hopscotch on the sidewalk. Hopscotch? Didn't they ban that stupid game a long time ago? Heat rolled off the ground, seeping into the soles of my feet.

Kara opened the trunk and pulled out the cooler. "Yes. Marta said it might be packed. We have to walk to the north field." She smirked at me. "Help me with the cooler, and don't complain."

"This is bullshit," I mumbled under my breath.

"I heard that."

I wasn't going to last the entire day. I hated large crowds. "Did Paul opt not to come?"

"You should stop being so nasty to him, Nicole. He's a nice guy."

"I'm not nasty to him." She didn't answer my question. I glanced at her. She was making a point not to make eye contact with me. "What's going on, Kara?"

She frowned. "He came over this morning to confess that he was in love with me."

"What did you say?" That saved me from having to tell her.

"I told him that he should find someone to make him happy. It would be very stupid of me to wait for a man to get his homosexual fling out of the way before he decided to date me." She smiled. "I need to get back on the market."

I maneuvered around a group of teenagers smoking pot and had a brief pang of nostalgia. That used to be us. "You were never off the market, Kara."

"Very funny, Nicole." Kara glanced back at the group of teenagers. "Maybe we should say something to them."

"Like what? Don't do drugs?"

"Yes," she said.

"Would you have stopped way back when if some random stranger told you to?"

She laughed. "I probably would have cussed them out."

"No, you would have used the first letter of every curse word and sounded like an idiot."

"Shut up. And by the way, Paul will be here today." She glanced at me. "Whatever your issue is with him, tell me already. Or let it go."

I shook my head. "It's... okay."

She studied me for a minute. I kept my eyes averted. I couldn't tell her I wanted Paul to leave. As irrational as it was, every fiber in my being was screaming at his intrusion.

Satisfied, she continued. "One of my students, Trisha Greenhaven, has an older brother playing today. She gave me a handmade invitation for the game. So, I'll be bouncing between José's game and her brother, Carl's. Paul is going to Carl's game."

How nice of him. Fucking suck-up.

We walked onto the field and made our way to the bleachers.

"He won't intrude on our reunion," she said.

Before I could respond to her, Maria came running over, carrying a doll almost as big as her.

"Aunt Cole!"

She had always called me that. When she was younger, it was hard for her to say Nicole. Of course, it sounded more like, "Coe," but I understood her.

I had barely enough time to drop the cooler, drop to my knees, and brace myself before the little ball of energy launched herself at me. Moisture filled my eyes as I squeezed her, inhaling her strawberry scent. It was hard to speak, partly because of the emotions that were lodged in my throat, and partly because of the enormous doll she had pressed into my stomach.

I was really surprised she remembered me.

"Hi, sweet girl," I finally managed to say.

She peeled herself off of me. "Did you bring me a present, Aunt Cole?"

I glared at Kara.

"I brought you something, Maria." Kara opened the cooler and pulled out one of the many bite-sized, cellophane-wrapped cakes she had stashed inside.

I got to my feet. "Oh, so I can't bribe them, but you can?" I whispered.

"Sugar is the one thing the kids and I have in common, Nicole." She pinched my arm. "Don't hate."

Marta came running around the corner near the bleachers. "How many times have I told you not to run off, Mejia?"

Maria stared up at her mother innocently. She had managed to inhale the entire cake in less than thirty seconds. "Seven," she said as she opened the cooler and pulled out another cake. Her doll lay abandoned at her feet.

"She is so much like you, Nicole. I would swear you were her mother." Marta pulled me into a hug. "Come see José before he has to go to the field."

I grabbed one of the cooler handles, and Kara grabbed the other.

"Where is your friend Paul, Kara?" Marta asked as she picked up Maria's doll in one hand and took Maria's hand in the other.

Maria's face was covered in frosting.

Kara avoided my gaze. "I'll introduce you later," she said.

I didn't care what Kara said, she wasn't done being fixated on Paul. It bothered me that she felt the need to lie to me. I never gave any indication that I had a problem with Paul. Well, not until today, at least. I rattled the cooler to get her attention. She turned.

"I'm sorry," I mouthed.

She smiled. "Me too."

"THE OTHER TEAM has better players than us. But we have a secret weapon." José pointed to a tall kid standing on the field, swinging the bat back and forth. "Leonard flunked twice, but they still let him play, so he's got skills."

Leonard didn't sound too bright, but I didn't tell him that. "What about you?" I asked as I squeezed him. I hadn't been able to stop hugging him. He had grown so much since the last time I'd seen him. In another year, he'd probably be taller than I was.

He looked up at me, his dark brown eyes filled with conflict. "I'm good. But Leonard is better." He shrugged. "I'm glad he's on our team."

It wasn't healthy for him to think so little of himself. I made a mental note to ask Marta about it; not that I was any authority on mental health but hearing him put himself down like that bothered me. Didn't kids usually believe they were the best at everything?

"You should head down now, mi hijo." Marta said.

José pushed up. "Watch me shine, Aunt Nicole." He ran

down the bleachers to join his team on the field. That was much better.

"Go get 'em!" I yelled.

A pang of guilt seized me. I should have kept in touch with them as well as let go of my petty grudge a long time ago. I'd missed a lot of their lives, and most of Maria's. Marta told me that she kept a photo of me in Maria's room, explaining why Maria—who had been one when I stopped coming around—still remembered me.

I glanced over at Juan and Kara. He sat pressed up against her side, drawing in his art pad. He had refused to acknowledge me when I first walked up. While his siblings had forgiven me, Juan hadn't. I needed to find a way to fix that.

Isabel sat a little down from us with her boyfriend Richard, or, as Marta referred to him, her friend from school. Isabel slanted a glance my way, a smile playing across her face. I winked and smiled back.

"I feel like we should go down there and glare at the boy Isabel is sitting with," I said. Maria dragged her doll over and climbed on my lap.

"They're just friends, Nicole," Marta said as she leaned over and wiped Maria's face. Marta was in denial.

"I want another cake, Aunt Cole."

"You've had enough, Mejia."

"I only had four," Maria pleaded.

"Four is enough." Marta narrowed her eyes at Kara. "Why did you bring all those cakes?"

"She was trying to bribe the kids." I poked Maria in the side. She giggled and kissed me on the cheek. "I told her it wasn't a good idea to bribe them, especially with sugar, but she didn't listen."

"I'm sure you did, Nicole," Marta said.

"The cakes are for me," Kara said as she helped Juan color a picture he had drawn.

Juan sneaked a glance my way; I smiled, and he looked away.

Marta told me not to push him, said he would come around eventually, but I'd wasted enough time already. Besides, I didn't operate that way. I shifted Maria to the bench and moved down to sit next to him.

"That's nice, Juan," I said.

No response.

I leaned in and kissed the top of his head. "I'm sorry," I said.

He sat there, silent. I struggled with what else I could possibly say to make him understand I really did mean what I said. I glanced over at Kara. She gave me a small, sad smile, broadcasting what Marta had said earlier. It would take time.

"Can I help you color?" I asked.

At first, I believed he wasn't going to respond. I even held my breath. But slowly, he reached into the pack of crayons and withdrew a red one.

After handing it to me, he said, "Don't leave, Aunt Nicole."

If I hadn't been leaning toward him, I would have missed his barely audible plea.

"I promise I won't."

After leaving the kids in a sugar and fast-food coma and apologizing to Marta for helping put them in that condition in the first place—she was never going to forgive me for that—I spent an hour at the mall. I arrived home at a little after seven with a short red dress that showed an obscene amount of cleavage. I had gone back on my promise to myself to avoid using credit cards. However, the rules of first-date etiquette dictated I needed to look my best, all but requiring me to purchase something new.

The dress had long sleeves and a deep-cut V-neck that came all the way down to my belly button and hugged my body like a glove. It barely covered my ass. If things went right on the date, as I hoped they would, the dress would serve its purpose beautifully, making the hundred and fifty dollars I spent on it more of an investment. At least, that was how I chose to interpret it. An investment into the overall enjoyment of the evening. The lie sounded good and a bit uplifting.

Freshly showered, I spent the next twenty minutes saturating my hair with mousse and pulling it back into a tight bun, leaving a few tendrils out along my face. Of course, by the end of the night, the bun would come loose anyway, but at least it would start out looking nice.

I applied a few swipes of mascara and some deep crimson lipstick and went into the bedroom to put on the dress. After rubbing some gold body glitter along my chest and spraying on my favorite perfume—"Fancy" by Jessica Simpson—I stood back and examined myself in the mirror.

Ronald wouldn't know what to do with himself.

I dislodged my favorite gold sandals from the bottom of my closet, along with a small clutch purse to match. I'd just put my phone in it when the doorbell rang.

My heart skipped a beat as I made my way to the door. Before I opened it, I glanced over my shoulder at my living-room. I probably should've spent a few minutes straightening it up, or at least putting away the boxes scattered all over the floor. Oh well, too late now.

I opened the door and did a double-take.

"You look beautiful," Ronald said.

"Damn," was all I could manage to say as I took him in.

The dark blue, casual suit he wore set off the blue in his eyes nicely, and he'd slicked back his shoulder-length hair into a pony-tail. I could have sworn he used some kind of lip-thickening cream to rub on his lips, because at that moment, they were downright irresistible.

He moved toward me, and I stepped back to let him in.

"Are you ready?" His eyes made a slow trek down my body. "I like that glitter on your chest. Please tell me it's edible."

"It's... it's edible." I shut the door behind us. Heat spread down my body, and my stomach quivered.

He moved in closer, and this time, I didn't move back as he ran a finger down the curve of my breast. When he placed his finger in his mouth, moisture pooled between my legs. Damn, this man was sexy as hell.

"I know what I want for dessert," he said and leaned down and claimed my mouth.

I sighed as I wrapped my arms around his neck and tilted my head to deepen the kiss. His hands were all over me, and before I knew it, he had turned me around and inserted his hand inside the front of my dress. My head lay on his shoulder as he kissed me and massaged my breast. He tasted like brandy and mint.

I reluctantly pulled away. "Maybe we should go before we miss our reservation."

"Maybe you're right." He kissed the side of my neck. "It's chilly outside. Did you want to get a jacket?"

"Um... yeah, hold on." I rushed back into my bedroom.

After grabbing my black cardigan and draping it across my arm, I retrieved my gold bracelet from the dresser. I fumbled to secure it to my wrist without success. The clasp was broken and one of the charms—a fleur de lis with a phoenix flying behind it—was also damaged. When did that happen? The other charm—an ankh, was intact. I never left home without it secured to my wrist. I'd have to get it fixed soon, which meant spending even more money.

A rustling sound coming from the living-room startled me. I placed the bracelet on the dresser, its absence already bothering me, and made my way back to the living room.

"Searching for something?" I asked, catching Ronald going through one of my boxes.

He let the flap fall back in place and smiled. "Just curious." He took the cardigan from me, wrapping it around my shoulders.

After locking my apartment, we made our way toward the front. Fragrant scents of shrimp and spices wafted out of Mr. Wan's apartment. Ronald opened the front door and stood to the side to let me walk out. He looked over my shoulder as I walked past, and I just knew Wade had come out. Nosey bastard.

"Nice car." He opened the passenger door to his black Jaguar convertible for me.

I slid inside and sank down into the plush leather seats. He shut the door, cutting off the sound from outside. After climbing in the driver's seat, he slid a hand up my leg and leaned over and kissed me. Once he succeeded in making me wet again, he turned on the car.

"Do you want me to turn on the seat warmers?" he asked as he backed out of the spot.

"Yes, otherwise I might have to go inside and change my underwear."

He turned on the heater. "You could take them off."

I smiled. "Maybe later."

Lucina's was located off the coast of Alice and built on a pier that extended one mile out onto the ocean. By 2004, all of the shops had gone out of business, leaving the pier abandoned. Jean Paul Puissant—a French chef from Louisiana—bought the pier and built an elaborate restaurant that he named after his Aunt Lucina, who was an Italian woman with a thirst for rich food and good wine. The restaurant served variations of French, American, and Italian cuisines.

We arrived fifteen minutes before our nine o'clock reservation.

As we made our way up the boardwalk, Ronald put his hand possessively on the small of my back. "It looks like rain." He gazed up at the darkened sky, the moon completely covered by clouds.

"Yeah, two nights in a row," I said.

Hushed voices and lights set to promote an intimate atmosphere greeted us when we entered the restaurant. The scantily dressed, dark-haired hostess beamed at Ronald and completely ignored me. I wasn't the jealous type, so I let the slight go. Besides, I was the one going home with him tonight.

The hostess led us out to the patio to a spot that overlooked the ocean. After handing us our menus and lingering over Ronald's shoulders a little longer than necessary, she finally took our drink order and sashayed away.

"This is a nice spot," I said as I opened my menu.

"Have you been here before?"

"Yes, a few times. It's a popular date spot—expensive, but popular."

"Well, order whatever you want."

I tipped the menu down. "Oh... I planned to."

I wasn't extremely hungry, having filled up on hotdogs and popcorn, but I did want to draw the teasing out a little more. It made the sex at the end of the evening so much better; all that pent-up desire suddenly being released.

The bottle of Asbach Uralt that Ronald ordered arrived along with two glasses. He poured both of us some and sat back to savor it. I took a sip. The same brandy he had served me in his office on Wednesday. I picked up the bottle and examined it.

"You always drink this stuff?" I asked.

He closed his eyes and slowly nodded his head. A small smile creased his mouth. "I had a German roommate in college who swore by it." He opened his eyes. "The guy stayed drunk. He couldn't function sober."

I was starting to wonder if maybe Ronald was the same way.

The waiter, a tall, Caucasian man with long dark-brown hair and a slender build, set down a basket of bread and butter. "Are you ready to order?" He had a strong French accent.

We both placed our orders. I got the shrimp rémoulade salad with a side of dirty rice, and Ronald ordered the catfish court bouillon with white rice.

"So, tell me about yourself," Ronald said when the waiter walked away.

I laughed. "Not much to tell. Besides what I told you in your office on Wednesday." I didn't like the whole get-to-know-you portion of dating. If I was being completely honest, I didn't like dating period. Going out to eat and having sex was what I enjoyed. Spending time with someone in hopes of starting a relationship was not my style. So, I avoided the question and answer portion like the plague.

He smiled and poured us both another glass of brandy. The wind blew over the fire pit next to our table, causing the flames to dance. "Maybe we should have gotten a table inside. It might start raining soon."

I gazed at the sky. "Nah, not yet. Probably a few hours off." I took another sip of brandy. It warmed me better than the fire.

"How can you tell?"

I reached inside the breadbasket for a roll. "I take it you haven't lived here long."

"No, I moved here five years ago after college."

"Well, you get used to it the longer you live here," I buttered the warm roll.

Ronald stared at my mouth, transfixed. The flames from the fire pit danced in his eyes.

"What?" I asked.

"I love your mouth," he said. "I have a very vivid picture of what I want you to do with it." He took a sip of his brandy, regarding me over the rim.

"You're forward." I glanced at the other guests sitting near us. Ronald wasn't exactly keeping his voice low. "You said Emilia liked to watch you. Is that because you sleep with all the female employees?"

His mood shifted as he poured more brandy into his already full glass. "No, I don't know why they feel I need someone to babysit me," he started. "But it doesn't really matter, anyway." He upended his glass and filled it again. The question obviously unnerved him for some reason. "My family"—he chuckled without humor—"are a bunch of idiots."

"Why are they idiots?" So, it was his family that had Emilia watching him. Interesting.

He smiled. "Because they believe the lie I told them about the blood."

I paused with the glass of brandy halfway to my mouth. "What do you mean you lied about the blood?" I set the glass down on the table and leaned forward.

He studied me for a moment. Anger danced in his eyes briefly before he averted his gaze in an obvious attempt to hide it.

"Ronald?" What the hell was wrong with him?

He touched my hand. "I apologize, Nicole. I'm usually better at keeping the rift between my family and me at the office. Let's just say I don't agree with some of their practices and leave it at that."

I pulled my hand back. "You took blood from me on Wednesday. The implication that you're lying about it is concerning." I paused. "As you told me on Wednesday, the art displayed on the wall is from the Gerzean culture. I know they practiced blood magick." I leaned forward. "Does your family practice blood magick, Ronald?"

He sighed. "No, they don't." He poured another drink for himself. "I don't agree with their 'everyone must be healthy to work here' mandate. So, I have, on numerous occasions, lied about the health of an employee." He leaned back in his chair and stared at his full glass of brandy. "Minor illnesses that I detect in a potential employee's blood, I have omitted from the reports my brother, Thomas, insists on." He reached for my hand again. "Nicole, I really don't want to further taint our time together. Please accept my apologies."

"Did you detect anything in my blood?"

He smiled. "You're perfectly healthy. And very damn sexy."

I smiled, despite the feeling in my gut that Ronald wasn't giving me the entire story. Besides, although I couldn't prove it, I still believed Lisa had performed some sort of spell on me Friday.

"To be honest, I might not be returning to work on Monday."

He frowned. "Please don't make a decision based on my issues with my family. You stated you needed the money." He reached for my hand. "I don't want to be the cause of your leaving."

Our food arrived before I could formulate a diplomatic way to explain my trepidation. Even though my uncertainty was grounded in something real, I still needed to understand it. And to do that, I'd have to dip into my savings and pay Luisah. Damn.

Obviously, taking my silence as consent, Ronald changed the

subject and told me about his years in college and the trips he had taken. He asked me a few questions here and there, but mostly, he spent the time talking about practicing medicine in another country. His face glowed as he spoke about his desire to continue with the passions he had enjoyed before his family hoodwinked him into working at the company.

Through it all, he managed to polish off not one, but two bottles of brandy. By the time we finished dinner, he was in no condition to drive, so I ended up having to get us to his place. I didn't complain. I knew we'd end up there anyway. With his address pre-programmed into the GPS, I maneuvered that powerful vehicle through the streets. And since Ronald slept the entire way to his house, I pretty much ignored the speed limit.

Dulean was an upscale settlement with large, lavish houses that sat on the border of the Tulare River. Most of the homes were nestled inside of gated communities. The remaining residential area was closer to the manmade lake in the center of the settlement that had a beautiful view of the small mountain range that sat on the border. They even had houseboats on the lake and cabins near the shore.

All of the settlements, except Brunswood and Perry, had collections of mountains separating them. But only Dulean took advantage of this, using the scenery to over-price the homes in the area.

I had a view of the mountains as well, only I wasn't paying out the ass for it.

I pulled up to the boatyard and glanced over at Ronald. He had fallen asleep with his hand on my thigh. If we had hit any speed bumps along the way, he would have been holding on to more than my leg.

I shook him gently. "We're here."

He jolted awake and slid his hand up my leg the rest of the way. His pinky grazed me, and I removed his hand from between my legs—an impulse that was a bit confusing. Especially since I'd come here for one reason only. So why did his touching me suddenly make me uncomfortable?

He blinked a few times and stretched. "The gate number is 4435."

I didn't move. Surely, he didn't expect me to get out and open it.

"I'll get the gate." He climbed out of the car.

"You're damn right, you will," I said to his receding back.

After he opened it and climbed back in the car, he directed me along the narrow driveway to a houseboat made of wood and glass that sat nestled in between a grouping of cypress trees.

The glass allowed an unobstructed view of the entire dwelling. The entire top floor featured a massive bedroom and bath area. Sliding doors opened up to a large balcony right off the bedroom. Ronald was a voyeur. I could actually picture him standing, in all his glory, in front of those glass doors, sipping a cup of coffee laced with brandy while he stared out at the lake. The bottom floor comprised of a living-room, dining-room, and kitchen.

I parked on a small wooden driveway next to the boat and climbed out of the car. Warm wind blew, rustling the trees. The briny scent of the lake engulfed me. A frog croaked nearby.

Ronald placed his hand on the small of my back. I pressed my body into his. After helping me up on the platform, he opened the door. The boat rocked gently as I followed in behind him.

Once we were inside, he turned on the lights. The space was all clean lines and functional, with no adornments on the wall or knick-knacks on the shelves. Impersonal. And very different from the passionate, sexually charged man standing next to me. It was almost as if he had designed his home to fit someone else's idea of him—a sort of illusion for the real man underneath.

"Did you want a drink?"

"No." I slipped my shoes off and walked over and peered outside at the water. Some of the lights were on in the houses surrounding the lake. "You're not shy about letting people see you?"

He moved behind me, pressing his erection against me. "I don't like hiding. Unfortunately, I'm forced to on a daily basis." He kissed my neck, sending shivers down my spine. He'd found my sensitive spot. "I refuse to hide who I am in my own home."

He moved away from me. I turned around. He removed his coat as he made his way to the couch.

After sitting down, he patted the space next to him. "Come here."

As I started toward him, he held up his hand to stop me.

"Take off your clothes first." He stared at me, his eyes full of heat, as he undid the buttons on his shirt.

Heat pooled between my legs as I slowly worked my dress down.

"Leave the panties on and sit on the coffee table." He removed his shirt and undid his pants.

I sat down in front of him, and he pushed my legs apart.

"I've been waiting to taste you all night, Nicole."

I shivered and my eyes grew heavy with lust.

He pulled my panties to the side and slid a finger inside of me. I moaned as I opened my legs wider. He pushed me back; my head dangled off the side of the table. Mouth warm, he bit the inside of my thigh, and I whimpered. After pushing my legs as far as they would go, he ripped my panties off and bit down on me. I bucked under the onslaught of both pain and pleasure.

Sliding his arms underneath my legs, he lifted me up off the table and brought me to his mouth. His bites were hard, and his tongue worked feverishly. When he suddenly stopped, I thrust my hips forward, my body aching for his tongue to return.

"Do you want to go upstairs?" He kissed my inner thigh and stood.

"Yes," I breathed.

He pulled me up. "Then take off my pants."

I slid his pants down his thighs. His erection pushed out between the folds of his boxers, large and ready. I bent forward and drew it into my mouth. He held my head steady as I gently worked it.

"I'm not ready to be done with you yet, Nicole." He lifted me up. "Come with me."

I followed him up the winding steps to the second floor. The bed sat flush against the wall directly across from the sliding glass doors. Ronald ran his hand down my back as I sat down on the edge of the bed. I slid back toward the headboard.

"Open your legs wide." Easing in between my thighs, he grabbed the back of the headboard and entered me with enough force to rock the bed.

I dug my nails into his back as he thrust hard inside of me. Pounding. Pushing to the point of maximum pain. I had this sudden, overwhelming need to be in control. I lifted up, forcing him to sit back, and placed one hand on his shoulder and one on the headboard for leverage. I elicited guttural sounds from him as I rode him hard.

My skin overheated. Sweat coated my body. Ronald leaned forward, licked my skin, grabbed my hips, flipped me over onto my stomach, and placed his hand on my neck to hold me still. As he shoved inside of me, I screamed out. Placing his free hand on my left leg, he pushed it out as far as it would go. Stretching me. The pain was intense. Ronald continued to ram himself inside of me. Punishing me.

I shifted, trying to get comfortable in the awkward position he held me in, but his grip tightened on me, stalling my progress.

"Hold still," he commanded as he let go of my neck, placed his other hand on my right leg, and pulled me back toward him. "Just hold the fuck still." He slid his arms underneath my legs and lifted me up in the air so that my breasts were pressed against the mattress. I gripped the sheets as he dug his nails into my thighs and increased his thrusts.

I couldn't move, which was both erotic and scary at the same time. I had never felt this kind of pain and pleasure in my life.

I placed my fingertips on the bed and held on while his thrusts became frantic. My orgasm rushed to the surface. I yelled as I came, my body convulsing. A few seconds later, Ronald bit my leg hard, and he emptied himself inside of me.

After a few moments, he laid me back down on the bed and rolled to the side. I shifted, pulling his sweaty body into view. His arm was stretched out to the side while his chest heaved up and down.

"I do need a drink," I said. My throat was dry.

He glanced over at me.

"Of water," I amended.

He smiled, got up, and made his way downstairs.

I turned over onto my back and lay there, my body still humming from the orgasm. I was sore and would no doubt feel it in the morning. Ronald came back into the room, and I surveyed him through hooded eyes as he brought me a glass of water.

"Damn, you have a nice body," I said.

He sat down beside me and took a slow perusal down my body. My nipples hardened.

"So do you. As a matter of fact"—he ran his fingers over my nipples—"if you stay, I can promise you that I will show you just how much I loved fucking you."

I eased up on my knees and moved to straddle him. "You have shown me that already." I nipped his ear. "Besides, I need to get up early." I wanted to stop by Vincent's house before I met Kara at the dojo for Krav Maga at ten.

He grabbed my ass and pulled me closer. "Not nearly enough." He took my breast into his mouth.

I arched back as he bit down on my nipple. "Damn!"

"Are you ready for more?" he asked.

"Are you?"

He pushed his erection against me to accentuate how ready he was. He picked me up and walked over to the sliding glass doors.

I slid down his body as he deposited me in front of the doors. "Face the glass."

I did as I was told. Ronald spent the next two hours taking my body to the brink. I tried not to think about the lights coming on in the houses directly across from his, nor did I dwell on the fact that I really liked that they had.

When Ronald finally fell asleep, I went downstairs and called a cab. It had started to rain by the time the taxi arrived. I made a mad dash to the vehicle to avoid getting completely soaked.

"Nice house," the cabbie said.

I shut the car door. "Yeah, it's nice."

I gave him my address and leaned back against the seat, captivated by the distorted images caused by the rain drumming on the window. I was falling back into my old patterns. Why did I sleep with Ronald? It wasn't like I had a hard time finding willing bed partners. What I told Paul on Friday night was correct. I enjoyed variety in my life and got bored really easily. How did that saying go? *Don't shit where you eat.* Well, tonight, unfortunately, I had managed to do just that.

Kara always asked me why I didn't try to find someone to settle down with. I told her the same thing I told Paul. Only it was a lie. Truth was, I had loved someone once, but a shard of broken glass ended all possibilities of me ever acting on those feelings. Even to this day, I still blamed myself for Steve's death.

Melancholy set in, and I blinked a few times, fighting back the tears. I didn't have any regrets about my decisions. And I wouldn't let anyone else's ideals color how I lived my life. When my pep talk didn't stop the pain brewing in my chest, I closed my eyes and blocked out the world.

"Is this your place?"

I jolted awake.

The hypnotic melody of the rain beating against the roof must have lulled me to sleep. Momentary confusion settled over me as I stared through the curtain of rain at my apartment building. My surroundings seemed unfamiliar. I'd moved so many times that home was more of an illusion than reality, and right now, that illusion was bathed in a watery distortion. Making me wonder if I really belonged here. And if not here, where?

"Are you alright?" the cabbie asked.

"Yes, thanks, this is my stop." I pulled myself together and shook off the last residuals of sleep and melancholy. *Get your shit together, Nicole.*

After handing the cab driver a twenty, I climbed out of the cab and into the pouring rain. By the time I was under the awning, I was completely drenched. I shivered as I reached for the wooden handle to pull open the door. As I did, the hairs on the back of my neck rose, and unease settled over me. I looked through the curtain of rain that ran off the roof of the awning. The pitter-patter of it was loud as it hit the ground.

I moved back to the walkway and into the downpour. The mousse in my hair made a sticky trail down my back, and my hair lay flattened against my face. I pushed it away from my eyes so I could see.

Rain pelted down and outlined a male figure standing across the street. He was insubstantial, appearing only as a black cardboard cutout or a silhouette. Making the bushes behind him visible. I shielded my eyes with my hand and stared at him standing there motionless, watching me. Car lights flashed as a car drove by, momentarily blocking my view. The rain eased up suddenly, and when I looked back at the spot where the figure had been standing... he was gone. I stood there shivering for a while with my new dress plastered to my skin.

I tried to convince myself that it was a hallucination brought on by fatigue, but I couldn't. He had been there. I would bet my life on it. I stood there a while longer, trying to come up with a plausible explanation for what I'd seen. In the end, I dragged my tired ass inside. I would worry about it tomorrow.

Once I got inside my apartment, I locked the door and went into the bathroom. After peeling off my ruined dress, I hung it up over the shower rod. I didn't feel like drying my hair, so I wrapped it in a towel and made my way to my bedroom.

I turned on the small lamp on the nightstand, peeled off my bra and underwear, and let them fall to the floor. Once I pulled my earrings off and set them on the dresser, I shut the door and lay down heavily on the bed. I pulled the covers over me and tried to quiet the unease in my gut.

*It was only a hallucination, Nicole.*

I slept, but not for very long, opening my eyes after what felt like a few minutes. Something was wrong.

As I shifted, I felt someone lift up off the bed. I watched as the indentation in the mattress slowly filled back in. It was as if someone had been sitting there and, when I moved, decided to get up. I bolted off the bed and scrambled to the corner, grabbed the metal pole I kept for protection, and frantically searched the dimly-lit room. My heart raced as I waited, plastered to the corner, sweat dripping down into my eyes. The only sound was the whirring of the refrigerator. Adrenaline flooded my body as I made my way to the door.

I eased out of the room, turning on lights as I went—bathroom, hallway, living-room, kitchen—all of them were empty. I stood in the kitchen, trying to calm my heart. My throat was dry, so I reached into the refrigerator for a bottle of water. After I emptied it, I went to the front door to make sure that it was locked. Satisfied that I was alone, I went back into the bedroom and sat down on the bed. I glanced at the clock on the nightstand and sighed. I'd been asleep for only an hour.

I moved back under the covers and lay down on the pillow. My heartbeat was still pulsating rapidly. I laid my hand on my chest and took a deep breath, closed my eyes, and opened them again. The bedroom door had been opened. I'd shut it before I had gotten in bed the first time. But when I'd been awakened, the door was wide open. Even if I believed that some sort of spirit or ghost had been sitting on my bed, watching me sleep—as unnerving as that thought was—I doubted that it could ever harm me. But something with the ability to open doors could.

And that something... had smelled like blood and sand.

According to the address listed on Vincent's driver's license, he lived in Perry. Thankfully, his house was located closer to the border of Pleasanton, about a mile from Greenwood Apartments that sat in the middle of what most people on the island called, 'the war zone.' Any closer, and I would have opted to forgo my curiosity and wait until Monday to ask him why and, more importantly, how he put his ID in my bag.

I pulled up to the dilapidated, once blue-colored house and rechecked the address on Vincent's ID. This couldn't be where he actually lived, could it? Even though Perry wasn't the most lavish of areas, the homes outside the crime area were still pretty decent. Vincent's house, however, was a damn eyesore.

The square-shaped house was covered in faded blue siding with patches of yellow in various areas. It was as if someone attempted to fix up places where the siding might have come off and decided to go with a different color altogether. One of the shades from the two front windows lay against the house, caked in what I assumed was mud, while the other one hung on by a thread from the rusted metal hinges, waiting for a single stray breeze to knock it over.

The yard looked as if someone had stopped in the middle of mowing it to take a break and never returned, leaving a large patch of long grass to dry up and eventually die despite our rain show-ers. A reddish-brown, iron-oxide-covered tricycle coated in dirt sat in the midst of the un-mowed grass, playing hide-and-seek; or maybe it was just hiding. I almost felt sorry for the rusted thing. The flowers around the base of the house had pretty much given up and died, a few inches from a spigot that still had the water hose attached to it, hanging on for dear life.

A rusted gray metal fence surrounded the monstrosity. I got out of my car and made my way to the gate. The smell of wet, dead grass and shit assaulted my nose, and I sneezed. I did not want to enter that yard. Unfortunately, if I wanted answers, I would have to.

The gate creaked as I opened it.

Throw-up mixed in with some dirt from the yard coated the walkway leading up to the house. I tried to watch where I stepped, but it was useless; the only clear areas on the concrete were not big enough to step in, so I was forced to step in some of the mystery filth. I would have to buy myself a new pair of shoes when I got paid.

The screen door was made of wood and covered in dirt. I doubted anyone would really be able to see out of it. I pulled the frame open with the tip of my fingers and pounded on the door hard. I hope he heard me the first time, because I wasn't going to touch that damn thing again.

Who the hell would want to live like this?

Heavy footsteps shook the porch, and the inside door banged open.

"Who the fuck is pounding on my door?" the person on the other side of the screen said.

"Hi, I'm sorry to bother you. Is Vincent here?"

An eyeball appeared in the middle of the muck.

"I don't know you, and I doubt you're Vincent's girlfriend. He's too damn fat!"

When the woman opened the screen, I got my first view of what I assumed was Vincent's mother. She wore a white cotton housedress from the '70s with bright orange, yellow, red, and green flowers printed on it. I doubted she had washed it since the day she bought it. Her hair was a greasy mop of gray and black that lay plastered to her head. She had on at least two pounds of make-up and bright pink lipstick that flaked off when she talked. She completed the outfit by bathing in a vat of cheap, floral-scented perfume that didn't hide her obvious aversion to bathing.

Poor Vincent.

"Are you a hooker? Is that where all his damn money goes? On hookers? Well, I'm gonna put a stop to that right now! I need supporting, and if he can't do it, then he should move his useless ass out of my house! This is the thanks I get for letting him live in my house for all these years? He should have left right along with his useless daddy."

She continued on her tirade of just how useless Vincent was for a long while. I stood there, eyes glazing over, trying to keep calm and remember that I was taught to respect my elders. It took two minutes for my mind to yell, *Fuck that*.

"Either go get Vincent, or I will find a train to throw you from." At least I didn't curse at her.

She stared at me for a moment. I doubted she got the reference to the Danny Devito movie.

"Hussy," she said as she took in my jean shorts and red halter top.

"Excuse me?"

"He's not here. I got back from the casino, and that fat fuck wasn't here. He didn't even have the decency to be home to make sure I had my breakfast. What kind of son does that to his own mother?"

I wasn't going to answer that question.

"Do you know when he will be home?"

"I'm not telling you!" she yelled and slammed the door in my face.

I counted to ten—something I learned from my mother. When that didn't work, I flipped off the door. I knew she saw my extended finger as I pressed it against the peephole. Her labored breathing gave her presence away.

After I was satisfied I'd made my point, I left.

Once I got back in my car, I removed Vincent's ID from my back pocket and put it in my purse. I glanced at the decrepit house. I wouldn't come home, either. Hell, I probably would have run away when I was two, diaper bag and all. I might have even taken the tricycle with me to save it from its pitiful death.

Damn, I would have to wait till Monday to return his ID and get an answer to my question. If I believed she would give it to me, I would ask his mother for his phone number. But that would mean another trip through that yard, and that wasn't going to happen. Besides, I needed to get to the dojo to meet Kara for class.

Frustrated, I started the car and pulled away from the curb.

When I reached the end of the block, a niggling on the back of my neck made me pause. A white, nondescript van had pulled up to the curb in front of Vincent's house. Three men climbed out and made their way up to the door. A fourth man stood by the van and casually surveyed the neighborhood. When he zeroed in on my car, I drove off.

I STOOD outside of Ezra Abijah's dojo, located in the settlement of Tulare in a strip mall five miles away from Tulare River and two miles from the border of Coeur D'Alene. It sat adjacent to Haller's Grocery Store and Ming Ling Donuts and Ice Cream, and was actually two storefronts combined into one. According to Kara, the previous tenant—Bartholomew Steinberg, who sold rare clocks—told the owner that he refused to work next to a rag head, which was what he so lovingly called Ezra. He had demonstrated his racial dislike by peppering the entire strip mall with hate posters. The owner eventually asked him to leave and leased the space to Ezra.

Munching on a croissant while I waited for Kara, I cursed

myself again for allowing her to talk me into taking this damn class in the first place. I'd told her on numerous occasions that I didn't need to improve my fighting skills. I wasn't at war with anyone and didn't see the need to learn Krav Maga.

"Pummeling someone to death is not fighting, and you need to learn some discipline and technique," she had advised me.

Apparently, learning martial arts together was a good way for me to learn it.

As I stood there baking in the heat, my head feeling as if someone was massaging it with steel gloves, I thought about the encounter with the entity I'd had last night. It had that same acrid scent I'd smelled when I first entered Tribec Insurance on Wednesday.

Before last night, my interest in the references to magick at Tribec were only a mild curiosity. One I would have eventually gotten around to finding out more about. But after the events of last night, I could no longer ignore the nagging feeling in my gut that something was off about the way they brazenly displayed the artifacts related to blood magick. Nor could I dismiss the possibility that Lisa used magick on Friday. At least, I believed she did.

The little bits and pieces were working out to be something. But the picture of it wasn't clear.

I'd once gone to this yard sale—some interesting buys were often found there—where this woman had set up a table full of odds and ends. Piles of junk. Well, amongst this junk was a zip-lock bag full of puzzle pieces, with the word PUZZLE written on front. There was no picture to show what the puzzle was supposed to be, just the pieces.

That was what I thought about the oddities that I had been confronted with thus far. The obelisk on top of the building, the smell of blood and sand, power circles, wards, Vincent's ID in my bag—I was still perplexed as to how he had managed to get it in there in the first place—the entity from last night, and lastly, Lisa using magick on me on Friday. I could add Doc to that list, but I was still trying to figure him out.

A sharp pain on my wrist pulled me out of my pondering. When I had eventually dragged myself from bed this morning—I was unable to fall back asleep after last night's scare—my right wrist had felt very hot. Now the heat had dulled to a discomforting ache with occasional flares of sharp pain.

As I took a sip of my coffee, wishing like hell I had a cigar, Kara came bouncing up—red hair pulled back, gym bag thrown over her shoulder, and Jackie O sunglasses perched on her nose. I tried to smile.

"You look like crap," she said.

"Well, it's definitely a step up from how I feel." I moved to give her a one-armed hug.

She plucked the remainder of my croissant from my hand and took a bite. "Sorry I'm late." She reached for my coffee. "You haven't by any chance decided to start using sugar this morning, have you?"

"Hell no." I glanced at my watch. "You have time to get some from Ming Ling."

She dropped her bag next to mine on the sidewalk and crouched to get out her wallet. "Why didn't you go inside?"

"I'm in a bad mood, and I really don't want to talk to anyone right now."

Kara pulled money out of her wallet and looked up at me. "Good, you can channel that bad mood into fighting." She stood up. "I need fuel. I'm going to get some donuts and a coffee. Did you want anything else?"

"Yes, a less chirpy best friend who will be very understanding if I tell her that I would like to go home, soak in the tub, and crawl into bed and go to sleep for the rest of the day."

"I will be back in a minute." She rushed off without even acknowledging my very reasonable request.

Class started at 10 a.m., which left us with only fifteen minutes to change. *Fuck this.* I was too damn sore to deal with this shit this morning. I picked up my bag, ready to start for my car, when Kara came bouncing back with a bag full of donuts and a coffee. Too late.

Kara frowned. "Where the hell are you going?"

I sighed and pulled open the door. "Nowhere."

The dojo was enormous, with light brown walls and a large floor mat that almost took up the entire space. A punching bag, a set of free-standing weights, and a water cooler that always needed to be filled ran along the back wall. The backroom was comprised of a short hall that had an office, a changing room with a shower, and a door marked "private." The inside of the changing room had a free-standing wall that allowed men and women to have privacy.

After making our way back to the changing room, I set my bag down on the bench, took a deep breath, slid out of my shorts and eased into my black Lycra bodysuit. We weren't allowed to wear shoes in the dojo, so I slipped on some black socks. I extracted my gloves and a bottle of water from my bag and stowed the bag in our shared locker.

I turned around. Kara was sitting on the bench, scrutinizing me. "Why are you moving so slowly?"

"Doc was trying to rearrange my insides last night."

"Translation, he was a little rough." She slipped on her gloves, pulling the Velcro straps tight against her wrists.

"He created a new category of rough."

She got up from the bench and threw an arm around me. "Well, let's go out there and work out that soreness. Beating someone up always makes me feel better." She said this as if I should feel the same way.

"Have you considered adjusting your lithium intake?" I asked. We walked out to the training area.

"Funny, Nicole."

We sat down on the edge of the mat and waited for class to begin. Ezra—six feet tall with short, dark, wavy hair that had no style or definition; a permanent five o'clock shadow; tan skin; dark brown eyes; scars all over his well-defined chest; and a large lion tattoo covering his entire back—stood in the center, waiting for everyone to settle down.

"Today, we will work on our *Muay Thai* technique," he began. "For those of you who are new to the class, Krav Maga is a combination of many fighting techniques." Ezra held up his fingers and ticked them off. "Boxing, Savate, Muay Thai, Wing Chun, judo, jujutsu, wrestling, and grappling." He paced as he talked. "You will master each technique separately. Others teach by combining all of them at the same time. This is *not* how I will do it in my dojo." He observed the class to see if there were any objections.

The speech was for the three new girls who, at the moment, were staring at Ezra with an unveiled hunger in their eyes. I'd had that same awe on my face when Kara had brought me to the class for the first time.

"Kara," he said.

Kara jumped up. "Yes, Sensei."

"Demonstrate."

Kara went to the center of the mat as Ezra surveyed the class for another volunteer. If I shrank back, he would pick me, so I sat there like everyone else with a look of indifference on my face. I did not want Kara to demonstrate on me.

"Cedric."

Cedric—bald head and too much chest hair—jumped up and joined Kara on the mat.

Ezra took us through a series of punches, kicks, and elbow and knee strikes. After each technique was demonstrated, we all stood in a semicircle to practice while Kara, Ezra, and Cedric walked around correcting our techniques.

I was doing fine until we got to the kicking part. It was a little hard to bring my leg up without experiencing a sharp agony running down my inner thighs, so I went about my kicks half-assed.

"Bring your leg up," Ezra said.

Damn, this was going to hurt. I bent my legs a little.

"Good, now push out." He moved behind me and gripped my upper thighs.

I moved forward and kicked, blinking rapidly past the pain. I was doing it wrong.

"You need to build up more strength when you kick. Your boxing is fine, but your kicks are weak. I can work with you after class." He moved on to the next student.

Great, more paid-for torture. I had to quit. The only thing was, I didn't have a sufficient excuse to do so. I couldn't blame it on not having enough money. Kara was paying for it. And I couldn't say I didn't like it. I did like fighting; I just didn't need to learn how to. In my opinion, I already knew plenty.

For the last twenty minutes of class, Ezra paired us off for matches.

He paired me up with Tanner Everett—a short, white man in his early forties who smelled like he was on the verge of having his deodorant expire, and who, I believed, had a deep-seated hatred for women. Or people in general, because every time he came to class, he was angry and went to great lengths to demonstrate how irritated he was by putting way too much force into his matches.

I was going to get my ass kicked.

When it came time for our match, I moved to the middle of the mat and tried hard not to show any fear. Tanner smirked. My bravado obviously wasn't working.

"You will be using the elbow techniques," Ezra began. "Remember"—his eyes bore into Tanner—"you will use only minimal force when executing your blows." He kept his gaze on my opponent for a few minutes and, after a short beat, turned to me. "Nicole, you start."

Since Krav Maga philosophy was to neutralize threats before they occurred, we didn't get into any type of stance. I attacked. Twisting my shoulder, I moved in the opposite direction, aimed my elbow toward his chin, and struck. Tanner countered by raising his elbow and thrusting forward before I could make contact. He struck my arms with enough force to make me stagger; I started to yell foul but was met by a double elbow chop to my shoulders that forced me down.

I recovered and countered his next move—another forward thrust that I blocked with my left elbow. I brought my right elbow across his chin. I didn't wait for him to recover. Instead, I repeated the strike, and since he opted not to pull his punches, I returned the favor by using all the strength I had to essentially pummel him to death with my elbow. I would have succeeded in doing so if Tanner hadn't viewed me as his own personal anger-management doll.

My skin heated. I narrowed my eyes and pulled strength from the adrenaline suddenly flooding my body. This bastard was not going to get the best of me.

My next strike was met with air as he turned around in a spinning elbow move and struck me so hard that my arm smashed into my face. I couldn't bring my right arm back up to strike, so I reversed the defense position, using my left elbow to strike with and my right to defend. It turned out to be my undoing, because my arm was in too much pain to effectively block anything.

His next move—a double elbow chop—brought me down to my knees. But he didn't stop there; as I fell, he spun around and elbowed me in the face. Blood sprayed from my mouth. I turned to defend myself against another assault, but found Tanner on his knees, warding off multiple kicks from Kara. I would have laughed, but it hurt too much to even move.

After Kara landed one more blow to the side of Tanner's face, Ezra pulled her off him. She wasn't even winded. Tanner glared at both of them. It was obvious to everyone—from the amount of damage that Kara had done to Tanner's face—that Ezra had taken his time before intervening.

"You know, this is very familiar." I held a pack of ice to the side of my face.

We were sitting outside of Ezra's office, waiting for him to finish talking to Tanner. I had to rinse my mouth several times to get the taste of blood out. I'd bitten the inside of my cheek. Hard.

"Yeah, Tanner is a stupid face," Kara said, mirroring her comments about David and Peter from when we were eight.

I chuckled. "Don't make me laugh. It hurts."

The door opened and Tanner stormed out with a murderous look on his face. His eyes found mine. His nostrils flared and his fist clenched. Kara swung her leg out dramatically and smiled. Tanner narrowed his eyes in anger and started for us.

Ezra came out and stepped in front of him. "Leave now." He turned to us. "You two, in my office." He left without waiting for us to respond.

I stood and made my way toward Ezra's door. Tanner stepped in my path. He was one bold son of a bitch. I would give him that.

"Bitch," he whispered through gritted teeth.

"Asshole," I hissed right back, stepping around him.

"If you don't move, I'll kick you again," Kara said.

After one last hateful glance, Tanner walked away.

We entered Ezra's office at the same time.

White walls with a single Krav Maga poster hanging behind him, a black filing cabinet with a missing lock that sat in the corner behind a metal desk that was a few dents away from unusable, and three metal chairs made up the entire space.

Kara and I sat across from Ezra, waiting for our dressing-down.

"Your kicks are good, Kara."

"Thank you, Sensei."

"Now, I have to reprimand you for attacking a student. Consider this your reprimand."

Okay, maybe this wasn't going to be so bad.

His eyes dipped to my wrist. The corner of his eye twitched before he met my eyes again. "Nicole, if you would like to continue coming here, I would like to offer you some additional training so that what happened today doesn't happen again."

"Is Tanner coming back?"

"No."

That explained his slow reaction to Kara kicking the shit out of Tanner.

"I'd like you, however, to stay. And with a little more dedication and discipline, you could reach the same level as Kara and Cedric."

There was that damn word again... discipline. Why the hell did everyone believe I needed discipline?

"Um... sure." I removed the ice pack from my face. The cold was becoming too much.

Ezra glanced at Kara. "Excuse us for a moment."

Kara got up. "Yes, Sensei."

Ezra moved to the chair that Kara had vacated. "Do you want to take this class?" His tone suggested he already knew the answer.

"No," I said. I wasn't in the mood to bullshit.

"Then why are you here?"

I shifted in my seat. "Kara wanted me to take the class with her." Damn. I sounded like an idiot.

"Do you do everything people tell you or want you to do?"

His gaze was too intense, studying every single movement I made. So I was trying really hard not to move. But maybe that was telling as well. Shit.

"No, I don't," I said. "Kara wanted—"

He raised his hand to stop me. "I don't like wasting my time. If I didn't have a business to run, I would tell half the people in the class not to come back. They are wasting my time. I would put you in that category as well if you didn't have skill. Your problem is you lack follow-through."

"Did Kara tell you that?" My face heated with both embarrassment and anger.

"She didn't have to." He got up and moved toward the door. "Get up."

I got up reluctantly and followed him out. He strode onto the mat and turned to wait for me, all the while scrutinizing my every move. I would say he was checking me out, but there was no heat in his eyes, just a steady watchfulness—like a predator watching his prey.

A few people stood around the mat, all of a sudden becoming really interested in what was going on.

"Class is over; leave the building," Ezra barked.

Everyone moved quickly toward the door like ants swarming toward a piece of food. He looked over at Kara and dipped his head once. She sat down at the edge of the mat and waited.

"Nicole, you will demonstrate all five kicking techniques that we learned today until I'm satisfied you know them. You're moving as if you're in pain. Channel it!"

He moved to the center of the mat and waited. I stared at Kara. She gave me a look that said, *Do it.*

"Yes, Sensei," I said, feeling bullied. I moved in front of him.

"You will kick me with all your strength. If you execute the kick wrong, I will defend. Do you understand?"

"Yes, Sensei, but why—"

"Tae Tad, demonstrate!" he said, demanding a side kick.

I bent my legs and twisted my hip as I attempted to kick the back of his knee. He blocked it with a hard strike to my hip. I yelled as my knee buckled and I fell to the ground.

"Again!"

I glared up at him, and he glared right back. I started to turn to Kara but remembered what he asked in the office. I didn't need her to help me. I pushed up from the floor and reluctantly put weight on my leg. I gritted my teeth through the pain and attempted the move again. This time, he didn't defend, and I was able to make contact with his knee. He didn't flinch. Tough bastard.

"Tae Chiang, demonstrate!" he again ordered, indicating a diagonal kick.

Was he going to yell at me the whole damn time?

I inclined my body a little in the opposite direction. This one was going to hurt, but I kept my mind off the pain and focused on kicking him as hard as I possibly could. I swung my leg upward at an angle, making sure I was executing correctly—I didn't want him to hit my leg again. As my foot sailed toward his neck, I twisted my foot so that the arch faced down. Before impact, he moved to block me. I brought my leg down before he could strike it and got into position again. He nodded and moved back. I repeated the steps, and this time, I was able to hit him on his neck.

"Good. Tae Kod," he said, this time not yelling.

I started to smile but thought better of it. The down round kick was mostly used when someone was bending down. Ezra bent down slightly. I brought my leg up, twisted my hip, and kicked. He knocked me down on the mat before my foot could make contact with him.

"Again!"

I got up and limped into position. And once again, he knocked me down—hard. I attempted this move ten more times before I was lying on the ground, unable to move and panting like I'd just run a marathon.

"Are you giving up?" He stood over me like a damn tyrant.

If I could have moved, I would have gotten up and beat the shit out of him, which was funny because he'd given me the opportunity to do just that, and I'd failed miserably. And except for the light sheen of sweat coating his skin, he wasn't even winded. I, on the other hand, was drenched in sweat and braying like a horse.

"Yes... yes... Sensei."

"Do you trust that I could teach you enough to help with your fighting technique?" He still stood over me, now with his hands on his hips.

"Yes. But I don't need it." I lay on my back trying really hard to stop the burning in my lungs.

"Why?" He extended his hand to help me up.

"I've never been in any war-like situations where I've had to constantly defend myself. And if situations ever arise that I need to, I know enough to get by." I took his hand and painfully stood.

"Learning martial arts is not always about fighting. You lack self-discipline. The first time you attempted the Tae Kod, you failed. And each subsequent time, you failed again. But instead of learning from your prior mistakes, you continued to repeat them."

Damn. His assessment of me sounded suspiciously like my life thus far.

"I can't do it." I glared at him. Sweat ran down the side of my face. I wiped it away with my sleeve.

"And since you have told yourself that, your mind will not allow you to consider otherwise. I told you I wanted you to demonstrate all five techniques." He held up five fingers to accentuate his point. "You only completed two and a half-assed third. No follow-through."

"I'm leaving." I turned around.

Kara was gone. I rubbed at the sudden pain in my chest. Why did she leave?

"Last question. Will you let me teach you? Not in a class session, but one on one."

I whipped around. "Why do you want to?" Kara had abandoned me, leaving me with an ache in my heart.

"You could benefit from it."

"You just said I wasn't any good."

"Apparently, you don't listen very well." He moved closer until he was standing over me. He smelled like sweat and an earthy scent that I couldn't place. "I said I don't like to waste my time. You would not be a waste of time. I would like to teach you for various reasons, but mostly because you need it."

He glanced at my wrist again, drawing my eyes to it as well. It was still sore and emanating heat, but there wasn't any bruising on it.

"How often do I need to come?" I was more than a little curious as to why he wanted to teach me outside of class.

"Tuesday and Thursday mornings at five."

"There is no way in hell I'm getting up that early in the morning."

"That will be your first test. Getting up and making a commitment to come here."

I sighed. I had essentially gotten my ass handed to me twice today, and possibly embarrassed Kara. The former was troubling. Of the two fights I've had in my life, I was able to hold my own pretty good. True, they were girl fights with a lot of hair pulling and screaming, but I always won. And the latter was really bothering me. Kara's absence at the moment hurt.

"How much?" I asked finally.

He placed his hand on my shoulder. "I'm not charging you."

I took a deep breath. "Okay." I closed my eyes and silently cursed myself. "Okay." I opened them and stared at his chest. He shifted under my gaze. "How did you get the scars?"

He glanced at his chest as if he'd forgotten they were there. "Defending my life." He moved away.

"Sorry, I didn't mean to make you—"

"I will see you Tuesday morning at five."

I nodded, even though he couldn't see it. "Thank you, Sensei."

I watched him pick up a few items off the floor before I made my way to the back to change. It was odd that he wanted to teach me alone. In my experience, people usually had a reason for helping others. And now I just needed to figure out why, after three weeks, he had suddenly taken an interest in me.

And why had he kept looking at my wrist?

"**I**s that your balance?" Kara asked as she leaned over my shoulder at the ATM inside Haller's Grocery Store.

When I'd come out of Ezra's, Kara was waiting for me. She'd refused to make eye contact, and I'd refused to let her see just how much her leaving me alone had affected me. It was a song and dance that we'd perfected over the years. And I hated it. But I also had no clue as to how we could fix it.

"Yes, sadly, it is," I said finally, stuffing the money and receipt into my bag. I was down to thirty damn dollars.

"What do you need a hundred dollars for?"

"I need to pay for some information."

Kara grabbed a cart, and we made our way down the aisle to the meat counter to buy some ground beef for nachos.

"What information costs a hundred dollars?" She picked up a box of Ding Dongs and Twinkies and tossed them in the buggy.

"I only need forty for the information; the rest is for me. I want to find out about the Naqada culture from Egypt. I doubt a regular library has any useful information, so I have to go to Luisah's for it. I haven't paid my annual dues in four years."

"Is it that D important?"

"You know, you sound really stupid trying to avoid the word 'damn.' You're not religious, and I know you don't have any delusions of being a proper woman, so why not just say 'damn?'" I picked up a bag of tortilla chips and put them in the buggy.

The argument was an old one, but I loved having it with her. Besides, I was cranky and sore, and my damn arms and legs hurt like hell. I needed something else to focus on. If I ever saw Tanner again, I was going to introduce him to my style of fighting—pound my opponent until they didn't move anymore.

"And you sound like a drunken sailor's whore mother," Kara said.

"You used the word 'whore.'"

We stopped at the meat counter.

"Whore, slut, skank, and tart are fine. But the B word is not." Kara focused on the man behind the counter, who was trying really hard not to laugh at our exchange. "Hi, can we have two pounds of the ground chuck, please?"

He smiled. "Sure thing, miss."

"I can't believe I have to get up at four in the morning twice a week to have Ezra give me extra training on Krav Maga. The only reason I agreed to it was because I had looked like an idiot getting my ass kicked."

Kara laughed. "You'll do better next time." She bent down and examined the rest of the meat.

"Did you set that up?" I eyed her with suspicion.

She turned and rolled her eyes at me.

"Here you go, ladies. Can I get you anything else?"

"Yes, I would like four chicken breasts, two steaks, and four pieces of catfish," Kara said.

"How long is your grandmother staying?" I leaned against the glass case. The cold felt good against my back.

"I don't know." She turned away from me. "Maybe I should sign up for one of those online dating services."

"Do you want to stay with me?" I ignored her attempt to change the subject.

She cast her eyes down to the floor. "I can handle her, Nicole." Her voice quivered.

I really wished she'd tell me what the problem was between them. "No, what you should do is stop falling in love with unavailable men," I said in response to her previous statement. "Besides, you're supposed to be in love with Paul."

"Here you go, miss." The butcher handed her the meat with a smile on his face and hope in his eyes.

"Thank you." Kara placed the meat in the buggy and shook her head at me. "I can't help it. Every single man that I like seems to have some type of hang-up or issue. And I told you yesterday, Paul and I are just friends."

"The butcher is available." I grabbed a can of cashews and opened them.

She gave me a sideways glance. "Don't be funny." She reached for the cashews. "And don't eat in the store," she whispered harshly.

"Damn, shit, fuck, Kara! Why can't I eat in the store?"

"Nicole."

I turned and found Emilia from work, wearing a short green dress, staring bug-eyed at me. All she needed were some wings and a wand to complete the look.

"Um... hi." I placed the can of cashews in Kara's outstretched hand. "Sorry, I get pretty delirious on no sleep. This is my best friend, Kara. Kara, this is Emilia; she works at Tribec."

They exchanged hellos.

"How are you?" Emilia asked.

"Fine. I'm really excited to get back to work tomorrow."

She cocked her head to the side. "Really? Because I got the impression on Wednesday that you weren't too happy about the job."

I glanced at Kara. "No, I was just—"

"She's lying," Kara said. "Nicole has an aversion to working." She regarded me like a proud mother. "But we are working on it, along with her sudden profanity outbursts."

They both laughed at my expense.

"Funny, Kara, very funny." I turned back to Emilia. "You live around here?"

"Yeah, in a complex around the corner. I was doing my shopping for the week."

I looked inside her empty cart, and she followed my eyes. "Well, I better get going. It was nice meeting you, Kara. Maybe I will see you tomorrow, Nicole." She rushed off before I could respond. How would she see me unless she went to lunch at the same time the trainees did?

"She must not eat much," Kara said. "She's got no place to put it, though. I can't believe how tiny she is. She's like a porcelain doll."

"Yeah," I said, but my mind was miles away.

Doc told me his family had Emilia watching him. He never explained why, and I didn't ask, either. Was she aware I went out with him last night? Was she watching me now? If so, I was going to have to have a long talk with the both of them.

We finished getting the rest of the ingredients to make nachos, along with a few packs of Black & Mild for me, making a big dent in my hundred-dollar allocation for the week.

"Maybe you should give them up altogether," Kara said.

I shoved my change in my purse. "It's just one more thing for us to work on. Along with my aversion to working and sudden profanity outbursts." I smiled at her.

"You're horrible, Nicole."

"I love you, too, Kara."

ONCE OUTSIDE, we loaded the groceries into Kara's car. As I made my way to my vehicle, Emilia came walking out of the store without any bags in her hands. I stopped. I wasn't going to let this intrusion into my personal life go unchecked. She was welcome to watch Doc all day long. She wasn't, however, welcome to spy on me.

I started toward her, only to come to an abrupt halt. Rachel—the girl from my training class—walked out of the store, also without any bags. She slipped a pair of shades on and made her way to the same dark blue Buick LeSabre I saw her get out of on Friday. It sat idling in the handicap spot near the front of the store.

I stood there in the middle of the parking lot, trying to decide which situation disturbed me more—Emilia's obvious meddling or the sudden appearance of Rachel.

As the Buick passed by, Rachel turned her darkened gaze toward me.

Funny thing was, I couldn't figure out if she was following me or Emilia. And more important, why would she be following either one of us?

THE RINGING of my cell phone greeted me as I opened the door to my apartment. I rushed over to where I'd left it on the floor by the sliding glass door, charging.

"Hello," I said, out of breath.

"Where have you been? I have been calling all morning."

"Hi, Doc," I said.

"You left last night and didn't wake me," he said in a chastising tone.

"Sorry." This was one of the reasons I avoided relationships—too much accountability to another person. "I told you I had to get up early."

"I want to see you tonight."

"Um... I need a two-day rest period before we have sex again." I glanced at Kara.

She was holding her mouth, trying hard not to make a sound as she laughed at me. I threw her a dirty look and turned around.

"You're a little too rough, Doc."

"The noises you made suggest you liked it."

Smug bastard.

I entered the kitchen, opened the box on my counter, and pulled out my cutting board. Kara followed me in and started unpacking the groceries. She was still trying hard not to laugh.

"We don't have to have sex. I just want to see you."

I didn't believe that for a second. "I have a few things to take care of today. It will have to be late. Say, around eight."

"That sounds good. Did you want to go to dinner?"

"Nah, I don't feel like getting dressed up. We can order pizza."

"I'll bring some clothes over so I can stay the night," he said, and hung up.

I stared at the phone in shock. "He just invited himself over to spend the night." I set the phone down on the counter.

She laughed. "How bad was it?" She pulled my frying pan out of the same box, rinsed it, and put it on the stove.

"It wasn't bad... just rough, but not the whole time." I washed the veggies. "I mean, it was good... really damn good. He has this style." I placed the lettuce and tomato on the cutting board and opened the drawer to get a knife.

"Details." Kara dumped the ground beef into the pan. "I need lots of details. Make sure not to leave anything out."

I relayed to her what had happened from the time I opened the door until the time I snuck out of his house.

"He's a little intense," Kara said.

I set a saucepan on the stove and dumped a jar of salsa into it to simmer. Kara handed me a plate with slices of Velveeta cheese. I placed a few slices on top on the bubbling salsa, turned down the heat, and turned to her. "Yeah, but in a good way," I said, stirring.

Kara dumped the meat into the salsa and cheese mixture. "So, is it going to be just sex, like you and Jordin? Or are you going to try dating him?" She leaned against the counter.

I turned off the stove, set the pan to the side, opened the refrigerator, and pulled out two Samuel Adams. After handing her one, I opened mine and emptied the bottle. "No, Kara. I don't want to date him."

She scrutinized me with concern in her eyes.

"I don't want to have a pity party today."

Kara wrapped her arms around me. "Nicole, you know I don't pity you. I just wish you were happy."

"Who says I'm not happy?" I opened another beer.

"Sarcasm is not happiness, and"—she jerked the beer from my hand—"stop hiding behind alcohol when you have to talk about something serious."

I sighed heavily. "I'm not hiding, Kara. And sex is not a serious conversation."

"Do you think it was smart to sleep with him? I mean, he is your employer."

I stared at her, not hiding the hurt in my eyes. "You sound like Marta."

She flinched.

I had no illusions that my lifestyle bothered Kara. But in all the years I'd known her, she had never said anything to me about it. It was in that moment that I understood why it had bothered me so much when she left me in the dojo. The belief that one day, my carefree attitude about life would become too much for her, and she would no longer want to be my friend. Changing one's behavior to please others was not a good idea. I understood that. However, I really didn't want to lose my friend.

"Sorry," she said. "I worry about you."

I sighed. "To answer your question, I like the way my life is, Kara. I know it bothers you." I grabbed her hand. "But I don't want to change."

She smiled. "I wouldn't change you, Nicole. Promise."

I smiled and turned away from her; I was afraid she would see the lie in my eyes. It wasn't that I didn't want to change. I just didn't know how to.

FOR THE NEXT TWO HOURS, we watched *Columbo* while shoveling nachos in our mouths as if it were our last meal. Kara polished off her bag of donuts and most of her Twinkies, and I finished two cigars and three beers. When the credits started to roll, we were both leaning back against the couch, rubbing our distended bellies.

Kara glanced at me. "You know, you should really unpack if you're going to have company tonight."

"I can't move."

"What about your errands?"

I groaned and climbed to my feet. "I'm going to take a shower."

"I'll clean up." Kara got up and stepped over my boxes. "You've been here two weeks, Nicole. It's time to unpack."

"Don't touch my boxes, Kara." I've never liked people going through my things. It is way too personal. "Besides, I don't have anywhere to put anything. I got rid of most of my furniture when I moved the last time." I sat down on the couch. Damn, I was stuffed.

Kara sat down beside me. "Well, at least put them in the closet."

"Fine." I didn't move.

"If my grandmother leaves, we can do this at my house next week."

"Not a good idea; Elizabeth doesn't like me. I'm positive she's plotting my demise. Every time I visit, she sits in the middle of the floor and stares at me."

Elizabeth was Kara's gray Chartreux cat who, every time I came over, would stop what she was doing—or torturing—and sit, wrap her tail around her legs, and stare at me. Every time I moved, she would follow me with her eyes. I honestly believed that cats were only putting up with humans until we all killed each other off and they could take over the world.

She laughed. "She does that to everyone. You two just need to have a play date."

"And you need to have your meds adjusted."

Kara moved to the floor and opened a box. "What do you need this for?" She held up my yellow and brown, chipped ceramic ashtray.

I snatched it from her. "It was my first ashtray!"

"It's junk." She reached into the box again.

It was no use trying to stop her. Once Kara set her mind to something, she wouldn't stop until she finished. I silently relented and joined her in sorting through my belongings.

Kara helped me unpack two boxes and stow the rest in the hall closet. It was a very big exercise in patience on my part, because she questioned everything. Most of the stuff I had was basically junk, but it was my junk. And I didn't appreciate anyone telling me what to do with it.

Once the kitchen was cleaned, she left, and I went to take a bath to ease some of the soreness in my body.

I lay back in the warm jasmine-and-lavender-scented water and thought about what I was going to do for work. I had to quit Tribec Insurance; too many strange occurrences, including the recent development of Emilia and Rachel following me. And if I didn't find something soon, I would lose this nice apartment and be forced to move in with my parents again. I really didn't want to do that. My life seriously sucked right now.

Once I finished washing myself, I climbed out of the tub and went into my bedroom to get dressed. I stared longingly at my bed. If I laid down, I wasn't getting up again. I turned away.

Besides stopping by Luisah's, I wanted to get my bracelet repaired. As I reached for it, something snagged my attention. It was now fixed and resting inside a shen ring that had been etched into the wood.

A shen ring—shaped as one continuous loop that had no

beginning nor end, with a sun disk in the center of it, symbolized eternity, and was used as a symbol of protection in Egyptian culture. It was often associated with the falcon god Horus and the vulture goddess Nekhbet, and also with Isis.

I traced the perfectly carved symbol with my finger. A slight vibration pulsed through it. Chills ran up my spine and goose-bumps broke out on my arms. I glanced behind me at my messy room. I hadn't been dreaming last night. An entity had entered my home and carved a symbol of protection on my dresser after fixing my necklace. Who or what did it think I needed protection from?

I pulled my phone out of my purse. My hands shook as I took a picture of the symbol. I hesitated and swallowed hard. The nachos were threatening to come back up. Once I secured the now-mended bracelet around my wrist, I left in search of answers with an icy fear in my heart about what I just might find.

Stifling a yawn, I pulled into the parking lot of a convenience store around the corner from my apartment. I needed something a lot stronger than coffee to keep me up.

If not for the fact that I believed my life was in jeopardy, I'd have gone back home and gone to sleep. But that wasn't an option. I'd been unwillingly thrust into a situation from which I had no idea how to defend myself, making it imperative that I learn more about blood magick—the very principle my father and Luisah kept from me.

Today, I would get the answers I needed.

The bell over the door chimed as I walked in, maneuvering around the tightly packed aisles to the back where they kept the energy drinks. I opened the cooler and stared dumbfounded at the massive variety that lined the racks. How can there be ten varieties of the same fucking drink? I grabbed the first can my fingers came in contact with and kicked the door shut with my foot.

A short Chinese man wearing a Hawaiian shirt stood up when I set the can on the counter.

"Tylenol, please?" I reached into my bag for some money.

"You buy for boyfriend?" he asked as he rang up the items.

I glanced up at him. "No." I handed him a twenty.

"This a man drink." He smiled and handed me my change.

"Well, thanks for sharing." Why the hell did people always feel the need to supply me with information I didn't ask for? It wasn't like it had been shelved in the 'men only' aisle, next to the condoms.

Outside, the glaring sun threatened to burn my retinas. I slid my sunglasses back into place while simultaneously sucking down a huge gulp of the putrid energy shot. Distilled piss. What a fucking waste of money. The clerk was right—no woman should ever be subjected to this shit.

I popped two Tylenol tablets in my mouth and washed them down with the last sip remaining of the bottled water in my cup holder. The travel-size pack cost almost as much as a full bottle. Damn rip-off.

I lit a cigar and took a long drag on it, letting the soothing apple and woodsy smoke coat my tongue to ensure that the industrial taste of the energy drink was completely gone before I blew the smoke out the open car window. Satisfied, I started the car and left.

As I crossed the border of Brunswood into Tulare, I glanced over at Ezra's dojo, where several people moved inside, repeating what my class had done earlier this morning. An image of Ezra standing over me, asking if I was giving up, slammed into my mind. The weight of his words suddenly struck me for a brief moment, making me focus on my decision to quit my job at Tribec.

Was I giving up?

I had no real, solid proof of what the Stewarts were doing; only assumptions. The only physical proof of strangeness associated with Tribec was the shen ring carved on my dresser, as well as the entity from last night. Was I absolutely sure they were responsible? Did I truly believe Doc when he said his family wasn't practicing blood magick?

Fatigue was causing me to second-guess myself, so I'd wait until I got the answers I was searching for before I made any decisions.

So no, Ezra, I wasn't giving up. At least, not right now.

The road narrowed, and the street changed from Williams Avenue to Route 73.

A handmade sign—a piece of wood painted white with black lettering that was nailed to a long, wooden pole—indicated that I was entering the town of Coeur d' Alene. A plethora of scents—eucalyptus, lavender, and salt—wafted through the car.

A small cluster of shops crowded both sides of the highway. The parking areas were asphalted—a rarity in this town where the rest of the walkways and personal driveways were covered in crushed seashells that, when the sun hit them just right, glinted a brilliant iridescent color. That's why I collected them when I was younger, filling small mason jars on my bedroom's windowsill, so that when the first rays of morning sunshine hit the shells, brilliant colors danced over my walls.

Most of the locals referred to Coeur d'Alene as the town that time forgot. The small, scrap-wood homes with tin roofs and dilapidated brick chimneys were a testament to that. The history was damn intriguing, though, and the subject of a poem written by Louis Badet in 1880. "The Land Guarded by People of Colour" explored the two land bridges' mysterious creation in 1875. It also told the story of the free Creole people who'd moved from New Orleans and populated Coeur d' Alene, as well as the Gullah people who populated Sandpoint. Two years after it was published, Louis was found murdered in his rented room in South Carolina, and after his death, all southern schools and libraries banned the poem due to its perceived satanic content. Finding the missing poem had always been my mission, but the many fruitless searches always ended in disappointment.

I passed my father's shop—Henri Fontane's Herb Shoppe—located on the left side of the road along with a shoe store, a jewelry store that sold hand-crafted Cherokee Indian jewelry, and a clothing store.

I pulled up to Luisah's, my tires crunching on the gravel, and parked right in front. She was washing down the windows with a mixture of rosemary, sage, and lavender—herbs she'd once told me were for cleansing.

I was eleven years old when I first wandered down the road from my father's shop and found Luisah leaning on the front of a moving van, smoking a hand-rolled cigarette outside a grouping of recently built houses in a bright yellow scarf, faded blue jeans, black t-shirt, and boots. Besides my mother, she was the most beautiful woman I'd ever seen; her skin color, the same as my father and me, blending seamlessly into her dark green eyes. Her gold hoop earrings glinted in the sun as she stared at the houses.

After a moment, she cut her eyes in my direction. "Come here, girl."

Either fearless or stupid, I continued the last few steps and stopped in front of her. Aromas of vanilla and tobacco swirled in the air between us.

"What's your name, girl?" Her accent was strange, not southern or the familiar Creole I'd heard from my family in New Orleans. But it did have some subtle similarities.

"Nicole Fontane."

She dropped her cigarette and ground it out with the heel of her boot. "Well, Nicole Fontane, my name is Luisah Pleasant. You can call me Luisah."

"Okay."

"Where are you coming from?"

"My daddy's shop."

"What's your daddy's name?" She looked up the road.

"Henri."

She nodded her head and waved at someone behind me. I turned. My father stood in the road, watching us. He dipped his head once and headed back inside.

"You wait right here while I go inside and make sure that fool, Leonard DuPont, followed my directions on how to clean up the shop. My lazy nephew, Raphael will be here in a minute." She looked down at me. "Can you do that, Nicole Fontane?"

"Sure," I told her.

From that day forward, I spent more time in her shop than anywhere else. At first, it was because I'd developed a crush on Raphael, but when he stopped coming around, I still continued to gravitate there.

Luisah told some amazing stories about her life in the old countries, which were considered the birthplace of magick—places like Egypt, Ireland, Scotland, Romania, China, and Japan. The tales fascinated me.

Her shop was also where I first met Steve.

I glanced at my watch; it was a little after four. Luisah normally closed the store at five on Sundays but would stay there longer if a customer was still inside. I climbed out of the car, and Luisah turned. As she shifted toward me, one of her gold earrings caught a beam of sunshine, causing her whole body to momentarily light up. I stopped and stared at the effect.

I'd always believed she was in her early thirties. However, seeing at her now, in that beam of sunshine, she appeared both young and old simultaneously. And her eyes, which had darkened, appeared... ancient. I glanced up at the sun. Maybe something had covered it to cause the effect in her eyes. It blazed without a cloud around it, a big, fiery ball of gold.

I shielded my eyes and stared at her. The momentary shift in her appearance was gone.

I continued toward her. "Hi, Luisah."

"I have not seen you in so long, girl." She hugged me, and her familiar scent wrapped around us. "You owe me forty dollars."

I pulled back and smiled. "I have it right here," I said, reaching into my purse.

She shook her head. "Inside." She turned toward the door.

I followed.

"You want tea for your pain?"

"Yes, thank you." I'd forgotten about her ability to read when someone was sick. She once told me she was a healer in another lifetime, and after what I'd just witnessed a minute ago, I wondered if that was a literal statement.

The floorboards creaked as I walked inside the familiar store. It was still the same—books crammed into the shelves in no discernible order, walls covered with tribal masks from different cultures, a display case filled with Egyptian, Greek, Roman, and other cultural jewelry, as well as ceremonial daggers and magick-fused stones. Long, wooden, highly-polished tables ran down the center of the aisle, with brass reading lamps on top. The cookie tray she kept on a small chestnut bureau along with a pitcher of tea sat by the door, along with China teacups and saucers.

Artwork lined the walls—all portraits of Coeur d' Alene families except for one that hung near the folk magick section. Steve's junior high school picture, protected in a hand-carved wooden frame, with an inscribed golden plaque just beneath.

*Solas geal imithe go luath agus*

"Bright soul gone too soon." As written in his Irish ancestors' language.

Steve was killed at a party when we were sixteen. We were all a little too drunk that night, but Steve had been sober, and when he attempted to help one of our classmates avoid a glass table he was going to fall into, Roger shoved him away, causing Steve to fall on it instead.

A piece of glass had pierced his heart, killing him instantly.

His death changed us.

Kara let go of her "Fuck the System" attitude and took on this dogged sense of focus that consumed her. She wanted to make something of herself, so she decided to become a teacher. Marta stopped drinking and started dating Manuel Martinez. And at sixteen, she got pregnant. They married as soon as she graduated.

I, however, clung to my youthful rebellion, hiding behind sarcasm, foul language, and sometimes even drugs.

I blamed myself for Steve's death.

I was the one who'd convinced him to go to the party in the

first place. He'd given me a letter that night that I still hadn't opened. I wasn't ready to read his last words to me.

I probably never would be.

My throat seized up, and I choked back the tears. Luisah patiently waited for me behind the register.

"You miss him still?"

I nodded, unable to do more than that, and walked over to her, pulling out the forty dollars I owed her.

She stared at me. "I won't take your last. If you promise to not stay away so long again, we will call it even." Sadness filled her eyes, telegraphing that my absence had affected her deeply.

I hesitated, my hand still extended, holding the money out to her. "I don't want to owe you—"

She cut me off with a wave of her hand, came around the counter, and stood in front of me. She placed a cool hand on the side of my face and peered into my eyes.

I shifted under her scrutiny.

"You have too much pain, girl, too much." She shook her head. "Lock up the store while I go mix your tea." She turned and started down the aisle leading to the back room.

I took a deep breath as I went to lock the door. After flipping the sign to closed, I stared at the money in my hand. Guilt gnawed at me. I hated owing her. I needed to start paying my debts. Her refusing to take the money only made it worse. I sighed and placed the money back in my purse. Maybe I could leave it on the counter when she wasn't looking.

Luisah carried a tray with a steaming teapot to the counter and set it down. After pouring hot water over the satchel in the cup, she pulled a hand-rolled cigarette from beneath the counter and lit it. Once she blew out the smoke, she addressed me. "Drink it while it's still hot."

The first time I'd seen Luisah smoke inside her library, I asked her if she ever worried about the books being damaged by the smoke. She assured me they were protected but never explained how—just that they were.

"I need to sit." I took my tea to the nearest table.

Luisah sat down beside me and pulled a gold ashtray toward her. "What do you need?"

"Information on blood magick and if power circles are used in it. I also need information about the Naqada culture."

"Before I answer, you must promise not to stay away so long."

There was something more behind her words. Like the promise had weight. And I'd heard that phrase before. Unfortunately, I couldn't readily place my finger on just where. The hairs on the back of my neck rose. Luisah's gaze bore into mine. Why was she making me promise again?

"Nicole?"

"Promise," I blurted out.

The room shifted, and I grabbed the table. I blinked a few times, trying to orient myself. I stared at Luisah, trying to figure out what the hell had just happened.

"Tell me why you need this information."

"Luisah," I started.

"Tell me, girl."

After a brief pause, I catalogued the events of the last few days, the shit-ton of stuff that happened in such a short period. She never interrupted me, only stared, patiently listening while she smoked her cigarette.

By the time I finished, the lethargy and headache had vanished. Damn, that tea worked fast.

"Alone, the thirteenth floor is considered bad luck. Superstition. When used in magick, it adds power to the spell a practitioner is working." She got up and walked over to the bookracks.

That had to be it. They were powering some sort of spell. Doc said his family wasn't practicing magick. An obvious lie. I paused. Well, maybe not. I'd only asked if they practiced blood magick. My mistake. I should've asked about magick period.

While Luisah searched the racks, I grabbed my purse from the counter.

"Most of the history regarding the Naqada culture was lost."

She pulled out a book from amongst the stacks. "Sit." She placed a thin volume down on the table and walked away.

I pulled a notebook and pen out of my purse and examined the small, black, gold-embossed book. *Naqada*; written by Professor Shukuma from Morehouse University.

"Naqada is the name of three interlinking time periods that involve the same people. Amratian, Gerzean, and Semainean. These time periods were referred to as Naqada I, II, and III. The people constantly warred, using magick to settle disputes. And when a new ruler conquered the old, the people's way of life changed, leading historians to believe a new tribe had taken over the land. They were wrong." She set another book down in front of me.

*The Principles of Earth Magick.*

I'd studied it from cover to cover. It was the only book on magick Luisah had ever given me access to, limiting my knowledge of the other three principles. Knowing it like I did, I couldn't recall anything in there regarding blood magick or the Naqada culture. Maybe I'd missed something.

I flipped through the pages, which mainly focused on different aspects of earth magick, from common spells to all the herbs used in the practice. It also broke down the different types of practitioners—mage, latent, and apprentice.

Earth magick had three levels of abilities: healing—working with herbs and infusing them with magick with the intent to heal someone; growth—allowing the earth practitioner to stimulate herbs and other plants in nature to make them grow faster; and defensive, which was mainly used to break curses and spells placed on practitioners and, on rare occasions, to harm. But that was not something that was widely practiced, and almost considered taboo. Holistic healers could achieve some basic healing when using the right herbs. However, they didn't have enough magick in their blood for more advanced healing rituals. Mostly, they cured the common cold or helped with pain.

Mages had all three abilities, while latents only had one, and apprentices mostly studied the application of earth magick. Holistic healers were classified as apprentices.

"There is a reference to Naqada II or Gerzean culture in here when they were at their bloodiest." Luisah sat down and pulled the book on Naqada closer.

As I reached for the book, Luisah grabbed my wrist.

"Where you get this?" Her voice filled with dread.

I turned to her as she studied at my wrist, her fingers rubbing over the surface and a slight discoloration marring my skin.

I pulled my hand away to examine it. "I don't know."

There was a symbol carved—no, not carved, branded—into my skin, so small a casual glance would've missed it completely. Shaped like a shen ring, only different. The circle wasn't complete; it only barely touched the opposite end. And there was a design in the center that was difficult to make out. Almost as if whoever was branding me had been interrupted and wasn't able to finish the design.

Luisah's eyes narrowed in on the mark. Smoke curled around her head in a dizzying pattern, circling her, gathering in strength. The primordial cast shadowed her eyes once again as if something very old and ancient was peeking out, shedding its mask.

"An Old One has marked you again, girl," she said, her voice deeper and huskier. "It is protecting you." She touched my head as if there were a symbol branded there as well. "But it is different than this."

A sudden chill traveled up my spine as I ran my fingers over the spot she had touched. I didn't feel anything; no raised skin or rough patches. An image of Ezra's eyes dipping toward my wrist earlier today popped into my head. He'd been fascinated with my wrist, too. Had he noticed the mark as well?

"What is an Old One?"

Luisah shook her head, took a deep breath, and reached for the Naqada book. She flipped through the pages until she found the one she was looking for, then turned it toward me.

It was a drawing of a figure, which could be a man or a

woman; there were no distinguishing features to allow me to determine which. The figure stood with its arms crossed across its chest, holding two items. In its right hand was the flail that most Egyptian figures are depicted holding, but instead of the crook, in his left hand was a staff that had the head of a jackal on top—the sign of Anubis. Painted on his chest were the shen ring and other symbols that were vaguely familiar, along with the same symbol that had been branded on my wrist.

I glanced toward Luisah. Smoke continued to curl around her head, only this time, it didn't circle around her as if it was being powered by some sort of spell. I pulled my phone from my purse. After flipping through the pictures, I turned it around and showed her. "I found this carved into my dresser this afternoon."

Luisah studied the picture for a moment. "A shen ring. All cultures take on symbols from the past. They also take on some of the religious beliefs. Naqada were the first to use blood magick to create gods." She set her cigarette on the gold ashtray and got up. "It was not supposed to be used that way." She made her way down the narrow hallway to the back room again.

I drew my eyes back to the drawing of the man. My mind kept saying that it was a man no matter what my eyes said.

Could this be the figure I saw standing in the rain?

Luisah returned, carrying a large tome covered in a red velvet cloth. "Blood magick, like all the other principles, was created for a specific reason." She set down the massive tome.

"How do you create a god?" I eyed the book. It was one of the ones she'd refused to show me when I was younger, no matter how many times I begged.

"Some knowledge should always remain hidden," she had told me after escorting me for the hundredth time out of her forbidden room. Curiosity always got me in trouble.

She stared at me for a moment before answering. "All cultures create their gods, or what they perceive as gods. That is why faith magick was created. The Naqada created thirteen gods with blood magick." She removed the cloth from the book and closed her eyes. Her lips moved as if she were praying, but I couldn't hear the words she was saying. "I cannot let you handle this book for too long. It's too powerful."

She picked up her cigarette and took a long drag. After placing it back in the ashtray, she blew the smoke in a slow, steady stream as she opened the book. The smoke bowed around the book, soaking into the pages. The smell of cherries and old parchment saturated the air, and my lungs raged with fire.

Luisah handed me her cigarette. "Pull some smoke into your lungs and hold it."

My hands shook as I reached for her cigarette. My ears rang. Softly at first, but eventually, the sound grew louder. The pressure on my eardrums threatened to explode them inside my head. I stared at Luisah, directly into her ancient eyes, while I pulled smoke into my lungs.

I expelled the smoke. "What are you?"

"You are not ready for that answer, girl."

Suddenly, the ringing stopped, and the smell evaporated as if it had never been there in the first place.

"Luisah—"

She raised her hand. "Not today, Nicole. Today, I will only give you the answers you need to make the decision that is warring inside you." Pain etched across her face. "This is all I can do." She turned the book around. The page contained drawings of thirteen figures. "These are the thirteen gods that were created."

No names labeled the drawings, only symbols. Whorls of different colors—blue, green, red, yellow, and black—all interlinking and covering the beings' skin.

"What do these patterns on their skin represent?"

"Their names."

I glanced up at her. "I don't understand."

"All the patterns—none are the same."

As soon as she said it, the distinctiveness became apparent. It was as if my mind had been momentarily blocking the information from actually being processed. Whether it was the colors that interlinked or the pattern itself, the differences were there, but I had to concentrate on them to notice. One of the figures was the same one depicted in the Naqada book.

"Do the patterns represent a language?" I asked.

"Yes, but not one that is spoken." She pointed to one of the figures. "The patterns give off a musical vibration that associates the god with its power."

"Why did they create these gods? And why would two of them mark me for protection?"

"They wished to rule over all the tribes in Egypt. They twisted their earth magick abilities, using them to kill, by poisoning their enemies' land. When that didn't work, they created thirteen gods to destroy them." She pulled the book away from me abruptly, wrapping it back up. "It's better that you do not expose yourself too long. I promised your father I wouldn't teach you about blood magick." She turned to me. "You are hidden from these things for a reason. The marks will cause you no harm."

"Why would they—"

Luisah held up her hand to stop my next question. "You have free will. I can't make a decision for you. My binding prevents it. I've shown you what I can." She got up and took the book to the backroom.

The cryptic statement confused me. My free will? Something about that seemed... familiar. And why did she promise my father not to teach me about blood magick?

I pulled the Naqada book closer and once again studied the picture of the man. Yes, this could be the same being I kept having encounters with. Like Luisah said, an Old One created by blood and faith magick.

For the next few hours, I scrutinized every detail of the small amount of information she'd provided. From what I could discern, the Naqada people were bloody and ruthless and wished to take over the entire region of Egypt. But they were stopped, even after the creation of the thirteen gods and goddesses. I couldn't find any reference to how, only the end result. Nor did it say what happened to them.

There was only a brief notation that, three days after the gods were created, the Zero Dynasty began. So, what had happened in those three days to wipe out an entire civilization? And more importantly, who had the power to do so?

After shutting off the light on the table, I got up, stretched, and grabbed my things off the table. I was tired and really wanted to get going.

"Remember your promise, Nicole," Luisah said as she watched me walk toward the door.

"I will." I paused with my hand on the door. "What should I do, Luisah?"

"I cannot answer that for you."

"Why?"

"I am bound," she said, repeating her earlier statement.

Doubting that I would get more information out of her, I reluctantly left.

THE SUN WAS CASTING the last of its orange rays across the ocean, filtering light through the trees. Heavy, gray clouds hung low, threatening rain, and a slight breeze caressed my arms and legs as I walked to my car. My headache was gone, thankfully, and my mood had somewhat improved. But I was still restless.

Despite what I'd learned, I craved more. Curiosity bubbled in my gut. Pushing me toward a better understanding.

After climbing in my vehicle, I lit a cigar and drew smoke into my lungs. I needed a plan. Luisah didn't deny or confirm the Stewart family practiced blood magick. She only validated my suspicions about the relics they displayed.

Was that enough?

One could argue the Stewarts simply collected art and weren't aware of the pieces' association with a bloody society.

The only thing lacking plausible explanation was the Old One who had branded me last night. Why would he brand me for protection? Was he associated, somehow, with the Stewarts? Did Doc send him to protect me? And if he did, that would open up a whole other set of questions I really didn't need to add to my growing list.

Before any rash decisions—a common mistake I'd made repeatedly in my past—I'd make absolutely sure my assumptions were correct. After all, it wasn't only me in danger. Marta could be as well, and there was no way I was leaving her there if it turned out that the Stewarts were practicing blood magick and involving their employees in the rituals.

I looked over at Luisah's. The lights were off. Several things about my visit with her troubled me. Her being bound was at the top of the list. Bound by whom? And for what reason? More importantly, what did they have to do with me? There was genuine concern in her eyes, as well as pain, when she delivered her cryptic message. Like the binding was a physical weight she couldn't go against.

Also, why had she pulled out *The Principles of Earth Magick*? Especially since she didn't point anything out in the book. It was as if she was trying to tell me something without saying it.

I sighed. Luisah would have to be a puzzle for another time. Right now, I had to figure out what was going on with me. Besides Doc, there was another person I desperately wanted to speak with, so I made a U-turn and headed out of the town of Coeur d' Alene.

Ten minutes later, I drove into the empty parking-lot, slowly making my way toward Ezra's dojo. Maybe this wasn't such a good idea. He could have gone home already. To be honest, what was I going to say to him? *Why were you staring at my wrist? Why did you suddenly want to train me outside of class?* The former question sounded stupid, and he had touched on the latter already.

*Stupid and impulsive, Nicole.*

But it had to be done. As I picked up my phone to call Doc and let him know that I was going to be late, I received a text from him. Unease settled in my gut. I stared down at the very curt message.

DOC

Have to cancel.

No explanation and no apology. If I'd cared, I would have been offended. Instead, paranoia gripped me. Had he become aware that I was investigating his family? I glanced around the empty parking lot. Was Emilia still following me?

*Get it together, Nicole.*

I glanced over at Ezra's.

I really wasn't cut out for this investigative shit. Mainly because I didn't know what the hell I was doing. The only experience I had with investigating came from a slimy private detective named Bernardo Diaz for whom I had worked two years ago. We spent the majority of our time in his truck, watching cheating husbands. The job didn't last long, and the only thing I learned from him was how to effectively damage a man's balls. Bernardo had a real hard time keeping his damn hands to himself.

I couldn't use my usual techniques. They were, I admit, a little abrasive. Most people didn't like being hounded with an abundance of questions. Unfortunately, it was the only way I knew how to get to the answers I needed. I blame it on too much Columbo. Now he was a great investigator. Pushing the suspect to the brink of cracking always worked for him.

Images of me lying on the mat in the dojo, panting like a dog, popped into my head. I was not going to pepper Ezra with questions. I would, no doubt, end up on that mat again.

I glanced in the rearview mirror. I looked like road kill. No, more like road kill after it had been run over fifty times. My skin was sallow and sickly. The bags under my eyes had bags of their own, and my lips were past the point that ChapStick would even make a difference. My hair resembled an out-of-control bush that had been oversaturated with water. Why couldn't they make a product for my type of hair that actually worked all damn day?

I patted the bushy mess, trying to ease down the worst of it. It sprang back up, and I sighed. Oh well, there was nothing I could do about it now. I popped a mint in my mouth. At least I wouldn't knock him unconscious with my breath.

After lathering my hands with jasmine-scented lotion to cover up the cigar smell, I slid my phone back in my purse. Movement in front of me made me look up. Ezra stood in the doorway of his dojo, watching me. How long had he been standing there? Had he been watching my attempts to wrangle my hair? Or my checking myself out in the mirror?

"Damn," I muttered and got out of the car. I could only imagine what he was thinking.

"Hurry up, Nicole." He waited inside the darkened doorway.

The frustration in his voice suggested he might have been standing there for a while.

He held the door open for me as I walked inside. The familiar scents permeated the air, along with the smell of spicy meat. A faint light illuminated a single path along the practice mat to the door in the back. The one marked *private*.

The click of the locking door echoed in the empty room. Ezra brushed up against me as he stepped around me and made his way across the mat. A slight shiver ran down my spine at the contact. That strange, earthy scent radiated off of him. I had a sudden image of me running my nose all over his sculpted chest. Damn. Where did that thought come from?

After shoving that image out of my mind, I removed my shoes and followed him.

He didn't make a sound, while my feet swished loudly on the warm mat. He turned around, his eyes blazing in the darkness. "Pick up your feet. You sound like prey."

I stopped. "Does that make you the predator?"

He shifted, his body straining forward as if he were ready to pounce. I started to step back but stopped. Predators react to fear. I stood my ground. Waiting. My gut twisted. I flexed my fingers, trying to distract myself from the chilly feeling crawling slowly down my spine.

"In another time," he said, turning and continuing his trek across the mat, staying within that shaft of light.

I focused on the tattoo covering his back. The lion's golden eyes flashed in the darkness.

Ezra was a dangerous man, a completely different animal outside of the classroom. I pushed down the urge to run, afraid he might actually hunt me down like prey. Instead, I focused on the small band of light—a lifeline in the midst of the cavernous space. I wouldn't dare step out of its path.

While the mat was warm, the tile floor was freezing cold. I stopped, put my sandals on, and then rushed to catch up.

"You live here?" I asked as I followed Ezra inside the room.

On the right, a kitchenette with a microwave, small refrigerator, and a hot plate for cooking. A small saucepan with steam rising up currently sat on the surface of the hot plate. And on the left was a small desk with a built-in bookshelf crammed with books about war and combat. The back wall held a full-size bed covered in a drab, military-issued, gray fleece blanket tucked in so tight I could have bounced a quarter off of it.

The walls were covered with various posters of martial-arts events and a few gold medals. The medals were in a small wood and glass case and hung on the wall near the door. There were no photos of family or friends, or even a girlfriend. It was all very tucked-in and neat and completely devoid of anything that would give me some indication of who Ezra really was. Unless the space itself was the indication.

"Yes," he said and grabbed a bowl from the small cupboard above the kitchenette.

He removed the lid from the saucepan sitting on the hotplate, and the aroma filled the space. After dishing up some of the contents into the bowl, he reached into a small dishpan, retrieved a spoon, and handed it to me.

I accepted the bowl from him. "Thanks." Odd that he would give me food without asking if I wanted some. Filled with ground beef, pasta, tomato sauce, rice, lentils, caramelized onions, garlic, and chickpeas, I put the bowl to my nose and inhaled. Damn, it smelled good.

He pulled a chair out from under the desk and indicated for me to sit.

"Aren't you curious..." Ezra left the room before I could finish my question. *What the hell?* I sat and placed the bowl on the desk, along with my purse, while I tried to think of a tactful way to question him.

Ezra returned with another chair and set it opposite mine. After he dished up some food for himself, he sat facing me, his legs spread wide. "Why are you here?"

"I wanted to know why you really wanted to teach me." *Or I could go with the blunt approach. Way to go, Nicole.*

He spooned some food into his mouth, watching me as he chewed.

*Awkward.*

"I don't need to learn martial arts," I said, filling the silence.

"You may not need the technique, but you damn sure need the discipline."

Why was everyone trying to discipline me all of a sudden? Was I that out of control?

"Did Kara put you up to this?" She never did give me a straight answer when I had asked her about it earlier.

"She didn't need to, and you rely too much on your friend. You all but gave up when you fought Tanner today." He ate more food... or rather, upended the rest of his food into his mouth.

"He's better than me." I sounded like José when he made the comment about his teammate being better than him. Maybe I did need counseling. Tanner wasn't necessarily better than me. He was, however, more determined to inflict as much pain as possible.

"You need practice," he said.

Ezra stood up. "Part of learning any type of martial arts is learning your opponent. Tanner's weakness is his anger. When you fight out of anger, you lose the ability to observe your adversary. Cats are excellent predators. They watch and learn, never striking until their prey is vulnerable." He dished up some more food. "You were weakened today from pain, but you still fought back." He looked down at me. "You have skill; you just need to hone it."

"We don't know each other well enough for you to assume anything about me."

I hated the way he studied me, as if he could see right through all the layers of bullshit I'd built up around myself over the years. I didn't appreciate it at all. It took great effort to camouflage my pain. Fucking bastard.

"Enough to know that you didn't come here to learn why I wanted to train you."

It was like he was inside my head! I averted my eyes from his. The reason I'd really come here was important, but I couldn't find a way to casually bring it up.

"I sized you up the minute Kara brought you to class three weeks ago. We had this discussion this morning. I seem to recall telling you I don't like wasting my time. Now, choose, did you want me to fuck you or train you?"

My head snapped up. "I didn't come here to ask you to fuck me!"

"Didn't you?" He glanced at my hair.

My face heated with embarrassment, and I looked away. Damn. He had been watching me attempt to groom myself. And it looked exactly how I assumed it would. That I'd come here in the hopes of seducing him. I couldn't even imagine what he thought of my grooming efforts. No, I could, and the thought was humiliating.

"Why do I have to come so early?" I asked after a short while. I refused to continue with that conversation.

"It's when I do my one-on-one training, so you will come at that time," he said, still studying me as if he knew there was more to my visit.

*Just ask him about his interest in your wrist, Nicole.*

"You're a pushy bastard."

"Yes." He got up and put his bowl on the counter.

"Fine, I will let you train me." I picked up my bowl—like a petulant child—and took a bite of food.

He leaned up against the counter, eyes still trained on me. I tried really hard not to stare at the way his white gi pants hung low on his hips. Or the way his muscles bunched on his forearms. It was true I found Ezra attractive, but I never even considered trying to sleep with him. I put him in the category of off-limits out of respect for Kara. But sitting here, with his smell enveloping me and the spices from the food heating my body, it was getting really hard to hold on to reason. I shouldn't have come here.

"This is good. What is it?" I asked.

"Kushari. An Egyptian dish that is a mixture of Italian, Latin, and Asian cuisines."

"Did you grow up in Egypt?"

"Yes."

Was it a coincidence the mystery I suddenly found myself in the middle of involved the same part of the world Ezra was from? I didn't think so. *Just ask, Nicole.*

"Why did you move to Tulare?" I was acting like a coward. In my defense, Ezra scared the hell out of me.

"It wasn't by choice."

"You said you got those scars defending your life. What happened?"

"Someone tried to kill me. I decided I didn't want to die, so I killed them."

"Wow! A lot of detail there. Maybe you can try cramming it all into one word next time." I took another bite of Kushari.

"You barged in on me."

"How did you know I was out there in the first place?"

"I looked." He reached over me and pulled a book off the shelf above my head.

I polished off the rest of the food in silence.

"So, what do you do at night?" I got up and put my empty bowl next to his in the sink.

"Mostly read." He glanced at me. "Sometimes I go play pool around the corner."

"Do you want to go play?"

"Why are you really here, Nicole?"

I glanced at my wrist. The brand was no longer visible. Maybe being around Luisah brought it to the surface somehow, as if her very presence intensified it enough to make it visible.

I held up my wrist. The movement drew his attention. "Do you see this?"

He studied my wrist for a moment, his body rigid, eyes fixed. Nothing in the way that he gazed at it gave me any indication of whether or not he saw the mark there.

"Someone told me I was marked," I said, breaking the silence.

His eyes tracked up to mine, locking me in place. "Who?"

"It doesn't matter. You looked at it twice in class, and I assumed you might have more information about what it is."

"And you assumed, from a few casual glances, that I could see it as well?"

After he said it, my stomach plummeted. He was right; I had assumed that he saw it.

"Then why did you keep glancing at my wrist?"

"You kept rubbing it."

That made sense. Damn. I shifted. I had no reason to stay any longer. He had answered my questions. But still I didn't move, realizing in that moment that I was afraid to return to my apartment. Afraid the entity that had been haunting me would be there. Despite Luisah telling me it was a mark of protection; I still didn't want to encounter it again.

"Something else bothering you?" he asked.

My throat seized and my skin grew clammy. I sat, refusing to make eye contact with Ezra.

He was watching me, waiting for a response.

"I'm scared." I blurted out.

"Of who?"

I swallowed. "Not who, what."

"Explain." He straddled the chair opposite me.

Funny thing was, I felt safe around Ezra. Similar to how I felt around my father. I took a deep breath and launched into my story. Baring my soul to a perfect stranger. It was comforting to be able to unload all the issues that concerned me, taking the weight off my shoulders. I could never do this with Kara or my parents. Never let them see the scared little girl that I'd buried so deep inside of me.

"Do you believe me?" I asked once I was finished.

"I'll find you something to sleep in." He got up.

I stood up and followed him over to the dresser. "Why won't you answer me?"

Fear that I'd made a mistake wormed its way inside me. *Why did you come here, Nicole? Why did you allow this man to really see you?*

Strange, since up until today, Ezra and I had not said more than a few words to one another. However, when he stood over me and asked me if I was giving up, something changed. It was like a switch had flipped inside my mind. I was finally able to see my life much more clearly. All the mistakes. All the times I'd actually given up and not pushed myself further. And suddenly, I didn't want to continue down that road any longer.

He handed me a t-shirt and silently watched me. His gaze settled on my wrist. Was he lying when he said he couldn't see it? No, he didn't say that—he'd turned the question around on me. And I'd been too eager for an answer that I failed to really digest what he'd said. What was he hiding?

"Ezra, please answer me." My voice was barely a whisper.

He stared at me, his eyes pinning me in place—but still he said nothing.

I squirmed at the intensity of his focus on me. He'd pushed past my barriers and could see me for the fuck up that I was.

So, I did the only thing I could to regain my comfort.

I stripped.

And stood there, exposed. Waiting for him to say something. This type of exposing was easier for me; no uncomfortable feelings of vulnerability to deal with. Maybe my nudity would elicit a response.

Silence.

He picked up the t-shirt I'd set on the bed, bunched it up in his hands, and waited, his eyes never leaving mine. After a brief hesitation, I raised my arms over my head. Goose bumps broke out on my skin; my body shook as he slid the shirt over me, effectively covering me up.

I'd never been so turned on in my life. Or so confused.

"Yes, I believe you," he said finally, his voice flat.

"Stay with me," I whispered, hating myself for even considering trying to sleep with Ezra. Especially when it was so evident he didn't want to sleep with me. And, honestly, I really didn't want to sleep with him, either. I just really needed someone to comfort me right now.

"Not tonight." He made his way to the door. Stopping at the threshold, he turned around. "Promise me you will quit tomorrow."

"I promise." He was the second person I'd given a promise to today. Did his have the same binding weight that Luisah's had?

Ezra turned out the lights and left the room. I stood there staring at the open doorway, hoping he would come back—knowing that he wouldn't.

A strange thumping sound woke me up. Since there were no windows in Ezra's room, I lay in the empty bed, staring at the unfamiliar shapes, slowly coming into focus. The only light came from an alarm clock sitting near the bed. Its bright red numbers showed it was just after five. I ran my hand over the cold space in the bed beside me. Ezra hadn't come back to his room last night. A pang of embarrassment seized my heart.

I got up and turned on the light. My clothes lay folded on the table. So he had returned last night. Only, he didn't sleep in his bed. After getting dressed, I eased out the door and made my way toward the front. The thumping sound was coming from an open door on the left. I peered inside. Ezra, covered in sweat, wearing only gi bottoms, pounded on a punching bag in the middle of the room. I hesitated. Debating whether or not I should say something as I watched his back muscles flex with each blow. He had to know I was standing there.

"I will see you tomorrow, Nicole," he said, without turning around. His voice startled me.

I nodded, knowing he couldn't see me, and left. I had no plans of ever returning again.

After taking a quick shower, I got dressed, downed several cups of coffee, told Wade to shove it up his ass when he just so happened to meet me at the front door, got in my car, and headed out. Today, I was going to quit my job and hope I could find another one within a week.

It wasn't likely, but I still held out hope. After all, hope was all I had at this point.

Once I'd taken my place in the line of commuters heading to work, I reviewed all of the information I'd learned thus far. Damn. In the midst of all my running around, trying to find answers to what the Stewart family was up to, I failed to ponder the one thing that was most important. Why me? Why was I suddenly immersed in the middle of something I still couldn't quite put my finger on?

I couldn't figure out the one factor that tied all the situations together.

Unless that factor was me.

The blare of a car horn brought me back to reality. I slammed my foot on the brake, narrowly missing the car in front of me. Damn, I was tired. It would be two days in a row that I'd gotten minimal sleep.

I'd texted Marta this morning, asking her to meet me in the parking lot before work.

She still hadn't responded.

Thirty minutes later, I pulled into the parking lot of Tribec Insurance and wheeled into a slot. I turned off my car and listened to it ping, while I leaned back and rested my head against the seat. I needed a moment to compose myself.

I glanced over at the building. How was I going to handle this? Walking in and quitting was the obvious answer. However, something told me it would be better if I provided a valid reason

—one that didn't draw any more attention to me, if that was even possible.

I reached in my purse and retrieved a cigar. As I lit it, I brought up memories of my actions from last night. I'd made an idiot out of myself. I wasn't used to feeling vulnerable, and the only way for me to combat those unfamiliar feelings was to hide behind sex. The fact that Ezra hadn't responded only compounded the embarrassment. I added apologizing to my growing list of things to do and pushed the thought away.

I glanced at my phone. Ten minutes before I would have to go inside and quit. I was really starting to hate that damn word. I would give Marta another five minutes.

MY SANDALS SQUEAKED on the highly polished floor as I made my way toward the guard station. I didn't dress completely down; I did have on a decent enough skirt and blouse that matched. I might have forgotten to comb my hair and put on deodorant, but it really didn't matter. I wasn't staying long.

Oliver stood as I walked toward him.

"Good morning," I said, sounding fake even to myself. I hated this asshole, so why was I being so nice? I set the manuals down on the counter, along with their stupid red sales shirt. I should have burned the ugly thing.

"You're not wearing your badge," he said, staring at my chest. It would seem Oliver was a creature of habit and really hated when people didn't wear their badges. Or, he just liked staring at women's breasts.

"Yes, well, I came to return these."

He looked at the manuals and then back up at me. "You will need them for your training."

I assumed my wanting to return the manuals would at least

clue him in to the fact that I was quitting. Apparently, when they hired Oliver, they weren't necessarily looking for someone who used more than one brain cell. His only qualifying attributes must have been his size and menace.

"Never mind; can you call Francine Delaporte down? Also, I would like to speak with one of your employees." I reached into my purse and retrieved Vincent's ID. "Vincent Merkatz."

"He no longer works here." Oliver narrowed his eyes as he reached for the ID.

I quickly shoved the ID back in my purse and smiled. I'd made a very big mistake. I should have thought this through more. Vincent gave me his ID for a reason. And I just announced that I had it. My plan to not draw any more attention to myself just blew up in my face.

Someone touched my shoulder, and I whipped around, ready to defend myself.

"Good morning, Ms. Fontane," Doc said, taking in my disheveled state.

I patted my hair as if it would somehow miraculously lay down by sheer will alone. Of course, it didn't. And the sudden sticky feeling under my arms had me backing away out of sniffing range.

"Good morning," I said.

His eyes cut to the manuals sitting on the guard station. He smiled. "Are you quitting again?"

That fucking word.

"No, I..."

"She wanted me to call down Mrs. Delaporte. And she was also looking for Mr. Merkatz, sir. Should I call her down?"

I dug my fingernails into the palm of my hand and fought a silent war inside my head. I was dangerously close to turning around, picking up the manuals, and throwing them at Oliver. Doc must have realized this, because he stepped forward and quickly removed them from the counter.

"I can walk Nicole to the training room," a male voice said.

I glanced around Doc. Daniel stood there, poised, hands stretched out toward Doc. I was once again struck by the notion that he looked out of place. Like he should be somewhere barking orders or running secret missions. He definitely didn't belong in a call center selling insurance. Hell, I didn't belong in a call center selling insurance.

"I can carry my own damn... sorry, my own manuals." I snatched the manuals from Doc and picked up my shirt. Fuck. Did I have to mess up everything?

He leaned down and whispered in my ear, "I would love to help you tame that glorious head of hair later today. Wait for me outside after work." He strode off.

I didn't even have time to tell him no.

"Nicole," Daniel said as he extended his arm in a gesture that said I should go first.

Was he trying to protect me? I didn't need a fucking knight in shining armor. I needed to quit! Why couldn't I manage to walk the hell out of this damn place? I wanted to throw a tantrum but seriously doubted that would work. They would probably send me to their creepy medical clinic in an attempt to assess my health. They might even decide to pump me full of the same stuff they gave Lacy, making me pliant and stupid.

After debating with myself for a few minutes, I made my way reluctantly to the training room. How the hell did I manage to screw up quitting? Once the outer doors to the hall closed, Daniel leaned in close.

"Be careful what you say here," he said.

"What the fuck is that supposed to mean?" I demanded, bearing down on him, happily letting my frustration out on the first available person I could.

He held his ground. "It means you need to be careful. They are watching you."

"Like you?" I asked. "I saw your friend Rachel yesterday. Was she following me?"

He entered the training room without answering. Bastard. I

checked my phone again. Marta had finally returned my text. However, her response was troubling.

MARTA

Call you later.

I sent a quick text asking why she wasn't at work.

No response.

A few seconds later, someone invaded my space. I turned. Our trainer, Andrew, loomed over me.

"Is there a problem, Ms. Fontane?"

If not for the warning Daniel had given me, I would have given him a very colorful and physical answer to that question. Instead, I shook my head and stepped into the training room. As I did, I mentally added Marta's absence to my list of concerns.

When I arrived home from work after a grueling day of training, the only available space to park in my complex was next to the dumpster. Since that accurately conveyed how I was feeling at the moment, I didn't mind.

I passed Mr. Wan's door and inhaled the scent of fried dumplings and rice. He opened the door, wearing his usual khaki pants and white t-shirt.

"Hello, Mr. Wan." I stopped at my mailbox.

He rubbed his stomach and ran his eyes over me. "You don't look so good, Nicole."

"Yeah, well, I don't feel so good, either." I pulled out a pile of mail, all of it for the previous tenant. "Do they know Jeremy Wright doesn't live here anymore?"

He stretched his hand out to me. "I take." He perused the mail. "Do you want some dinner? I make enough."

I smiled. "Maybe some other time." I shut the mailbox. "I have errands."

He nodded. "Well, get some rest, too, Nicole."

"I will."

I opened my apartment door, dropped my purse on the floor, and went to start the coffee maker. Once started, I made my way to the bathroom to wash the stink off my body.

Freshly showered and wearing a pair of jeans and a tank top, I returned to the kitchen and downed a few cups of coffee. I grabbed my purse and keys and started for the door. My cell phone rang. Dropping to my knees, I dumped the contents of my purse on the ground and searched frantically for the phone.

Once found, I looked at the display and groaned. *Sexy Doc.*

"Hey," I said. I shoved all my stuff back in my purse and climbed back to my feet.

"Hey, yourself. I couldn't stop thinking about you today. It was very distracting. Why didn't you wait like I instructed?"

"Like you instructed? Look, Ronald, I'm not returning to Tribec Insurance." Shit. I still had questions to ask him. "But I would like to continue seeing you," I said, softening my tone. "I have to check on my friend, Marta. She didn't show up today. Can we reschedule our date?" It would be more like an inquisition, but he didn't need to know that.

"That is upsetting, but I understand." He paused. "Can you find it in yourself to at least come in tomorrow? Maybe there is a way I can convince you to stay. Please. If you are still troubled after tomorrow, then I will accept your decision."

"One day is not going to change my mind, Ronald."

Why the desperation for me to work there? It couldn't be a desire to date me. I doubted Doc dated anyone. Fuck senseless? Yes. But date? No. I had a hard time picturing that. So, what was it? Was he trying to mess with his family? It was obvious I was a disruption and they really didn't want me there. So maybe he secretly enjoyed their discomfort. If I was right, Doc definitely had a bit of a sadistic streak. In any other circumstance, I might have stuck around to enjoy the show. But right now, I just wanted to get the hell out of there.

"Let me try, Nicole, please. And to answer your last question, how about dinner this weekend?"

"Okay," I said, omitting what I was agreeing to.

"Enjoy your evening." He hung up.

After tomorrow, I had no plans to ever see him again. I needed to ensure my safety, and that meant learning as much as I could from whoever was willing to give me answers. Complete answers.

So, if I had to make nice with Ronald, I would. After all, he'd been forthcoming before in answering my questions. Maybe he would do so again. Hopefully this time, he wouldn't leave anything out.

I texted Marta again, but she didn't reply. Next, I called. The phone rang seven times and then went to voicemail. Damn. I was starting to feel like a stalker.

And why was I so concerned about her? I wanted to attribute it to a bad feeling, but truthfully, it was probably my concern about our fragile friendship. I'd told her about my date with Doc on Saturday. And while, surprisingly, she didn't come right out and say she didn't approve, the look was there. And true to form, I chose to ignore it like I do all situations that make me uncomfortable. But now, it was almost like I needed to apologize to her and make sure we were okay. I could drive over there. That, of course, would mean traveling through Perry at night. I suppressed a shiver.

*Get over it, Nicole.*

Fuck. Decision made, I grabbed my purse and headed for the door. Before I could open it, my phone dinged.

MARTA

I'll **see** you on **Wednesday**

When I texted back asking why, she didn't respond. What the hell was going on? Maybe she really was upset with me. I needed a drink. All this self-reflection was pulling me down. I sent a quick text to Kara telling her to meet me at Jordin's and headed out.

WHEN I PULLED open the door to Jordin's, the savory scent of grilled onions wrapped me in pleasant cocoon. I loved that smell. I took a few moments to enjoy it before I ventured in. The buzz of conversation filled the air, while music played softly in the background.

A few of the tables were occupied—mostly by men who were staring into their mugs of beer as if it held all the answers to life. A biker sat in the corner by himself, staring fixedly at the front door. Maybe he was waiting for the rest of his gang to come back.

A barfly—that is the first thing that came to mind when I saw her—was sitting on a stool, sipping wine and chatting up a guy who was too inebriated to even keep his eyes open.

And the hussy committee was holding vigil on the remaining bar stools, staring rapt at Jordin as he mixed drinks. Their usual barely-there clothing hugged their bodies in open invitation.

Damn. Monday nights at Jordin's looked a little depressing.

Jordin looked up at me and did a double-take.

"Yes," I projected with my smile. "I'm here for some food and company on a Monday."

I thought about Doc's invitation to get together tonight, and a queasy feeling settled in my gut. Was I tired of him already?

I pushed thoughts of Doc aside and made my way to an open table. Jordin came over, leaned down, and kissed the side of my neck, sliding a Samuel Adams in front of me. I sat up straighter and turned into him.

"This is a welcome surprise." He brushed his lips over mine.

Butterflies filled my stomach, and an ache settled between my legs.

"Um... are you busy tonight?" I asked.

"No." He ran his hand down my back.

"Hey, Nicole," Paul said, taking a seat across from me.

Why the fuck was he here? Kara hadn't told me they were together when I texted her. Then again, she hadn't responded, either. I just assumed she would show up like she always did. But now, she seemed hell-bent on including Paul in every damn thing we did.

Jordin straightened and looked at him.

Paul took off his suit jacket. "Hey, Jordin," he said.

Jordin inclined his head. If I didn't know any better, I would have sworn there was some jealousy brewing in Jordin's eyes. But that wouldn't be right. He knew I had no interest in Paul. Anger, maybe?

Kara came bouncing in and made her way toward us. "Sorry it took so long; I had to pick up Paul from work."

"Why?" I asked before I could stop myself. Fuck.

Jordin ran his finger down my neck. "Come see me later," he said, and walked away.

"Nicole, what is..." Kara started.

I held up my hand. "Sorry, I'm in a shitty mood." I reached out and touched Paul's hand. "Forgive me?"

He smiled hesitantly. "Yeah, sure, I just... If I'm intruding, just let me know."

*You're intruding, Paul.*

Kara touched his arm. "No, you're fine." She looked at me. "Right, Nicole?"

She knew it wasn't fine. But if she wanted to pretend, I'd go along with it. Besides, she did ask me Saturday what my problem was with Paul. I never answered her because, truthfully, I didn't really know. He was nice. Kara really liked him. But... it was something.

Maybe I was turning into a conspiracy nut. There wasn't anything wrong with Paul. At least, not that I could see. Yes, he was hanging around more. And yes, that did disturb me. Hanging with us on Fridays was one thing, but including himself in our other activities was not okay.

I shook my head and took a swig of my beer. I could be a real selfish bitch sometimes.

"Besides, shouldn't you be in bed? You do have training tomorrow," Kara said.

Shit. I'd forgotten about my one-on-one training with Ezra in the morning. But honestly, after embarrassing myself last night, I had no plans of ever showing up there again. Now I just needed to find a nice way to back out of Krav Maga training altogether.

I took another swig of my beer. Thankfully, that was a problem I could solve later.

Jordin brought them drinks, and we settled into some mindless chatter. After a while, I zoned out, only making appropriate noises when necessary. I couldn't concentrate. My plan was to talk with Kara about Marta, but I didn't feel comfortable talking while Paul was there.

"Nicole? What do you think?" Kara said, pulling me out of my thoughts.

Shit. I'd missed something.

I shrugged.

"What's with you tonight?" she asked.

"Um... I'm afraid I'm not the best company right now."

She looked over at Jordin. "I get it," she said, anger lacing her voice.

"You know what?" I stood up. "I'm going to go. I'll call you later." Before she could respond, I set some money on the table and walked away. If I stayed, I would say something I couldn't take back.

Pushing down the guilty feelings trying to surface, I sauntered over to the bar. "Take a break," I said to Jordin.

He smiled and pulled his apron off.

I had an itch I really needed to scratch. Or, more accurately, some problems I needed to forget.

Jordin was between my legs, his tongue working overtime. My body thrummed with need. His window was open, and the sound of the rain pulled at me, making my heart ache. His scent was all over me, enveloping me in a tight embrace, mixing with the salty scent of the rain. It was heaven. And just what I needed. To just forget everything for a while. Bodies slick, we moved in synchronicity, so familiar with each other, we could anticipate the other's needs. He lifted up, his arms bulging, and slid inside of me. I groaned, squeezing my legs around his powerful thighs, pushing him deeper inside of me.

Too bad my mind was elsewhere.

I'd fucked up with Kara. Truthfully, I'd fucked up royally for the past week. But what else was new. I always fucked up eventually. Only, this time, I was afraid my actions had cost me something important. And if I dug deep and was truly honest with Kara, the possibility of her finding someone was what really scared me. So, unconsciously, I was pushing her away. Before she had the opportunity to pull away from me.

Jordin grabbed my wrists, bringing me back to the moment, and dug his thumb into the sensitive spot where the mark from the Old One had been branded into my skin. His pace quickened, and in a flash so brief I would have called it a vision, I saw him moving over me, his body bathed in a golden aura. My breath caught in my throat, and I pushed him away.

"Nicole?" He sat back on his haunches and stared at me.

What the hell just happened?

He reached for me, but I pushed him away.

He cocked his head to the side and studied me. The light from his kitchen bathed him in an almost eerie fashion. Like maybe he wasn't really there. That's all I needed right now. To be hallucinating while having sex with Jordin.

I reached for him, brushing my fingers across his sweat-slicked chest.

"Do you want me?" he asked.

I wanted to say yes. Any other time, I would have. But the response got lodged in my throat. After a brief hesitation, I got up from the bed. He didn't move. Didn't come for me. In that moment, that brief second that it took me to pick my underwear off the floor, I felt used. But hadn't I come up here to use him?

"Maybe some other time." I pulled my clothes on, and, for the first time in my life, shame devoured me.

He got up and went into the bathroom. I stared at the familiar tattoo on his back, suddenly feeling as if I was missing something. Like a neon sign was flashing in front of me and, since I was standing to close, I couldn't make out the words.

When the shower came on, I got up. There was no point in me staying any longer. I was no longer in the mood. After pulling on my clothes, I left—my mind preoccupied with the notion I was overlooking something dangerous. Something that would eventually come back to harm me.

My hand shook as I worked my key into the lock on my front door. I ignored the tears trailing down my face as I went inside and slammed the door. Everything was spiraling out of control. It was almost as if I'd been dumped in the middle of traffic, and in order to stay alive, I had to avoid all the cars rushing toward me. Only, I didn't have the ability to move.

Without turning on the lights, I slid down the wall and let the tears come.

Why was I suddenly so confused about my life? Well, that's not right. I've always been confused. Only, I'd gotten really good at avoiding acknowledging it. I'd built a wall around myself, and somehow, brick by brick, it was coming down.

I stared at the empty desk where Marta's place card still sat unclaimed. Andrew was a constant white noise in the background. I didn't want to be here. Life had handed me some lemons, and I just couldn't make any lemonade. I should have sucked up my unease with magick and went to work for my father. Then I wouldn't have to be here, listening to this idiot drone on and on about insurance.

Damn. This fucking job was making me feel as if I was trapped inside a jail of my own making, staring at bars that represented all the mistakes I'd made in my life. All I had to do was reach out and tear them down. One by one. Only, that meant facing my problems, and I wasn't ready to do that.

On top of all that, guilt gnawed at me for not showing up at Ezra's. Or at least calling. Despite not really wanting to, I'd have to stop by after work. And, if he wasn't too upset, I could ask him why he thought I should have quit. I also needed to apologize for my behavior.

"Ms. Fontane." Andrew straightened his ill-fitting, ugly brown suit. "Can you tell us what the three tiers of medical insurance represent?" He stood directly in the center of the power circle—I was going to call it what it was—lording over everyone.

"No, Mr. Snow, I can't." I stood up. "And I have to go to the bathroom." Or jump off the nearest bridge.

"I expect you to pay attention."

That's too damn bad, Andrew.

"Did you want me to pee on the floor?" Please say yes. "Or can I go to the bathroom?"

He bristled, and I waited.

A small dip of his head was his only reply. I walked out without a backward glance.

"Where are you going, Ms. Fontane?" Oliver stood behind his desk like it was a damn fort. Fucking asshole.

I flipped him off. A small measure of childish satisfaction filled me—only to be crushed by the sound of his chair being pushed back. I glanced back at him and scowled. If he wanted to fight, I was so ready to oblige him. No sense in quitting quietly. I would go down in blaze of glory.

"Do you have a problem?" I asked.

He smiled. It unnerved me that it actually reached his eyes. Was he really finding joy in my behavior?

"No. But I believe you have." He sat down and turned away from me.

What the fuck ever.

When the elevator arrived, I climbed on and used my badge to make the numbers display. The only floors I had access to were the third and seventeenth floor. Stupid. But on our first day, Andrew informed us we could only use the bathrooms on the third floor while we were in training. Despite there being perfectly good restrooms on the ground floor.

A short ride later, the elevator deposited me on the third floor, where human resources was. Ambient noise from hushed conversations and light music playing in the background greeted me. Like the lobby, the human resources floor also had an abundance of Egyptian art. I was surprised none of the employees had tried to make off with one of the paintings. Or at least been stupid enough to try, only to be stopped by Oliver.

I walked inside the restroom and inhaled the scent of cherries.

This building oozed odd smells. Gripping the side of the sink, I stared at my haggard appearance in the mirror and tried to find some control buried deep inside me. What the hell was wrong with me? I was like a damn two-year-old throwing a tantrum. It wasn't their fault all my bad decisions had led me here. My last resort, sort of, and I was throwing it away like spoiled food.

Yet no matter how much I tried to reign myself in, I just kept digging that fucking hole.

A toilet flushed, and I glanced in the mirror at the bathroom stall door opening. Lisa. Damn.

"Ms. Fontane, shouldn't you be in training?" She moved toward the sink, captivated by her own appearance.

Icy bitch.

"Are bathroom breaks allowed?" I asked, not hiding the disdain in my voice. If she wanted to fire me, I didn't care. And honestly, I expected to be fired by the end of the week, anyway. No sense dragging it out. Blaze of glory and all that.

She cut her eyes in my direction. "If you plan on continuing to work here, you will need to work on your attitude, Ms. Fontane."

"Do you think it's a medical condition?"

"What?"

"If so, I could always have Doc help me with it. That is covered, right?"

Her mouth opened, then closed. Fear crept into her eyes, swimming in those icy blue depths. She was afraid? Why? Before I could ponder it further, she shook her head as if the motion would remove the fear.

She turned away from me and looked at herself in the mirror. "You know, Ms. Fontane..." She reached into her pocket and pulled out a tube of red lipstick. After applying enough for two people, she slid it back in her pocket and turned to me. "If I were you, I'd be extra careful around my brother. He has such"—she smiled on her way to the bathroom door—"delicate taste."

The door closed before I could respond. The way she said *delicate* implied Doc had some sort of strange fetish when it came to women. Yes, he was a bit overwhelming in bed, but not too out of the ordinary. So why the warning? I doubted she was truly concerned about my safety. There wasn't an ounce of compassion in her voice or her body language.

I washed my hands and made my way to the door as I tried to ignore the sudden chill rolling down my back.

THE SUN HAD ALREADY STARTED to set by the time I arrived at Ezra's. After leaving work, I texted Marta again. I couldn't shake the feeling of dread in my stomach, and I really needed to hear her voice and know that she and the kids were okay. She still hadn't responded.

I checked my watch; it was later than I thought. My actions at Ezra's Sunday night and the fact that I hadn't shown up for training had been plaguing me all day. Despite my decision to never return, I wanted to know why he'd told me to quit. He had to know something about Tribec Insurance. That was the only explanation I could come up with. Especially given his aversion to my giving up when I fought Tanner on Sunday. The man didn't like quitters. So why tell me to quit?

Maybe if I asked him nicely, he'd tell me what he knew.

I parked my car in the same spot I'd parked in the other night. After shutting it off, I stared at the darkened building with anxiety and fear brewing inside me. This time, he wasn't waiting for me. Only a few cars were scattered throughout the strip mall. And only one car was in front of Ezra's. I hesitated before getting out. Maybe I should have called first.

"Get it over with, Nicole," I said aloud and climbed out of my car.

I glanced up at the darkening sky. Fat rain clouds partially covered the moon. It was the first time I thought about the unusual amount of rain we had had in the past few days. That, and the chill associated with it. Tulare had rain showers, but not every day. However, despite its peculiarity, I refused to dwell on it. I had too many real issues to worry about that were more important than our strange weather.

A slight breeze blew over the parking lot, stirring the debris. I walked at a steady pace to the door, rehearsing in my mind what to say.

Once I reached his door, I took a deep breath and pulled the handle. Locked. I checked my watch. The dojo closed twenty minutes ago. Cupping my hands against the glass, I peered inside. A beam of light coming from under the back-room door trailed across the floor.

Sudden laughter had my head whipping toward the sound. A group of guys had come out of the grocery store, carrying cases of beer. I stood there staring at them for a moment, unsure of what to do next. I could call and leave a message, but that was too... pathetic. I could wait for him to come back, but I had no idea when he'd left or how long he would be.

"Nicole."

I jumped, and a warm, calloused hand reached out to steady me.

"What are you doing here?" Ezra stood outside the open door.

"I didn't hear you open the door."

He studied me for a moment, and then stood to the side so that I could enter the dojo. The familiar lemony scent tickled my nose. He locked the door, the sound swallowed up in the darkness. I turned around and looked at him; the fading light was at his back, making it difficult to make out his face. For a brief moment, I thought about how Jordin had looked last night.

"I'm sorry," I said.

He stood there for a few minutes and then stepped around

me and started toward the back. Just like before, remaining in that small patch of light that stretched out on the mat. "You missed training. You'll have to make up the time Thursday," he called over his shoulder.

"So you still want to train me?" I removed my shoes and followed behind him. A sudden case of déjà vu overtook me, and I stopped.

"Yes." He stopped at the edge of the mat and turned. "You're stalling."

"Why did you tell me to quit Sunday night?"

"Did you?"

"It's complicated."

"Then un-complicate it. You can't stay there."

"Why?" I moved closer to him.

He looked down at me. "Some things are better left alone, Nicole."

"More cryptic bullshit, Ezra? If there's something you want to tell me, then spit it the hell out. How am I supposed to make a decision when all I'm getting is an ambiguous warning to quit?" I shook my head, frustrated, and dropped my purse to the floor. "Up until Sunday, you paid absolutely no attention to me other than to point out all the mistakes in my technique!" I sounded a little hysterical, as well as bitter, but sadly, that didn't stop me. "So then! Then, I throw myself at you. Baring my soul and all that shit. And all you have to say is I should quit my job?" I took a ragged breath.

He leaned down so that our faces were level with each other. "Do you still want me to train you?"

I leaned in. "Do you want to tell me why I should quit?" I bit out.

"I already did," he said, his voice going low.

"No the fuck you didn't." I slammed my chest into his. I was on a roll. Ignoring common sense and that part of me that tried to warn me when I was going too far. She was waving her hands like a mad woman, and I was ignoring the hell out of her. "Is your training going to be cryptic as well?" I asked, and before I could stop myself, I shoved him.

He had me on the mat before I could blink. I lay there in stunned disbelief while he stood over me. "Don't threaten me, Nicole. And if you want answers, come back in the morning for them."

I laid there, unsure of what to do next. I hadn't threatened him. Well, maybe I did push him a little and get in his face, but he got in mine first. I sounded like a whiny toddler, but in my defense, I was tired and very frustrated.

He extended his hand and helped me up. "Your ignorance is keeping you safe. I'm limited in what I can tell you. My encouraging you to quit, especially..." He looked down at my wrist, placing his thumb on the very spot that was branded. "I crossed the line on Sunday. But that's my problem, and I will deal with it." He rubbed my wrist with his thumb.

My skin heated; my stomach did a flip, and I sucked in a silent breath.

"You're protected. But knowledge might not keep you that way. Stop asking questions." He dropped my hand and stepped back.

I studied my wrist and Luisah's words came back to me.

*An Old One has marked you, girl.*

"You know something about the Old Ones? Who are they? Why has one marked me?" I moved closer. "I'm scared. Please, Ezra, give me something. Something more than 'it's better if I don't know anything.' You and I both know that's bullshit."

He stared down at me; his eyes darkened as he gazed at my lips.

My breaths grew shallow. My chest moved up and down rapidly, and he continued to stare. This was not what I'd come here for, despite my lustful advances Sunday night.

"Why do you always make me feel so vulnerable?" I yelled. I didn't understand why I was responding to him like this. My throat was raw. Tears traced down my cheeks. I squeezed my hands into a fist, my nails biting into my palms.

"Nicole, I already told you," he said, more an exhale than an actual sound. He tore his eyes from my lips. "I am unable to help. You should go." He stepped back and turned away.

I grabbed his arm and pulled him around to face me. "What the hell is going on? What do you mean you can't tell me anything? How do I protect myself if I don't know what's happening?" My chest heaved as I stood there staring at him, waiting for him to answer me.

He yanked me up so quickly that I didn't have time to process the movement. He pinned my arms to my side and kissed me hard. I wrapped my legs around him, and my body throbbed as he pressed his lips against mine.

I was so caught up in the heat coming off him that it took me a minute to realize he wasn't really kissing me.

Suddenly, the pressure from his lips turned painful. The heat he generated coated my face. Sweat broke out along my brow. I tried to pull away, and he ground his fingers into my arms, holding me tight. I squirmed, trying to get away from him as panic took ahold of me, and the next thing I knew, I was on my back with Ezra pressing down on me. His lips still on mine. I couldn't breathe. He was searing a symbol on my lips, the pain like a knife carving into the sensitive skin.

The now familiar sickly-sweet scent of cherries filled the dojo, muting the familiar lime scent that always hung heavy in the air. The aroma crawled across my skin, pushing its way beneath the surface. I writhed on the ground, moaning, caught up in a whirlpool of pain and pleasure.

An image flashed into my head.

*An ax coming down, blood spraying all over my bedroom walls. My mother's clothes, bloody, rage in her eyes.*

Suddenly, it was over. Ezra jumped up and stood over me, his chest heaving. His eyes darker, almost inhuman. A reddish haze surrounded him. Whorls of gold surfaced on his skin.

His name.

A booming noise rushed around the room as if the sound had weight. I covered my ears, trying to stop the pain the sound caused.

Ezra dropped to his knees and placed a strong hand on my stomach. The whorls moved under his skin, snaking up his arm. My vision blurred.

"Stay still. Let it take hold." His voice sounded layered, as if many voices were trying to merge into one.

My lips were raw. "What..." I started; my throat hurt, making me sound hoarse. "What did you do to me?"

"Something that I made a vow not to do."

"What do you mean?" I whined. The pain was too intense.

"I have violated your free will." He grabbed my wrist. "Like my brother did."

I struggled to get up; Ezra placed his hands on my stomach to keep me in place. I weakly pushed his hand away and sat up. "You are..." I cleared my throat. "You are the second person who has told me that. Luisah said she couldn't make a decision for me; it was my free will. What does that mean?"

Ezra quickly got to his feet, knocking me back down on the mat in the process.

"What the fuck?" I coughed. Although the burning had stopped, my throat still felt too raw. Like I hadn't drunk any water in weeks.

"The Historian," Ezra said finally. He extended his hand down and helped me to my feet. "You need to leave. Don't come back here unless I call you." His gaze and hands held me in place. "The less they believe you know, the safer you are." He sounded afraid.

Was he talking about Lisa? Her look today would suggest she was trying to tell me something, too. But that couldn't be right. No, the more I thought about it, the more I believed her look was more about my relationship with Doc.

"Did you lure me here? Did you tell Kara to bring me to

class?" I asked, my mind suddenly fixated on the unbelievable coincidence of the situation.

A look of confusion crossed his face. The gold whorls stopped moving. "No. I knew who you were when you came to class. But I had no idea she was bringing you. It was a coincidence. I kept my distance until my brother marked you." He dropped his hands from my arms. "You know what I am. My brothers and sisters and I have only two choices when it comes to those with magick like yours."

I didn't know if I believed him about it being a coincidence.

"What magick? I'm a latent earth practitioner. I have very limited power. And since I was younger, I haven't been able to access even that."

"Kill or protect," he said, ignoring my question. "I have chosen to protect you... if you return, I will be forced to kill you, despite my mark of protection." He sighed, the sound heavy with regret and pain. "I no longer have free will."

He stepped back, melting into the darkness—the gold whorls on his skin suddenly going dark. The moon must have finally been completely covered by the clouds, because all the light in the room vanished, leaving me plunged into complete blackness.

Frustration and anger warred inside of me to the point I thought I would burst. This was the second time I'd been given vague answers to my questions. It was as if everyone was conspiring to keep me in the dark. Yet, the pain in his voice was real. Maybe he did want to tell me more but couldn't. I needed to learn more about the Old Ones. And why people with my supposed form of magick were so dangerous to them. At least, that was how I was interpreting his statements. Why else would they make a vow to kill or protect?

But more importantly, I needed to understand what kind of magick he believed I had that would pose such a threat.

The lock clicked, and the wind blew the door inward. I took the hint. Scooping my purse up off the ground, I left with way more questions than answers.

I couldn't wait till Wednesday. In the midst of all my selfish introspection, I'd failed to really digest what Marta had written. Why Wednesday? Was one of the kids sick? Was she? I had to check on her. I wouldn't rest until I knew she was okay. I'd have to worry about the new mark and learning Ezra was an Old One later.

With security doors and bars on their windows, every house on Marta's street had their lights on. Was this her idea of "decent enough?" Did the residents really believe these extreme measures would prevent the unsavory characters in Perry from venturing onto their street? Wrong. Greenwood Apartments was only a few blocks away. The criminals in that war zone didn't care whether there were lights, bars, or alarms; nothing stopped them.

I'd broken into a few houses with Frank when I was high that weren't too far from here. I never told anyone about my brief stint in criminal activity. It was bad enough they knew about the drugs. But Marta's neighborhood, with its many lights, was similar to some of the neighborhoods Frank would take me to—although, we usually stayed away from cul-de-sacs since there was only one way in and out. He told me it was better for them to light the way than for us to use flashlights, since a person carrying a flashlight would stand out more than a person who was simply passing by.

Marta lived at the end of the cul-du-sac. Her yellow house with white trim and a slightly overgrown yard was the second-to-last one before the street wrapped around. I made the loop, pulled up, and parked my car directly in front. There was a basketball hoop over the garage and a basketball lying in the grass. It looked deserted.

I left the car running as I got out and ran to the door. A newspaper sat on the welcome mat. Not a good sign. I rang the bell and waited. No response. After knocking and still receiving no response, I returned to my car.

Disquiet settled in my gut as I stared at her house. Tapping my leg, I tried to think of what to do next. Maybe I should call Kara. I shook my head. No, not yet. Fuck.

I pulled my phone out and looked at Marta's text message again, as well as the ten I'd sent afterward.

Still no response.

My greatest fear was that her association with me might have put her and her kids in harm's way. Yes, that was irrational. But given what I'd experienced thus far, I'd say it was also plausible. I did everything in my power to draw attention to myself. Slipping back into my old familiar patterns of self-destruction. Antagonizing the Stewart family, who, despite what Doc said, were practicing blood magick. Or were at least deeply associated with it. Because of my behavior, I might have caused harm to not only myself, but Marta and her kids as well.

Were they really that vindictive? Wouldn't they just fire me? I thought about the confrontation, on my behalf, between Doc and his siblings on Friday, and his obsessive desire to keep me at Tribec. Maybe they would. Because if Doc was protecting me, then hurting my friend would be the next logical step. And I wouldn't put anything past Lisa. That bitch was cold as ice.

Sadly, sitting in my car in the middle of the night, staring at her house, was not going to help me figure it out.

A knock on my car window startled me. I jumped, hitting my head on the roof of the car.

"Sorry, miss," the man yelled through the glass.

I rubbed my head and took a deep breath—trying to calm my suddenly rapid heartbeat. I studied him while I kept my foot on the gas, ready to take off if he posed a threat. Late sixties, with rich brown skin and gray hair. He smiled; I assumed to reassure me that it was safe. I hesitantly smiled back.

"You alright?" he asked.

I rolled down my window and turned off the car. "Sorry," I said. "I hope I didn't wake you. I was…" I looked back over at Marta's house. "I was looking for my friend."

"Mrs. Hernandez?" he asked.

I nodded. "Do you know her?"

"Yes, yes, she and the kids left Sunday night. Haven't seen them come back yet." He looked down at me again. "Before you go thinking I'm one of those people who likes to spy on my neighbors, I'll tell you that I don't sleep much, so I'm usually up around this time of night."

I got the impression he might have been accused of being nosy on more than one occasion. Why else would he so readily volunteer that information?

He jerked his head, signaling something over his shoulder, as he rested his hand on the roof of my car. "Live over there. Yeah, I saw them leave around…" He tapped the car as he thought. "Maybe around six, somewhere in there. Not too long after they got home from church. Waved to them." He smiled at me. "I was just gettin' in myself from services at Ivory Baptist around the corner."

"So, did she speak to you when they left; maybe tell you where they were going?"

"I'd already gone inside by the time they piled up in that car of hers and left. I only saw the car leaving. Didn't see them get in."

That was strange. I looked at my phone again. Marta would have known when she texted me that she wasn't coming to work and told me why. Instead, she sent a vague text. Not like her at all. Marta had a tendency to go on and on. Sure, our rekindled friendship was fragile, but the history was there, and so was the love for one another. And she still hadn't responded to my question of why she would only speak to me on Wednesday.

"If you want, I can tell her you stopped by," the man said, jerking me out of my thoughts.

"No, I'll try and call tomorrow."

He knocked his knuckles on the roof of my car. "Well, you stay safe," he said, and walked away without a backward glance.

Something had happened to Marta and her kids. The problem was, I didn't know what I was going to do about it.

"Hey, so you're home," Wade said. He stood in the hallway by my apartment.

"Why are you standing by my door?" I inserted my key into my lock. My hands were shaking. I wanted to blame the copious amounts of caffeine I'd drank today, but the truth insisted otherwise. I was scared for my friend and her kids. And without a clue as to what I should do about Marta's sudden disappearance, I felt lost as well.

"Nah, I heard noise inside your apartment, and when I knocked, you didn't answer. So I... um... went around to your patio door and looked inside. I didn't see you, so I thought maybe someone had broken in."

"What!" I couldn't get the door open quickly enough. But as soon as I stepped inside, I wanted to leave again.

I smelled sand... and blood.

The Old One had been inside again, and this time, someone had heard him.

"Did you call the police?" I moved farther into the apartment. I wasn't scared. That would have been a normal reaction. Instead, I stood there surveying my apartment while anger boiled in my stomach like acid. It was too much. Everything that had happened since I walked into Tribec Insurance was an overload on my mind, and right now, I was having a really hard time dealing with it all.

"No. Mr. Wan went inside to check; said it seemed okay. I thought I would wait till you got home to let you know. Must have been a really..."

I slammed the door in his face. I didn't mean to be cruel, but he was seriously starting to rub me the wrong way. And I didn't have enough energy to deal with him at the moment. I would apologize later—after I told him to leave me the hell alone.

All my boxes had been removed from the closet and stacked neatly against the wall. Proof that someone had gone through them. What the hell were they even looking for? I shook my head in frustration as I went over to check if anything had been stolen. There was nothing valuable inside. A quick search through them confirmed that nothing had been taken.

I went through the rest of the apartment, turning on lights as I cleared each room. I pictured Marta's heavily-lit neighborhood and laughed. Damn. I was using the same logic as them. Only, they believed they were protecting themselves from human beings. I was trying to use light to keep an Old One out. I shook my head and went back into the living-room.

After pulling out a blank notebook, I plopped down heavily on the floor and dumped my purse out on the carpet in front of me. I didn't have the patience to search for a pen. My eyes landed on the scrap of paper that Vincent had stuck in my pocket. He had written "Gary and Anita Taylor," along with a phone number. I pulled up the memory of the phone call I'd heard. The guy never said his name. It was possible it was on the caller ID along with the phone number. But both his and his wife's name? At least, I assumed it was his wife's name.

Why did Vincent give it to me?

Guilt gnawed at me. I should have driven by his house again. After all, he lived only a few blocks from Marta. Yet, the situation with Vincent wouldn't be easy to figure out—especially since I had no way of contacting him. Besides, I needed a lot more brain cells to work with to solve it. As it stood now, I was only working with three, and they were barely hanging in there.

I looked through the items from my purse, the weight of fatigue pushing against me. I closed my eyes for a moment, trying to subdue the itchy feeling. When I opened them again, I was no longer sitting. Rather, I was lying on the floor with my head on my empty purse.

I pushed myself back up and reached for my phone. I blinked my eyes a few times to try and clear the blurriness and pulled up a search engine. I spent the next twenty minutes calling the three major hospitals on the island. No one had admitted Marta or her kids. There were a couple of Jane Does, but they turned out to be middle-aged, white, homeless women. I'd have to call the clinics in the morning when they opened. I briefly entertained the thought of calling the police but squashed it. I had no definitive proof that something had happened to Marta and her kids, and in my current state, the police might opt to lock me up instead—especially if I went in there ranting about ghosts and gods.

It was after midnight; Kara was most likely asleep already. I wouldn't call her. Besides, I wanted to avoid involving her in this until it was absolutely necessary. Hopefully, that time would never come.

I pulled the notebook onto my lap, picked up a pen, and started writing down everything that had happened to me since I first walked into Tribec Insurance. What I was writing was probably not making much sense, but I needed to do it.

Once I finished, I laid my head down on my empty purse again. I doubted I would make it all the way to the bedroom. My mind and body were too tired. Maybe a few hours of sleep would help me come up with a really good plan on what to do next.

I shut my eyes—floating, floating—in that moment of twilight sleep.

So peaceful.

Until a finger trailed across the back of my neck.

I shoved up from the floor, kicking items everywhere. My pulse pounded in my chest, the sound of blood rushing to my ears rendering me temporarily deaf. The shadows around the room pulsated, contracting in and out. I snatched my purse off the floor and ran out of my apartment. The door slammed behind me.

I escaped to my car and slid into the driver's seat, my back melting into the vinyl interior.

*Calm the fuck down, Nicole.*

The words ran on a loop in my brain as I clutched my shirt, fist buried between my breasts as I took a deep breath. Going to my parents' house wasn't an option—that would only involve them in this whole mess. I rifled inside my purse, fingers wrapping around the slender leather clutch. At least I had my wallet.

I maneuvered out of the complex parking lot, my heavy eyes blurring out the details. I blinked a few times and let off the gas. *Where the hell was the motel?*

A sudden bump rattled me, and my eyes shot open. Shit. I jerked the wheel to the left and narrowly missed a telephone pole before coming to a full stop straddling the center white line. A light flashed in a slow off-and-on in the windshield reflection. A neon sign. I glanced in both directions.

Rent by the hour.

Finally.

I pulled into the half-empty lot and parked in front of the Coke machine. After paying the clerk, I stumbled to the room, burning bile rising into my throat.

Maybe I should sleep in my car. Fuck it. I'd already paid, and I doubted that dirty motel clerk would give me my money back. I laid two bath towels on the bed and stretched out on top of them. After setting an alarm, I laid down and stared at the ceiling.

My life was spiraling out of control, and it all began when I first set foot in Tribec Insurance. I knew I should have left. But then where would I have gone? Tears filled my eyes. Turns out, despite my resolve to never work with magick, I was working with it anyway. But not by choice.

Light flooded the room, and the bass from a car stereo made the cheap night-stand shake. I closed my eyes, trying to block it all out. My life, the room, everything. Slowly, as if my mind was fighting itself, everything started to fade away.

The smell of sand tickled my nose, but I was too far gone to react.

Darkness.

An alarm sounded, tiny bells cycling loudly in my ears. I cracked one eye open, and light flooded my vision. My phone was lying right next to me on the bed. Only, it wasn't my bed. I bolted up and took in my surroundings. Every light was on in the dirty motel room. Memories flooded my sleep-deprived mind, suddenly making me recall the events of last night.

I snatched up my phone and silenced the alarm. It was after six in the morning. I didn't know how long I'd been asleep, but it must have been a really hard sleep; the bed had hardly been disturbed. I must have had some presence of mind to protect myself from a possible germ infection, since I was lying fully-clothed on several bath towels instead of the actual daisy-printed spread. It might have been white when they first bought it. Now, it resembled something that should be lining a dog bed.

Now that I was awake, I couldn't stomach being here any longer. I grabbed my half-empty purse—I must have left most of the contents on the floor of my living room—and headed out the door, wondering how many hours I'd actually paid for.

I ARRIVED home five minutes later and let myself into my apartment. Anxiety had me standing in the doorway, my eyes darting around. Debris from my purse lay strewn all over the floor, my notebook still open to the page I'd been writing on. What did the Old One want from me? There had to be a reason he kept visiting me. Touching me. My skin crawled with the remembrance of its icy fingers running across my neck. I thought about what Luisah had said. He'd marked me for protection. So why was I so afraid?

Pushing the unease and fear down deep, I stepped over my stuff and made my way to the shower. Once I was clean, I started the coffee maker and pulled up a search engine on my phone and located four medical clinics.

By the time I'd consumed three cups of coffee and several slices of toast, I'd called all four. No one fitting Marta or the kids' descriptions had been treated at any of them.

I was out of options.

Marta's parents had died in a car crash a year after Marta was married. Her mother was an only child, and both her parents were long deceased. Marta's father had only one sibling, whom they'd lost contact with. He, however, had an aunt who was still alive, but unfortunately, she suffered from Alzheimer's and would most likely not be of any help. And I didn't know any of Manuel's family.

In essence, Kara and I were the only family she had. A pang of self-loathing washed over me. Why had I been so damn petty and refused to reach out these past few years? She was right to worry about her kids and my influence over them. My life hadn't been stable. It still wasn't. Why couldn't I have seen that?

I pushed away my self-loathing—it wasn't helping—and tried her cell again. This time, the call went straight to voicemail. Maybe she would show up at work today. At this point, I was willing to hold on to that thin line of hope. At least, until I was proven wrong. If she didn't show up, I'd call Kara.

Yesterday, I'd shown up looking like a vagabond. Even

though I didn't intend to stay, I wasn't going to repeat that embarrassment. After pulling on one of the outfits I'd bought after I was hired, I grabbed my travel mug—filled with coffee—and left.

I didn't have a plan, so I'd have to improvise. Lucky for the Stewarts, I also didn't have immediate access to a gun. Otherwise, my plan would include gunfire and bloodshed.

As I drove into the parking lot of Tribec Insurance, I spotted Daniel casually leaning against his car. The space next to him was free, so I pulled in and parked. He was at my car door before I could even open it. He yanked at the handle, and I sat there, staring at him. What the fuck was his problem?

"Unlock the door," he said.

I ignored him.

He glanced over at the building and then back down at me. I would say he looked nervous, but that wasn't exactly right. Concerned, maybe? And definitely frustrated. The concern was what had me unlocking the door and pushing it open. He backed up while I climbed out of the car.

"What do you want?" I asked.

"I told you Monday that you needed to be cautious in there. You didn't listen. I also told you to not draw any more attention to yourself. Glaring at Andrew all day was not a good idea. And I won't even go into your behavior on Tuesday."

"My friend Marta is missing," I said in response to his unwelcome, bossy comments. "I believe they did something to her and her kids. So, I will be drawing as much attention to myself as I need to, to find out what happened to them."

"If that's true, running in there without a plan will get you killed."

How the hell did he know I didn't have a plan? And why had he taken an interest in my well-being? From the first day I'd met him, I got the impression something was off. What I found the strangest was the way he kept assessing the room, looking for threats. Did he know something about the Stewarts?

"Thanks for your concern," I said as I started toward the building.

He grabbed my arm. "Nicole. We can help you. You have to trust..."

I snatched my arm away. "I'm not going to sit in there and pretend nothing has happened. I don't operate that way. And what is this 'we' shit?"

"You're going to have to trust me—"

"I don't fucking know you—"

"Dev, we have to go in. We've been out here too long," Rachel said. She strolled up to us, her backpack secured over her shoulder and smiled at me.

"Who's Dev?" I asked.

Daniel touched my elbow. "She's right. Let's get inside; we can discuss this later."

"I'm not going to sit in there and pretend everything is okay."

"You have a better idea?" he asked.

Fuck. He was right... again. I didn't have a clue as to how to handle this situation. Sighing heavily, I reached inside my car and retrieved my training manuals. If I was going to play a part, then I might as well look it.

Rachel moved away first, making her way into the building before us.

I walked beside Daniel—or whatever his name was—at a slower pace. "So, I take it your name isn't Daniel."

He glanced at me. "No, it isn't. But while we're in the building, you need to keep referring to me by that name. Understand?"

I gritted my teeth. I could always call him "Jackass"—I didn't care for his aggressive tone, but that was counterproductive, so I kept it to myself. He stood there, eyes narrowed, waiting for me to respond. I bared my teeth as I moved past him and entered the building.

"GOOD MORNING, everyone. Please find your assigned seats so we can begin."

Andrew stood in the middle of the power circle and waited for everyone to find their seats. The little notecards with our names on them were placed on the tables. My seat had changed—again. This time from the west energy point to a focal point. Daniel's seat changed to the east energy point, and Rachel sat on the west, next to me. The focal point across from me remained empty.

I started to move my chair, as did Rachel. They were bolted to the ground. These people were getting brazen.

I glanced over at Rachel.

"Excuse me, Andrew," Daniel called.

Andrew continued to observe Rachel and me. I met his eyes in challenge.

"Sir," Daniel called out again.

Andrew ignored him. Bastard. I put a hand on the table and braced myself. My knuckles turned white from the pressure as I physically restrained myself from launching over the table. Rachel touched my arm, silently telling me to stop. Red haze coated my vision; adrenaline flooded my body. I pushed forward a little more. Andrew's eyes narrowed.

"Is there something you needed, *sir*?" I bit out.

"Take a seat, Ms. Fontane."

Rachel sat down, reached out, and yanked me down as well. I jerked my gaze toward her. She shook her head, a minuscule gesture that was barely noticeable.

Andrew smiled and turned toward Daniel.

"Careful, Nicole," Rachel mouthed and pushed a small cloth bag into my hand. "Keep it in your pocket. It disrupts their spell."

"You know what spell they're using," I whispered.

She pulled a tablet out of her backpack and wrote, *Athanasia.* What the hell was "Athanasia?"

At my puzzled look, she mouthed "Later," and turned and focused her attention on Daniel.

I looked down at the small burlap sack with a red symbol woven into the fabric. It smelled like clove and dandelions. I shoved it into the pocket of my dress pants. I would examine it carefully later.

After Daniel finished peppering Andrew with pointless questions—an obvious distraction—Andrew turned back to the classroom.

"Yes, well, I'm glad to see all of you today. We have a busy week ahead of us." He paused and rubbed his head. "Yes, well, first a bit of bad news." He glanced at me, and I could swear I saw a small smirk play across his lips. "Mrs. Marta Hernandez decided she didn't want to continue her employment with us."

I flipped him off under the table. When he glanced down and narrowed his eyes in anger, I realized he could see me. I wasn't doing a very good job of not drawing attention to myself. Surprisingly, Andrew decided to ignore my antics and continue with his instruction. His dismissal of my actions brought up another question. Why was he ignoring them? Any other employer would have shown me the door by now, but these people were actually acting as if my behavior was okay. It was further proof that Doc was indeed protecting me. But why?

I glanced over at Rachel. She was scrutinizing me. I pulled a sheet of paper out of my notebook and wrote: *What does the spell do?*

She didn't respond. Maybe this was not the best place to ask. I folded the slip of paper and shoved it into my purse. I'd have to wait till later to question her again. Along with her pushy friend Daniel.

About an hour into the training, a pulling sensation engulfed me. At first, it was subtle—a slight nudging. But then the intensity grew, sucking on me as if I were in a sudden whirlwind of pressurized air. I glanced at Rachel. Her hand was in her pocket; she dipped her eyes toward my pants.

I slid my hand in my pocket and palmed the small sack she'd given me. When my hand closed around it, the pulling sensation stopped, and Veronica gasped.

She and Jesse started gagging as if they were being choked.

My eyes flew to Andrew. On Friday, he'd looked on the verge of death. Except for his eyes—a clear blue. Now, his pasty skin had taken on a healthy glow. His wrinkles had all but disappeared, and his hair had a nice, healthy sheen to it. It is almost as if he was morphing into a much younger version of himself.

Suddenly, his hand flew to his throat. He drew in a ragged breath, bending as if he could pull air from the ground. He rose up and his eyes found mine. They were filled with accusations. As if I was the one who'd caused him to choke.

Veronica pulled in a ragged breath, and Jesse stood up and pounded on his chest. Andrew staggered back; his hand landed on the desk. After clearing his throat, he yanked his tie into place and straightened, trying to regain his composure. Veronica coughed a few more times and raised her hand.

"Yes," Andrew said, his voice sounding rough. "What is it, Ms. Lockwood?"

"I think I... I need..." She didn't get the opportunity to finish her statement. She suddenly pitched sideways and landed hard on the floor. Her body lay motionless, her chest perfectly still.

I jumped up and went down on my knees beside her. Daniel was by my side in an instant. I looked up. Andrew was still standing in the middle of the circle with a perplexed look on his face.

"She needs a doctor!" I yelled.

Andrew blinked a few times, as if he were coming out of a trance. He stared daggers at me for a brief moment and then rushed out of the circle and picked up the phone on the wall.

"She's been drained almost to the point of death," Daniel said, whispering to me.

"How do you know?" I placed two fingers on the side of Veronica's neck to check for a pulse. I breathed in a sigh of relief when I felt a small thump. She was alive. Barely.

He started to say something but stopped.

Andrew made his way over and knelt down beside us. "Please, everyone, return to your seats." He looked over at me. "Are you ill as well, Ms. Fontane?"

Anger pulsed through my body, flooding in like a tidal wave. Maybe it was the very deliberate way they had set up the power circle to use magick on their employees. Rachel said the spell was called "Athanasia." Once again, my lack of knowledge had placed me in a dangerous situation.

Multiplied by my lack of sleep, worry for Marta and her kids, frustration, and the realization that they were using magick on me, I answered without thinking. "No, but it isn't for lack of your trying." I kept eye contact with him, waiting for him to deny what we both knew he was doing.

The door opened, and Andrew looked away—guilt, anger, and fear were competing for dominance on his face.

Lisa strode in the room with a murderous look in her eyes. She was closely followed by both Ronald and one of the guards—Oliver Strong. I was somewhat surprised he'd actually ventured this far out from behind his fort.

Ronald met my eyes. His were filled with worry. Maybe he wasn't involved in all of this. There was genuine concern in his eyes. That meant they were keeping secrets from him. But given their relationship, I wasn't surprised. I smiled to let him know I was okay.

"I need everyone who is not ill to leave the room, please," Lisa said as she walked over to where Andrew and I knelt. She glanced down at the girl briefly and then zeroed in on me. "I trust, since you are upright, that you are well, Ms. Fontane?" She formed it as a question, but the look in her eyes told me she knew damn well I was okay.

I cut my eyes to Andrew, and he flinched. I didn't dare repeat my accusations. I'd slipped once; I wasn't going to do it again. Ronald came over, and as I moved past him, he let his hand briefly touch mine.

Jessie listed to the side, his eyes drooping. As I stood in the doorway observing this, Lisa came striding over and slammed the door in my face.

"What are we supposed to do now?" I asked.

"Is that your idea of not drawing attention to yourself?" Daniel whispered.

I shook my head. "Sorry. I just..." I glanced up at the black dome on the ceiling. They were watching us. But could they hear us, too? "Never mind."

The door opened a few moments later, and Lisa walked out. "Dr. Stewart would like all of you to be examined. Oliver will escort you to the clinic." She paused and carefully rearranged her face into a mask of worry. It looked painful. "I truly hope all of you are... okay. And that this little mix-up will not put you off Tribec Insurance."

Was she fucking kidding? I stepped forward, and Rachel touched my elbow, reminding me to be quiet.

"Do you know what caused everyone to get sick? Is it something we should be worried about?" Daniel asked, his tone even.

Lisa forced a smile. "We are looking into it. And it won't happen again. Once everyone is checked out, you may resume the rest of your training in the break room." She checked her watch. "Now, if you will excuse me, I need to call the building manager to have him come inspect the classroom." She glanced at me. "Once you are checked out, Ms. Fontane, my brother Thomas and I would like to see you upstairs. I will have one of the guards escort you." She turned and strode away without a backward glance.

"I guess I'm getting fired."

Daniel moved in front of me, blocking the camera's view. "Tell Dr. Stewart to send you home."

"Why..."

He shook his head. "You don't want to be alone with them."

I peeked over his shoulder. Oliver exited the room, carrying Veronica. He glared at us. "You three, follow me."

Jesse walked out of the room on his own, and we followed behind him. I brought up the rear, taking the opportunity to look in the training room. Andrew was standing there, his face red with anger, as Ronald berated him in a hushed tone.

Andrew started to turn toward the open door, and I quickly looked away.

Ronald rested his hand on my knee. "How are you?"

Cold seeped into my bones. I suppressed a shiver. After what just happened, his forwardness was making me a little... uncomfortable. I shifted on the exam table, trying to dislodge his hand.

"Fine. Just thought I would fake sick so you can send me home. That way, I could avoid going to see your brother and sister," I said. Daniel's warning kept popping up in my head. Would they really try to harm me?

A single drop of water splashed in the sink. I shifted my gaze toward it as I inched back on the table. I should have sat in the chair.

"If you agree to come over tonight..." He leaned in and kissed the side of my jaw.

I tried not to flinch. Despite his obvious concern, my awkward conversation with Lisa yesterday was now causing me some concern. I still didn't understand why she warned me about Doc's tastes. Was she referring to sex, or women in general?

He moved back and stared at me. "What's wrong?"

I sighed. "You know your family is using magick on the employees."

His eyes widened. "Nicole. We've discussed this."

"It was a spell that caused Veronica to pass out. Trust me."

He grew quiet, staring off in the distance. After he removed his glasses, he stepped forward and rested his hand on my knee. "I'll cover for you. Say that you had a really bad headache and needed to go home."

"Why do I get the impression that you knew?"

He looked away. "My family... it's complicated. My loyalty to them got in the way of my logic. I apologize. But I have tried to protect you. I hope you can see that."

"My friend Marta is missing. Did they do something to her?"

Confusion crossed his face. "No, we were told she quit."

Before I could respond, someone knocked on the door, and he moved away.

"Yes," he said and slid on his glasses.

Emilia walked in. "Thomas needs to see you."

Ronald nodded. "Yes, well, I will be there in a minute. Have you finished up with the rest of the employees?"

Emilia cut her eyes in my direction. "Yes." She turned back to Ronald. "They're ready to be discharged if—"

"I will handle it in a minute," he said, cutting her off.

She paused, her hand still on the door. "Nicole, if you would—"

"Leave."

"Of course, Dr. Stewart." She spared me one last glance before shutting the door firmly behind her.

He moved back in front of me. "Why don't we continue this in my office?"

I pushed him away. "I don't want to get you in trouble with Lisa."

He laughed. "She is... difficult. But Thomas is usually able to keep her in line."

"What about you? Does he try to keep you in line?" I asked, thinking about his admission that they had Emilia watching him. Maybe they didn't trust him to keep their secret.

"No, he just cleans up after me." He moved closer. "Now, let's go to my office."

"No, I'm going home."

He tried to cover his wounded look with a smile. "I will send you home, but I want you to wait in my office while I discuss some things with my brother."

"Why do we need to go to your office?"

"More privacy."

I wasn't buying it—too much desperation in his request. My gut was screaming at me that something was wrong with his sudden confession. Like it was all calculated for my benefit.

I shook my head.

"Fine," I said after a short while. Maybe I could get some more information out of him to help me figure out what was really going on.

I jumped down from the examination table and followed Ronald to his office. Once we were inside, he pulled his cell phone from his pants pocket and made a call. His desk phone rang, and he hit the speaker button.

"It's imperative that you remain quiet," he said as he made his way to the door. "And don't open this door." He shut the door.

What the hell was going on?

My question was answered a few moments later.

"That girl needs to go."

I recognized the speaker's voice—Thomas Stewart.

"What girl?" Ronald replied.

"Don't play dumb with me, little brother; you know damn well which one. The one you're fucking."

I covered my mouth to smother the gasp.

"Excuse me, Dr. Stewart; what do you want me to do about the rest of the employees?" Emilia said.

Where the hell were they? And why had Ronald left the line open for me to hear their conversation?

"Did you give them the herbs?" Lisa answered.

"Yes, Ms. Stewart."

"Then they should be fine. Send them to the break room, but before you do, have one of the guards tape off the training room. I don't want anyone nosing around in there." She paused. "I suppose we will have to call someone out to look at the room. Convince them it was some sort of gas leak." Another pause. "Order lunch for them. I don't want anyone leaving the building until the herbs have completely taken effect."

"Yes, Ms. Stewart."

A door closed with a click.

"That stupid witch is not doing her job," Lisa started, her voice taking on a chill. "We hired her to watch you, and now look what's happened."

Ronald cut her off. "Everything is fine. And I don't need Emilia watching me. I can manage my own love life."

"You haven't been able to manage it since you were a teenager. What has changed now?" Thomas said.

Why the hell were they so concerned with Ronald's love life? And what messes had they had to clean up for him in the past? Did he have a slew of bastard children out there? Ones the Stewarts didn't want to acknowledge? Typical rich assholes. No wonder he didn't want to work with them and drank himself to death.

"It doesn't matter. The point is that you can't fire Nicole."

A long pause ensued.

"That is why you asked to speak with her, correct? It's also troubling that, if that was your intention, why do it yourself? We have an entire human resources department to handle these types of things. What reason would you have to speak with her directly?" There was challenge in his voice.

"We can't have her disrupting the power circle upstairs—especially not so close to Harvest," Thomas responded.

Harvest? So this was why he had me wait in his office. To confirm his family was practicing magick without having to actually say it. Damn.

"Harvest is next week; she won't even be out of training."

"Save it. You have no say so in this, Ronald," Lisa said.

"I have as much say as the two of you. And I say Nicole stays. I will talk with her."

"And say what?" Lisa said.

He laughed. "I'm not stupid, Lisa. And I managed to dispel her unease when she was first hired. I can explain away anything she might have noticed. Besides, the problem is with Andrew. I told you he was using the circles. You should have done away with him a long time ago. He has always caused problems that you two have consistently ignored."

"I will deal with Andrew," Thomas said. "And you didn't inform us about her unease on Wednesday. She should never have been allowed to continue through the process."

"I dealt with it." Exasperation tainted his voice.

There was a long pause. Why was Ronald fighting so hard to keep me here? What game was he playing? He knew I no longer wanted to work for the company.

"She can stay," Thomas said, his words final. "In the meantime, I want someone to find out what principle she practices. There is no way she disrupted that circle by herself. Emilia was unable to determine it, so send Logan."

Who the hell was Logan? And why was Emilia trying to figure out what principle I practiced? As soon as I thought about it, I recalled our conversation from Wednesday. She had asked me about it, but I dismissed it when she didn't press further.

"You will not send Logan after her," Ronald said.

I flinched at the icy chill of his tone.

"She could have been sent by one of the other families for the Ark. Logan has ways of dealing with these types of situations," Lisa said, sounding much too enthusiastic about the prospect of sending Logan after me.

"Paranoid, Lisa?" Ronald said.

"I want her gone!"

Fucking bitch. I was more than willing to oblige her request. Right after I put my fist through her carefully made-up face.

"Shut up, both of you. Lisa's right, Ronald. You need to end it. Preferably without us having to clean up your mess. And I want her blood tested for the anomaly again. I don't trust you're being honest," Thomas said.

Ark? They actually had an Ark, too? What the hell did they use it for? And what anomaly could they be looking for in my blood?

"Despite what you two believe, I know how to do my job. And her blood doesn't have the anomaly. Allow her to return to training with the rest of the group."

I thought he was going to convince them to let me leave.

"Where is she now?" Thomas asked. "I don't see her on-screen."

Shit. Vincent was right; they did watch the employees.

"In the restroom," Ronald said.

I took that as my queue to leave. After securing my purse on my shoulder, I eased Ronald's door open and peeked out into the hall. Empty. And no black camera orbs on the ceiling. I soundlessly closed the door and made my way to the elevators.

However helpful the information I overheard was—confirming my suspicions completely about the Stewart family—it didn't give me a clue as to what happened to Marta and her kids. Why had Ronald chosen to suddenly be honest with me and provide an opportunity for me to overhear their conversation in the first place? Why had he decided to turn against his family? Well, actually, he'd already done that when he lied to them about the blood.

So, what was his motivation for helping me? More importantly, what the hell was the Harvest?

aniel stood in my kitchen leafing through my journal. My mind still preoccupied with trying to figure out what the Harvest could be, I'd reluctantly handed it to him when we arrived at my apartment after work. He had offered to go with me to Marta's house. So, while I changed out of my work clothes, he perused my notes. Not the most comfortable experience for me, having someone riffle through my inner most thoughts, but it was necessary. Besides, it would save time in me having to explain all my observations as well as what had been going on with me since I started with Tribec.

"Thanks for making coffee." I poured myself a cup. "So, do you think I'm crazy?"

He looked up. "No. And you're out of sugar."

"I don't like the stuff. Black is better. Gets into your bloodstream quicker."

He polished off the rest of his coffee and set the mug on the counter. "Is that a scientific fact?"

I shook my head. "No. It's bullshit. I don't like sugar and see no point in using cream, either. I don't need to gussy up my coffee to drink it." I leaned against the counter. "Shall we start with the easy questions?"

He nodded. "Fair enough." He refilled his mug. "My name is not Daniel Carter. It's Devlin Grey—thanks to my mother. She named me after one of her favorite stories."

"Dorian Grey. Your mother wanted you to be immortal?" I pulled a bag of Lays potato chips from the cabinet. I'd refused to eat the lunch they bought us. Something about eating the food of my enemy unnerved me.

He smiled. "Yeah, she always told me she wanted me to live forever."

Might be a really interesting story there. I would have to remember to ask him about it some other time.

"Anyway"—he flipped through my notebook—"I was never in the military. I was, however, a detective in the Los Angeles Police Department. I had to provide an alias in case they did a search. While Rachel could have created a false background for me—as she did with the name Daniel Carter—searching certain databases would raise flags."

"Is Rachel a former detective, too?"

"No, far from it. I worked on a case involving her. Hired her after I left the department."

"Why'd you quit?"

"Not important."

"I don't know you, Devlin Grey, so everything is important."

"Cautious. I can respect that."

"After what I've experienced in the past few days, yes. I don't need the full history. So give me the *Cliff's Notes* version."

He reached for the bag of chips. He and Rachel had opted to forgo the lunch as well. Smart. We didn't know what they'd put in the food. They'd already pumped us full of mystery herbs without us knowing. I was still trying to work out that one. Especially since I'd spent all my time with Doc. Air ducts, maybe?

"*Cliff's Notes.*" He handed me back the bag of chips and rubbed a hand down his face. After a few moments, he continued. "Rachel's father tried to kill her entire family. He was running for governor of California, and on the advice of his campaign manager, he decided that he had to get rid of his secret family." He stood rigid, his hands resting on the sides of the counter, while a vein pulsed on the side of his neck. "He opted to poison all of them over dinner."

"Fucking jackass." Poison was a strange choice for a man. Women were more likely to use poison as a method of killing, while men went for more aggressive tactics. Rachel's father was not only evil, but also a coward. "How did he expect to get away with it? Didn't they wonder why he wasn't eating?"

"He told them he wasn't feeling well. Hai Lin called us when her four children succumbed to the poison. Rachel's dad was still there, tied to a chair. Hai tried explaining what had happened while he ranted about being kidnapped.

"When my partner threatened to arrest her, Hai went after him with a knife. My partner shot her six times." He glanced up at me, his eyes filled with fury. "Hai weighed a hundred pounds. We could have easily restrained her. But my partner..." He shook his head as if he was trying to dislodge the painful memory from his mind. "After the incident, I was asked to leave."

"How did Rachel and her mother survive the poison?" I asked.

"They're immune to poison. A rarity for earth practitioners."

The mere fact I didn't know this was possible with earth practitioners shined a bright light on my limited knowledge of my own principle. Luisah implied my father elicited a promise from her to not teach me about blood magick. My parent's neighbor, Cherry, made the same promise about elemental magick. Apparently, he didn't stop with just the other principles. He failed to teach me about mine as well. Was my limited understanding the reason I had such a hard time using magick?

If not for the urgency to find Marta and her kids, I would've driven to my parents' house and asked. As it stood, I'd have to have that very difficult conversation later. Hopefully by then, the fury that was working its way through my body would have receded.

"What happened to her father?" I asked, curious.

"Rachel killed him four years later."

If I hadn't already been disturbed by what Rachel's father had done, the casual way in which Devlin relayed that information would have alarmed me. "How did she get away with it?"

"That's her story to tell." The tone of his voice conveyed I wasn't going to get any more information on the subject.

I let it drop. For now.

"Okay. Next question. Why are you helping me? And what are you doing at Tribec Insurance?"

"We came to Tulare to locate a young girl named Felicity Markum. Since her and her parents were estranged, they paid her boyfriend, Jesse Lombardi, to give them regular updates on her well-being."

"Jesse sounds like a winner. Fucking bastard was probably with her for the money," I said.

"From what the parents told me, Jesse genuinely cared for Felicity. And the money was for her. Anyway, two months ago, Jesse failed to call them at their prearranged time. They became worried and, a week later, hired a private investigator named Bernardo Diaz."

"What? I used to work for him."

He paused, regarding me with a curious look on his face. "The last report they received from Bernardo indicated he had a meeting with Lisa Stewart on April twenty-second," he said, not commenting on my knowing Bernardo. "They didn't hear from him after that. My firm was hired six weeks ago. Two weeks ago, Bernardo's bloated body was found in a secluded marsh area near Alice. He'd been strangled."

Although I really didn't like the sleazy bastard, news of his death was still disturbing.

"If Bernardo went missing in April and had only recently been found, where had he been all that time?"

"The coroner report indicated he'd been frozen for several weeks. So, someone kept him on ice before dumping him. They also couldn't find any evidence on him."

Why would someone go to those lengths? It almost seemed...
planned. Again, that eerie feeling overcame me that someone was
orchestrating the situation behind the scenes. Maneuvering pieces
into place, and I was one of those pieces. But that couldn't be
right. If I hadn't gone to Tribec Insurance in the first place, none
of this would be happening. At least, I was hoping that was the
case. If not, it would imply someone had purposely steered me in
that direction. But how?

"Is that the reason you're at Tribec? You believe they had
something to do with her disappearance?" I asked. At this point, I
was willing to believe it, too.

"Yes."

"That still doesn't explain why you're helping me."

"Rachel believes you might be connected to what's going on.
And if you're right about your friend being missing, it could give
us some clue to where they might be keeping Felicity."

I tried not to focus on the fact that they were essentially using
me. Instead, I concentrated on their willingness to help. Besides, it
was a little refreshing to learn I wasn't paranoid in my thinking
that the events from the last few days were centered on me.
Someone else believed it, too.

"That will have to be enough for now." He picked up my
journal. "I want to discuss the things you observed with my team
after we check on your friend Marta." He started toward the door.

I set my coffee mug in the sink. "You know," I said, as I
walked over and snatched my journal from his hands, "you're a
very bossy bastard. If I agree to work with you, you're going to
want to stop doing that. I don't respond very well to heavy-
handedness."

He invaded my space, his body vibrating. A small smile played
across his lips. "If you agree to work with me? Full disclosure,
Nicole—the only reason I'm allowing you to work with *me* is
because Rachel is convinced you can help us. And I'm concerned
for your friend."

"You don't know my friend," I said, pushing myself farther

into his space. Warning bells were going off in my head, urging me to stop. I ignored them. Bastard thought he could intimidate me.

"I know she's a widow, has four children—Isabel, Maria, José, and Juan—and the two of you had been estranged for a few years."

"Why the fuck were you spying on my friend?"

"We weren't; we were watching you. And right now, it's not important. If you want to stand here stewing and acting like a child, I can leave." To prove his point, he gripped my arms and forcibly moved me to the side.

My body trembled with anger. I reached out and snatched his arm, trying to pull him off-balance. His feet remained planted in place. Strong son of a bitch.

He studied me while I cycled through a slew of emotions—anger, frustration, guilt. He was right; we did need to move quickly. However, I was having a hard time dealing with the fact that he and his team had been spying on me.

His face softened. "Look. I don't trust easily. I needed to be sure you could be trusted, and that meant looking into your background. And yes, following you was part of that. I'm not going to apologize for taking precautions to ensure my team's safety. I will, however, apologize for the pain it has obviously caused you."

While I respected his honesty, I still didn't appreciate his intrusion into my life. First, the Old One and my constant encounters with him. Now, I learn Devlin and his team were also following me around, documenting my life and the lives of my friends.

My blood boiled as I stared at him. No emotion registered on his face. But I did notice a vein pulsing in his neck. Good, he was angry. If I wanted to be petty, I could stand here all day, locked in our silent war. But in the end, my worry for Marta and the kids had me relenting.

"When this is over, we're going to have a very long discussion about boundaries," I gritted out.

"I'm looking forward to it; now, let's go," he said and walked out the door.

Unbelievable.

ON THE WAY to Marta's house, I told him about my discussion with Doc and how he'd let me overhear his conversation with his family. Devlin remained quiet as he navigated the streets without my input.

"The Harvest," Devlin said. He pulled up in front of Marta's house and parked. "I guess that explains a few things."

"Like what?" I asked.

He looked out the window at the kids playing in the street. "They're collecting people."

"How do you know that?"

"It fits with what we've been able to decipher from Bernardo's notes. A lot of people have gone missing that were associated with Tribec."

"Could it have anything to do with the Harvest they were talking about? Do you even know what that is?"

"The name would imply it does." He shook his head. "I don't know what kind of ritual it is. This is the first time I've ever heard of the Harvest."

Damn. I was hoping he would know. I could ask Doc, but for some reason, his actions today, while intended to be helpful, still gave me pause. Despite him confirming his family practiced magick—he never said what principle—he still wanted me to work there. Why?

Devlin glanced out the window again. "It's better if you avoid telling her neighbors that you believe Marta and her children are missing. Someone might call the police, and involving them would be a bad idea."

I was willing to trust his judgment on the matter for a number of reasons. The most important being that if the Stewarts were collecting people, they had to have been doing it for a while. And if that was the case, they'd been able to cover their actions thus far. Drawing attention to ourselves could put us in the same predicament as Bernardo. Dead.

After a few minutes, we both got out of the car. Before we could make it up the driveway, a little girl—wearing a pair of blue shorts and a white t-shirt that proclaimed she was trouble—stopped from a game of hit-the-boy-and-run, and skipped over to us, her jaw working furiously as she chewed on a piece of gum.

She stopped in front of us, placed her hands on her hips, and looked up at me defiantly. "They're not home," she announced. "And Marta doesn't like anyone parking in front of her house. So you have to move your car."

I stared at *Terrible Tina*, as a smug little smile spread across her face. I seriously doubted that Marta had shared with the little brat in front of me that she didn't want people parking in front of her house. I also doubted she allowed her kids to play with her, either.

I had to bite my tongue to keep myself from responding with something that began with "Look here, you little fucking bitch."

"Renee!" A female voice called out.

I glanced across the street. A woman was standing on the porch with her hands on her hips, wearing a slip that she probably convinced herself was a dress. She was a thirty-year-old version of the delinquent in front of me.

"Get over here right now!" she bellowed.

Renee didn't move.

"Run along now, Renee," I said. I wasn't proud of the teasing tone that had crept into my voice. Nor was I proud of the way I was trying to stare her down.

Renee stuck her tongue out, flipped me off, and ran across the street.

"Fucking brat," I said.

"I don't know," Devlin said. "I get the feeling you were exactly like her." He winked at me. "Almost like looking in the mirror, huh?"

"Fuck you," I said with a smile.

"You back again?"

I turned around. The man I'd met last night stood a few inches away with a smile on his face.

"That one"— he jerked his head toward Renee's receding back—"needs a switch taken to her backside." He stuck his hand out. "Joe Magee." He inclined his head in my direction. "And I met your girlfriend here last night."

Devlin glanced at me with a questioning look in his eyes, not even bothering to correct the man on the assumed relationship. When I didn't say anything, he returned his attention back to Joe. "Devlin Grey." He shook the man's hand. "We were looking for Marta Hernandez."

I guess I should have told him on the drive over that I'd stopped by last night.

"Did she come back last night?" I asked.

"Funny thing, after you left, a moving truck pulled up. If I hadn't been up already, it would have woke me up. A couple of fellas, military men if I had to guess, got out of the truck and walked inside the house. I started to go over and ask what was going on, but thought better of it. After all, it was none of my business."

"She would have told me she was moving," I said, more to myself than anyone in particular. I glanced over at Devlin. "She didn't move."

He dipped his head in acknowledgement and turned back to Joe.

"I thought the same thing," Joe said. "But again, none of my business. Almost called the police, but..." He let his words trail off.

I started to press him on why he didn't but remembered the off-handed comment he'd made about not being a snoop. Maybe part of his "not snooping" involved calling the police at regular intervals. And maybe he'd cried wolf one too many times and had been warned against doing it again. At least, that was what I was assuming. Why else would he not call them if he thought something was wrong?

There was nothing more we could learn from Joe, so we thanked him for his time and returned to the car. Once inside, I pulled my cell phone out of my purse. My hands shook as I stared down at it, trying to think of what to tell Kara. Marta was missing. I had to tell her something. Yet, that would mean involving her, and I wasn't ready to do that.

"Sloppy," Devlin said, pulling me out of my inner turmoil.

I glanced over at him. "What do you mean?"

"How they took Marta. They had to know that you would start asking questions. And if you got the police involved, then that would eventually lead back to Tribec. Also, if they had planned to take her for their Harvest, then why do it after she started?"

Even though Doc indicated he didn't know anything about Marta, I was willing to bet his family was responsible for Marta and her kids going missing. And that they just didn't tell him. Again, why? Something about this whole situation wasn't making any damn sense.

"I'm guessing they select people with some sort of anomaly in their blood," I said eventually. "Which explains the physical they give everyone." I paused, thinking back to my date with Doc. He said he'd lied to his family about the blood. I looked over at Devlin. He was watching me, waiting for me to continue. If I was going to rely on him and his team for help, I needed to tell him everything. "Ronald is misleading his family about the blood tests."

Devlin drummed his hands on the steering wheel as he stared out the front windshield. After a few moments, he started the car. "I need to update my team. And we need to search Marta's house." He glanced across the street at Joe. "I will send someone over to do it. It's better if we don't come back here."

I looked down at the phone in my hand. I hadn't told Kara that Marta didn't show up for work yesterday. Keeping that information, as well as my assumptions that something had happened to her, was wrong. She would be mad when she found out. I slipped the phone back in my purse; I'd cross that bridge later. For now, I took comfort in knowing that she was safe.

We pulled up to a small, nondescript white house with dark green shutters, located on the border of Pleasanton and Alice. The Buick I'd seen before, along with a grey Chevy truck, were parked out front.

"Do you and Rachel live together?" I asked. I followed Devlin up the walkway.

He unlocked the door and stepped to the side so I could enter. "We're both staying in separate rooms at the Sandman Hotel in Alice. This house is being used as our headquarters. It's also where the rest of my team is staying."

The front door opened into a small, sparsely furnished living-room. A single blackboard lay flush against the wall. Several photographs were tacked up to the board. I moved over and examined them. Most of the pictures were of the Stewart family, and a good portion of them were of me—as well as Marta and Kara and I at José's game. I frowned. No wonder he knew where Marta lived.

"When did you stop following Marta?" I asked, trying to keep the ire out of my voice.

"After the game. We were more focused on you."

The casual way he said that disturbed me. It was a good thing we had already discussed it. I was prepared to turn away. But paused when one picture caught my attention.

It was a shot of Ronald and me on his houseboat—my naked body on full display.

I snatched it off the board. "Why the hell would you need to take a picture of me fucking?"

"I thought you were more observant than that," he said, and walked away.

Since it was difficult to yell at him when he wasn't in the room, I continued down the short hallway and was deposited into a family room. A few long tables covered most of the available space, computers resting on top of them. The room smelled like sweat, pizza, and a floral scent that I assumed belonged to Rachel.

Everyone looked up from what they were doing and stared at me. I completely ignored them, forgetting I still had a bone to pick with Devlin. I was too fixated on the large man sitting on the couch, with his arm strewn across the back. He stared at me with a small smile on his face.

I said the first thing that popped into my head. "You should have taken the tricycle with you."

"My mom hadn't let me ride it since the day my dad walked out," Vincent said.

I laughed, but there was no humor in it. I was relieved to see that he was okay. "I tried to return your ID on Saturday. Your mom was there. However, I didn't feel comfortable leaving it with her."

"So, you still have it?" He looked relieved.

"Yes. Is your mother okay?" I asked, remembering the moving van I saw pull up to her house when I was leaving. I was willing to bet it was the same one that showed up at Marta's. I sat down beside him. Despite my distaste for his mom, I still hoped she was alright.

"They took her," he said, sadness filling his voice.

I reached out and touched his arm. "I'm sorry. I didn't know enough at the time to help her." I took a deep breath. "I saw the van pull up. I wanted to go back." I sounded like Joe Magee.

Sitting on the sidelines and watching, all the while knowing that something bad was happening.

"It's okay; if you had tried to stop them, they would have taken you, too. I tried to warn you, but..." He shook his head. "I believe they knew I did. So, I went down to the medical clinic, told them I wasn't feeling good." He looked down at himself. "It wasn't hard for them to believe me. Dr Stewart wanted me to start on a diet."

I squeezed his arm.

"When I left, I met up with Alek," he said as he glanced over at the man who'd dropped Rachel off at work on Friday.

He stood to the left of the couch, a few feet away, leaning against one of the folding tables. Both his deep-bronze coloring and long, thick, curly black hair made me think he had some Roma blood in him. He wore a snug white t-shirt that showed off the muscle definition in his arms, and a pair of worn jeans that hugged his muscular thighs real nice.

He regarded me out of dark blue eyes.

I pulled my gaze away from him and looked at the man standing to the right of him.

He was a little taller than Alek and had rich-brown-colored skin, a bald head, and dark hazel eyes that reminded me of liquid amber. A very thin goatee surrounded his full lips. His arms looked as if he spent most of his time lifting weights. Chinese lettering was tattooed on one of those beefy monstrosities. Despite his massive size, everything about him screamed relaxed—except for his eyes. Brewing in that liquid amber was a tiger, ready to pounce. Like there was a barely restrained power raging inside of him—waiting not so patiently to get out.

He stood next to Rachel, who was surrounded by several laptops.

Devlin leaned up against a table near the sliding glass doors. He was watching me, waiting. "Now that the reunion is over, let me introduce you to the rest of my team."

I stood up. "You know, you're a fucking jerk." I walked over to Alek and stuck my hand out. "Hi, I'm Nicole Fontane."

He smiled. "Alexandros Vaduva, but you can call me Alek." He reached out and took my hand; warmth spread all over my body. He held onto it as he continued to study me. His eyes briefly dipped to my mouth. "Nice to meet you, Nicole."

It took a minute for me to process what he said. My hormones had decided it was time for them to join the discussion. Good lord, he was gorgeous.

"Vaduva?" I asked, as I tried to push the onslaught of desire down deep. I seriously hoped he wasn't related to Petronela Vaduva. That family really didn't like me.

"Yes," he said. "I have family on the island."

Shit. That cooled the lust inside of me really quick.

I'd worked at *Carnavalul de Fear* during summer break for two weeks until the matriarch—Petronela Vaduva—of the family had pulled me to the side, pointed one of her bony fingers at me, and screamed, "*Fată leneș ieși.*" Lazy girl, get out. Which at that point, I didn't mind doing since I really hated the job, anyway. And the only reason I took it was to find out if those mythical beasts they advertised were real. Sadly, I never did get the chance to actually see one up close because the bastards kept them sequestered and guarded at all times.

There was no way in hell I was going to tell him that.

"Alek, are you the pervert who took the picture of me fucking? After all, I've seen you more than once. Right?"

He tried to suppress a laugh. "No. And yes."

"So, no to the pictures. But yes to the following." I glanced at Devlin. "Good to know." I walked over to the next man.

"Hi. You must be the pervert that took the picture of me?"

He smiled. "Yes."

"Your name?"

He stared down at me. "Jonah West."

"No nickname?"

"Don't need one."

I glanced at his arm. "What's the tattoo say?"

"Patience."

"If you ever take another picture of me without my permission, I will give you another tattoo." I reached up and slapped his left arm. His eyes lit up with laughter. I ignored it, along with the sudden sting in my hand.

"I will put it right here. Can you guess what it will say?"

His eyes danced with humor as he shook his head no.

I leaned in close. "Pervert. So from then on, you will be known as the patient pervert."

Laugher erupted around me, but I didn't join in. Instead, I strode over to my purse to retrieve Vincent's ID. Of course, I couldn't find it. It had become buried under all the useless crap I'd shoved in my purse. My face heated with embarrassment as I moved to the table that Alek was leaning up against and set my purse down. Why the hell was I still carrying this thing? I looked like an idiot, rummaging around inside of it.

"That's why I don't carry a purse," Rachel said. "Too easy to put everything in it."

"Yeah, I've been meaning to change to a smaller one." After some frantic digging, I finally managed to locate his ID, along with the scrap of paper he had given me. "I wish you had told me why you gave me the ID." I handed it to him. "And the caller's information."

"Well, I hoped it might be useful," Vincent said. "And I wasn't sure whether they would let me leave or not. I had to get the information out of the building. They have a way of making people disappear." He handed Alek the ID. "I thought access to the elevator was encoded in the strips on our badges. So, I claimed that I lost mine and got a new one. I removed the strip and attached it to my ID," he said.

It took a minute, but my thoughts finally caught up to the situation. "Wait, were you working undercover at Tribec?"

"No."

The way he said it made me pause for a minute. He didn't

sound completely truthful. I glanced over at Devlin; he was studying Vincent with a contemplative look on his face. Devlin said he had a hard time trusting people, and from the look on his face, I wondered if he trusted Vincent. Even I could tell the big man was holding back some information. Like, for instance, why did he need to remove the magnetic strip from his employee ID and put it on his driver's license when he could just use his ID.

"I like her, Dev," Rachel said. She took the items from Alek, bringing my attention back to her. "She speaks her mind." She inserted the ID into a detached card reader.

Devlin eyed me. "She's also observant. Why don't you take them through the notes in your journal?"

"Yeah, sure," I said.

I relayed the information to the rest of the group, filling in some of the gaps in my thinking that I'd left out. Alek asked a few questions about the Old Ones, but for the most part, everyone sat back and absorbed what I was saying.

When I finished, Rachel turned her computer around so everyone could see the screen. "Blank, just like the other one."

"So, the magnetic strip is a decoy," Devlin said.

Rachel pulled Vincent's driver's license out and inserted an ID badge into the reader. "Yes. The actual card is what's read. It explains the texture and weight." She pushed a few buttons on her laptop, and the screen filled up with binary code. "It's both simple and complex. They have information embedded into the cards to identify each floor. So, all the floors are listed, but not the complete code to access them. That means this badge could access all the floors—once someone programs in the rest of the code for that floor." She grabbed a sheet of paper off the table and wrote it out. "Say the code for floor number two is 'FL2XXCPX9445.' Well, our badge would show 'FL2XXCPX'; the remaining numbers are left out, preventing us from accessing that floor."

"So, we need to obtain a badge with all the codes," I said.

"Or the codes themselves," Jonah said, rubbing his chin. He went over to a small table covered in left-over pizza boxes and a coffee pot and poured himself a cup of coffee. "Did you want coffee?" he asked, looking at me.

"Sure." I would take the gesture as a peace offering. Although I should've been the one making it. I can't believe I actually told him I would rename him 'patient pervert.'

After pouring me some coffee, he took a few sips of his own, sat down in the chair opposite me, and reached into a box of doughnuts laying on the table. "I want to start working on one of the guards," he said.

Exactly what did he mean by, 'working on?'

"I've put together files on all of them. Most likely, they have access. I could take the badge overnight and return it in the morning."

"Did you already pick someone out?" Devlin asked.

Jonah picked up a file folder and handed it to Devlin. As Devlin paged through it, I made my way over to him and started reading over his shoulder. He glanced up at me, and I stared down at him. After a short while, he turned back to the file.

The file folder held a dozen pictures of the guard who'd escorted me to the medical clinic on Wednesday. George Merced. Jonah hadn't limited his salacious photography to just me. He'd managed to take pictures of George in the middle of various sexual acts in an alley. I guess it was his way of letting go. Especially after spending the whole day being a dutiful soldier at Tribec. Well, good for him.

"I followed him a few times. He has a pretty set routine," Jonah continued. "He shows up for work at seven in the morning and leaves at five in the evening. He eats lunch at work, goes to Michela's for a few hours to drink. Picks up both male and female hookers. Then home by eleven." He finished off the rest of his doughnut in one bite.

Michela's? I wouldn't have been caught dead in there, despite it being ten minutes from my apartment and five minutes from Jordin's. The crowd was a little too rough for my taste. And a little too adventurous.

"I'd hoped to get access to their computers. However, after today's events, I'm not comfortable returning. It could put us at risk. So, we'll have to break into the building after hours," Devlin said.

"Why can't you hack into their servers and get the information?" I asked Rachel.

"I already tried. They don't keep employee or client information in their main system—only financial stuff. That's why I had to go undercover with Dev."

"They have something to hide," I said to no one in particular.

"Right," Devlin said. "But before we get started, I have a couple things I need to cover with you, Nicole." He pulled out a chair and sat. "All the evidence of magick at Tribec indicates they practice earth magick. However, you wrote blood magick in your journal. Explain why."

"Okay," I said, sitting down in the chair beside him. "The artwork is from a civilization in Egypt—pre-zero dynasty that practiced blood magick. Although Luisah didn't come right out and say the Stewart family was practicing, she did point me in that direction." I thought about the copy of *Principles of Earth Magick* she had given me. "She also implied there was earth magick involved." I focused my attention on Rachel. "You never told me what the *Athanasia* spell was used for."

"*Athanasia* is used to revitalize or extend life. Old druid priestess created the spell. I'll show you how it works later."

Didn't the druid faith consist of all males? Revitalize or extend life? How was that even possible? Could that explain the strange way they'd set up the power circle?

"Can someone have more than one principle?" I asked.

"Shamans practice both earth and mind magick," Alek said. "Did you say Luisah gave you the information on blood magick?"

"Do you know her?"

"We need to stay focused," Devlin said. "For now, we will move forward under the assumption that the Stewart family is practicing some form of blood and earth magick in a ritual that involves harvesting people. So, casualties are going to be unavoidable." He pinned me in place with his eyes. "If that is going to be a problem for you, then you need to let me know now. I can't have you freaking out in the middle of it."

I could guess the casualties he was referring to didn't include his team. I mean, who went into a situation hoping to get killed? No, the casualties would mean the people sitting in this room would use whatever they had in their arsenal to save not only Marta and her kids, but the girl they were hired to find as well. To be honest, I just couldn't muster up enough "give a fuck" to care if the Stewart family and all their ilk were killed. They'd taken five people I loved with the intentions of harvesting them in their sadistic blood magick ritual. And if this band of vigilantes was going to help me rescue my friend and her kids, then I was in.

"Okay," I said, because he was still staring at me.

"It's obvious that we are going to have to use magick. All of us in here, excluding Vincent, are mage-level practitioners." He looked at Rachel. "Rachel's principle is earth. On top of healing us when we're injured, she's also our computer expert, first line of offense, and back-up interrogator." He turned to Jonah. "Jonah's principle is faith. On more than one occasion, he's used his magick to change our circumstances, as well as provide the extra strength we needed."

"By praying?" I asked.

Jonah smiled at me. "More or less."

Okay, not an answer. But I'd let it go for now.

"He also runs surveillance and acts as muscle when we need it," Devlin continued.

"Aren't extra strength and muscle essentially the same thing?" I asked, thinking about Jonah's contributions to the team.

"For faith mages, no," Devlin said without further explanation. "Alek's principle is mind. He uses that when we need to interrogate someone with magick. He also works as back-up muscle and handles forced entry."

That was a nice way of saying Alek broke into places. Very politically correct. I added "thugs" to my assessment of the group.

"What's your principle?" I asked Devlin.

"Elemental."

"Figures. So, you've been fucking with the rain. What, was it not responding to your commands quick enough?"

"You must not know much about elemental magick."

"I know enough," I lied. He was right, of course. I really needed to learn more about the other magick principles. I could only imagine how inept I looked and sounded, and I didn't like it one bit.

"Elementals use the elements to work spells. We don't create them. However, we can harness them."

"Okay," I said. "And let me guess, you're 'Boss Man.'"

Someone chuckled.

"Which puts you in charge of everyone and—"

"And I do the planning and execution." He smiled. "Boss Man, huh?" He shook his head. "Well, Nicole, that leaves you. It's obvious you have magick. Rachel believes you're a mage. I can add that you're brash, have a quick temper, and have issues with authority. On the plus side, you're observant."

"What? Is it review time already? But I just joined the group, Boss Man. And to answer your question, my principle is earth, and I'm a latent practitioner. I'm also a pretty decent fighter." Or, as Kara said, I could pummel someone to death.

"A fighter?" He looked as if he was having a hard time swallowing that.

"If you like, Boss Man, I can demonstrate."

Alek, Vincent, and Rachel laughed; Jonah grinned.

"Maybe some other time."

I turned to Rachel. "I didn't know earth mages could see the magick in others?"

"Yes, our principle is more connected to the source. Mind mages can see it, too." She considered me for a minute. "You look stronger than a latent. You sure you're not a mage?" She glanced at Alek. "Powerful, huh?"

He studied me for a minute. "Yeah, but it's not complete. Maybe someone blocked your magick."

Rachel nodded. "That's what I think."

I chewed on that for a moment. Had someone blocked my magick? If they had, it would explain my difficulty practicing basic spells.

"I don't think I am," I said, still pondering it. If someone had blocked my magick, why would they do it? And more importantly, who would do it? A stray thought entered my head. Luisah touching my head, implying that an Old One had marked me. Could that be what she was talking about?

"Now, we can't forget there are non-magick users involved in this as well." Devlin got up and walked over to a black footlocker sitting near the kitchen doorway on the right. "Do you know how to use a firearm?" he asked, looking at me.

"I've used one before. I wouldn't say I'm an expert. But I know how to point the business end at the bad guy and shoot."

He handed me the gun. "This is a Glock 32. It holds thirteen rounds per clip." He eyed my purse. "I will have to get you a hip-holster later. For now, shove it down the back of your pants. It has a DAO—double action built in safety system—the lip depression, automatic firing pin safety, and the falling block safety."

"I don't understand a damn thing you just said. But I do get the gist of it." I stood up and shoved the gun down inside the back of my pants. The metal was cool against my skin. "I don't understand why we need guns. All of you are mage-level practitioners. Shouldn't that be enough?"

"The guards have no magick. When we get access to Tribec, you'll need a way to defend yourself. We won't be using magick on them," Devlin said.

Maybe he thought using magick against non-magick users was cheating. Funny that that was the one thing he had an issue with. I had no such issues. I'd use magick any day over a gun.

Jonah leaned toward me. "Dev used to work in law enforcement. They had a strict policy regarding use of magick against non-magick users. He's having a hard time shaking that doctrine."

"Do you have a hard time with it?"

He winked. "Not at all."

"I want to get the search of Marta's house over with," Devlin said. If he heard what Jonah and I were discussing, he didn't let on. Devlin rubbed the back of his head and looked over at the clock on the mantel. "What time did you go by her house last night?"

"It was close to midnight," I said.

He nodded. "The neighbor across the street could be a problem. But I noticed a small, wooded area behind the house. We can use that as an entry point." He looked at Alek. "You're with me and Nicole on the search. Jonah, I want you to get the key card from the guard; bring it back here. Once Rachel is done copying it, return it. We're searching Tribec tomorrow night. Once we finish, we'll all meet back here.

"Didn't you say you and I shouldn't go back?" I asked.

"Can't be helped." He looked at Vincent. "Keep working on the badges. And see if you can dig up some more information on Doctor Stewart. His letting Nicole overhear that conversation is not sitting right with me. And the fact they are having Emilia watch him is... troubling." He reached into the black footlocker and pulled out the same model gun he'd given me. "Also, dig up what you can on Emilia." He started to turn but paused. "Andrew Snow as well. He's a disgruntled employee. It wouldn't surprise me if he has some information on the company that we can use."

"Okay, I'm on it." Vincent pushed himself up off the couch. "I also have that list of properties compiled." He sat down at the table and opened the laptop. "I can divide it up. There's a lot."

Devlin looked at each of us. "Okay. Tomorrow, we look for information on their ritual." He glanced at me. "Would Luisah be willing to help us with information about blood magick?"

"Yes," I said, thinking about Luisah. However, I didn't know how helpful she was going to be since she was one of the people who I believed was keeping information from me.

Devlin glanced back at Vincent. "Divide up the properties into three lists. We can start hitting them after we see Luisah." He turned to me. "Again, if you are going to be involved, you'll need to pull your weight. We don't know how much time we have. And when the three of us don't show up for work tomorrow, it's going to set off alarms. So, we need to act fast. Last chance to back out."

"Why not go in to work?" I asked, surprised I was actually suggesting we go. "We might be able to get more information that way."

"I doubt we will learn anything else before their ritual. Taking Marta and her kids doesn't fit their pattern, and therefore, doesn't make sense. I have no idea if they're to be part of the ritual, and honestly, I have no plans to wait around and find out."

I had to agree on that one. Taking Marta seemed almost... I don't know, like an afterthought. Devlin said the woman he was hired to find went missing prior to her starting work. So why take Marta?

I followed them outside. As Jonah made his way to the black Buick, Devlin touched my elbow.

"The picture he took was not taken to capture you and Dr. Stewart," he said softly. "It was taken to capture an image of the specter standing behind the both of you."

My heart skipped a beat. Chills ran up my spine and my vision wavered. The Old One had been there when I was at Ronald's. Why? Was Ronald more involved in the events taking place than he let on? Were the two of them working together?

Alek placed his hand on my shoulder. "Are you alright?"

I lifted my hand to signal that I needed a minute. He backed away from me.

"Nicole," Devlin called.

I glanced over at him standing by the driver's side door. Impatience was wafting off of him in waves. I'd have to worry about it later, add it to my already growing list of things to worry about. Right now, I had to focus on Marta. And when we got back, I'd apologize to Jonah.

After a few deep breaths, I was able to regain some semblance of control. I climbed in the car and shut the door. A sharp pain seized my wrist. I looked down. The mark pushed its way to the surface—the image suddenly became clear.

The circle that the Old One had started was complete. The symbol in the center was still difficult to make out. But its familiarity sent chills down my spine. Now, it was a shen ring.

Despite fleeing from my apartment to escape the Old One, he still followed me. And while I lay in that dirty motel room, he had finished what he started.

I sat in the front seat next to Devlin, the cold seeping into my bones from the Escalade's leather seat, despite the warmth pouring from the vents. As I stared out the window, my mind kept going back to my time spent in that dirty motel room. What a waste of money. How come I didn't feel it when the Old One completed the shen ring? I'd felt it before.

The melodious thrumming of the tires on the asphalt, and the silence inside the car otherwise, threatened to lull me to sleep. No wonder babies always passed out in the car. But something told me it would be a long while before I was able to rest again.

"Is Vincent a member of your team?" I asked, rubbing my wrist.

"He's a distant cousin of mine. Very distant. On his father's side. I recognized him when he came out of Tribec Insurance a few weeks ago," Alek said.

Devlin remained quiet.

I peered into the back seat. "I get the impression he's been investigating them for a while."

Devlin glanced at me. "We think Vincent was working for a leftover fanatical faction of The Council of Principles. He might have been recruited before he got the job, or shortly thereafter. He hasn't confirmed this."

A fanatical faction of The Council of Principles? Why didn't my dad or Luisah tell me about this? Feelings of betrayal dug their claws into me. How could I ever trust my daddy or Luisah again? They should have armed me with enough knowledge about magick to protect myself. Yet, they didn't. Instead, they chose to dole out bits and pieces of benign information about herbs and symbols used in earth magick—keeping the dangerous aspects of all magick a secret. Like I was a damn child and unable to deal with it.

I pushed my anger down. I'd confront them later.

"You trust him?" I asked finally.

Alek shifted, drawing my attention back to him. "He's blood, no matter who he works for. Blood does not betray blood. He can be trusted."

"That's not always true," I pointed out, thinking about my own parents, who had been lying to me for years.

We rode the rest of the way in silence and, twenty minutes later, we pulled up and parked on the cross street next to Marta's. We climbed out of the car and glanced around the neighborhood. Marta's block still cast a beacon of light out into the darkened night.

"They believe the light will protect them," I said and dragged my purse out of the car.

"People have always believed that evil was afraid of light," Alek said. He secured a bag over his shoulder. "In some cases, they're right." He glanced at Marta's street. "Here, it just draws attention."

An image of me running through my apartment, turning on lights when I learned the Old One had been inside, popped in my head. Yeah, I guess he was right. Most people—including me, it would seem—believed light would keep away evil. Yet, did I really believe the Old One was evil? He hadn't done anything except mark me for protection.

"And makes our job harder," Devlin said and shut the trunk —bringing me back to the present. "Let's get moving."

We followed him to a small path behind the houses. The

wooded area wasn't deep. We could still see the houses on the next block. However, it did provide some cover.

Devlin turned on his flashlight when we got to the back of Marta's house. "Alek, get the door open. I'm going to take a look around the outside of the house." He turned and walked off.

"He's a bossy bastard," I mumbled.

Alek chuckled. "Yes, but he's good at what he does." He reached inside his nylon bag and handed me a flashlight. "Point this at the lock."

I took the flashlight from him and turned it on.

"The only reason someone would block your magick is if you're dangerous—or they want to keep something from you." Alek crouched down and examined the lock on the door. "I can look"—he reached in his bag and pulled out a slim leather case—"but it will hurt."

"I'm not real comfortable with you looking around inside my head. You and your band of merry men have already seen me naked. Exposing you to my inner thoughts is tantamount to seeing me naked all over again. Once is enough."

He looked up at me, his eyes dancing with laughter. "Merry men?" He opened the leather case and pulled out a small, metal tool with a hooked end, and another one with a flat end, and started in on the lock.

After a few seconds, the lock clicked. He stood up, shoving his instruments back in his bag. "If you were embarrassed, I'm sorry." His eyes dipped down to my breasts, and then back up again. "But trust me, you have nothing to be embarrassed about."

"I wasn't embarrassed." I sighed. "Devlin told me why Jonah took the picture. For a while, I was convinced that I had been imagining the encounters I kept having with it. Despite what Luisah said, a small part of me was still entertaining the thought that I was simply going crazy. It was easier to deal with it that way." I focused on him for a minute. "I get the impression you know Luisah."

He nodded. "She's known by my people."

"Care to elaborate?"

Devlin came around the side and moved past us and entered the house.

"Later." He tapped his head with his index finger. "If you change your mind about me looking inside you, let me know."

"Okay." I ignored how sexual his statement sounded, moved past him, and went inside the house.

The door opened up into the kitchen. I swung my light around the room. All the cabinets were open and empty. A few stray boxes and cans of food littered the floor, but for the most part, it looked as if they had taken everything.

"Alek, I want you to start upstairs. Spray the walls down in each room. And then come down here and do the same." Devlin handed me a camera. "Nicole, when he's done, take pictures of the walls."

"Why?"

"Let's get this out of the way. I work quickly, and I don't like a lot of questions. I understand you don't like being ordered around, but in this case, it can't be helped. We need to get in, gather what we can, and get out. There is a possibility they have someone watching the house. I don't want to linger." He moved closer. "So, when I give an order, follow it." He walked out of the room.

I stood there for a moment, thinking of various ways I could non-verbally express to him what I thought of his little speech. But in the end, I relented. There would be plenty of time later to help him understand. It would be a perfect opportunity to demonstrate my fighting skills.

The kitchen had a double-wide opening that led out to a family room. To the right were the stairs. I followed Alek. When we got to the top of the stairs, he pulled a can of spray out of his bag.

"What are you spraying?"

"Luminol. It helps detect traces of blood."

I swallowed. "He thinks they were killed in the house? The neighbor said he saw them drive off."

He must have detected the hysteria in my voice, because he stopped and turned to look at me. "Devlin doesn't leave any stone unturned. So, instead of searching for only one possibility, he searches for all of them. That way, we don't have to come back." He moved over and placed a hand on my shoulder. "I know she's your friend. But right now, you need to push the pain down and focus. It's the only way to help her."

I nodded, unable to speak past the lump in my throat.

"Okay." He took my flashlight. "Only take pictures of areas that start to glow. I'm going to do the other rooms."

After squeezing my shoulder, he moved into the first room on the right.

He was right. I needed to bury my feelings and concentrate. However, in my defense, in the last few hours, I had been over-loaded with information that any normal person would need time to process. So, in light of those facts, I believe I was holding it together pretty well. Yes, at any moment, I was going to snap, but I was still pushing through. On top of that, I was working with people I really didn't know.

Besides, no one was going to pat me on the back and tell me what a good job I was doing, nor were they going to stop and deal with my hysterics and overall lack of knowledge. So, I had to push through. If not for me, then for Marta and the kids.

I started off behind Alek, looking for areas on the walls that glowed. There were a few spots in some of the bedrooms, and several larger spots in the bathroom. Despite my knowing they were blood, I pushed on. Taking pictures as if on autopilot.

We repeated the process downstairs, and that was where we found larger concentrations of blood. Devlin, I learned, was going behind us and taking samples of the spots, as well as taking pictures of the overall house. There were a few scattered items that hadn't been taken, and after I finished taking pictures, Devlin had me gather them in plastic bags.

Once we were outside, I bent over and threw up. Thankfully, neither one of them said anything.

EVERYONE WAS HUDDLED in the war room eating pizza when we returned. I'd spent the ride back fighting the emotional turmoil in my gut. And trying to keep myself from crying. I needed to be strong. Thankfully, neither Alek nor Devlin said anything.

"There's a problem with the guard," Jonah said. He tapped his fingers on the table.

Devlin narrowed his eyes.

"He was awake. I had to secure him in his residence." He kept his eyes trained on Devlin.

"You know how to get in without being heard. What happened?"

"His company was a little late leaving," Jonah said. "Didn't know he was still in the house until I was in. Walked right into him. Gave him a few dollars and sent him on his way. George came out when the door shut."

Devlin looked at Rachel. "You done with the card?"

"Yeah." She pulled it out of the reader and handed it to him.

Devlin extended it to Alek. "Go over and fix it. We need to have access to the entire building."

Alek stood up, finishing his slice of pizza in one bite.

"I want to go with you," I said.

"Why?" Devlin asked.

"He can take me by my place after so I can get some clothes." Yes, I was assuming that I would be staying with them. And yes, I was lying about the reason I wanted to go with him. I was going to ask Alek to look inside my head. I really didn't want an audience for that.

Devlin glanced at Alek. "Your call."

Alek regarded me for a minute. "You better move if you're coming."

I grabbed my purse and a slice of pizza and hurried after him.

Alek opened the passenger door to the Buick. I practically crammed the entire slice of pizza in my mouth and fought hard not to choke. A smile spread across his face as he watched my jaws work overtime, trying to break down the mouthful of pizza. Why the hell had I shoved so much in my mouth?

I swallowed. "Sorry." I tossed my purse inside the car. "I'm a little hungry." I got in the car.

"Oh, I can see that." He shut my door and made his way around the car.

My cheeks flushed with embarrassment. *Real smooth, Nicole.* I could only imagine how I had looked trying to rapidly break down the food in my mouth.

"You should go easy on Devlin," Alek said after he started the car and pulled away from the curb.

"No, he should go easy on me. He's an asshole." I rubbed my chest. I should have grabbed something to drink as well. The damn pizza had become lodged somewhere between my mouth and my stomach.

Alek smiled. "He can be. You need me to stop for some water?"

"No, it will pass."

He studied me for a few seconds. "Now, tell me why you really wanted to come with me."

I looked out the window. This was going to be awkward. Not more than an hour ago, I'd told him I didn't want him looking in my head. Now, I was going to ask him to do just that. I'd also implied that it made me feel like I was exposing myself. Yeah, it was definitely going to be an uncomfortable conversation.

I reached into my bag and pulled out a cigar. After lighting it, I rolled down the window and blew the smoke out. I glanced over at him. "Shit, sorry. Is it alright if I smoke in here?"

He smiled and reached for the cigar. I gave it to him, and he took a drag. "My uncle used to smoke these," he said on the exhale.

"I was trying to quit. Had even managed to get down to one per day." I pulled in more smoke. After blowing it out the window, I continued. "But since taking the job at Tribec, I've gone back to smoking four a day. At this rate, I'll be chain smoking in no time."

He laughed.

I shifted in my seat so I was facing him. "How did you get mixed up with Boss Man?"

"He was investigating members of my family who had used magick to harm children." He glanced over at me. "They were already slated to have their magick blocked for their crimes. And the family would have taken care of it. But Devlin killed them before we got the chance to."

These people talked about killing as if it was something normal. As if everyone did it. Maybe, in their world, it was. Did I really want to work with them?

I glanced out the window as we made our way around the mountain, passing out of Pleasanton and crossing into Perry. The road narrowed and Alek made a right, putting us in the middle of the settlement.

"Wait, where does the guard live?" I asked, my palms suddenly sweaty.

"Off Carmichael Street. Anyway, he asked—"

I placed my hand on his arm. "Hold on a second. I don't..." I could have kicked myself. I should've asked him before where we were going.

Greenwood Apartments loomed up beside us like a massive beast. The five-hundred-unit building sat in complete darkness, looking out on the street. It was a monster sucking the surrounding area into a vortex of lost hope and destitution. The structure was also the demarcation point that let people know they'd entered the war zone.

The last time I was actually in this part of Perry was right after Steve's death. Deep into self-blame and unable to pull myself out of the depression I'd slipped into, I'd ventured into Perry searching for a way to forget. I spent my days with Frank, cutting school, having sex, and getting high. I tried every drug he gave me —weed, peyote, Ritalin, and acid. The only thing that kept me from continuing with acid was the fact that I didn't like the way it made me feel out of control.

I continued on that spiral dance for three months.

I was drunk, high, and naked when his Uncle Ray came into the room and shot him ten times in the chest over forty dollars. I still remember the sticky sensation of the blood on my skin, and the feeling of euphoric indifference as I tracked a single drop of blood as it made its way down Frank's side. It was the only thing I was able to actually focus on, since the rest of his chest looked like so much shredded meat from the ten bullet holes that had punched through flesh and bone.

My breaths grew shallow. A phantom clicking noise started inside my head, and just like that, Frank's uncle was trying to kill me all over again. Images of Frank's chest filled my mind. Sweat ran down my back. I'd put the gun Devlin gave me in my purse, but there was no way in hell I was going to dig for it now. That meant taking my eyes off the surrounding area. Not good.

Suddenly, Alek pulled to the curb. After turning off the car, he turned to me.

"Don't stop!" I gripped the handle on my door, pulling on it as if I could make it move in closer.

"What the hell is the matter with you?"

I looked out the window. A group of men stood near a red Chevy Impala; their eyes focused on us. When they started across the street, I turned to Alek.

"Keep driving."

He smiled. "You're scared of them."

"Yes." I looked out the front window.

The men had stopped in front of the car.

"Did you bring your gun?" I asked.

He tapped his fingers to his head and got out of the car. I guess his mind magick was his gun, and I was about to find out what a mind mage was capable of. Since I didn't want to look like a coward, I got out of the car and went to stand next to Alek.

*Stupid, Nicole.*

The air was filled with the smell of weed, alcohol, and poor hygiene choices. Broken bottles, trash, and discarded children's toys littered the streets. The native oak trees that grew all over the island had been ripped out of the soil and replaced with various car parts and furniture. Overflowing trash cans sat by the curb, waiting for a pick-up that would never come. Everything about the area screamed of abandonment and loss.

"You sellin' her?" the ring leader asked as he looked at both me and the car. He was a tall, lanky man with very pale skin and tattoos all over his bald head. He didn't wear a shirt. Judging from the various scars on his chest, I'd say he'd been shot a few times.

"No," Alek said.

There was a commotion behind us. Other people, both men and women, had started to surround us, blocking us in. Alek stood there with a smile on his face. Was he crazy?

"Then we takin' her." The man looked behind us. "More pussy for you to sell, Nia."

"She'll do," a woman said.

I turned and spotted Nia. An overweight woman with dark skin and bright purple eyes. They had to be contacts lenses. She wore a leather jacket, red lace bra, and tight black pants. There was a large scar running from her scalp along her jaw line, to her painted red lips.

She smiled at me.

I flipped her off. Not the smartest move, but I refused to show any fear despite the knocking in my knees. There was no way in hell I was going to let Nia turn me into a hooker.

The crowd started murmuring, and a few people inched forward, guns in their hands.

Alek laughed and turned to me. "This is what mind mages can do, Nicole."

"I thought Devlin said you didn't use magick on people who didn't have any," I whispered, then remembered Jonah said it was Devlin's hang up, not theirs. Good.

Alek started humming a dark melody. A feathery sensation crawled across my skin. I flinched and moved away from Alek, only to step back when I remembered where I was. I should've dug the gun out of my purse. At least then I wouldn't have felt so useless.

Someone in the crowd screamed.

I turned. A few of the people were clutching their heads as they backed away from the car. The man in front of us—the one who'd asked if I was for sale—was standing there, confusion etched across his face and blood trickling from his nose.

"Back in the car, Nicole," Alek said.

I didn't hesitate. I ran back to the passenger-side door and climbed in. I stole a peek behind me before I shut the door. All the people who'd surrounded the car, including Nia, were on the ground, clutching their heads as they rocked from side to side.

I was starting to rethink my desire to have Alek look inside my head.

The driver's door opened, and Alek climbed back in and started the car.

"What the fuck did you do to them?"

"Rattled their minds a little." He glanced at me. "They'll be fine in a minute." He pulled out and maneuvered around the twenty or so people lying in the middle of the street.

"And the leader, the one who is now bleeding from his eyes?"

He looked over at me.

"Did you kill him?"

"Do you care?"

I thought about it for a minute. Not caring would cross a line I wasn't sure I was ready to cross. Once I started excusing one act of vengeance, one justified death—then it would become much easier to excuse them all.

"Can you explain the levels of mind magick to me?" I said, changing the subject.

"Mind magick has four levels, for men. And in some rare cases, five, for women. The fifth being the ability to perceive the future. It's rare. The only woman I know that has it is Petronela." He glanced at me, and I looked away.

Damn. That meant she probably foresaw the reason I'd really wanted to work at the carnival. It also explained why I was never able to actually get a glimpse of the mythical beasts. I'd concluded a while ago that they were probably fake, anyway.

"The first," Alek continued, "allows you to alter someone's thoughts, their perception. But you have to use what is already there. I can't plant memories that don't have some basis in what a person has already experienced. Jonah left the guard tied up. So, I have to alter his perception of how he ended up tied to a chair. Since he liked picking up hookers, it should be easy.

"In the case of our friends back there, I can cause pain." He looked at me. "Temporarily. And to answer your other question, no, I didn't kill the guy. I only caused him pain. My guess, he has an undiagnosed tumor in his brain that might have ruptured. So, it's possible my fucking with his mind could have killed him." He shrugged. "I honestly don't know, and" —he glanced at me—"I really don't care."

I shifted around in my seat and glared at him. "Why did you let me believe that you did?"

He pulled up to George's—a small beige house with a well-kept yard—and turned off the car. "Honestly, I needed to see where your head was at." He shifted so he could look at me. "While I don't doubt your determination to help your friend, I don't know if you're willing to do what's necessary to eliminate a threat. And like Dev said, things are going to get bad. You have the guts; I'll give you that. Getting in our faces about that picture took some big ones. But can you follow through is the question."

"I'm here, aren't I? You have to understand, Alek, I've never seen anyone use magick to harm someone. It's going to take me a minute to wrap my head around the fact that you all seem to do this with ease. I will protect myself, and others, if necessary. But what happened back there, while justified, was a little... disturbing."

"Fair enough. So, let me be honest with you. Our team doesn't deal in black and white. In this world, there really is no way to protect yourself if you do. I don't make it a habit of using my magick to harm people, but in the situation back there, it was necessary. Those people would've had no problem killing me and taking you. So, I ask you, Nicole, why the fuck should I care if I gave them a headache or made their nose bleed?"

"Can you kill them with your magick?"

"That would be battle magick, and yes."

"Battle magick?"

"Yes," he said as he started to get out of the car. "It's better if you wait in the car. He knows you, so a part of his mind will hold on to your image."

"Wait," I said, placing my hand on his arm. "You said there were four levels."

He paused. "Looking inside someone's head. It's referred to as *scope*." He got out of the car. "It's what I offered to do for you. Now, wait here." He strolled up to George's house, never once looking back.

Despite my reservations about what I'd witnessed Alek do, I still believed it was a good idea for him to see if someone had really blocked my magick. He called it "scope." Interesting word choice. I surveyed the quiet neighborhood, my thoughts heavy. Battle magick? I'd never heard of that level of practice. I wondered if earth had a form of battle magick as well.

I glanced over at George's house and wondered how long it would take to manipulate someone's mind. I really wished Alek had let me see the process. I could've hidden in the shadows to prevent George from seeing me.

In answer to my question, Alek came out of the house a few minutes later. I glanced at my watch. Maybe five minutes. He opened the car door and climbed back inside.

"What happened?" I asked.

He started the car. "I planted a suggestion that he'd been tied up by the man Jonah paid."

I nodded. "I want you to look inside my head." I stared straight ahead. This was not going to be easy for me.

"Do you want to go back to Dev's house, or somewhere else?"

"We can go back to my apartment. I need to get a change of clothes, anyway."

"Alright."

"Why did you start working with Devlin?" I asked, after I gave him directions to my house.

I was nervous about him looking inside my head. And the more I learned about Alek, the more I might be able to put my mind at ease. I shifted around so I could face him as I reached in my bag for another cigar. Damn. I was out. I really needed to stop depending on the damn things. Especially since I couldn't afford them.

"My twin brother was one of the people he was investigating and later ended up killing. I made the decision to help him. I knew just blocking his magick wouldn't stop him. But my family refused to accept it." He paused. I reached out and touched his arm. His muscles jumped. "After his funeral, I joined Devlin's team."

"Were you upset you had to kill your brother?"

He glanced over at me. "No. I should have killed him sooner."

I couldn't imagine the pain he must have felt at having to kill his twin. Despite my wanting to comfort him, his body language suggested he didn't want to talk about it anymore. And I would respect that.

I turned and looked out the window—my mind now suddenly drawn to my own dilemma. Alek was right; the only reasons to block someone's magick were to keep a secret, or to prevent the person from using it. Since magick itself wasn't a secret, I was going to guess that whoever blocked mine was trying to prevent me from using it.

Now I just needed to figure out why.

"Are you sure you want to do this here?" Alek asked as he pulled into the parking lot of my apartment complex and parked.

"Yes, it's better for me to deal with it alone first." I glanced at him. "Well, not completely alone."

He smiled and took my hand. "I'll be as gentle as I can, but I do have to warn you again—it will hurt."

"You know, this conversation sounds very similar to the conversation I had with the boy who took my virginity. Almost word for word."

"Was he gentle?"

I shook my head. "No, he was clumsy. Thankfully, it didn't hurt, and it only lasted thirty seconds."

He laughed, which caused me to smile.

I opened the car door. "Let's get this over with. We don't want to get Boss Man's feathers ruffled."

When I got to my door, I noticed a small gift bag sitting on the floor. I picked it up and looked inside. Unease crept up my spine as I pulled out a bottle of Asbach Uralt.

Doc had been to my apartment.

"Who's that from?" Alek asked as he studied my face.

It was on the tip of my tongue to say nobody, but since he already knew I'd slept with Doc, there was no reason to withhold the information. So, I told him.

He took the bottle from me. "Dev doesn't trust him. Do you?"

"I don't know," I said, debating. "Maybe not. It does seem a little..."

"Suspicious?"

"Yeah. But I guess it really doesn't matter. I don't plan on seeing him again." I took the bottle from him and put it back in the bag. There was a card inside. I pulled it out and read it.

*Thinking of you.*

I put the gift bag back on the floor and opened my apartment door.

The blow caught me off-guard. I staggered back and fell into Alek. Before I could recover, I was yanked forward and thrown across the floor. I crashed into the stack of boxes near the far wall. Pain exploded inside my head, and as I tried to orient myself, someone yanked me up and slammed me against the wall. The room spun, and pain raced down my back. I blinked a few times and was barely able to make out three men fighting near the door —one of them had to be Alek.

The man holding me leaned in close, and his stale breath made my eyes water.

"We were paid to kill you," he whispered, "but I want to have a little fun with you first." He wrapped one meaty hand around my throat.

I looked down. He was fumbling with his pants. No fucking way was I going to let this smelly bastard rape me. I swung my knees up and pushed against him. When there was enough space between us, I kicked him with all my strength, hitting him in the stomach. He grunted and released me. My hands hit the carpet. Hard. I scrambled to get up, but he was quick. He grabbed my left arm. I made a fist with my right hand and swung around, hitting him in the jaw. My bones crunched and pain flared; I shook my hand to ease the pain. It didn't help.

My attacker staggered back, catching himself at the last minute on the couch.

I rushed forward, intent on landing another blow.

He lunged, wrapping his arms around my legs and pulling me down to the floor. He flipped me over and straddled me, pinning my arms with one hand. Someone yelled, but I couldn't tell who. The sound of his zipper going down was like a death blow. Once he pulled himself free, he reached down and grabbed my zipper. I bucked, putting as much strength as I could behind it, but it was no use; this guy was strong.

He yanked my now open jeans down my legs, his nails ripping into my skin. He fumbled for a few minutes while I continued to buck, my heels pounding on the carpet. When he realized that he couldn't pull my jeans off with one hand, his grip on my hands grew slack.

I yanked my arm away, reached forward, and grabbed his dick, squeezing it with all my strength. He bellowed. His fist came down hard on my jaw. My eyes watered, but I didn't let go.

He continued to pound on me, splitting my lip; the pain was unbearable, but I kept my hold on him. If I let go, he would be able to hold me down again. My vision waivered. I was close to passing out. He had switched from hitting me in the face to hitting me in my arms, so I squeezed even harder, yanking and twisting it; blood oozed between my fingers. Finally, he fell off me, slapped his hands against himself, and curled into a ball.

I could have run or gone to check on Alek. But whether he was winning or losing, I would still need to watch his back. The guy was down and in pain, but not incapacitated.

I straddled him and started pounding. In the process, the mark Ezra branded on my lip heated and my body flooded with not only adrenaline, but power. A raw sort of energy that kept building, increasing my strength as I continued pummeling the guy's face. Despite my hand being broken, I still kept going, plowing into my attacker's doughy face. The rage felt good. I embraced it, and a spray of blood flew up and coated my face.

While I was taking out my anger, fear, and frustration, someone walked up behind me. I whipped around, my bloody fist balled up, ready to attack.

Alek stared down at me with a mixture of horror and awe all over his face. "Are you done?"

I looked down at what was left of the man's face and grimaced. His eyes were halfway out of their sockets, his lips had been reduced to mush, and every surface of his face was covered in blood. I didn't even want to think about what his dick must have looked like.

"Were you trying to give him a sex-change?" He crouched down and took my hand in his. "Your hand is ruined."

I winced as he probed it. "I think it's broken." I looked up at him. Blood trickled from a cut on his lip, and a patch of red marred his temple. It looked as if someone had punched him really hard in the head. "Why didn't you use your magick?" My mouth wasn't working right, so the question came out slurred.

"It's a little hard to concentrate when you're being attacked." He studied me for a moment. From his wince, I guessed I looked pretty bad. "I'll call Dev; we need to get this place cleaned up." He glanced over at the other two men lying on the floor. "We also need to find out why they were in here waiting for you."

"To kill me. This man"—I moved so that I was no longer straddling my assailant—"believed raping me was an added bonus." My entire body felt as if I'd been run over by a truck.

"What the hell? Nicole, are you okay?"

I whipped my head back to the door, causing a wave of nausea to hit me. Mr. Wan stood in the doorway, eyes wide with his hand covering his mouth. Shit.

Alek stood up and walked over to him. "She's fine." Pause. "I'm Detective Russo." Pause. "I need you to return to your apartment." Pause. "I will be by shortly to take your statement." Pause. Alek's voice sounded layered and far away.

Mr. Wan wavered, and his eyes turned glassy. He looked at me one more time, confusion etching across his face.

"Go wait in your apartment," Alek said.

After one more sway, Mr. Wan turned and left.

Alek rubbed the side of his head and spit blood out on the floor. I started to fall over, and Alek rushed over and wrapped his arms around me, trying to keep me upright. My eyes snagged on a body in the corner.

"My neighbor," I mumbled.

"I'll take care of him in a minute."

"No... no... my other neighbor." I lifted my shaking arm and pointed to the corner where Wade lay, his body twisted in an impossible angle—blood pooling beneath him from the slash across his neck.

Fuck. I should've been nicer to him. Or, rather, I should've explained to him that I wasn't interested. If I had, maybe he wouldn't have come to my apartment hoping to see me whenever he heard a noise in my place. Because that's exactly what he'd probably done, surprising the men who'd broken in.

I lay there for a minute, letting Alek hold me. The warmth radiating off his body and his spicy scent pulled at me. Made me forget for a minute that someone had sent three men to kill me. Did they believe I was that damn dangerous?

"Do any of them have magick?" I asked, staring at my attacker.

Alek signaled with his chin to the man lying against the wall. I shifted so I could follow his line of sight. I didn't recognize the man. "That man is a mind mage. Despite his battle magick being weak, it took me a minute to overpower him." He rubbed his head. "But not before he did some damage."

"Are you going to be okay?"

He smiled at me. "You look worse than I feel."

I tried to smile, but my mouth refused to work right. "Can you turn the other man over so I can see his face?"

He hesitated, his eyes roaming over me.

"I'm sure I can manage to sit here by myself without falling." I wasn't completely positive about that; the room was still spinning. "Besides, I'm sure a few bottles of Sam Adams and a twenty-four-hour nap will fix me up just fine."

"I'm sure it will." He got up.

After helping me stand and depositing me on the couch, he went over to the man who was facing the door. When he turned him around—none too gently—I gasped.

"That's Oliver Strong. One of the guards that works at Tribec." That fucking bastard had actually come here to kill me.

He looked down at the unconscious man. "Why would he and his buddies be waiting inside your apartment to kill you? And do you think it has anything to do with the bottle of liquor that Ronald left for you?"

I pushed up from the couch, waited for the room to stop spinning, and went out to get the package. When I came back in, Alek had his cell phone to his ear.

Since I couldn't use my right hand, I set the bag on the couch and pulled the card out. The inscription didn't sound ominous. The fact that he hadn't signed his name was suspicious, but I was having a hard time picturing him sending a group of men to my apartment to kill me. So then the question was, who would send them here?

From the conversation I'd overheard between the Stewarts, they were not going to bother with me. But honestly, they could've changed their minds and not shared the information with Doc. That left the timeline. Obviously the men had been here awhile; at least, that was what I was guessing. So, when did Doc actually drop off the bottle of liquor?

"Devlin says to wait here. We need to question them. Find out who sent them."

I nodded, still caught up in my own thoughts.

A scary thought came to mind. Obviously Doc's siblings felt he needed to be watched. But why? Was this some sort of game for him? Seduce an employee, sleep with her, leave a parting gift, and then send a group of people to kill her? If that was the case, it would explain their comments about having to clean up after him. It would also make him a sadistic bastard.

I set the card down. Alek watched me with concern in his eyes.

"What's wrong, Nicole?"

I told him what I was thinking.

"That doesn't make sense," he said.

"This whole damn situation doesn't make sense." My head throbbed and my eyes twitched. Why did someone want me dead?

Pain radiated from my temple to my jawline. I glanced at the clock on the wall. Damn, almost one in the morning. I should be sleeping. When I tried to sit down on the couch, I ended up on the floor. I would've laughed at myself, but suddenly my lips grew warm, followed by my wrist. Pressure built inside my head, and I rubbed my temples to try and ease it.

"Nicole," Alek said, sounding far away.

My lips burned as if they were being roasted. And the heat on my wrist flared—spreading up my arm as if there was fire beneath my skin.

"What is that?" Alek asked, staring at my lips.

My mouth moved, but no sound came out.

"Nicole?"

I closed my eyes. A solid wall of pure blackness pulsed inside my mind. Carved in the center of that dark mass was a golden glyph of a phoenix, outlined in red. A fleur-de-lis rose up behind the mystical bird. The entire mark was enclosed in a shen ring. Outside the ring were hands, held up as if in prayer. The image looked alive as it beat against my mind.

It had to be the mark Luisah said the Old One gave me. But when? More troubling was it was also one of the charms that dangled from my bracelet. And instead of burning, like the ones on my lips and wrist, the pulsing caused a pain so excruciating, I could hardly breathe.

As the pressure increased, a small fissure cut the through the blackness. The pressure turned to pain. I screamed as more fissures opened up, leaking light into the darkness. My body jerked, and I slammed my heels against the couch. Pain radiated down my legs.

"Nicole, what's wrong?" He put his arms around me, stilling me, as he scooped me up and secured me in his lap.

I wanted to tell him what was going on, but I couldn't stop screaming. The pain was too intense. Memories overtook me.

*"...she's keeping him alive, Henri. Make her stop... please!"*

*My mother holding an axe, blood dripping on the floor. A man lying on the floor, bloody, his eyes open and trained on my six-year-old self, lying underneath him.*

*"Nicole, baby girl, stop. Let him die..."*

*"She can't keep this power..."*

*"Help her, please..."*

*"...there is always a price."*

*"I hurt, Daddy..."*

"Nicole, Nicole." Alek's voice was frantic.

"Make it stop!" I finally managed to scream.

*My father was holding me. Tears in his eyes. "...hush, baby girl; it will be alright..."*

*"...she's so cold," my mother said as she knelt beside a woman I didn't recognize, while my still form lay in a tub of water.*

*"There is always a price," the woman said as she gazed down at me. Her eyes started to glow, leaking a reddish light into the room.*

"Hold on, Nicole." Alek shifted so I lay across his lap, my head on the floor.

His warm hands encircled my head, and the snatches of memory kept flashing through my mind as if they were a montage.

"Sleep, Nicole," Alek whispered.

All of a sudden, the pressure inside my head receded. But the black mass continued to pulse.

"Sleep," Alek said, his voice taking on a melodious tone.

The phoenix beat its massive wings, stretching out to cover the mass. Darkness crept around the edges of my vision. The hands turned, palms out, as if warding off an attack.

The last thing I heard was Alek roar in pain.

"What the hell happened to this man's dick?"

My eyes flew open, and I jumped, knocking a green jar to the floor. Rachel grabbed my arm to steady me. Strips of bandage dangled from my broken hand.

"Careful. I'm almost done," Rachel said.

I blinked a few times, bringing the room into focus. I was sitting on the couch next to Rachel. She smiled at me and resumed wrapping my hand in a white bandage that smelled like juniper and rose.

I settled back and looked around my apartment.

Jonah stood staring down at the man who attacked me with a horror-filled look in his eyes. Devlin was in the middle of the room, surveying the damage. All of my boxes were upended, the contents spilling out, and there were holes in the walls.

"You do good work, Nicole. Real good work," Rachel said. She secured the bandage with tape.

I was surprised there wasn't any pain in my hand, and that my face no longer felt as if someone had run over it with a lawn mower.

"How long?" I managed to eke out. My throat was raw.

Alek handed me a glass of water. "Here, drink this."

I reached up, my hand shaking, and took the glass from him. After a few measured sips, I looked up at him. "What happened?"

He knelt down in front of me. "Someone did block your

magick like we suspected. And I'm guessing a few memories as well. Someone very powerful."

"I heard you scream." I took another sip of water, the cool liquid soothing my throat. How long had I been screaming? And why weren't the cops here? The rest of my neighbors had to have heard me shouting.

He nodded. "Whoever put that block on your magick also put something in place to make sure it couldn't be removed. My suggestion for you to sleep was viewed as an attack and"—he rubbed his temple—"the spell lashed out to defend you."

"I guess it's a good thing you didn't go rummaging around in my head."

He smiled. "Do you have any idea who put it there?"

"I have an idea, but I want to confirm it before I say." I looked over at Rachel and watched as she stuck a small, green jar in her bag. "What is that stuff?"

"A healing salve. It should help for a while. When we get back to the house, I will have to work on you some more." She touched the side of my face. "You were hurt pretty bad."

I closed my eyes to see if I could still see the black wall inside my head. It was there, but most of the fissures had been filled in again, leaving only an extremely thin one, running underneath the mark. Why had I not been able to see this before?

"Do you need to lay down?" Devlin asked.

"I'm fine," I said.

He dipped his head in acknowledgement and looked over at the two men they'd propped up against the wall near my front door. "We need to wake one of them up." He glanced over at my attacker lying on the floor. Jonah was still studying him with a repulsive look on his face. Like he couldn't quite figure out how the man had ended up like that. I winced. I couldn't believe I'd managed to tear his dick up like that.

"He won't be much use," Devlin told Rachel. "Unless you want to heal him."

"No, he can stay like that. He's dying anyway." She studied the other men. "We can use Oliver."

Damn. I really wished I could help them with Oliver. I had a score to settle with that bastard.

Alek knelt down in front of Oliver, placed his hands on either side of the man's face, and started humming. After a few seconds, Oliver's eyes fluttered open.

Jonah placed a chair in the middle of the floor. Once he and Alek had secured Oliver to it, Rachel got up from the couch, picked up her backpack, and made her way to the bound man. She dragged the coffee table over and set the bag on top.

"Hello, Oliver," Rachel said. "I don't like explaining more than once, so please listen. I'm going to ask you a few questions, and then, if you answer, we let you go. If not, we have to hurt you really bad." Rachel smiled at him as she opened her bag and retrieved a slim black case. After pulling out a small vial and a needle, she turned back to him. "I know you won't give me whole truth, so I'll inject you with my version of Amobarbital—truth serum—to help you."

"You're not injecting me with that shit!"

She filled the syringe with a burnt-orange solution, set it on the table, and pulled out a roll of duct tape. "Yes, I am, Oliver." She ripped off a piece of tape and slapped it over his mouth.

How was he supposed to answer with tape over his mouth?

He tried to lunge forward, but Jonah held him in place. Once he was secure, Rachel moved to his left side and jammed the needle in his neck. Oliver jerked, his body going into a sudden spastic attack. Jonah held on while Oliver continued to buck violently.

Alek stood with his hands down to his side, his feet planted. His eyes remained transfixed on the man in the chair. The only indication that Alek might have been in any pain was the strain around his eyes. I wondered what kind of backlash he'd experienced when he attempted to put me to sleep. His eyes met mine, and he came over and sat next to me.

"I thought you did the interrogations?" I asked.

He rubbed his temple. "I need to give my mind a rest. Besides, Rachel has been pestering Dev to let her interrogate someone for a long while."

I glanced over at Rachel. "She's enjoying it a little too much."

"Yeah." He grunted. "She's a little unbalanced, but..."

I turned to him. He was watching me, his face filled with worry. "I'm fine. Whatever Rachel did worked. So, you can stop looking at me like I'm about to kill over and die." I stared at his head. "I'm more concerned about you."

He shook his head, wincing at the movement. "I'll be okay."

We stared at each other for a minute, the air between us charging. Butterflies swarmed in my stomach, and my eyes grew heavy. His eyes dipped to my lips. I swallowed, not liking the emotions raging through me. Alek started to reach for me, but stopped when Oliver let out a loud moan.

We both turned and looked at him. He was blinking rapidly and moving his head from side to side. The strong smell of urine filled the air. After a few moments, his head slumped forward.

What the hell was in that shot?

"I will remove tape now so you can answer," Rachel said.

I noticed she spoke in broken English again. She'd done that a few times since I'd met her. It was almost as if, when she was angry or deeply emotional, she couldn't quite find the right words or phrases.

As soon as she ripped the tape off, his head shot up. "Fuck you, you stupid Chinese cunt!" Spit flew everywhere.

"Okay, that not nice." She reached into her bag and removed some brass knuckles. "I get you some of these, Nicole." She pointed at my hands. "Protect your hands better." She turned and belted Oliver in the stomach twice.

Alek was right; Rachel was a little unstable.

Oliver bent over and coughed, pain etched across his face. He spit blood on the floor and glared at Rachel with challenge in his eyes. "Untie me, and we'll see who beats who," he garbled.

"I don't fight fair. So, I ask again. Do you understand?"

"Fuck—"

She belted him again. Tears filled his eyes. He stared at her with a look that promised payback.

"Do you understand?" she asked again.

He didn't respond.

Rachel continued her persuasive attempts to get Oliver to talk.

During the process, Devlin glanced over at Alek. "You said you convinced the neighbor that you were a detective."

"Yes," Alek said.

"Go talk with him. See if he saw anything."

Alek touched my cheek. "You going to be okay?"

I smiled and pushed my face against his hand. His warmth was comforting. "Yeah, I'll just sit here and enjoy the show."

He chuckled, gave me one last concerned look, and got up and left.

Rachel came and sat back down next to me. I turned toward her, and she beamed at me.

"We both do good work." She dipped her head in Oliver's direction.

I didn't readily know how to respond to that. I mean, yes, I'd pretty much pulverized the man who attacked me, but I'd done it in self-defense. Rachel had tenderized Oliver to make him talk. And despite my elation at him getting his ass kicked, there was a pretty big difference between what Rachel and I had done. But I wasn't going to tell her that. I nodded, adding a smile to reassure her.

"Who hired you?" Devlin took Rachel's place in front of Oliver.

"Oh... well... Andrew wanted to know why the Stewarts... protect her... well, Dr. Stewart, anyway. Andrew thought... he..." Oliver laughed. "He wanted to fuck her, like he did the others..." He looked behind Devlin and blinked a few times before focusing on me. His eyes roamed over my body—stopping at my breasts.

Even in the midst of getting interrogated, he still had the audacity to stare at my breasts. Un-fucking-believable.

Devlin moved to block his view.

"Why does he think she's being protected?" Devlin asked.

Oliver shrugged, causing him to waver a bit. He smacked his lips and looked around the room. "I need some water," he said.

"I'll get you some after you answer the question. Why does he think she's being protected?"

"Andrew got caught using the circles, and he took too much... he blamed all of you." He looked at Devlin, Rachel, and me.

So, the three men had come for all three of us. But why would he assume that Devlin and Rachel would be here with me?

"Andrew sent you here for all three of us? Why?" Devlin asked, drawing my attention back to the horrific scene taking place in my living-room. Oliver looked as if he was on his last leg. Blood leaking from his eyes slid down the side of his face, mixing in with the spit on his chin.

"He told us to kill all three of you... he figured you all would be together." He looked at me and smiled. "Lance and I wanted to fuck her first. I knew Ronald had had a piece..."

*Smack!*

Rachel had moved so quickly from the couch that it took me a minute to register she was gone from my side.

"Don't talk about my friend like that, or I let her rip your dick off, too! Now, answer the question!" Rachel yelled.

Oliver stared at her through eyes covered in a white, filmy substance. His mouth opened and closed as if he were trying to pull air into his lungs. Finally, he laid his head forward, resting his chin on his chest. After a few minutes, he started mewling, and spit spilled out the corner of his mouth. "They told him... he couldn't take anymore," he mumbled.

"Couldn't take anymore what?" Devlin asked.

Oliver's head jerked up. "Life."

Devlin continued asking questions. According to Oliver, the Stewarts performed their harvesting ritual every four months and used the employees to fuel the magick, as well as provide them with strength. It fit with what Rachel had said about the *Athanasia* spell. Maybe that was why Luisah had pointed me toward *The Principles of Earth Magick*. There had to be a spell in there. Or at least a spell to counter it.

He also told us the guards and managers weren't allowed to participate in the Harvest. When the ceremony did take place, the managers were required to keep the employees in a trance until the Stewarts finished their ceremony. Once the employees left, the guards disposed of the dead bodies that had been used in the ritual.

The people they used in their Harvest were not from the island. He said they'd made a deal with the mayor to limit the amount of island citizens they took. So that was why they offered mainly medical insurance. It gave them a reason to screen applicants for the anomaly in their blood. If an applicant did have the anomaly, and the family members didn't, it was up to the guards to get rid of the family, including the children. However, Andrew had paid the guards a very large sum of money so he could take over the job of disposing of the children. Unfortunately, Oliver didn't know where Andrew got the money or what he did with the children once he collected them.

"Why is Andrew working against the Stewarts?" Devlin asked.

Oliver looked like he was ready to drop. His eyes were completely white now, and his skin looked grayish.

"What's happening to him?" I asked Rachel.

"He's dying. Dev, he won't last much longer."

So, it wasn't her own variation of truth serum in the vial, but rather some sort of poison. If I'd known this prior to Oliver admitting his and his buddy Lance's plans for me, I might have said something. What, I didn't know. But I felt someone should have at least objected to outright murder.

Devlin glanced at her and then back at Oliver. "Answer the question."

"He's working for the Sinclair family."

That name sounded familiar. However, I couldn't readily put my finger on it.

"Who are the Sinclairs?" he asked.

"Dev," Rachel said with urgency in her voice.

"Tell us about Dr. Stewart."

Oliver actually smiled. "He likes…" he started, then slumped forward—letting out a long sigh before he lay still, dead.

"Shit!" Devlin said.

Alek walked back in the room. His attention focused on me—a questioning look in his eyes. I nodded to let him know I was okay. I was way too caught up in what I'd just witnessed.

"Anything?" Devlin asked.

"Mr. Wan said he heard someone come in around midnight. Thought it might have been Nicole. And when he heard her neighbor Wade's door open, he didn't think anything of it." He looked at me. "He said it was normal for Wade to come over when you got home."

I looked over to where Wade lay in the corner, now covered in a pink sheet. "Yeah, he was a pest. But…" I shook my head. "I should have been a little firmer with him." I took a deep breath and pushed myself up off the couch.

Rachel reached out and took my hand. I was really proud of myself for not flinching.

"It's okay, Nicole. It's not your fault," she said.

I glanced down at her. There was a concerned look in her eye. I was trying really hard to hold onto that image, replace it with the one of her belting Oliver and injecting him with poison as if it were normal. True, I had wanted to hurt the bastard myself. But there had to be a line, right?

I had to get out of the room. Away from these people for a little while. I was having a really hard time distinguishing the good guys from the bad. I'd had this internal debate when Devlin first mentioned what they would have to do, and again when I witnessed Alek fuck with those thugs' minds. But between now and then, the situation had gotten really intense, and I needed a few minutes to myself. I snatched my hand away from Rachel. I felt a little bad about it when I did, but it didn't stop me from running out of the room.

"Okay, looks like our timetable has changed. Apparently, Andrew is concerned about Nicole, as well as Rachel and me. Once he finds out his henchmen weren't successful, he might send some more."

Devlin's authoritative voice carried into the room. I turned around and slammed the bedroom door to drown him out, then slumped down heavily on my bed.

My door opened a couple minutes later.

"What the fuck?" I yelled.

Devlin walked in and stood in front of me. "Last chance—do you want out?"

"You fucking people are cold!"

Devlin ran his hand down his face, frustration leaking from every single pore. He knelt down in front of me. "I was there for Rachel after her four siblings were killed with magick. She was so out of control, I thought she might kill everyone in sight. Jonah had to tattoo 'patience' on his arm to remind himself that he needed to think before he acted; otherwise, he could risk getting more people killed—besides the few hundred he'd already gotten killed. I helped him control the beast inside of him. Alek had to turn away from his family because of their archaic practices." He paused and considered me for a minute—frustration and anger brewed in his eyes. "There are no checks and balances when it comes to magick, Nicole. I, along with my people, have decided to become that balance. We may blur the line, but at least we know there is one. Trust me; we're able to pull back before we completely cross it."

I frowned at him. It still didn't make it right—or did it?

He took my shaking hands into his. "I don't have the luxury of being soft. I can't. But don't think for a second I don't understand how you're feeling. I've been there. And I'm never going back." He stood up, pulling me with him. "So, are you in or out?

And Nicole, please understand, this will be the very last time I ask you this question. Your hesitation and objection to what we have to do can cost someone's life. I won't let that happen."

Sanity dictated I should have been disturbed by the events that had taken place in my apartment. But given the circumstance, I was well past the point where reasoning played any part in my decision making. I just needed a minute to accept that fact. It helped, however, learning why Devlin and his team were the way they were. And now that I knew, it made it easier for me to accept what had to be done.

Devlin was right. There were no checks and balances when it came to the use of magick—not since the destruction of the Council of Principles. If the mayor of Tulare knew that this was going on and made deals to keep it quiet and contained instead of doing something about it, there really wasn't anyone to stop it, either.

I brushed away the tear that ran down my face and thought about Marta and the kids. For them, and everyone else I loved, I would set aside all judgement and reason. "I'm in," I said.

"Good, pack up what you need. We head out in five," Devlin ordered as he walked over to the dresser.

While he studied it, I grabbed an overnight bag and started shoving items into it.

"You can't pinpoint when this was carved?" Devlin asked.

I stopped packing and glanced over at him. "No, and it's freaking me out." I resumed my haphazard packing. At this point, the shen ring carved into my dresser was so far down my list of priorities, I'd stopped caring about it. I knew it was important, but Marta and her kids were more important. So, I'd worry about it later.

Devlin took out his phone and took a picture of the carving. I went to the bathroom for my toiletries.

When I came out of the room, Jonah and Alek both had one man each draped over their shoulders in a fireman's hold, heading for the door.

"Did you kill the last man?" I asked.

"Yes," Alek said as he walked out.

As I watched them go, it suddenly dawned on me that I'd offi-cially left the world of reason and morality behind and plunged head-first into the world of insanity. And for the time being, I had to be okay with that.

I was six years old when I walked into the kitchen of our Louisiana home on the bayou and found my parents washing blood off their hands. They didn't see me, because I'd hidden behind the tall kitchen cabinet—my usual hiding place —and watched as my mother's hands shook and my father, the strongest man I knew, cried softly while he wiped blood from my mother's cheek. She cried as well, but the tears were too fast for the sounds she was making—a deep, guttural anguish that had her whole body trembling. In some of my recollections of that moment, I felt pain, and in others, I felt a detached sense of wonder. Almost as if I'd momentarily stepped outside of myself.

The next memory I have was of me wrapped in a towel, fresh from a bath that I didn't remember taking, with the smell of rosemary, lemon, and verbena coating my drying skin. My father was holding me. His familiar apple scent tickled my nose, overpowering the other smells, and the heat he always radiated warmed me as he rubbed my back in a soothing gesture.

"Shh... baby girl, it's gonna be alright," he said as my little body trembled in his arms.

I could never quite remember if I was crying or not. But the fact he was trying to soothe me suggested that maybe I was.

I remembered we'd stopped outside my bedroom, because the portrait of my two-year- old self always hung directly across from my bedroom door. I heard sounds behind me, and when I started to lift up, my mother placed her cool hand upon my head and eased it back down on my father's shoulder. I never understood why, in that moment, her hands were so cold, when usually they were always too hot.

I turned my head slightly so I could see her. She was crying again.

"It's going to be alright, *ma fille*," she said, and moved to shut the bedroom door.

But she didn't close it quickly enough. I'd spotted the man lying on the floor—an ax lying beside him. That was where the memory faded. I never remembered what happened before I caught my parents in the kitchen. Nor did I have any recollection of them finding me. All my memories restarted with the bath they gave me; the details of even that were fuzzy.

A chunk of the day... gone. I'd tried numerous times to recall what happened on that day. But the memory always stayed hidden and locked away in my mind. Sometimes, when I was sleeping, I could remember distorted scenes, but they never made any sense to me. And when I awoke and tried to piece them together, they seemed to fall away, leaving me with nothing but a deep sensation of loss. That was why I started keeping notebooks, afraid that I might forget something else one day.

Exactly one week later, we moved to Tulare Island.

And now I knew why.

Rain pelted my car window. The drumming, in any other circumstance, would have been soothing. But now, it just added to the melancholy. A lump had formed in my throat on the way to my parents' house. Now the raw emotion that had restricted my air broke, as I stared through the hazy windshield at their house. I needed to go in and talk with them, ask them why they had blocked not only my magick, but my memories as well.

But I didn't move.

Facing them would be just too much right now.

I glanced across the street at Cherry's house. It was one of those nights again. Where a stranger was more suited to help me than my own flesh and blood. Funny thing, though. Cherry was no longer a stranger. Not really.

Decision made, I climbed out of the car and made my way to her house. Besides, I could really use one of her famous glasses of lemonade right about now.

I STARED rapt at the fireplace. The heat buffeted me, drying my damp clothes. I sunk my toes into the plush tan carpet, trying to warm them up. Flames danced over the porcelain dolls on the mantel, making them appear alive. I used to be afraid of those life-like cherubs and their shifty black eyes—always begging Cherry to put them away when I came to visit.

Cherry handed me a glass of her special lemonade and, without taking my eyes off the fire, I took a long swig. Heat coursed down my throat. I closed my eyes to the sensation. Damn. I'd forgotten how potent her concoction was.

She hadn't asked why I'd shown up at her house. Just opened the door—wearing her tattered green robe with her silver-blonde hair hanging in two braids down her back—and let me in, giving me a towel to dry myself with.

We sat in silence, watching the fire. So familiar. I could remember many nights just like this. Only, this time, I didn't have to sneak back into my house to avoid having to explain why I was drunk and where I'd been.

Despite my reassurances to Devlin—so much indecision still consumed me. So, I'd come to the one person who would understand the war inside of me at having to take someone's life. True, I'd killed my attacker to stop him from raping me. But it didn't stop the hollowness that had burned its way into my soul. Like I'd started down a dark path and there was no way I could ever go back. Yet, despite this, I felt... elation and satisfaction. And if I was honest, drunk with power. All these feelings had to be wrong.

"Did you ever regret killing him?" I asked, still watching the fire. Was it like this for her when she'd burned down her husband's mistress's house? Did she watch the fire in a hypnotic trance?

"I regret him making me."

I glanced over at her. Cherry sat in her favorite brown recliner, staring at the only clock in the house. The one sitting over the fireplace. She'd told me once she refused to put more than one reminder of time in her home. I thought it was a weird statement, most likely brought on by copious amounts of alcohol. But now, I sort of get what she was saying.

Time reminds you of all the mistakes you've made and that you could never, no matter how much you wanted to, go back and fix them. At least, that's what I assumed she meant.

"How did he make you?"

She looked at me. "I never told you about my father."

"Is this the long way to my answer?"

"Always so pissy. Haven't learned much about life yet." She took a sip of lemonade, studying me over the rim of her glass. "But I think you're learning. You want my help? You listen to my damn story."

I swallowed the lump in my throat and chased it with a sip of lemonade.

"He knew I had magick," she said, picking up where she left off. "He hated it. Preacher man with a devil daughter." She laughed. "My mother's family gave me my power. So, he had to know his wife had magick, too. But did that stop the ole' bastard from making my life miserable?" She shook her head, anger dancing in her eyes.

She suddenly cackled, startling me. "I burned him once. Best damn day of my life." She clenched her fist. "Until that evening. He made my mother burn me." She lifted the sleeve of her bathrobe. A large burn mark ran up her left arm. I always wondered why she never wore anything without long sleeves.

"What'd you do?" I asked, setting the now empty glass on her coffee table.

"I found a gullible man, had sex, and then faked a pregnancy. I was sixteen. He was eighteen. I couldn't stand him." She looked at me. "He was my way out. I didn't have to face anything else. Not deal with my parents or my magick."

I shifted on the couch and looked away. Why was her story suddenly sounding so similar to my own life? Minus the pregnancy and asshole father. My parents loved me. Hers, from what it sounded like, despised her. Yet somehow, we had both taken a wrong turn in life. The key ingredient being, neither one of us could face our problems. Cherry and I, it would seem, were kindred spirits.

Damnit. I'd come over here to get help dealing with my taking someone's life. Now I was trapped. Cherry was forcing me to face things I didn't want to face. I never remembered her being this blunt when I used to visit before. Or, maybe, like most things in my life, I had blocked it out.

The walls closed in. Beads of sweat peppered my upper lip. The porcelain dolls seemed to be laughing at me, their black eyes piercing me with judgment.

I got up.

"Sit down, Nicole. You wanted my help."

"How do you know that?" I asked, glaring down at her.

"You've always wanted. Just too damn stubborn to ask. Now, sit down."

A tear slipped down my face, and I angrily wiped it away. "Did you know he blocked my magick?"

"Yes," she said.

The dam broke. I couldn't get enough air in my lungs. The next thing I knew, I was enveloped in a lemony, alcohol-smelling embrace. Cherry rubbed my back as the sobs tore my insides out.

"I could see your magick when you first came to visit me," she said as she continued to rub my back. "Elemental magick was once a part of earth magick. Closer to the true source of power that fuels magick. It took me a while. But when I realized you were a mage, I confronted him."

I pulled back and stared at her. "You confronted my daddy?" No wonder he didn't like her.

She smiled. "Most magick users on this island fear him. I'm made of tougher stuff than most. I told him if he didn't tell you one day, I would." She got up and sat back down on her recliner. After taking a long sip of lemonade, she continued, "I warned him. And now you know. You're strong, Nicole. But you have to learn how to use your magick properly." She glanced at the fire; it danced in her eyes. "Otherwise, its seductive power will consume you."

We sat silent for a while more. Eventually, I got up to leave. My buzz had worn off enough that I was comfortable driving.

When I opened her front door, a blast of warmth blew across my skin. "Did you notice the rain showers have changed?"

She looked up at me. "Yes. The calm before the storm."

A puzzle pieced had just clicked into place. Something was happening, and I was at the center of it.

WHEN I ARRIVED at Devlin's, he was standing on the front porch, talking with Rachel. As I got closer, he intercepted me and took my bag.

"Where am I sleeping?" I asked.

He opened the door and I walked in. A muted television played somewhere in the back of the house. Its light flickered down the hallway.

"Choose whatever room you want." He set my bag down inside. "We'll see you in the morning."

He left me standing there. I walked to the first door on the right and opened it at the same time Alek came walking out of a mist-filled bathroom, a towel wrapped around his waist. I was too emotionally drained to appreciate the view, but I did catalogue it for later consumption.

I made a beeline to the bathroom and jumped in the shower.

At first, Alek said he would sleep out in the living room on the couch, but I told him that we were adults and that we could share the room. I didn't want to displace him. Besides, he looked as tired as I did.

When I came out of the bathroom, Alek was stretched out on a blanket on the floor—minus his shirt. I took a moment to enjoy the view of his very well-defined chest before I moved toward the bed.

"We can share the bed," I said.

He opened his eyes and looked up at me. "That's not a good idea."

I smiled. "Get in the bed, Alek. I promise I won't attack you."

He hesitated and stared at me, as if he was trying to ask permission.

"Suit yourself. That floor doesn't look comfortable." I laid down on the bed. Despite my fatigue, I couldn't close my eyes. When I did, images of Oliver kept invading my thoughts, so I stared up at the ceiling instead. "Rachel is intense."

"She's good at what she does." The bed moved as he lay down beside me. "Rachel really likes you. I wouldn't be surprised if she asked Dev to give you a job. She hates being the only woman on the team." He paused. "Devlin has a bit of a soft spot when it comes to her. She can convince him to do just about anything. Which is the reason you're here with us."

So, it was Rachel who convinced him to help me. Good to know.

"Rachel is a little detached from sanity." Did that mean they wanted me to work with them permanently? The prospect of that had my heart beating fast. It would be a paycheck, at least. Maybe they'd let me file papers and make coffee.

He chuckled. "You get used to it."

"Devlin told me a little about all of you."

"He said you were having a hard time with everything. I think you're holding it together pretty good."

"Actually, I'm not. But I'm too damn exhausted to freak out. I will reserve my meltdown for when I've had more than a few hours of sleep." I turned on my side, facing him. "What did you do with Wade?"

"We put him in his apartment. I planted the suggestion in Mr. Wan's head that he should check on him in the morning."

"And the men?"

"Dropped them off in Tulare, near the water. It will be a while before they're found."

I nodded.

He reached out and ran a finger down my cheek. Heat spread throughout my body. "You should get some rest, Nicole. I doubt we'll have the opportunity to do so later."

"I can't sleep. I'm tired, but I can't erase the images in my mind. I'm scared that my friend and her kids are dead. And it feels like I'm running around in circles, getting nowhere."

"A couple hours will do you some good. Rachel healed you, but..." He touched his finger to my forehead. "She can't heal that war going on inside your mind. It's better to let it rest."

I lifted my now-healed hand and studied it. I'd removed the bandage when I got in the shower. "I knew earth magick could heal you, but I've never seen it mend broken bones."

"Like I said, she's good at what she does."

I tried not to think about the concoction she'd given Oliver.

Alek reached out, hesitated, and then gathered me in his arms and pulled me to him. I gasped, and he smiled. "Relax, I'm not trying anything. Now, turn around."

"Please don't start sounding like Boss Man; I can't take two of you."

"Somehow I really doubt that. What you did to that man's dick was just... damn," he said, grinning.

I smiled and then turned around so he was spooning me. His warmth soothed me. I relaxed against him and let out a sigh.

"I'm not going to attempt to use magick to put you to sleep, but I can hum a little of the spell."

"Alright." I was willing to try. Even if I couldn't fall asleep, I was really enjoying the feel of Alek's body up against mine.

"Close your eyes."

I closed my eyes, and Alek started humming. The sound of his voice caressed me, cocooning me in a warm embrace. The melody sounded like a lullaby. I sighed and relaxed into the feeling.

"Nicole."

"How am I supposed to sleep if you keep talking?" I said, trying to move back so I could feel his body.

"It's time to get up."

I cracked one eye open. Alek was no longer lying behind me. He was standing on the side of the bed, looking down at me. His hair was damp, and he had on fresh clothes. There was a mug in his hand.

"Why did you take another shower and get dressed?" I blinked a few times. The outside light was now flooding the bedroom.

"I always shower twice a day. And you've been sleep for almost four hours."

I shot up so fast, my head spun. "Wait, what?"

He handed me the coffee. "Get up. We're heading out in a few minutes. Rachel made breakfast. Better get in there before Jonah eats it all."

I shoved the covers off me and got up. I felt like shit. Four hours of sleep didn't even put a dent in my sleep deficit. I needed at least forty more to do that. But it would be a really long time before I could crawl under the covers and ignore the rest of civilization—a very long damn time.

I set the mug of coffee on the dresser and groaned. I kicked my way over to my overnight bag and dug out what I hoped would be a matching outfit. I was somewhat surprised I was able to find at least one pair of jeans and a tank top amongst the party dresses, t-shirts, and casual pants that I'd shoved into my bag. What the hell had I been thinking when I packed this shit? Thankfully, I'd packed my low-heeled boots in case I needed to kick the shit out of someone. My hand needed a rest.

After getting dressed and doing what I could with my hair—I forgot to bring my gel—I downed the cold cup of coffee Alek had given me and went out in search of more caffeine and food. In that order.

Everyone was sitting in the kitchen, drinking coffee and eating eggs. Just like the rest of the house, the furniture and décor were sparse. White walls with faded wallpaper trim around the borders. If they planned to stay here long, I'd suggest they remodel. The place was a little depressing.

"You look like shit," Jonah said, staring at my hair.

I flipped him off and poured myself another cup of coffee.

"Now that we're all up, let's get moving. Nicole, you're with me," Devlin said.

"Damn! Do you have an off button?" I interrupted and then took a large sip of my coffee. "And what kind of coffee is this?" I really hadn't tasted the first cup, since I'd drank it so fast in hopes of getting some caffeine into my system. But now that I was able to, a bitter, somewhat sweet aftertaste filled my mouth.

"It's not coffee. It's my own invention. Helps keep you up for hours," Rachel said.

I spit out the concoction, sprayed Devlin in the process, and ran to the sink to rinse out my mouth. There was no way in hell I was going to drink something Rachel had concocted. Laughter, followed by a chuckle—which was probably Jonah's—came from behind me as I guzzled tap water like a fish.

"There's nothing wrong with it," Rachel said.

I lifted my head from the sink. Water ran down my chin and coated the front of my tank top. The look on her face made me feel like an ass. There was so much pain in her eyes, it was almost like an actual physical weight bearing down on me.

To appease her, I decided to ignore common sense and walked over to pour myself another cup of... whatever. It took a lot of guts and determination, along with a dose of stupidity, but I managed to drink the entire half-filled cup.

"It's good," I lied.

She smiled. It was halfhearted, but at least she wasn't looking like I'd kicked her puppy and stolen her favorite doll anymore. "I understand. You think I poisoned it."

"Um... Well, I just..." I shook my head. I hated this. How the hell did I end up having to apologize to the crazy chemist in the first place? "Sorry, Rachel. I was thinking about that stuff you gave Oliver and overreacted," I said sheepishly.

She smiled; this time, it lit up her entire face, and she gave me a hug. "I know."

After an awkward pause, I hugged her back.

"Okay, now that that's settled..." Devlin started.

I looked down at Rachel. "He really doesn't have an off button, does he?"

She smiled. "No, but I can make something to shut him up."

I laughed.

Devlin glared at us, shook his head, and then continued. "As I was saying, Nicole, I doubt we need to talk with Luisah about the ritual. From what Oliver said, I got a pretty good idea of what's going on. So, we're going to start with Andrew's condo. I'm willing to bet he has some information we could use. Alek, you're with us." He glanced at his watch. "My guess is, he's already at work. Our not showing up today could give him a false sense of hope that we've been taken care of. Yet, Oliver not showing up could be a problem. So, we'll need to work fast."

He picked up his mug of coffee and took a sip. After he swallowed, he continued. "Jonah and Rachel, check out Oliver's residence. See if there is anything in there we can use, and then get started on the list Vincent compiled. We want to start eliminating possibilities. Vincent, see what you can dig up on the Sinclair family."

"I already know who they are," Vincent said. "They run an at-risk youth program in Perry."

Everyone paused and looked at him, the implications of what he was saying sinking in. If Andrew had recently started taking care of disposing of the kids that didn't have the anomaly in their blood, and he was working for a family that ran an at-risk youth program, then chances were, he was either selling or giving the kids to them. It also explained where he was getting the money to buy them. Fucking bastard.

"They have a location in Perry near where I live."

"The address?" Devlin asked.

After Vincent gave him the address, Devlin changed the plans. Jonah would go to Andrew's condo, and the rest of us would visit the Sinclairs' at-risk group home. A small sliver of hope wormed its way into my heart as we walked out and piled into Devlin's car.

Along with a healthy dose of terror as to what we might find.

The group home was located on Carson Street. Four blocks from Vincent's house, and two blocks from the area Alek and I had driven through last night. Three houses occupied the entire block, with the group home taking up the majority of the space. It was painted an off-white color, with dark blue shutters and a well-maintained yard. A black wrought-iron fence surrounded the entire property.

We parked in front and got out of the car.

"We going in with finesse?" Alek asked.

Devlin opened the trunk. "We don't have time for finesse."

Rachel pulled two sheathed blades and a small belt with several pouches attached to it out of her backpack. After securing the leather sheathes—one around each leg—she strapped the belt on and twisted her hair up so it was out of her face.

Devlin shut the trunk and rejoined us. He was wearing a belt similar to Rachel's, only his had an array of small vials with varying substances attached to it.

I looked at Alek. "Where's your superhero utility belt?"

He tapped his head and smiled. I guess he didn't need one. If I hadn't witnessed him incapacitate twenty people last night, I might have called him a cocky bastard.

I dug the gun out of my purse and shoved it down the back of my jeans.

"Are you sure you can pull that out?" Alek asked as he looked down at my jeans. "Those look pretty tight."

I reached behind me and yanked out the gun, suppressing the sudden flare of pain as the barrel scraped my bare skin.

He smiled.

"Nicole, keep the gun out. Rachel, stay with Nicole. We don't know what to expect, or if any of these people have magick. Alek, you're in front. If you can't convince them to cooperate, use force."

Alek inclined his head as he pulled open the gate. We proceeded single-file up the walkway.

There was a "Welcome to Our Home" sign above the door, and a large potted plant hanging from the porch ceiling. Alek opened the door, and we walked into the reception area. A tall, dark-haired woman stood behind the desk with a smile on her face. The smile dropped as soon as she got a good look at us.

"Can I help you?" she asked. Her gaze dropped to the gun I held down at my side.

Too late to hide it behind my back now.

"We have a few questions," Alek said, his voice taking on that melodious tone. "Are you in charge?"

The woman's eyes fluttered, and her hand went up to her forehead. "No... that would be Nickolas. He... just a moment." She picked up the phone sitting on the desk. "There are some people here to see you."

She hung up the phone and focused her attention on Alek. He stood there calmly, watching her. Holding her captive with his eyes.

While we waited for Nickolas, I took a few minutes to look around. Directly behind the woman was a wall of cubbyholes that were filled with two sets of white towels. There were numbers affixed to each cubby, along with a single key dangling from a peg underneath them. Both the left and right side of the house were identical. Each side had a small reception area and an archway that led to a hallway.

Nickolas—a tall, slender man with short black hair and dark brown eyes—came from the left. "Can I help you?"

"Mage." Rachel said, shifting to block me.

The man's eyes narrowed. "What do you people want?"

Alek moved so he was right in front of him. "We're looking for some missing children."

The man smiled and looked over Alek's shoulder. I turned. Three more people came into the room from the right—one additional woman and two men. Reinforcements. I put my finger on the trigger of the gun and waited for a signal from Devlin. If they wanted to fight, I was more than ready to oblige them. Damn, I sounded brave. Too bad I didn't feel it.

Rachel turned and took in the newcomers. "All of them are mages, Dev."

"There are no children here. So, it's best if you people leave."

"Funny, I was led to believe that this was an at-risk kids' facility." Alek moved closer to Nickolas. "What type of *at-risk kids' facility* doesn't have children?"

"I don't know who sent you here. And frankly, I don't care. Either leave the premises, or we'll remove you by force."

"We'll leave after you allow us access. If you don't, we'll access it by *force*."

If we weren't in the middle of a very serious situation, I would have laughed at the way Alek was goading him. The man looked like a cornered rat, his eyes darting between us and his people. His hand shook slightly as he pulled on his suit jacket.

Nickolas glanced over at the woman behind the desk. "Your service will be rewarded."

The woman's face stretched into the gleeful smile of an acolyte happy to finally be able to do her master's bidding. She pulled a knife from behind her back and drew the blade across her arm. No pain registered on her face, only the maniacal glee of a crazy fanatic.

My breath caught in my throat. I studied her face, trying to find some small spark of self-preservation. She looked at me, her eyes swimming with madness, and I flinched. There wasn't any humanity in her gaze. I looked away.

Nickolas lifted his hand, and blood bubbled up from the cut on the woman's arm. It flew toward him. He let it circle there, building strength, and in one quick motion, he flicked his hand out and struck Alek across the face with a blade made of blood.

Blood magick.

A small cut opened on Alek's cheek, and Nickolas smiled.

Rachel pushed me back, reached inside her pouch, and pulled out a handful of yellow powder. Alek stepped back, and Rachel stepped forward, almost as if they'd synchronized the move. She lifted her palm and blew the yellowish powder in the man's face. The smell of black licorice hung in the air, mixing with the scent of copper. It had to be Henbane; most often referred to as 'killing dust.' Lucky for us, the herb was inert in its powder form until an earth mage infused it with power and intent.

Rachel chanted; her voice echoed around the room, filling the small space.

Before the dust could reach him, he lifted his hands, blood dancing around them, and made a wall of blood. But he wasn't fast enough. Some of the dust was able to reach his exposed skin, causing it to sizzle, burning its way to the bone. The smell of over-cooked beef and pig fat rose from his skin. He bellowed as he covered his arm, backing away from Rachel.

Devlin stepped forward and regarded the newcomers with a stony gaze. His body was poised and ready to attack. They drew rivulets of blood from the woman's arm. He lifted his hand and turned up his palm—a small tornado circled inside. As it grew, he started chanting, his voice building and resonating inside the room. When he stopped, a boom sounded as he flung out his hand and threw the tornado at them.

Blood mixed in with the wind, spraying across the walls. They staggered back but gained their footing quickly as a wall of blood shot up, stopping the gust of wind. The smell of ozone and iron saturated the air. I coughed, trying to get the sudden taste of it out of my mouth. Please don't let me have swallowed any of it.

I rubbed a smudge of blood off my cheek and glanced at the woman, standing there in a mindless rapture as blood continued to flow out of her arm. There was no way her small body contained that much blood.

Someone yelped, and I turned. A new woman was squaring off with Rachel, her face bubbling as if it were being burned with acid. There were too many smells now, filling up the small space. Rachel had unsheathed one of her knives and thrust it toward the woman, narrowly missing as the woman leapt backward.

Alek stood in front of another man, who threw lances made of blood at him, all the while jerking his head from side to side as if he was trying to dislodge something from his ears. Suddenly, the man stopped and grabbed the side of his head. Alek sang in that melodious voice of his, the song dark and deep. After one last shake of his head, the man fell at Alek's feet—blood oozing out of every orifice on his face.

I wanted to run. I was foolish to think a gun would make me brave. Magick played by its own rules. And sadly, I didn't know them. I was not prepared for the torrent of power being thrown— my own being so damn weak. Nor was I prepared for the fear it would cause. What did I really believe I could do to help?

I started to move back toward the door, when suddenly, a large hand was around my neck. A man lifted me off the ground, and I raised the gun, only to have him slap it away. Blood crawled up my face, pushing its way inside my nose and mouth. Just as my air supply was cut off, a strong force built inside my head, and the marks on my wrist and lips heated, scorching me. The phoenix-mark inside my head beat its massive wings, pushing at the darkness that coated my mind. Fissures appeared, and a thick, jagged line streaked across the blackness. The hands turned out from the prayer position and pulled at the black mass, as if they could pull it back in. But it was useless.

An alien-like power spilled from me, forcing its way out of

every one of my pores. The man holding me screamed and let go. In awe, I watched as his body flew back and hit the opposite wall with so much force that his head nearly cracked wide open, spraying blood everywhere. His chest caved in as if someone was pulling his insides out of his back. He pitched forward and landed at my feet.

His wounds had given the blood mages more fuel for their spells.

Shit.

My head pounded as more and more cracks opened up, cutting through not only the red mark, but the darkness as well. I stumbled over the leg of my attacker—falling on him, my hand slipped into the hole in his chest. Bile rose as I scrambled off of him and landed on my back. I rolled to my side and pushed myself away from him. My eyes landed on the single eye remaining in its socket, devoid of life. His other eye had slid down his face, resting on the hollow spot that used to be his right cheek.

I screamed.

Alek stopped his assault on Nickolas and turned to look at me. I'd fucked up.

The distraction gave Nickolas the opportunity he needed. He pulled another stream of blood from the woman and flung it at Alek's back. Rage filled me as I watched Alek flinch when the blood made contact.

I snatched the gun off the floor and ignored the warm, slimy blood coating the handle. Alek wouldn't have been distracted if it wasn't for me. It was past time I stepped up and helped.

I lifted the gun, wrapped both my hands around it, and fired. It wasn't a really good shot, but I did manage to clip Nickolas's shoulder, causing him to drop the second lance of blood. As it splashed onto the floor, Alek recovered and rushed him. Nickolas stumbled backward, trying to move out of his way, all the while reaching for more blood. Thankfully, the woman had finally fallen—drained of blood.

Alek got to him before he could lift up his hands. He placed his hands on either side of Nickolas's head, and with one quick twist, he broke his neck.

Alek turned back to me. His entire body was outlined in an orange hue. It slithered along his skin. Was this what the magick in others looked like? I swiveled my head toward the group. They had similar auras surrounding their bodies as well, only in different colors. Rachel had green pulsating around her, and Devlin had blue. How was I suddenly able to see this?

I turned away from them. Their power was starting to burn my eyes.

Most of the darkness inside my head was gone. Light shone through, and with the light came horrendous pain. My body thrashed, and in the process, I grabbed onto the dead man's leg again. As soon as my hand clasped on, his body jerked. The man's mouth unhinged. An eerie scream reverberated from him, piercing my eardrums.

Power continued to surge through me, and a bright light filled the room. I bucked on the floor. Thrashing. But still I held on to the dead man's leg.

Alek dropped down to the floor and pulled me into his lap. "Try and control it, Nicole."

I wanted to scream at him that I couldn't—that it had taken complete hold of me—but I was having a hard time formulating a coherent sound. A dam, held back for too long, suddenly broke free inside of me, and there was nothing I could do to stop it. Pain engulfed me. Memories flooded my mind once again.

*Me in the tub.*

*A woman, holding me down.*

*My mother crying.*

*My father holding me.*

*A familiar man, pulling down my panties.*

*His dead form, moving, jerking, while I held on to him.*

"Dev, the dead are moving," Rachel said.

"Alek, you need to stop her!" Devlin screamed.

Bodies pressed against me; the coppery scent of their flesh

coated my tongue. A man stared down at me out of long-dead eyes. Alek shoved him away, but he kept moving. As if he was trying to reach me.

My heart seized with the sudden knowledge that I'd done this before. Used the strange power to keep someone alive. To keep their soul trapped in their body. Most likely suffering in anguish. Only, the man who I'd kept alive twenty-two years ago was the very one who had raped me. The one who my loving mother had killed with an ax.

I closed my eyes against the gruesome display and the pain and focused on the bright ball of light inside of me. The red mark pulsed frantically, as if it were trying to stop the influx of power surging through it. The black mass crept around the edges, trying to fill in the light. I stayed focused on that, willing it to move faster. I didn't want to face these memories. I didn't want this power.

Alek started humming the same tune that he'd used to help me sleep. He couldn't use his magick. If he did, the power inside me would lash out and hurt him. Something crashed to the floor, and Alek pulled me closer, so my head was buried in his neck.

"Rachel, move back!" Devlin yelled.

"Please, Nicole, try and control it," Alek whispered urgently.

I wanted to scream at him that I was trying, but no sound came out of my mouth. My head pounded. The mark expanded, covering the light, and in one quick surge, the black mass rolled over it, completely covering it again. The mark settled back down to its normal size. However, the hairline fracture underneath it still remained. As if the break was no longer able to be repaired.

I opened my eyes; Alek was cradling me in his lap. He'd moved me from the crook of his neck and stared down at me, distress in his eyes.

"I'm okay," I croaked as I swallowed the lump in my throat.

He turned toward the others. "Get her some water!"

I looked over his shoulder.

Rachel stood there, covered in blood, dismay etched all over her face. "How did you do that?"

I shook my head. I really didn't understand it myself. Why, after all this time, was my magick suddenly trying to break free?

Devlin returned with a bottle of water and handed it to me. "Can you move?"

I reached up and took the water from him. After emptying the bottle, I shifted so I could get up.

"Careful," Alek said.

Surprisingly, I wasn't in pain. And my head no longer hurt. After he helped me up, I looked around at the front room.

Bodies lay on top of one another, all facing me. Blood coated the walls, along with the killing dust Rachel had used. Cracks ran up the walls, like fissures caused by a massive earthquake. There was a large hole in the middle of the floor, with dirt and weeds pushing up into the room.

So much destruction.

"What now?" I asked, still trying to gain some semblance of balance while I pushed down the pain and feelings of betrayal. My parents had lied to me.

Devlin pulled his phone out of his pocket and punched in some numbers. After a short while, he said, "Jonah, I need you here." He paused. "Okay, take what you found back to Vincent. Let him sort it. Then get over here." After he hung up the phone, he looked over at me. "Nicole, I need you to explain how you're able to raise the dead."

I shifted under all three of their questioning gazes. "I don't know."

I couldn't give voice to what I'd done. I didn't understand it myself. What kind of earth magick raised the dead? At least, that's what I believed my principle was. I could be wrong.

"How many times before yesterday did it happen?"

"Yesterday was the first time."

"Can you think of what might have triggered it?"

"I..." I paused. The only thing that had changed in my life, besides the events at Tribec, was the additional marks put on me by two different gods—or Old Ones. I looked down at my wrist and could barely make out the small shen ring. I touched my fingers to my lips. I'd never had a chance to look at the one Ezra put on me, but I knew it was there. I'd felt it, burning into my skin. I glanced at Rachel. "You don't by any chance have a mirror?'

She shook her head. "Why?"

I went over what Luisah had told me about the marks. I even confirmed for them that the entity Jonah had taken a picture of was, in fact, an Old One.

Devlin rubbed the back of his neck, and Rachel contemplated me for a minute.

"It sounds like another level of earth magick," Rachel said. "One I never heard of."

"We'll have to discuss this later," Devlin said after a while. "In the meantime, we need to split up and search the house."

After moving the bodies behind the large reception desk and covering them with the towels we found in the cubbyholes, we split up in twos. Maybe Devlin believed hiding the bodies would be enough to disguise what had happened here. I was too damn tired and emotional to tell him no one but a blind man who had no sense of smell would ever believe there was nothing wrong here.

Except for a few occasional glances at me, Alek was quiet as we walked down the right-side hallway. I wished I could read his mind. Or get up enough nerve to ask him what he was thinking.

Seven rooms lined the hallway. Each of them contained the same furnishings. A trash can with a clear plastic liner sat just inside the door. A full-sized bed with a plain white bedspread and no pillows lay flush against the wall in the center of the room. And a bucket of toys that smelled like they'd been saturated in bleach with the faint scent of rotten cherries and fire simmering underneath, sat at the foot of the bed. Inside the nightstand drawer was a box of condoms and a bone-handled ceremonial knife made of silver.

Images kept popping in my head of children in those rooms, helpless, while adults did unspeakable acts to them. "Fucking bastards," I said.

I pulled on my stiff, blood-soaked shirt, and continued down the hallway.

At the end of the hallway, we veered to the left and ran into Rachel and Devlin.

"Anything?" Devlin asked.

Alek shook his head while he studied a massive bureau sitting flush against the wall at the junction of where the two hallways met. Made of oak and covered in silver pieces, the bureau had hieroglyphs drawn all over the surface of the wood.

Alek looked behind it. "We need to move this."

Devlin braced the opposite side, and they both pushed. It took a few tries, but they did manage to slide the bureau out of the way, exposing the hidden door behind it.

"Steel." Devlin stood there, studying it.

"I doubt we'll be able to kick it in," Alek said.

"I'll be back. Alek, check the rear of the house. I don't want any more surprises. Rachel, stay with Nicole."

I guess I needed watching now. We both stood there in silence as Alek went off to search the back of the house.

Rachel snuck glances at me. When I caught her, she turned away, looking down at the floor—a frown etched on her face.

"Are you mad, or scared of me, Rachel?" I finally asked. The silence was getting to me.

She met my gaze. "Neither. Are you sure your principle is earth?"

"Yes. My father's is, and so is his family's."

"What about your mother?"

"She doesn't have any magick." At least, that's what I believed. I'd never outright asked her. However, if she did have magick and passed on some of that principle to me, that might explain the anomaly in my own abilities. As far as I knew, there were only five principles. Maybe I was wrong. Sadly, it wouldn't be the first time.

"You got that ability from someone," she said. "But no, I'm not mad or scared. Just need time to understand."

I could appreciate that. My newfound abilities were scaring the hell out of me, too.

"So, I assume Boss Man is going to want to drop me off at the nearest intersection," I said.

She smiled. "He's not like that. If he can take Alek in, he can take you in."

I wanted to ask what she meant by that, but Devlin had returned, carrying a crowbar, Alek trailing behind him.

Once the door was open, we started down the stairs.

The walls were made of gray brick and covered in wards written in red. A cherry smell hung heavy in the air, mixed in with a citrus and earthy scent. Dirt, or maybe some sort of compost. When we reached the bottom, the hum of a generator filled the silent void. Silver candelabras lined the hallways; flames licked the walls, illuminating the space and casting shadows in the corners. The stench of dirt grew as we continued down the corridor.

At the end of the hall was another metal door, and on both sides of the hallway were two additional rooms without doors. I glanced inside one as we passed. In the center of the room was a large power circle. Candles sat at each energy point and four focal points. Child-sized manacles were bolted to the floor inside the circle, and a large dais sat outside the circle, covered with a red velvet cloth.

I blocked the image and its meaning from my mind and caught up with the others. If I dwelled on what I'd seen in that room, focused on what they might be doing in there, I wouldn't be able to continue.

Devlin had managed to get the door open. He reached inside the dark room and fumbled along the wall for a light switch. Something rattled, and Rachel gasped.

I pushed her out of the way and walked into the room.

A cold, dark fury took over every fiber of my being. Every reservation I had about working with Devlin and his crew completely drained from me. Anger boiled in my gut as my body shook. My ears rang as I stared at the twenty cages filled with naked children. Their eyes, filled with fear, looked back at us, pleading.

"Aunt Cole."

My head whipped in the direction of the small child's voice. Four-year-old Maria stood there, naked, with lacerations along her legs and blood running down her inner thighs. Isabel, José, and Juan moved with Maria toward the bars. I ran to them, pulling at the cage. Someone's hand covered mine.

"Let us pry it open," Alek said.

"I want my mommy, Aunt Cole."

I couldn't speak, and after a while, I could barely see past the tears as they ran freely down my face. My heart felt heavy in my chest. My breathing grew shallow. Why? Why would these monsters do this to kids? And how had they managed to get away with it?

When Alek finally managed to get the cage open, I reached in and pulled Maria's tiny, shaking body to mine.

"I hurt," she mumbled into my shoulder.

I rubbed her back, fighting for control of my emotions. Another body pressed up against mine. Juan, covered with blood.

"Don't leave," he whispered.

I pulled him to me, smothering him against my chest. His body shook as he cried.

"I promise I won't," I said, sadness choking me, making it really hard to breathe.

I vowed in that moment that I would kill every last one of the people involved in this madness, every person who ever visited this sick place. They would feel pain—slow, sweet pain—before I allowed them to die.

When we finally managed to open all twenty cages, the kids, the ones I assumed had been there the longest, shuffled over to a large, arched doorway, their bare feet slapping against the dark concrete floor, and stood single-file in line with their eyes cast downward and their bodies rigid. It was systematic and learned, and most likely drilled into them brutally.

I moved past them and peered into the room.

It was a communal shower covered in pristine white tile with silver-plated shower heads jutting out from the walls. The shower heads were spaced three feet apart and rose four feet off the ground. A six-foot black cabinet sat in the corner, towering over everything. Gold hieroglyphs covered the surface. The cabinet had no doors, and each shelf contained a stack of white bath towels and a single scrub brush.

The room smelled like honey and rainwater and something more acidic underneath that I couldn't place. The children all stood there, not registering me or anyone else in the room. It didn't matter that we weren't their captors; all they knew was if they were freed from the cage, they had to wait their turn to be washed.

A scream lodged in my throat. I clenched my fist, my nails biting into the palm of my hand, causing the skin to break. I glanced down. A single drop of blood fell on the floor, staining the white surface a ghoulish red.

The kids shifted. Their moans of distress filled the room, echoing off the walls. Maria, who had refused to leave my side since being released from the cage, pushed her small, clammy hand against mine. I wrapped my fingers around hers in an effort to reassure her this terrible nightmare was over.

As I swallowed down the lump in my throat, I pushed away the rage boiling underneath my skin. Agonizing pressure built in my chest. I was going to explode. I couldn't do that right now. I had to keep myself focused. Not think about the fact that, in two days—*forty-eight hours*—Marta's kids had been victimized. I had to focus on the fact that they were safe now. And soon, their mother would be, too. I needed to hold on to that bit of hope.

"They wash us before, but not after," Isabel said. She moved closer to me, her brothers right beside her crowding around me.

If the people who ran this place weren't already lying dead upstairs, I would have gone upstairs and killed them. I picked Maria up and walked away from the room. I refused to allow her in there. Refused to allow any of the kids to enter that room, despite their filthiness.

Devlin stood in the middle of the floor, rubbing the back of his neck as he kept his eyes averted from the children. A war was playing across his face; the vein on the side of his neck jumped, and his eyes were hard. The sheer force of his control looked painful.

"We need to move, Dev," Rachel said. She reached out for the first child in line—a little Romani girl no more than six years old. "We need to get them out of here." She tried to steer the child away from the door, but all she succeeded in doing was prompting the little girl to step into the room and move to the first spout.

Rachel stared at me, as if I somehow held the answers. I was just as lost as she was on what to do. No one would be able to fix what had been broken in these kids. Who knew how long they'd been down here, being abused and bled for those sadistic bastards' rituals? The woman who'd allowed herself to be drained dry was a willing participant. These kids, however, were not.

Isabel moved away from me, her small feet slapping against the hard concrete floor as she walked into the shower room and took the little girl's hand. "Come on," she said.

The girl started mewling as she frantically tried to pull away from her. She became crazed, and when she reached out to strike Isabel, I moved in quickly and grabbed Isabel by the waist, moving her away from danger.

Alek stalked over and entered the room, his face filled with fury and pain. He went down to his knees and reached out to the little girl. Her head turned slowly toward him. Her deep brown eyes regarded him with mistrust and fear through the curtain of her long, dark hair.

"You are safe," he said. He pulled off his shirt and wrapped it around her.

Her eyes remained fixed on him, but she didn't respond. It was as if all life had been drained out of her, leaving only a robotic shell behind.

"*Sunteți în siguranță*," he whispered as his eyes filled with tears.

She said something to him, but I couldn't hear it. Tears traced down his face as he pulled her tiny frame to him. Her body remained rigid as he continued to speak to her in their language. I wished there was something I could do. Some way I could erase the horror of what I was seeing. What sort of animal would do these horrific things to children?

It took some doing, but we finally managed to move the other children upstairs. Rachel found some clothes for them, and once they were dressed, Devlin called in a tip about the situation to the island police. He said we couldn't remain there, at least not in sight; we were still trying to limit our exposure.

Maybe he believed the Stewarts didn't know we were investigating them. It was possible he was delusional, or maybe even filled with false hope. However, I wasn't going to question his logic. He'd been doing this a lot longer than I had.

I did, however, insist that we take Marta's kids with us. He started to protest, stating it might tip our hand, but thankfully, Rachel intervened. Jonah elected to stay behind and watch from a distance to ensure the remaining kids were safely rescued.

As we pulled away, I finally texted Kara. As much as I wanted to shield her from what was going on, I couldn't. She would never forgive me if I did. Once I gave her Devlin's address and asked her to meet me there, I pulled Maria closer and silently wept.

"WHAT'S GOING ON, NICOLE?" Kara stood in the doorway of Devlin's house.

I moved back to allow her entrance, and when she was safely inside, I shut the door and pulled her into a hug. I was having a really hard time keeping it together, and I needed the comfort of familiarity, someone who would understand the turmoil that was wreaking havoc inside of me.

Kara squeezed me as I cried. When my eyes wouldn't produce any more tears, I pulled back and filled Kara in on what had transpired in the past few days. Once finished, the look on her face mirrored the chaos inside of me.

"I won't scold you for not telling me." Kara shook her head as she sat down heavily on the metal fold-out chair. "I won't." Her eyes roamed around the room, taking everything in. "Not right now..." She looked up at me with a mix of fury and sadness. "Where are the children?"

"Sleeping," I croaked. I cleared my throat. "I want you to take them with you; we..."

"The 'we' in that statement includes me as well, Nicole."

"Kara, I can't let you get involved. I don't want you to get hurt."

Kara stood up abruptly, causing me to jump back. Waves of anger rolled off of her, and her eyes narrowed. "When have I ever given you the impression that I couldn't take care of myself? That I couldn't fight for my friends? I am so pissed at you for not telling me that Marta and our godchildren were in danger. You think you could relegate me to babysitter? There is no way I'm standing on the sidelines when there are monsters holding my friend hostage. No. F'ing. Way!"

I had screwed up royally. I should have called her in the beginning. Every single time I started to, I'd decided against it. Rationalizing that decision with bullshit excuses. Kara was right, and I needed to fix this.

"Kara..." I started.

"Hi, I'm Rachel."

I turned. Rachel stood in the hallway. How long had she been there? She was studying Kara the same way she had studied me when we first met.

Kara moved past me and walked over to Rachel. "Kara. What's the plan?"

Rachel looked at me and then back at Kara. "What principle do you practice?"

"Earth. I've been trained in battle magick."

My mouth dropped. "You never told me you practiced magick."

She took a deep breath and let it out slowly. Not more than a few seconds ago, she had been scolding me about keeping secrets from her, and now I find out she'd been lying to me throughout our entire friendship. Fucking hypocrite.

Devlin walked into the room with Jonah right behind him. "You must be Nicole's friend. You can stay here or take the kids with you. We need to get moving..."

"Not now, Dev," Rachel said as she pushed him backward out of the line of fire.

"What do you mean, you've been trained in battle magick?" I repeated through clenched teeth.

"Nicole, now is not the time. I..."

"Who trained you?" Devlin asked.

I glared at him. "Can you please give my friend and me some damn space?"

"We need to move," he started.

Rachel grabbed his arm and pulled him out of the room.

When they were gone, I turned back to Kara. "Start explaining." I held up my hand before she could answer. "But first, you can apologize for lying to me as well as for making me feel like shit just a few minutes ago."

"I won't apologize for being honest," she said.

"Oh, so you know what honesty is, then?"

"Don't, Nicole. You and I both know we don't have the time." She sighed, and a single tear slid down her cheek. "When it's over, I will tell you everything." She reached out and took my hand. "Promise."

I wanted to remain mad at her, but I couldn't. There was so much pain in her eyes. "Okay," I said finally. "We rescue Marta first."

"I don't like this," Devlin said, walking back into the room, Rachel following behind him.

Rachel glared at him. "Doesn't matter, Dev. We can use the extra help. Kara is a mage, and battle trained. She stays."

A silent war ensued between them. The vein in Devlin's neck beat rapidly.

"I said she stays."

"Fine," he said. "What about the kids?"

"They'll sleep for a while and can stay here with Vincent," Rachel said.

I preferred to get them somewhere safe, but the only other place we could take them was to my parents'. And since I wasn't in the right frame of mind to deal with them right now, I decided the kids could stay there for a little while longer.

"Okay," Devlin said, drawing our attention back to him. "We're going to need to split up." He looked over at the stacks of boxes in the corner that Jonah had collected from Andrew's house. "It's obvious Andrew has some information that might help us. I need to find out what he knows." He looked at Jonah. "I want you to search the last two properties." He reached into his pocket, pulled out the list, and handed it to him. He ticked his head toward Kara. "Take her with you."

"Kara," she said.

"What?" Devlin asked.

"My name is Kara." She walked over and stuck her hand out for the list. Jonah smiled and handed it to her.

Devlin nodded and focused his attention on me. "You're with Alek, Rachel, and me on the interrogation of Andrew."

"I'd like to help with that," Kara said.

"Tough. Let's get moving; time is not on our side."

Kara opened her mouth to say something, and Jonah wrapped his arms around her waist to stop her. She glared daggers at Devlin. And yes, I did smile as visions of Kara wiping the floor with him floated into my mind. Such a glorious sight.

T he complex Andrew lived in was a new, up-scale development in Dulean that still had a sales office on the premises. There were four completed buildings, with six units per building, and one building still under construction.

Devlin's phone rang as we pulled up in front.

"Anything?" he asked the person on the other line. "Alright. Meet us back at the house. Start going through the boxes." Devlin hung up and looked at his watch. "It's after seven. He should be home by now." He looked at me in the rearview mirror. "Will you be able to control yourself in there?"

If we did run into someone, could I keep my magick in check? So far, the only times it had manifested were in situations where my life was in jeopardy.

"As long as no one tries to kill me, I should be fine." I didn't want him to tell me to wait in the car. Because if he did, I would refuse, and it would get ugly.

"She'll be fine," Alek said.

Rachel didn't say anything. Ever since she'd witnessed what I could do, she hadn't looked at me the same way. A few times, I'd caught her studying me when she thought I wasn't looking. It was unnerving. Eventually, the time would come when we would either talk it out, or—judging from what she had done to Oliver —fight it out. All I could do was be prepared when that time came.

Devlin dropped Alek and me off in front of the complex and drove his car around the block. He and Rachel were going to enter from behind, while Alek and I went through the front.

Alek reached out, took my hand, and started for the office.

"Maybe we should have gone around back with Boss Man and Rachel?" I tried to retrieve my hand and ignore the sudden eruption of butterflies in my stomach.

He glanced back at me, tightening his hand around mine. "Something tells me you're not good at climbing fences. Now, wipe that confused look off your face. We're a couple looking for a new place to live."

"I'll ignore that assumption you made about my physical capabilities. I really doubt the salesperson is going to believe that." I took in his outfit. After his shower, he'd put on a pair of snug jeans that rode low on his hips, and a red sleeveless t-shirt that looked as if it was a second skin. He had a single gold hoop earring in his left ear, and his long, dark hair pulled back with a strip of fabric. "This is an uptight community. I doubt they would believe we actually wanted to move here."

Alek stopped. A small smile creased the corners of his mouth as he took a slow perusal down the length of my body. I'd showered and changed, too. Due to my limited options, I was wearing pretty much the same thing I wore earlier, only a different color tank top.

I narrowed my eyes at him. "When you're done, we can discuss a better plan. One that doesn't involve us pretending we want to buy a condo."

He stepped closer. "You keep forgetting what I can do."

He was right. I had completely forgotten that he could fuck with someone's mind. "I'm anxious."

He took my hand again. "If you hang around us long enough, you'll get used to it. Now, we need to move."

His statement implied that I would be working with them longer. Had Devlin said something to him about it? Or did Alek just like me being around? I glanced down at our joined hands. Maybe it was the latter. I didn't know how I felt about that, so I let it go.

When we arrived at the office door, Alek paused. Something was wrong. It was well after seven at night, and the sign on the door indicated they closed at five. The salesperson was sitting in her office with a blank look on her face. Even when we opened the door, she remained in that passive posture, staring off in space. If not for the obvious rising and falling of her chest, I would have thought she was dead.

"A mind mage has been here," Alek said as he made his way to the woman. He placed his hand on her forehead and started humming.

"Wouldn't it be better if we left her there?" It was a selfish thought, and honestly, I felt bad about it. But as long as she wasn't dead, she really wasn't my priority.

Alek stopped humming and looked at me. "She might be able to tell me who did this to her." He straightened and looked around. "Nothing is disturbed." He glanced back at her. "Someone planted a suggestion deep inside her. One that left her mind confused. Otherwise, she wouldn't be catatonic."

"Why would they?"

"Probably someone she would recognize. And when they tried to erase that memory, it broke her mind. Sloppy. They should have known better."

More like they knew they were breaking her mind and didn't care.

Alek examined her. "Nothing we can do for her now."

Damn.

He took my hand and pulled me out the door.

We followed a dimly-lit path to the rear of the complex. Andrew's condo was on the top floor. We climbed the stairs, and Alek walked over and rapped his knuckles on the door three times.

"Is that the secret knock?" I asked.

He watched me. "Nervous?"

"No, just... frustrated."

"So, you make jokes when you're frustrated?"

I glanced down at our joined hands. "Why are we still holding hands?"

The door opened, and Alek let go.

"Andrew is dead. What took you so long?" Rachel asked.

Fuck! I really wanted to hurt him for what he did.

Alek moved past her, and I followed him.

"Someone planted a suggestion in the salesperson's mind. I wanted to see how deep it was," he replied. "See if I could find out who did it."

"He's in the bedroom," Rachel said and shut the door. After a brief glance in my direction, she turned and made her way to the back of the condo.

"I don't think she likes me anymore," I said as I followed Alek.

"She's worried. And truthfully, Nicole, we all are. Your magick is unknown. One we don't have time to figure out. The fact that Devlin is still letting you work with us is out of character. He doesn't like unknown variables."

"Understood." I pushed past him. Even though I did understand their concerns, it didn't stop his words from stinging a little.

I entered the bedroom and came to an abrupt halt. Something about the scene in front of me seemed familiar.

Andrew was hanging from a rope attached to an exposed beam on the ceiling. His dark suit was disheveled. And there were a few drops of blood staining the front of his yellow shirt. His eyes were open, all the life in them snuffed out. A small part of me wanted to feel sorry for him, but I couldn't. He was responsible for what had happened to my godchildren. I had been robbed of my revenge.

I glanced around his bedroom. There wasn't anything for him to stand on. The bed was up against the wall at least three feet away, and the only other furniture in the room was a large oak bureau near the balcony door.

"This was how they found Louis Badet," I said, finally putting my finger on the familiarity of the situation.

They all turned and looked at me.

"You know, the author of that poem, 'The Land Guarded by People of Colour.' He was found hanging in his hotel room in the exact same fashion." I waved my hand around the room. "There is nothing close enough to Andrew for him to stand on. So, how did he manage to hang himself?"

Devlin nodded. "Interesting." He walked around Andrew. "Someone is doing damage control—meaning Andrew might have had some information that could have helped us. Or information that could have linked the Sinclair family to that group home."

"But any halfway decent detective would spot the obvious signs of murder when they entered the room," I said.

"It might be a message," Alek said, looking around the room.

Devlin gazed at him, his mind working. "You think we're compromised."

Alek studied him for a moment before focusing on Andrew. "They might know something. We found the kids a few hours ago. It's quick. Almost as if..."

"We should go, Dev. If they staged this for us, then they might be back," Rachel said.

Devlin took one last look around the room. "Yeah. Something's not right about this." He walked out of the room with Rachel and Alek following behind him.

I stood there for a moment, looking up at Andrew as he slowly rocked from side to side. I felt cheated. I wanted to be the one to hang him. Right after we got all the answers we needed. I pulled my phone out of my back pocket and scrolled through my contacts.

Maybe there was someone else who could provide us with information.

"Ronald, call me. It's important."

I didn't hold out hope that he would call back. There were still questions as to why he had helped me in the first place. But at this point, I was willing to take all the assistance we could get. Even if that help came from someone I was beginning not to trust.

We'd picked up burgers on the way back to Devlin's house. Mine lay on the floor half-eaten, along with a heaping pile of fries. It was very unlike me not to devour food, but I just couldn't eat. After feeding the kids and reassuring them that we would find their mother, Kara had taken them to my parents' house. It broke my heart to have to let them out of my sight. However, my parents would be able to protect them if need be. There was no guarantee we would all make it out of this alive.

The information Jonah had collected from Andrew's house lay scattered all over the floor. Three boxes contained alphabetical records of people who'd been insured by Tribec Insurance dating back to 1907. Attached to each folder was a spreadsheet with six columns listed—name, age, blood type, health score, nationality, and one with the heading H77-1.537 ratio. The H77-1.537 ratio column dated back to 2010. The ratios ranged from 0.375 to 0.923. The ones with the scores below 0.47 were all crossed out in red ink. The health scores had a high, medium, or low rating. The insured with the higher H77-1.537 ratio, along with a high or medium health score, were all highlighted in yellow.

Another three contained a list of employees dating back to 1907 as well. Just like the files on the insured, the folders all had spreadsheets attached to them, only they had three additional columns. Ritual viability, duration of employment, and date of death. Some of the employees met their criteria, but they weren't highlighted. Instead, they remained employed for exactly ten years; and the ones who didn't, only one year, which explained their high turnover.

The last three had personal information. Unfortunately, the information was useless in determining where they were keeping Marta. It did, however, confirm that Devlin's client, Felicity, had been killed along with her boyfriend and his uncle. Her name was crossed out in red, with a single notation next to it—"clean up."

"I don't understand why they haven't been caught." I pushed the last file away from me. "Or why Andrew collected all of this stuff to begin with."

Devlin looked up from his pile and focused on Rachel. "When did they first open Tribec, Rach?"

Rachel flipped through a few pages of her notebook. "They started Tribec on the island in 1947. Before then, they were located in New Orleans." She closed the notebook. "They were still a small company at that time."

"I don't remember them saying that," I said.

"You weren't paying attention. You were too busy assessing the room," Devlin said. He set the folder he was looking through with the others he had viewed.

"Yeah, well, either way, they have been getting away with it for a while, and nobody has noticed."

Alek stood up and stretched, his shirt riding up and giving me a real nice view of his hard, well-defined, bronze-colored stomach. I tried to keep my eyes averted from the sight. Tried and failed.

"It's safe to assume they have some connections on the island." He walked over to the coffee pot. "All the files I've been through are for past employees who died *naturally*. And in each case, the coroner who made that judgment call was a Stewart." He poured another mug of coffee and handed it to me.

I stared at it for a minute, contemplating my options. The last mug of *mystery coffee* had kept me up all day. From the looks of things, we were most likely going to be up all night. It wouldn't hurt to have some help with that. "Thanks." I took the mug from him. "The same coroner. How is that possible?"

"No. Different coroners, same last name."

I glanced up at him, and he smirked at me.

"Of course, I knew that," I said. Actually, I didn't. While my body could run a marathon around the world, my mind was sluggish. Looking at what Tribec had been doing for over a hundred years was just too damn overwhelming.

"Of course," he said and went back to his pile.

I pulled the medical files to me, a thought brewing in my head, a puzzle piece finally starting to fall into place.

"They didn't start looking for an anomaly until a few years ago. Before then, they just... sacrificed people." I thought back to my date with Doc. "He said he lied about the blood. So maybe he lied about the anomaly. But why?"

"Who, Nicole?" Alek asked.

I glanced at my phone. Still no call from Doc.

"Nicole?"

I focused on Alek. "Sorry. I called Ronald earlier." I rubbed my forehead. A headache was starting just behind my eyes, making it hard to concentrate. "I thought, since he helped..." I lifted my hand up to forestall Devlin's comment. "I know it didn't make sense for him to help me in the first place. However, since he did, I wanted to see if he would just come right out and tell me where his family was keeping Marta. He has to know."

"If he was going to do that, he would have done so already. Now, what did you mean he lied about the blood?"

"He told me on our... date... that he lied to his family about the blood. When I pressed him on it, he said he lied to his brother Thomas about the employees' health." I glanced around at the boxes. "It was a lie. I know that. He all but admitted it in his office on Wednesday. But what I don't know is if he's involved, or if he's an unwilling participant in what they're doing." I locked eyes with Devlin. "Don't you think it's important that we find out? He could turn out to be a useful ally."

Devlin held my gaze, his eyes distant, as if he were working something out in his head. Honestly, I wasn't completely convinced that Doc was an ally. Something about him suddenly being truthful was... strange. All the properties that we knew of had been searched, and the only other person who could have given us more information was dead. We were out of options.

Another thing that was disturbing me was the H77-1.537 ratio. Doc admitted he lied about the blood. So, how would he know to look for an anomaly in people's blood in the first place? It suggested he had some knowledge there was something he needed to look for to make their rituals work. Who would have given him that information?

"This box has information on the Sinclairs," Jonah said, drawing our attention to him. "Along with four other families." He pulled out a list. "Hamilton, Smith, Young, and Peterson. The Hamilton family owns a pharmaceutical company; the Smiths have a foundation that helps find homes for immigrants and refugees; the Peterson family runs an all-girls school in Alice; and the Young family..."

"Runs the Better Day Church. Or, more accurately, the Better Day *Cult*," I interjected. "I heard about them a few years ago. They were involved in some sort of scandal."

"What do they all have in common?" Devlin asked.

"Access to a lot of people," I said. I looked around at the piles on the floor. "This isn't helping. And now we know that what we're dealing with includes six prominent families on the island."

"We stay focused," Devlin said. "And worry about the rest later."

That was a lot easier said than done. If Andrew had a file on those families, there had to be a reason. We already knew that the Stewarts and Sinclairs practiced blood magick—I had to assume, given the evidence that they all did. They also had people willing to sacrifice themselves to fuel their blood spells.

"That woman who sacrificed herself. Do you think she really did it willingly? Or was she used as a slave?" I asked.

"Blood slave," Alek said, nodding. "Yeah, it would have to be something like that."

Although Devlin and Rachel agreed, we all had to know it was a lie. The woman had been more than happy to be used. Sure, she could have been brainwashed. But the joyous look in her eyes was real. Her whole face had lit up when Nickolas thanked her for her service.

"I need more coffee." I got up and made my way to the pot.

"You shouldn't drink any more. It's not good for you."

I paused, turned around, and stared at Rachel. "What do you mean, it's not good for me?"

She looked up at me. "It not good to drink more than four cups in forty-eight hours. We drink it when we expel a lot of magick. If we didn't, we wouldn't be able to function. I have to drink it every day. I'm constantly expelling magick."

I ignored the last comment and focused on the rest. I would have to ask her later how she expelled magick constantly. "What the hell is in the coffee?"

Devlin narrowed his eyes. "Later, Nicole. Right now, we need to find out where they are keeping Marta. There's regular coffee in the kitchen." He studied me for a minute. "But I don't think you need it."

It was on the tip of my tongue to call him a bastard, and I was two seconds away from throwing my coffee mug at Rachel.

"Nicole," Alek said.

I didn't look at him. Because if I did, it would force me to calm down, so instead, I focused on Devlin. "Unfortunately, *later* doesn't work for me. So, someone better fucking explain just what the hell I've been drinking," I gritted out.

"In order to explain it in a way that you understand," Alek interjected, "we have to go into a magick lesson. And you have to admit... Nicole, look at me." His voice, normally smooth and soothing, had risen.

I turned my head slowly toward him.

He stared at me for a moment and then continued. "We don't

have time for that right now. But trust me; I wouldn't give you something that would harm you." He continued to stare me. "Do you trust me, Nicole?"

I took a deep breath and willed myself to calm down. "Yes," I said, turning away and focusing on Devlin. "After this is over, we are going to have one *long* conversation, *Boss Man*." Of course, the person I should've been angry with was Rachel, but for some reason, I just couldn't bring myself to be mad at her. Maybe it was the look on her face when I first drank her concoction and spit it out.

"Just stay away from my dick," Devlin said.

The fact that he said that with a serious face caused an inappropriate bubble of laughter to burst out of me. I tried to contain it, but once it got going, I couldn't stop. Eventually, the laughter turned to tears of frustration.

Alek placed his hand on my back. "We're all frustrated, Nicole, but we need to keep it together."

"You're right." I wiped tears from my cheeks. "Fuck, I'm sorry, I just... How the hell do you all do this and not go insane?"

"Patience," Jonah said.

"I found something, Dev," Rachel said. She handed him a photograph.

I moved so I could see it.

The picture, taken in a dark room, depicted a solid block of black marble. If not for the wooden handles on either side, that's what I would have thought it was. There were figures drawn into the sides that resembled Egyptian hieroglyphs. The object lay on bare concrete with minimal light filtering in the room. "Ark of Horus" was written on the back. The Stewarts had mentioned something about an Ark. This must have been it. How in the hell did Andrew get access to it?

"There is also mention of a ritual of blood," Rachel said, handing Devlin a piece of paper.

That was a strange way to reference it—'ritual of blood' and not 'blood ritual.' The wording sounded important. However, I didn't have any concrete reason why, just a gut feeling.

Devlin reviewed the paper Rachel handed him, confusion crossing his face. "It keeps repeating the phrase, 'of the blood.' But everything else..." He shook his head and handed the paper to me.

I read the first paragraph and understood exactly what he meant. The writing was just random words that didn't make any sense, all strung together, except for the repeating phrase.

I took in the scattered piles of paper on the floor. "Why was he collecting all of this?" I asked again.

"Best guess," Devlin started. "Blackmail. He must have thought all of this would get him something. But what? From what you overheard, they were going to deal with him soon. My only problem is that everything he's done, from gathering information to selling those kids, just doesn't make any damn sense. And we have no way to question him about it." He stood up. "And you're right; none of it is helping us locate Marta or the other people they took."

He looked down at me. "We might just need to understand more about blood magick. Chances are, after outing the Sinclair family, the Stewart family will figure out someone is coming for them. We were lucky back at the group home. I don't want to chance us walking into something we can't handle. Sitting here, trying to sift through all this information, is eating away at our time."

I checked my watch. It was late, but I knew Luisah would be there. My only concern was whether she would give us the information we needed? I stood up and stretched.

"Jonah, Rachel, call Kara and have her meet us at Tribec. When we're done with Luisah, we'll meet you there. Vincent, compile some info on these other families. I want as much information as possible. If they're all practicing blood magick, I'm not leaving this island until we stop them."

"Damn," Vincent said. He turned the computer around for

us to see and turned up the volume. A tall man in a dark blue suit stood behind a bay of microphones affixed to a podium.

*"We are looking into the activities of our employees and want to assure everyone that, after carefully reviewing everything, none of our other facilities were involved in the practices of the one located on Carson Street. We are actively searching for anyone who might..."*

"Turn that shit off," Alek said.

"When was that interview done?" Devlin asked.

"Around noon. It's Bradley Sinclair." He turned the monitor around.

"So, only two hours after the police found the children, they're trying to get ahead of the situation." Devlin rubbed the back of his neck. "Nothing we can do about it now. And we just ran out of time." He looked at the piles of boxes on the floor. "Fuck. We'll be going in blind."

"We handled them before, Dev," Rachel said.

She was right. Despite the lack of understanding of blood magick, we had won. We'd have to rely on what we'd learn so far to win again.

After I texted Kara to meet us at Tribec, we climbed in Alek's car and headed out.

When it was all over, I'd go see Luisah. And maybe my parents, too.

We arrived at Tribec Insurance fifteen minutes later. Kara made her way over to us.

"I should have listened to you," Kara said. She stood by Alek's car, waiting for me to get out. She was wearing jeans, a tank top, and black boots. A belt similar to the others was secured around her waist, and a long, elk-handled knife was strapped to her thigh.

"Damn, you have a superhero utility belt, too?"

She smiled, but there wasn't any joy in it. I hated to see that dead look in her eyes. When I continued to stare, she looked back over at the building.

"That day at Jordin's, when you said you felt there was something off with Tribec…" She looked back at me with sadness in her eyes. "I should have listened."

I shook my head. "I blame myself for that, Kara, not you." I took her hand. "I'd cried wolf one too many times. Telling you that something was wrong with this job or that one. I don't blame you for dismissing it as my usual bullshit. But I do blame myself for not following my instincts." I turned and looked up at the obelisk on top of the building. It was the first indication to me that something was wrong. That, and the smell of blood. I turned back to Kara. "All that matters now is that you're here and together with the other superheroes. We will solve this."

"There is something wrong with you, Nicole," she said, shaking her head.

"Yeah, there is. But you love me."

"Nicole, you're with Alek. Kara with Jonah. There are twenty floors in this building. Rachel and I will take seven floors, Jonah and Kara take seven, and Alek and Nicole, you take six. We meet back here in the parking lot. I don't want to be in there longer than we have to," Devlin said.

"They have an entrance in the back that's used by the guards," Jonah said. "Two cars in the lot belonging to Duncan Glass and George Merced."

Devlin looked at me. "Where's the gun I gave you?"

I dug it out of my purse, put my purse back in the car, and shoved the gun down the back of my jeans.

Devlin glanced at Kara. "I should have given you a gun."

She smiled. "I don't need one."

"The guards might have guns."

The look on Kara's face telegraphed, "I don't give a fuck."

Devlin started to say something but turned and started toward the back of the building.

What the hell had Kara been taught that made her believe she could stop a bullet?

W e entered from the back. Silence settled over the group as we moved inside. The clicking from my boots echoed inside the dimly-lit space. The lobby was clear. The doorway that led to the training room stood open, as if it was waiting. As we moved toward it, I glanced over my shoulder at the elevator. The black marble looked as if it was moving. Like suddenly it had come to life. I rubbed my bare arms and kept moving.

We split up and searched the rooms. I entered the employees' breakroom. The smell of burnt popcorn and coffee hung heavy in the air. Despite the room being empty, I could still feel the presence of... something.

"Nicole," Alek said as he walked up behind me.

I turned. "You scared me," I said, clutching my chest.

He took my hand and led me back to the lobby. I suppressed the butterflies that erupted in my stomach at his touch.

"Rachel and I will take the top seven floors," Devlin announced, as Alek and I joined the rest of the group. "You and Alek take the middle six. Kara and Jonah, you take the remaining floors. We will all ride up separately." After handing us our IDs, now programed for all the floors, he signaled for Rachel to get on the elevator. "Stay alert," he said as the doors closed.

I thought it was a complete waste of breath, since it was

obvious the guards were somewhere in the building, but I managed to keep that comment to myself.

"Did you notice that Devlin keeps pairing us up?"

Alek glanced at me sideways. His full lips stretched into a crooked smile, exposing the small dimple on the right side of his face.

Damn, he had a nice smile. "Maybe he thinks you can control me."

"I've already tried that, remember?"

Yeah, I remembered.

The elevator opened on the thirteenth floor. Damn, I didn't even think about the fact that our six floors would include the thirteenth one.

"Looks like a storage area," he said and stepped off the elevator. When I didn't immediately exit, he turned around. "What are you waiting for?"

"This floor is unlucky." I looked out over the large expanse. "I don't see anyone, so there's no need for us to search it."

Alek shook his head. "Nicole, that's superstition, not fact. And yes, we do have to search it." He grabbed my hand. "Now, come on, time is wasting."

A dim light from the ceiling shone on a stack of boxes in the middle of the floor. White labels with black lettering were lined up on the right side of each box. Tan filing cabinets lined the right side of the room. Old computers, sitting on pallets, lined the left.

Coldness seeped up from the gray concrete floor as I made my way toward to boxes. "This must be where Andrew got all his information." I quickly flipped through the boxes, and remembered Rachel saying that they didn't keep anything on their main servers—only financial stuff and other frivolous things about the company. Smart. Especially when there was a chance their computers could be hacked.

After searching the next three floors, we made our way to nine.

Unlike the other floors' wide-open spaces, the ninth floor had a long gray wall stretching the entire span of it, with two openings that I assumed were hallways on both sides. Devlin said for us to not split up, but since we were on the same floor, I didn't see any harm in searching alone. Besides, I had a gun. Didn't know how to really use it, but I had it.

I'd just left the third to the last office when a muffled noise came from down the hall. I quickly ducked back inside the office, sat down heavily on the floor, and pushed my back up against the wall. The gun bit into my back, but I ignored it. I pulled out my cell phone, ready to turn it back on, and paused. I didn't have Alek's number.

Shit.

Heavy footsteps moved my way. I eased forward and pulled out the gun. My hands shook as I flipped the safety. I was sitting under the window facing the desk. Even though the person wouldn't be able to see me if he decided to check the office, I wasn't in a position to shoot. I scooted over so my back was against the wall and I was facing the door.

*Please be Alek.*

A large man came into view, blocking the light behind him and my exit. The guard whose arms resembled tree trunks filled the space. Duncan Glass. As if in slow motion, he turned his head in my direction and zeroed in on me. I raised the gun just as he started to walk into the room and fired. The recoil slammed me against the wall, and the sound pierced my eardrum. Damn. I'd missed him completely. He smiled, then advanced. I tried to get another shot off, but he lashed out and knocked the gun from my hand. But before he could do more than that, Alek stepped into the room.

Duncan Glass was a large man—much larger than Alek. But it didn't stop Alek from reaching out, wrapping one hand around the man's neck, and wrenching him back. He lifted the larger man off the ground and slammed him against the wall. Duncan beat at him with his fists, but Alek didn't flinch. His hand continued to squeeze as he hummed his dark melody. Blood slowly began spilling from every orifice on Duncan's face, trickling down and coating Alek's arm.

When his eyes rolled back in his head, I jumped to my feet and reached out and grabbed Alek's arm. He didn't budge, almost like he was rooted in place.

"We need to question him," I yelled, trying to get his attention.

Alek turned to me, his head moving slowly as if it were pushing against a very strong current. "I am."

He was fucking with his mind.

Alright, then. I picked my gun up off the floor and waited for Alek to finish his brand of questioning. Based on the blood flowing down Duncan's ashen face, it looked more like he was shredding the man's mind, but I wasn't going to complain. Duncan was involved in all this sickness, so he deserved every bit of torture he got.

When Duncan crumpled to the floor like a deflated balloon, Alek turned to me. "Eighth floor." He stepped out of the room.

I rushed to catch up with him. As we stood waiting for the elevator, I glanced over at him. Beads of sweat were dotted all over his forehead, and his eyes were bloodshot.

"What did you do?" I asked.

He turned to me as if in pain. "Something I shouldn't have." He wiped his forehead. "We don't have time for niceties."

The doors opened.

"Come on." He stepped into the elevator.

I hustled in after him and the doors slid shut. He reached out and took my hand. I moved closer, trying to soak up the heat coming off of him. This would be the third time I'd been attacked in the past few days.

I chuckled, but there wasn't any humor in it. "You know, when Kara was talking me into taking Krav Maga with her, I told her I wasn't at war with anyone and didn't see the need to learn." I glanced at him. The focus in his brown eyes was too intense. I looked away, and he squeezed my hand. "Turns out, I was wrong."

The elevator doors opened, and I froze.

The smell of blood and sand rushed at me as if an invisible wind had sent it hurtling into the elevator—flooding the small space. We stepped off and looked around. The entire floor was covered in a series of power circles in an array of colors. Three green, three gold, three black, and one large red one in the middle of the room, all drawn so that they intersected each other. Directly in the center of the red one was a raised, bone-colored, marble dais. A black satin cloth lay around it, along with four small ceramic jugs. The Ark was nowhere in sight.

My footsteps echoed as I moved farther into the room. "I guess we found their power source. They must have moved the Ark."

"It would appear that way." Alek pulled out his phone.

A conveyer belt, with at least a hundred chains hanging from it, covered the ceiling. At the end of each chain was a long, metal hook. I didn't want to think about what they hung from those hooks.

The elevator doors opened, startling me. I whipped around, gun already extended.

Kara and Jonah stepped off the elevator. Kara's clothes were disheveled.

She lifted her hands. "Careful, Nicole."

I studied Kara for a minute. She kept her eyes averted from me. Her mouth twitched as if she was fighting the urge to smile. Jonah stepped away, watching her from the corner of his eyes.

"What happened?"

She looked at me, and I stepped back. I'd never seen that look in her eyes before. She smiled, but it didn't reach her eyes.

"Kara," I said and moved toward her.

"We ran into George," Jonah said. He glanced at Kara. "She took care of it."

She looked away from me and continued her trek into the room.

"Did you call Devlin?" Jonah asked.

"Yeah, he and Rachel are on their way," Alek said.

Jonah walked around the room. "The configuration of the power circles..." His voice trailed off as he moved to one of the black circles. "This is an old faith magick ritual. The mages stand here to center their power. Green circles are for the latent practitioners, and gold for believers, but..." Jonah twisted around, studying the circles drawn on the floor. "The red circle is to contain our combined power, and it shouldn't be touching the others."

The elevator doors opened, and we all turned.

"They're using a ritual to bring something into existence," Jonah said, as Devlin and Rachel made their way toward us. "However, they're doing the ritual wrong."

Devlin studied the lines on the floor and then glanced up at the ceiling.

"What are they trying to bring into existence?" I asked. All of the rituals they were using—that we knew about—were being done incorrectly. Was it because they'd received the wrong information? Or were they trying to change the spells?

Jonah turned to me. "In ancient times, the ritual was used to speak with the gods that faith magick had created. Now"—he shook his head—"I have no idea why anyone would use this ritual. Particularly not like this."

When Luisah had told me all religions created their gods, I thought she meant on a spiritual level. But what Jonah said suggested that the lesser gods that had been created by faith magick were actually real. Tangible. Able to be seen and conversed with. Up until today, I'd also believed those were the only gods in existence. The ones that were worshiped in the different religions across the world. That belief, too, had been proven wrong.

"What happened to the gods?" I asked.

"People stopped believing in them," Jonah said.

Devlin looked at Alek. "Do your people have any information regarding the Ark?"

"It's never been mentioned. But I can check with my cousin."

Devlin scrutinized the floor one last time, then turned to us. "We need to check and make sure they don't have any other properties besides the ones we already searched. They are hiding these people somewhere, and if we don't find them tonight..."

He left the obvious unsaid. Chances were, the Stewarts would kill everyone they took.

I pulled out my phone and turned it back on. I needed to try Ronald again.

My phone beeped, indicating I had several missed messages. Five missed calls and one text from Ronald.

**_Meet me at my place._**

The text had come in twenty minutes ago.

"I might be able to get us some information," I said, showing them the text.

"You're not going alone," Devlin said, and glanced at Alek.

I shook my head. "No, I don't think he will open up if I bring another guy with me. Besides, if he wanted to hurt me, he would have already." I shoved my phone back in my pocket and glanced at Alek. "I'll go, see if I can get some information out of him."

He looked worried and just a tad possessive. I didn't even want to think about how his look made my heart skip a beat.

"I'll be fine." I made my way to the elevator.

"Of course she will," Kara said. "Because I'm going with her."

"I'd prefer if Alek went with you," Devlin stated. "He could—"

"Kara can handle it," Jonah said.

Devlin glanced at him. "Are you sure?"

Jonah nodded.

"Alright. I want you to text the address when you arrive."

I saluted him. "Yes, sir."

Kara climbed on the elevator with me. "You are such a smart A."

I breathed a sigh of relief that the old Kara was back. I couldn't deal with another revelation right now. And from what I'd seen in her eyes when she and Jonah had stepped off the elevator, I knew that revelation was coming soon.

The doors opened and we stepped off.

Kara pulled me to a stop. "Are you sure this man isn't going to try to hurt you? We could be walking into a trap."

I shrugged, because truthfully, I didn't know what Ronald's agenda was. All I knew was, if he was willing to help us, then I would do whatever it took to get that help. And if he refused, I was sure Rachel would get it out of him somehow.

After giving Kara directions to Ronald's place, I sat back in my seat and stared at the message on my phone, willing it to give me some clue as to what we were walking into. It yielded none. Despite my reassurances to the others, I was more than a little apprehensive about going to Ronald's. Warning bells had started sounding when he'd so graciously allowed me to overhear the exchange between him and his siblings. Puzzle pieces had started falling into place, and the scribbled note on the entry next to Felicity's name was really starting to bother me.

They said they had to clean up Ronald's mess in the past. Was Felicity one of his messes?

I glanced over at Kara; she had worry lines creased across her forehead and a frown on her face.

"What happened with my parents?" I asked softly.

Kara glanced at me. "I had to tell them what happened. And it took a lot to convince them not to follow me. Well, convince Henri; Anne was really worried about the kids. She looked"— Kara pulled onto the bridge that would take us to Dulean— "scared, maybe. But..." She shook her head. "It was more than that." She glanced over at me. "How are you holding up?"

"I don't know. I'm frustrated. We know who's responsible; we know what they're doing. We also know where they live. But we can't do anything about it. I understand if we did confront them, there is the chance they would kill everyone before we could rescue them. Even with magick, we're essentially powerless. Our power should be enough, damn it!"

"It should be." She paused. "I'm scared for you, Nicole. I'm scared for all of us. That guard…" She shook her head. "I killed him, Nicole. And what disturbs me most is that I liked it. I liked watching the light go out in his eyes. Watching him suffer as I slit him open and blew killing dust inside of him." She paused as tears streamed down her face.

Well, that explained the look she had in her eyes. I reached over and squeezed her hand. "All our emotions are running high, Kara. You did what you had to. Besides, I don't think anyone would have spared his life knowing what we know."

She swallowed. "Magick is like a drug to me. I long to use it. I…" She let go of my hand and put hers back on the steering wheel.

"Kara?" This was the first time she had ever said anything like that to me. I always believed she hated magick.

"Not now." She turned and gave me a half smile. "Later. I promise."

We rode in silence the rest of the way. Kara was struggling with what she had done. Hell, even I was having problems with all of it. But as hard as I tried, I couldn't come up with an alternative way to handle the situation. Devlin said there were no checks and balances with magick practitioners. Bradley Sinclair giving a news conference—attempting to shift the blame of what his family was responsible for to his employees—only proved that point.

On the way over, I tried calling Ronald. I'd forgotten the gate code to get into the slip-yard. He never answered. I started to get worried, but when we pulled up, the gate was wide open. He must have left it open. Why did that suddenly send a chill up my spine?

I directed Kara to his boat. Two differences caught my eye. One, his car was gone, and two, there were shades covering the glass walls, and all the lights were on inside; the brightness was leaking around the edges of the shades, casting an eerie glow out onto the blackish water.

I stared at the spot he'd parked in the other night.

"Something's not right," I said as I climbed out of the car.

"Why do you say that?" Kara came around the car and stood next to me.

I looked over at the neighboring houses. All the lights were out. I pulled out my phone and checked the time. It had been a little over forty minutes since he'd texted me. I didn't text him back and tell him I was coming, so maybe he'd left. Or maybe something had happened to him.

"It's going to rain," Kara said, looking up at the sky. "We should check the house." She turned to me. "Maybe you should call him."

I dialed his number. The call went straight to voicemail. I stood there, staring at the brightly-lit house, contemplating whether I should knock. I paused, then frowned. How odd. The front door was ajar. The gate being open was understandable, sort of, but the front door being open... not so much.

I glanced up at the sky. Rain clouds hung like water balloons ready to burst. She was right; it was going to rain. I could even smell it in the air.

"Let's check the house," I said as I started forward.

"How much do you trust this guy?"

I turned to her. She was scanning the area around us.

"I don't," I answered truthfully. Truth was, I hadn't trusted him before, either.

Kara focused on me for a moment, then pulled her blade out of its sheath. "I've got your back."

I smiled. "I know."

The only sound was the water lapping against the boat. The silence filled me with dread. We stepped up onto the deck and made our way to the front door. As we got closer, I got a whiff of something strange emanating from inside the house.

"Do you smell that?" I asked.

Kara inhaled deeply. "Smells like alcohol."

I pushed the door open slowly. "What the fuck?" I said as I got my first look at his house.

Every piece of furniture had been destroyed as if a tornado had touched down inside.

The leather couch looked as if someone had used a knife to shred it. All of his wood furniture lay broken in pieces strewn about the room. The few pictures he had on the walls were piled in the corner, the frames broken. Liquor bottles lay spilled, their dark liquid saturated into the carpet.

Whoever had done this had either been searching for something or filled with rage. There was no other explanation for it.

"Ronald?" I called out.

There was no answer. Rain started pelting down, hitting the houseboat, tapping out a static rhythm. It reminded me of the last time I'd been here and the feeling of melancholy that had suddenly overwhelmed me.

"Do you think they did something to him?" Kara asked.

I thought about Andrew hanging from the ceiling—the only indication of violence in his entire condo. Nothing else had been disturbed. Not like here. This place looked as if someone had taken out a lot of pent-up rage on every viable piece of furniture.

"I don't know," I said finally. "Let's check the rest of the house."

"Nicole," Kara said, pointing.

I looked to where she was pointing. A massive amount of blood was pooled at the foot of the stairs. I pulled the gun from my waistband and started for the stairs. Kara followed closely behind me. Each step leading up to the second floor had deposits of blood on it. It looked as if someone had purposely deposited the blood there leaving a trail to follow.

My stomach lurched when we reached the top. Acid rose and coated my throat. My vision wavered as I fought a tidal wave of revulsion. Warm air leached into the room from the small fissure in the glass. The smell of death hung heavy in the air, along with the scent of human waste.

My eyes tracked to the body lying exposed on the bed—flies swarming around it. My brain didn't want to acknowledge what I was seeing. It was almost as if my mind was trying really hard to protect itself from the nightmare before me.

"Oh my God!" Kara said. She stepped around me and made her way to the bed.

I couldn't move. I just stood there, frozen in place. The person on the bed was familiar—Ronald, despite doing such horrific things to her body, had left her face intact. The small pixie woman looked like a macabre wax replica of the woman I'd met a week ago.

"This is the woman we saw in the grocery store the other day," Kara said. She stared down in horror at what was left of Emilia.

She lay in a pool of blood, her body mutilated and twisted in ways no human body should be twisted. Her insides looked as if they'd been ripped from her torso. Her legs were spread wide, and a foreign object had been shoved deep inside of her, only the black handle showing. Her thighs were shredded, and her feet... I couldn't figure out what had been done to them. Several parts were missing—toes, half of her ankle.

"Who would do this?" Kara asked.

"Ronald," I said, because in that moment, I knew. The brutal scene in front of me pulled the final piece of the puzzle into place. He didn't have illegitimate children spread out all over the place. He had bodies that needed burying and messes to clean up. And Lisa, subtly, tried to warn me about it. She didn't do a very good job.

"There's a letter addressed to you," Kara said, holding out a sheet of paper, along with a photograph.

I finally managed to uproot myself and move forward. My hand shook as I took the items from her. The picture was of Devlin, Rachel, Alek, and I leaving Andrew's house. Did that mean that Andrew had been working with Ronald this whole time? It would explain his ability to obtain so many records. But that didn't fit. Why, if he was working with Ronald, would he send those men to kill the three of us? And why did Ronald encourage his family to take care of him?

No, I got the feeling that Andrew was working alone. Ronald had cut whatever nefarious plans he had short when he killed him. Alek was right; the scene at Andrew's condo had been staged for our benefit.

Either way, Andrew wasn't our problem anymore, so I focused on the letter. It was written in an elegant cursive. Almost romantic in nature. Sick bastard.

Nicole,

I had to substitute Emilia for you. She wasn't quite as fun, but then she was a substitute. I have enclosed a map to my siblings' ritual site. I will give you two hours from the time you set foot on my boat to find them. After the time is up, I will call my brother and sister and inform them of your arrival.

I had to take Marta and her beautiful children. While Andrew took care of the young ones, I enjoyed Marta for a short while before I convinced my brother that she had a higher ratio of the anomaly in her blood than all the others they had collected. I apologize if news of this upsets you, but it is your fault. You threatened to leave, and if you did that, my family might not have been exposed. I needed a way for you to continue asking questions, and Marta was my best opportu-

*nity for that. I wanted to be free of their sick-
ness and pursue my own dreams.*

*When we meet again, I will fuck you. And
when I'm done, I will have you for dessert.
Emilia didn't taste as good as I thought. Maybe
your flesh will taste better.*

*Think of me.*

*Ronald*

"What does it say?" Kara asked.

A scream lodged in my throat, and my hands shook violently
as I handed her the letter and ran out of the room. My skin
suddenly felt dirty as it slowly dawned on me that I'd slept with a
monster. And had come very close to being one of his many
victims.

Once I made it outside, bile filled my mouth and I threw up
into the brackish water. My body trembled as rage consumed me.
My fault. Everything that had happened was my damn fault. If I'd
only listened to my instincts and walked out that first day, Marta
and her kids would have been safe.

Images of what he might have done to Marta swam in my
head, and I threw up again. I kept throwing up until the only
substance coming out of me were streams of acid.

"Nicole," Kara said, placing her hand on my back.

"No, Kara. It's my fault. You were right. Both you and Marta
were right. I make one damn bad decision after the next." I turned
and faced her, swiping my mouth with my hand. "Only now,
those bad decisions have hurt the ones I love!"

"We don't have time for pity parties, Nicole. He gave us two
hours." Kara rubbed her arms as she stared off across the water.

I snatched my phone out of my back pocket. "I'm not having
a pity party." I punched Devlin's number into the phone.

"Then what are you doing?"

"Waking the fuck up."

I could no longer sit back and wallow in my stupidity. No longer allow events to unfold around me and let anger at my lack of knowledge keep me from stepping up to the plate. I'd made mistakes, true, but it was time I got the hell over it. Essentially, it was time I put my big girl panties on and did some damage.

I would deal with the lies and deceit once Marta and the rest of the captives were safe.

An image of Ronald's living room swept over me. The rage he must have been consumed with when he tore apart every piece of the furniture in his house. Shedding the crippling façade that he'd been forced to adopt. My original impression of the cold, drab interior not being like him at all was true. He kept the real him tucked away behind a rumpled suit and ill-fitting glasses. I'd thought the intensity of his lovemaking—if I could even call it that—was both intoxicating and thrilling. I had no idea that, just below the surface of that passion, was an inhuman monster, waiting to break free.

Unfortunately, he'd used me like a human chess piece. Moving me into position without appearing to do so by stoking the embers of my curiosity and mistrust.

Kara and I climbed back into the car. She glanced over at the boathouse, its lights still leaking from the creases behind the shades.

"He really is a sick man," she said.

I didn't respond.

"What should we do about Emilia?" she asked.

I glanced over at Kara. While there was anger lining her pretty face, there was also pain. I understood that agony. Emilia didn't need to die. Her death served no purpose. He could have easily slipped away and left her alone. Instead, he used her as a message to me. Making her death also my fault.

"Nothing now." I settled back in my seat. Despite the seething anger in my body, I was tired. "We have to deal with it later."

Would there be a later?

In all likelihood, we were walking into a trap. One we really couldn't avoid. If, by some miracle, we survived this fight, I would come back and deal with Emilia's body. Did she have any family on the island? She had mentioned some friends. It was good that she would at least have someone to mourn her death.

Kara started the car and backed out of the parking spot.

Yes, if I did survive, I was coming back here. Once Emilia's body had been taken care of... I was going to burn that bastard's boat to the water line. I'd sit in a lawn chair, drinking some of Cherry's lemonade, while I watched the flames engulf his fucking houseboat. Preferably with him inside.

I just needed to find him first.

S mall marshlands, which most believed were uninhabitable, lined the roads that connected Sandpoint and Alice to the main island. No one to my knowledge had ever ventured past the dense patches of trees and water for fear of gators and snakes. Ronald's directions indicated we needed to do just that. Was it his sick way of making us suffer? Was there possibly another way to reach our destination? I wish we had time to find out.

I'd called Devlin and instructed him to meet us at the junction between Alice and Sandpoint. It was located only a half-mile from Tribec Insurance. We'd been so damn close to where Marta was being held.

Kara, in an attempt to get us there quickly, was trying to break the sound barrier by driving her small car at its maximum speed. Under normal circumstances, I might have been a little worried for my safety, but these weren't normal circumstances. Besides, enough time had already been wasted, running around the island and searching one property after the next. If I could have flown to the location, I would have.

"Didn't they find that private detective, Bernardo Diaz, in that same area?" Kara turned toward me. "The one you used to work for?"

"Yes. Now, please keep your eyes on the road."

Kara focused on the road.

We had assumed Lisa or one of the guards had killed Bernardo. Now that I was aware Ronald was behind everything, I wasn't convinced she was the one who had killed him. I had had a feeling that someone was behind the scenes, orchestrating the events of the past few days, and believed it may have been related to magick and the Old Ones.

I was wrong.

"Ronald had something to do with his death," I said, shaking my head. "He wanted to break free of his family. But they must have had some sort of hold over him. Something keeping him in place."

I still hadn't been able to decipher what that hold might be. His sick activities would have hurt them, too. I doubted they truly believed Emilia could keep him in check. So, what was it that kept him under control?

"Anyway," I continued, "in walks Bernardo, asking questions about a girl I'm positive Ronald killed. So, what does Ronald do? He kills the private detective and places his body in a location that would draw attention to, and possibly expose, his family's secret ritual location."

"Only, it didn't work," Kara said.

I pondered that for a moment. If they did find Bernardo in that area, why hadn't they discovered the Stewarts' secret location as well?

"Anyway. After that obvious failed attempt, here I come along with my numerous questions and skepticism about Tribec, and he must have danced with joy." I thought about how hard he had worked to keep me there. Yeah, I was definitely a willing pawn. The sex must have just been a bonus. "Now, he has found another way to expose his family's secrets. Feeding me implausible stories that explained my concerns." I turned to her. "He must have known how ridiculous they sounded and must have figured out that I would keep asking questions. Only, when I told him I was going to leave, he had to adjust his plans again." I swallowed the lump forming in my throat. I'd let the guilt and sadness feed my fury instead.

"Don't blame yourself, Nicole. It's not your fault."

"I'm just stating the obvious," I said, ignoring her statement.

"But why would he go through all that trouble?"

"That's the one thing I just can't figure out."

We grew silent. The streets whirred by in a blur. A few minutes later, we arrived at the junction of Alice and Sandpoint. The road curved off onto a small dirt road. Devlin had parked his car up against the guardrail. The yellow reflector lights lit up as Kara pulled in behind him.

We climbed out of the car and made our way to the others.

"Where's Jonah?" I asked when I handed Devlin the letter from Ronald.

"Getting us some waders. The water's a little deep." He pulled a pen light out of his pocket and read the letter.

"There aren't any stores open this late…" I glanced at my watch. "Excuse me, this early in the morning."

"I know," Devlin said, still reading.

"Then how is he… never mind." Apparently, his procurement of the waders was going to come with a discount. Well, I guess it really couldn't be helped. We needed them.

I took in the haggard appearance of everyone. We were all tired. At least, I knew I was. Along with hungry, sticky, and frustrated.

Alek came over to me. "You alright?"

I looked up at him. "Learning that I was a pawn in a sick, sadistic bastard's plans is doing my self-esteem wonders. And knowing that my best friend was taken because of said plans is downright disturbing. But don't worry. I'm focused."

He pulled me into a hug.

I wanted to push away, but the feel of his strong arms around me felt too damn good.

"Not your fault. Remember that," he whispered into my ear.

"I'll try to," I mumbled into his chest.

Headlights flooded light in the area we were standing in, and I reluctantly pulled away from the warmth and safety of Alek's embrace.

Jonah climbed out of his truck and grabbed some bags from the back. "They didn't have small, only medium and large." He handed out waders to everyone.

"I can't believe there isn't a road we can use to get us to the location." I pulled off my boots and jeans and stepped into the rubber pants. "Just how did they get everyone over there in the first place?" I stopped. "And how are we going to get them out?"

"Um… Nicole," Kara started.

I glanced up at her. Everyone was watching me.

"Yes?"

"You're supposed to put them on over your jeans."

I shook my head. "I'd rather err on the side of caution." I glanced up at the sky. "It's going to rain again." The rain had stopped when we left Ronald's house, but clouds still covered the sky.

After a brief hesitation, everyone else followed suit.

I got my first awe-inspiring glimpse of all three men in their underwear. Drool pooled in my mouth as I unabashedly watched Alek slide his jeans off of those powerful thighs. My stomach fluttered and heat spread all over my body as he slowly slid the waders on over his black boxers. They weren't doing a very good job of covering his manhood. I had this sudden desire to write a letter to the manufacturer and thank them. When it finally dawned on me that he was in fact sliding them on slowly, I glanced up and caught the heat and laughter in his eyes. He winked at me and slid them on the rest of the way.

I wasn't going to apologize for ogling. I deserved a little something enjoyable after all the shit I'd been through in the past forty-eight hours. True, I wasn't going to act on my attraction to him. However, it didn't mean I couldn't enjoy the view.

After everyone had stowed their shoes and jeans inside their bags—I had to share with Alek—Devlin turned to us.

"First off, we don't know how many people they have, so it's possible we will be outnumbered." Devlin scrubbed his hand down his face. The lines around his eyes had gotten deeper. "There's nothing we can do about it. We have to go in. So, we'll worry about it when we get there." He shoved a few additional items in his duffle bag and looked at me and Kara. "Second, we're not taking prisoners. We're not calling the police. This is our fight. Understand?"

"Understand," Kara and I said in unison.

Honestly, he really didn't need to say the last part. Neither one of us had any plans on leaving those bastards alive.

"No plan, Dev?" Rachel asked.

He handed her the letter. "We have no way of knowing if this bastard changed his mind and warned his family of our arrival. We need to move just in case he did."

"Could be a trap." Rachel handed the letter back to him. She glanced at me. Anger danced in her eyes, along with a small dose of insanity.

I was thankful that that look wasn't directed at me. If I didn't kill Ronald, I had no doubt she would. I was seriously entertaining the thought of letting her question him first. Before I slit his throat.

"We'll have to deal with it." Devlin regarded me for a moment. "I can't imagine what's going on in your head but know that we are going to get this sadistic asshole real soon."

"Does that 'we' include me, Boss Man?" Yes, I was petitioning him to allow me into his crew. Very unlike me. However, I had killing plans I couldn't carry out on my own. It would be beneficial to have Devlin's band of superheroes on my side.

He smiled. "Yes, it does." He cut his eyes in Kara's direction, a silent question playing on his face.

"Don't worry, Boss Man; I was going to join the team even without your approval," Kara said.

Rachel beamed at the two of us. "Good, now we're best girlfriends!" She reached into her backpack and pulled out a set of brass knuckles. "Here, Nicole. You can use my old pair until you get your own."

She handed me a pair of worn brass knuckles that probably still had remnants of blood imbedded in the metal. I smiled at the kind gesture and turned to Kara.

"Those are cool," Kara said as she studied them.

She was obviously lying to spare Rachel's feelings. I had to admit, despite the scary condition the brass knuckles were in, the gesture itself was a nice one. Morbid, but kind.

"Let's get moving. Alek, I want you out front with Nicole." Devlin handed the letter back to me. He had put it inside a protective plastic cover with only the map showing. "Jonah and Kara, bring up the rear." He reached into his bag and pulled out a gun. "Kara, we don't know what we're up against in there, so I want you to take this."

Kara took the gun from him.

"Do you know how to use one?" he asked.

"Yes." She shoved the gun into her bag. "It was part of my training. Although, I do prefer to use my blade or my magick."

He glanced down at the belt secured around her waist. "Do you have Henbane?"

Kara smiled, the gleam in her eyes showing just a touch of unrestrained madness.

Devlin, obviously taking the crazed look in her eyes as consent, started toward the break in the trees with the rest of us following close behind him.

Moonlight filtered through the branches, providing us minimal light to see by. There was a slim chance that Ronald had kept his word and not told his family about our coming, so we weren't going to announce our presence. At least, not until we had to.

The rain had started up halfway through the trip. My hair was plastered to my head, and the waders had filled up with water, rendering them useless. It was a good thing I'd removed my jeans. Sweat ran down my back, and I was being eaten alive by a horde of mosquitoes. The smell emanating from the water was a mixture of dead fish, algae, and human waste. I had moved on from disgust to a quiet, soothing rage. I tried not to visualize Bernardo's dead, bloated body floating in the water we were now trekking through. Instead, I focused on the many ways I was going to make the Stewarts pay for my discomfort.

After a few minutes of wading, we started up an incline and were deposited onto a small parcel of land heavily saturated with trees. We wound our way through it and eventually ended up on an even larger area. Maybe a few acres' worth. It had two structures on it—a small white house and a large red building, partially hidden behind a grouping of large cypress trees, that resembled a barn.

I stared at the structure, my left eye jumping. I was such a fucking idiot. Ronald had told me they had a barn. Proof that that sadistic bastard had been playing me since day one. Dropping little breadcrumbs along the way to see if I could figure out what his family was up to. There was no way I was going to tell them I had the answer all along. It was too damn humiliating.

Alek placed his arm across my chest, pausing my advance. "Hold on."

Devlin waded up beside him and pulled out a pair of binoculars. "Nobody in the house. They must be in the barn." He turned to Rachel. "You and Kara need to neutralize their source of power. I want you to poison all the blood slaves." Seems we had settled on a name for them. He glanced at me. "You and Jonah need to keep any guards they might have busy, while Rachel and Kara work. Alek and I will handle back-up."

We all stripped out of our water-logged waders and slipped on our dry jeans. I pulled off my heavily drenched tank top and wrung it out. Everyone's eyes were on me, but I ignored them. Besides, they had already seen me naked. I retrieved my gun from Alek's bag, making a mental note to get myself a bag along with a superhero utility belt as well, and started up the incline toward the barn.

As we walked, we came upon a narrow road leading around the small plot of land that curved toward the inland. A school bus sat off in the distance, just off the road.

"That bastard made us go the long way," I said.

Alek glanced at me. "Figured he did. And we should also assume that he didn't wait two hours to call his family."

"We'll deal with him later," Kara said.

I smiled. "Yeah, we will."

We moved along the road. Everyone's steps were silent but mine. Devlin glanced over his shoulder at me, his eyes conveying that I was making too much noise. Unfortunately, it couldn't be helped. I didn't know how to be stealthy. But I did make a note to learn. There had to be a trick to it. Hell, even Kara was moving without making a sound.

The barn-like building was a lot bigger up close. It had large bay doors and no windows, and sat on a small, hill-like formation. The bay doors were open, and the inside was pitch black.

Devlin pulled a flashlight out of his bag and shined the light around the area. Nothing. No indication of life whatsoever. The eerie quiet was disturbing. Not even the crickets were making a sound.

Yes, definitely a setup. Regrettably, we had no choice in the matter. We had to push on and enter that building.

As we moved inside, the smell of human waste and blood made my eyes water. We were standing on a hard, wooden floor. A crackling noise filled the air as we advanced inside. Chains rattled above us. Devlin shined his light up at the ceiling.

The first thing I saw was her hair. Hanging down, as she dangled from a chain around her feet. Naked. Bloody. Her chest —covered in intricate carvings—was barely moving.

Marta.

Something inside of me broke. Instantly, Kara moved up beside me.

Suddenly, a light blazed on, causing me to jump.

Lisa stood in the middle of the barn, wearing a pair of black leather pants, a leather halter top, and a pair of black, lace-up, leather boots. She had gold arm cuffs circling up her biceps. Her long blonde hair hung in two braids on either side of her head. Some sort of golden twine-like material had been woven into the braids. She looked like some deranged warrior from another time.

There were nine people crowding around her, including her brother, Thomas who was wearing a business suit. Seriously? I couldn't figure out who was the crazier of the two. Lisa in her warrior-woman costume or Thomas with his dark green suit. Lisa, at least, was dressed for combat. Thomas, however, looked as if he were attending a business meeting or a hostile negotiation. I pulled the gun from my waistband, broadcasting just what my talking points were going to be during the meeting.

Naked people crouched beside Lisa and her band of warriors —their eyes cast down to the floor, with long, jagged cuts running down both arms. Thick metal collars were secured around their necks. A long chain ran from a hook on their collars to a thick metal band on Lisa and her peoples' wrists. I wondered again about their practices, and just what type of person would willingly allow someone to use their blood to fuel a spell.

I glanced up at the ceiling. There were close to fifty people all hanging from their feet, naked with glyphs carved into their chests. I fought hard not to charge forward and mow Lisa and her sadistic crew down in an attempt to free the people. The effort was exhausting.

"You know, I was very suspicious of my brother's intentions when he took your friend. But Thomas foolishly thought he was just coming around." Lisa stared at me. "He called us over an hour ago."

His betrayal didn't surprise me. We had expected as much.

I showed Lisa my teeth as I chambered a round.

She laughed at my display and began twirling her index finger in a circular pattern. Tiny rivulets of blood began pulling from the cut on the arm of the man chained to her. Thomas moved into the shadows, and the other blood mages spread out, moving into position, covering the massive, almost empty, space.

I zeroed in on the Ark resting in the center of the room on a slab of black marble—the lid open. One of the captives hung directly over it, blood slowly flowing down from a deep gash on his leg, trickling into the Ark. I felt helpless as I watched this morbid display. We needed not only to save the man—if we could—but we also needed to get the Ark. Which meant we'd have to go through those blood mages and their slaves to do it.

Damn.

"I need fuel, ladies," Devlin said as he lifted his hands, summoning wind from the vial around his waist.

Kara and Rachel stepped forward, Henbane coating their hands. They blew the dust, covering the room with tiny particles as they started chanting, their voices rising and falling in a hypnotic melody that sent chills up my spine.

Jonah moved next to me, reminding me that we were supposed to keep the blood mages on the defensive. We both raised our guns and fired.

Before my bullet could make contact with Lisa, a wall of blood rose up at the same time as the man beside her roared. I continued firing at the rest of the blood mages, keeping them busy while Kara and Rachel worked in tandem, moving toward the other blood slaves.

My gun clicked. I was out of bullets. I should have asked for another clip. Too late now.

The wall of blood fell, and Lisa gasped. The slave chained to her clutched his throat as his neck started boiling, and blood and mucus ran down his chest.

Another slave entered the room and knelt at her feet. How many damn blood slaves did they have?

Lisa focused on me. "I couldn't figure out what principle of magick you practiced. Ronald said you didn't." She looked at the gun hanging uselessly in my hand. "And that just confirmed it." She unclipped the chain from the dead guy's neck and kicked him aside. After clipping the new guy to her, she focused on Devlin. "Mr. Carter. How surprising."

"Here's what's going to happen," Devlin said, not bothering to correct her about his name. "My associates and I are going to remove the people you have hanging from the ceiling and give you an opportunity to get a head start." A small tornado circled in his hands. "If you stay, it will be painful."

"An elemental. Tell me, Mr. Carter, do you know anything about blood magick?"

Rachel advanced on her, weaving like a snake. A small smile creased the corners of her mouth. She reached into the pouch tied around her waist and pulled out more Henbane.

Lisa watched the entire scenario with a smug expression on her face. She must have believed she was invincible. Crazy people often suffered under that delusion. I was really looking forward to bursting her bubble.

Rachel blew the Henbane into the new slave's face, all the while chanting that hypnotic melody—her voice rising and falling. The slave fell forward, his entire torso burning away. A smile remained plastered on his face as his flesh sizzled. His eyes grew vacant and, finally, he curled into a ball and died. There was no blood left in his body.

I shuddered and turned away.

Alek stepped forward and Rachel moved back, their moves again looking choreographed like they did at the Sinclairs' house.

Lisa grabbed the side of her head as Alek pushed into her space.

"No more talking, bitch," Alek said, standing in front of her.

Someone yelped, and a large stream of blood ran down in a straight line, making its way to Alek's back. Without thinking, I ran and shoved him out of the way. There was no way Alek would die on my watch. The lance sliced across my arm. My eyes watered, but I swallowed the pain. Alek pulled me toward him, his eyes narrowed on the deep gash on my arm.

"Why the fuck did you do that?" he asked, his voice laced with both anger and concern.

I shook my head. "He would have killed you!"

"Nicole..."

Before he could finish his statement, a clinking noise drew our attention to the ceiling. We had eliminated their blood slaves but had completely forgotten about the hostages chained above us. Not good.

Kara moved in front of me and extended her hand toward the ground. The wood planks rumbled and then cracked down the seam. Dirt began swirling around her as she hummed. A lance made entirely of the substance sliced through the air, slamming into the chest of the man standing next to Lisa, piercing his stomach. His blood slave was already dead, and he was in the process of pulling blood from one of the people hanging above us. Kara moved so fast; it was almost a blur. She rammed her fingers into the man's throat and yanked hard. Blood flew everywhere.

Maybe her ripping his throat out was overkill, especially since I was pretty sure he would have died from the wound on his stomach. However, I wasn't particularly troubled by the gruesome display. I was too caught up in what had just taken place. For a split second, I remained focused on her, mystified as to how she was able to summon and manipulate the dirt.

That second cost me.

Someone rammed into the side of me, knocking me onto the floor. I twisted, trying to keep my attacker off of me. Thomas wrapped his hand around my throat, the crushing pain immediate. Bastard. I should have known he was planning on sneaking up on someone when he moved into the shadows.

"Do you know what my brother would have done to you, Ms. Fontane?" he sneered in my ear.

*Thanks for the reminder, asshole.* I lifted up, wrapping my legs around his torso. My vision wavered as he increased the pressure on my neck. I squeezed with all the strength I had. Unfortunately, it wasn't enough.

My marks pulsed. Adrenaline flooded my body, and my skin heated. The sound of sizzling flesh rang in my ears.

Thomas quickly let go. He stared down at me, clutching his burnt hand. "What the fuck are you?" he said.

I didn't hesitate; I pushed up off the ground, and Thomas stepped back. His fear worked in my favor. I rammed my fist into his face, cutting into his eyes with my bare knuckles. Too late I remembered the brass knuckles that Rachel had given me. It didn't stop me. I continued pounding his face, ignoring the sudden flare of pain in my hand, as well as the sticky sensation of blood trickling down my arm from the cut across my bicep.

Suddenly, my arm went numb. Tiny rivulets of blood started pulling from the open wound. Shit. Thomas smiled. His mouth was saturated with blood from the many teeth I had broken in my tirade. His fingers danced; he continued to pull blood from my arm.

Between one blink and the next, Jonah appeared behind him, as if he had somehow managed to teleport himself there. He wrapped his arms around Thomas and lifted him into the air. The sound of Thomas's ribs being crushed didn't sound real. Thomas's hands stilled, and my arm went slack. Jonah dropped Thomas to the ground, grabbed his head, and wrenched it off his shoulders. I glanced up at Jonah; something slithered behind his eyes. Like another soul existed inside of him. What the fuck?

"Jonah?"

"Don't be afraid. I'm in control."

Before I could respond, a noise from outside had me whipping around and looking across the expanse of the barn. Two additional people entered with blood slaves chained to them.

A whisper of metal slicing across leather echoed, and I glanced over at the sound. Kara had unsheathed her knife. Devlin stepped in front of her, fire circling his hand. The new arrivals' steps faltered as a stream of fire shot out and engulfed the new blood slaves. The air filled with the smell of burnt flesh.

Lisa grabbed my hair and yanked me up. How the hell had she

gotten away from Alek? Across the room, he pushed up; deep cuts marred his body. Despite my saving him a minute ago, he still managed to get hurt. And although it was clear he could handle himself, it didn't stop me from worrying.

Lisa twisted my hair again, and my eyes watered. Seriously, we were going to fight like *girls*, now? Fuck that. I twisted, ignoring the pain and the feeling of my hair being torn out, and kicked Lisa in the stomach.

The bitch didn't even flinch. All my Krav Maga training was useless!

She grabbed my shirt. "We should have eliminated you—"

Suddenly, Alek wrapped his blood-covered arms around her waist, pulling her back toward him. I fell and landed on Thomas.

The black mass inside my head cracked. Fissures opened up, and the phoenix beat its wings against the darkness. My vision narrowed—the light began saturating my mind. My nostrils flooded with the smell of sand. When Thomas's headless body started twitching, I scrambled up and moved away from him. Almost immediately, he lay still. What the hell? Up until now, my magick had only responded when I was being attacked with magick. Thomas was dead, and Lisa no longer posed a threat. I inhaled. Sand. I looked around, trying to find the entity. He had to be here.

Devlin and the two men who entered the barn were fighting. Blood continued to stream down from the ceiling as Devlin threw blades made of water at them. It was almost as if the mages were immune to the injuries he was inflicting.

Lisa stood nearby, shaking uncontrollably while blood spilled from her eyes. Alek stood in front of her, fixed upon her dying body and blazing with a strange orange light.

Kara fought another man, her face and arms covered in gashes. She no longer used her magick. Instead, she was striking blow after blow with her fist and feet, beating him into submission. She'd said using her magick felt like a drug. Maybe her resorting to using her physical strength was her way of keeping herself in check. I admired her ability to call upon her training. Maybe one day, I'd be able to do the same.

Rachel danced around a woman whose skin was boiling in several spots. The eerie chant still emanated from her mouth. She didn't have a mark on her.

As for Jonah? He was holding another man's head between his hands, ready to wrench it off his shoulders. He had left a trail of heads all over the barn. Where the hell did he get that strength?

The scene was pure chaos, and before I could go and assist Devlin, I suddenly went airborne, flying through the barn doors and out into the night. I landed on my back in the middle of the muddy field almost fifty feet away. I lay still, trying to minimize the pain that was radiating down my back and legs.

When my breathing was under control, I tried to sit up, only to end up slipping and falling down again. The rain pelted down hard on my face. I was beginning to wonder if someone was in fact controlling it. It had never rained like this before. I looked over at the barn; nobody had come out after me. They must still be in there fighting. I needed to go back in.

I managed to get to my knees as I ground my teeth against the pain. Before I could climb to my feet, I saw the entity—or rather, the Old One. He knelt in front of me, his insubstantial form, outlined by the rain. I could see the barn behind him. But the image wasn't completely clear, more like a hazy out of focus picture. I shifted to the side, and he mirrored my movement. Almost like a pantomime.

Up until this point, he hadn't shown any indication he was trying to harm me. But that could have changed. Especially after what Ezra had told me.

"What do you want?" I asked. It was a stupid question. I mean, did I really expect him to answer? He wasn't even solid.

He disappeared. As I started to turn, his body pressed up against me from behind. The coppery scent of blood flooded my nostrils as he circled his arms around my waist. Phantom lips trailed down my neck. I couldn't breathe. Darkness crept around the sides of my vision. I started hyperventilating, trying to get air into my lungs. My skin felt hot and feverish, and the mark on my lip turned ice cold. Dormant. Images started running through my mind, too fast at first for me to see what they were.

Suddenly, they stopped. I was no longer in the field with the rain beating down on me. Instead, I was in the middle of the desert, staring at dozens of people lying in the sand, their blood draining into the center of a large hole. Heat sizzled on my skin. The taste of sand filled my mouth. It was almost as if I were really there.

A small child emerged from the blood as gold glyphs began forming on his body. A large gathering of people stood off to the side, chanting.

The image changed.

Suddenly, my body was being pulled as if through a web of time, as more images flashed.

The desert again, this time with even more people—thousands of them, their blood running down into the hole in the sand that was now occupied by a black and gold Ark. Thirteen naked figures, all covered in gold glyphs, stood in the middle; one of them was restrained. He was fighting.

"Free me," he whispered inside my head.

Abruptly, I was pulled from the desert and once again was pelted with rain.

"You are of the blood, and if you free me, I will save your friends," the Old One said. His voice, layered as if many voices were trying to merge into one, crawled across my skin. While it was similar to the way Ezra's had spoken when his power came out, there was a darker note underneath. Something cold and evil.

I tried to push away from him, but his grip was too tight.

Screams erupted from inside the barn, and I turned toward the sound. Dozens of people carrying weapons rushed inside. Gun shots rang out. Again, I tried to move forward, but he stopped me.

"Let me go. I need to save my friends!"

"They are dying," he said, "and only I can save them."

More gunshots and more screams, this time much louder. An image of my friends lying dead flashed into my mind. My nails bit into my palms as I tried to shove those images from my head. The black mass started cracking, spilling out light; the fleur-de-lis expanded—almost hiding the phoenix, and the mark on my lips remained cold.

"Yes," he whispered.

A long, jagged line appeared in the mass. I could feel the frustration rolling off of him. Could feel him digging inside of me with ghostly fingers. And I suddenly realized, the only thing keeping him from taking what he needed from me was the mark inside my head. The one placed there to block my magick. He was after my magick. I just didn't know why. And honestly, it didn't matter—I knew I had to fight him. To stop him.

Another image popped into my head of Ronald raping Marta while she was being held down by the guards.

More fissures opened up, and the phoenix beat its wings rapidly.

Another image of the kids in the basement chained to the floor.

I gritted my teeth, willing myself to fight. He was doing this. Showing me my worst fears. I buckled under the onslaught of false images. At least, I hoped they were false. Please let them be false.

I pounded my fist on the wet ground, trying to force him out of my head.

Another image of little Maria being raped.

"Stop!" The realization that I couldn't protect myself threatened to pull me under.

*Fight, Nicole.*

Another image of Alek being shredded to pieces by lances of blood.

And then the mass broke apart.

The Old One shoved me to the ground and flipped me over.

He ripped at my skin, feverishly tearing into me as if he could dig his way to the magick that lay inside of me. My body thrashed as I fought a wave of dizziness brought on by blood loss. He continued to dig. The pain was too much. My fingers dug into the mud.

Suddenly, the mark on my lips heated; the Old One abruptly stopped and flew off of me.

Booted feet came into view. I looked up through the rain. Ezra stood there; his skin glowing. His eyes blazed their dark brown, now looking more amber in color. He wore a strange gold cloth tied around his waist and held a short sword in his right hand.

"You can't have her, brother," Ezra said, his voice layered as if many people were speaking and not just one.

A naked woman stood beside Ezra, her body aglow from the marks etched across her skin. She looked down at me. Her dark green eyes were feral, as if no part of her had ever been human. She smiled, showing me perfect white teeth. An overwhelming feeling of familiarity came over me. The scent of jasmine wafted off of her, and then the memory rushed to the surface.

*"There is always a price," the woman said, her voice melodious like a lullaby. As she gazed down at me, her eyes started to glow, leaking a reddish light into my bedroom.*

I remembered now. She was the Old One who had bound my magick twenty-two years ago.

She knelt beside me. "Sleep, little one. Sleep," she whispered.

Darkness swirled around the edges of my vision, caving in like a tidal wave. The woman's voice continued to push at me, lulling me to sleep. Until all there was... was blackness.

Voices pulled me out of the fog. Pain shot through me like a lance. A spasm ran down my body, and I bucked under the onslaught. My torso felt tight as if something was restricting me, holding me down. I tried to lift my right arm, but it wouldn't move. A scream ripped through my throat.

"Hush, baby girl, it will be alright," my father said.

"Daddy," I mumbled, cracking open my eyes. The room was too bright. Figures stood around me, but I couldn't make out their faces. My body was cocooned in a pillow-like softness and my skin was icy, as if I'd been submerged in sub-zero temperatures for a long time. I could barely breathe past the agony ripping through my abdomen.

"She needs to remain sleeping," a familiar female voice said.

Images started to come back to me. A torrent of pictures running through my mind. Too fast. I needed them to slow down.

*Ezra standing next to me.*

*A naked woman covered in glyphs. Her name. The glyphs were her name.*

*"Sleep, little one. Sleep."*

*Me laying on the ground, cradled in Alek's arms.*

*The Old One ripping into my body.*

*Men rushing into the barn.*

"Make it stop!" I screamed.

"She will die if she stays awake!" the woman cried.

"Then put her back to sleep," my father yelled.

His voice made me flinch. I'd never heard such anger coming from him.

Someone lifted my arm. Their hands were warm, almost feverish against my too-cold skin. Something was being secured to my wrist. The metal as it lay against me was solid, unforgiving.

"Do not let her take this off," my mother said, her voice filled with sorrow and agony.

I reached out and touched her arm, ignoring the painful burn of her skin.

"I am here, *ma fille.*"

"I will make sure she keeps it on," Kara said. Her voice sounded full of pain. Was she crying?

"Kara," I whispered.

"I'm here, Nicole. I promise I won't leave your side. Just rest." Her voice was soft, cradling me in a warm embrace. She linked her fingers with mine.

I sighed. The people I loved the most were here.

The scent of jasmine surrounded me. I wanted to tell them no —don't put me back to sleep. But the pain had finally robbed me of my voice. The Old One moved in close, the brightness of her skin threatening to blind me. I closed my eyes.

"For now, you sleep."

Darkness enveloped me once again.

"Are you awake?" a male voice said.

My eyes fluttered open. I turned my head toward the speaker. Alek sat in a chair beside the unfamiliar bed I was laying on. I blinked a few times, bringing the rest of the room into focus. No, not unfamiliar. We were in his room at Devlin's house. An IV pole stood near the bed. I glanced down at my hand. My bracelet was back on, the metal cool against my skin. The charm that was a rendition of the mark inside my head stood out, as if the metal had been polished recently.

"What..." I couldn't finish. My throat was too raw from not being used. How long had I been laying here?

He picked up a glass of water and shifted so he could help me up. "Take small sips," he said as he tilted the glass against my lips.

After taking a few agonizing swallows—the water stung my throat—he laid me back down on the pillow. I stared at him. His eyes were swollen and bruised, and his beard had grown out. A white bandage was wound around his arm, and a long scar ran along the side of his neck. He regarded me out of weary eyes.

"What happened?" I asked, my voice barely audible.

"When you left the barn, a few more people showed up. It was close. Everyone was hurt pretty bad. They had started using the captives' blood. Kara and Rachel had to poison most of them." He shook his head. "We only managed to save ten out of the fifty they had hanging."

A tear slid down the side of my face. "Marta?"

"Your friend is fine." Alek smoothed back my hair. "Nicole..." He shook his head as if he was trying to dislodge something painful. His eyes filled with tears. "You should be dead. No one..." He ran his hand through his hair. "Your entire chest cavity was open. I almost lost it when I found you lying there."

"How long?" I reached out for the water. After taking a few more sips, I continued. "How long have I been asleep?"

"Five days." He sighed heavily. "Can you move?"

I tried to lift my arm, but it wouldn't budge. "No," I said.

He laid down beside me and pulled me into his arms. "You need more rest. We will talk later."

I mumbled my reply, my eyes already growing heavy. Alek started humming, the same tune he'd used on me before when I couldn't sleep. I tried to fight it, but I couldn't focus. My mind started to drift. It didn't take long for me to fall asleep. When I did, I noticed the mark inside my head was no longer surrounded by darkness.

# EPILOGUE

A week later, I pulled into my apartment complex and parked in my usual spot.

"Did they assign you this space?" Alek asked as he pushed open the door, moving slower than he usually did.

"It would seem like it." I made my way around to him.

He leaned against the car, watching me as I approached. "You're moving better. But..."

I stopped in front of him. "But what?"

"You look scared."

The block on my magick had been removed. I'd shared with the others my theory that someone was working behind the scenes, moving pieces into place for something big. Despite their skepticism, I just couldn't shake the feeling. And eventually, they all agreed that recent events would suggest something bigger was definitely going on. However, they still didn't buy into my mastermind theory.

We did decide, however, that if it was true, I needed to learn more about my form of magick. Unfortunately, that training would involve Alek's family. They would need to delve into my mind. Even though the darkness surrounding my mark was gone, the mark was still there. And it would take a great deal of power to get around it. Sadly, that meant I had to work with Petronela Vaduva. I wasn't looking forward to that. It had taken Alek over a week to convince her to see me.

"I am scared," I said eventually. "Of Petronela Vaduva."

During his negotiations with her, she had told him about my short employment at the carnival and went over every single detail of my failure. Thankfully, he didn't hold that against me. Nor did he tell Boss Man.

He pulled me to him. He was doing that a lot lately and hadn't left my side since I woke up. He ran a finger down the side of my face. Now, that was new.

"I'll be there with you," he said in an extremely husky voice. "So don't worry."

I stepped back. "Alek. We can't do this."

He moved forward, resting his cheek against mine. I inhaled his scent. His closeness sent heat throughout my body, settling low in my stomach.

"Do what?" He brushed a kiss across my cheek.

I sighed deeply. My hormones were screaming at me. *Yeah, why not, Nicole?*

I reluctantly moved back. "Because..." *Keep it together, Nicole.* "I will be working with you, and I don't want it to get awkward." It was already awkward. I wanted Alek. Bad.

His sexy lips slowly parted, spreading into a crooked smile. "We will do it your way for a while." He pushed off the car. "Then we'll try it my way forever."

He left me standing there with my mouth wide open. He had just issued a challenge. I didn't particularly like challenges.

When we entered the building, I glanced over at Wade's door. The authorities believed his death might have been connected to the tenant before me, and I wasn't going to correct them. It was better that way.

The usual smells of food wafted from under Mr. Wan's door. He'd been talking about selling the building in the last couple of days, said the building was bad luck. I couldn't argue with that, especially based on its history.

We entered my apartment. I set my bag on the couch while Alek went into the kitchen.

A few days ago, I started unpacking my boxes. Kara was right; it was all junk. And most of it ended up in the dumpster. I kept my first ashtray, though. I doubted I would be able to get rid of it. At least, not yet.

I went into the bedroom to get a few changes of clothes. Kara and I were staying with Marta and the kids. It had been over two weeks since we rescued them, and Marta was still not herself. And the kids were constantly battling nightmares. It had gotten so bad that Kara had to give them herbs to help them sleep.

I still hadn't talked with my parents. My father had saved my life; he and my mother had sat by my bed, waiting for me to heal. Yet, they had lied to me about my magick. As well as their part in blocking it. When I knew what to say and how to say it, I'd call them.

Devlin had found a reference to The Oren Group buried in a stack of documents he'd gone through. According to Kara, it was the same group her grandmother worked for. After putting two and two together, we figured out it was the same group Andrew had been working for as well. They were a fanatical group of assassins who were rumored to be the reason The Council of Principles had been destroyed. If that was true, we had many more enemies to deal with besides the Old Ones, the five remaining families involved in blood magick, and, of course, Ronald.

He still hadn't been found, but he'd sent me another bottle of liquor along with a note saying he would see me soon. I was eagerly awaiting that reunion. I had a new set of brass knuckles to break in.

"Do you want some water?" Alek called out.

"No, I'll just get my things so we can leave."

After filling a bag with clothes, I went out into the living room and rummaged through my box of notebooks. I'd started journaling again, trying to keep my thoughts as well as the discoveries I made in order. When I pulled out an empty notebook, the thick, unopened letter Steve had written me fell to the floor.

"What's that?" Alek asked.

I glanced up at him. "A letter an old friend wrote me twelve years ago."

All these years later, I still hadn't read it. I was too afraid to read his last words to me; too afraid to confirm what I'd already known: that Steve had been in love with me, and that some small part of me had loved him just the same. I'd been running for most of my life from memories and other situations that made me uncomfortable. However, if I was going to set out on this path of discovery, I needed to deal with the past.

So, I opened the letter and read it.

Nicole,

I really didn't want to go to this party, but since you asked so damn nicely, I will. I wanted to tell you... shit. I wanted to say this in person, but I didn't think you would listen. Please don't make fun of me after you read this.

I love you. I know you said we should only be friends, but I don't agree. I'm hoping that you will change your mind and give us a chance.

And since you don't like flowers and any of that other sappy shit, I hope the letter will be enough.

Luisah gave me the enclosed pages the other day. She said you would need them one day soon and that I should stick close to you. Guess what? It's not a poem.

-Steve

I set the letter aside and stared down at the documents he had enclosed. Five thick sheets of paper, worn and yellow. They resembled parchment.

I read the title twice, trying to digest what I actually held in my hands. *The Land Guarded by People of Colour.*

It wasn't a poem. That was the first thing that jumped into my mind. The pages looked as if they had been torn from a book. And the words—written in cursive—appeared raised, as if the author used heavy ink. I sniffed the pages. Cherries. And some sort of herbal scent I couldn't place. They were from the blood book.

"Is that what I think it is?" Alek asked, reading over my shoulder.

I nodded, unable to speak as I read through the material in front of me. It explained in great detail not only how the island was created, but why. They had enlisted the help of what they referred to as 'The Keepers of Earth' and performed a ritual infusing these chosen people with immortality. Before leaving, they made them swear to never allow anyone on the island.

They obviously didn't listen.

There were diagrams of all the Old Ones in much greater detail than the drawings in the book Luisah had shown me. By each of their renderings were their original names, and also what they were known as when they had been altered by the blood spells. The one who had marked my wrist was known as "The Trickster."

I continued down the document, absorbing all the information, and stopped suddenly at a set of familiar patterns and sucked in an audible breath. The symbols looked like musical notes.

A deep shiver ran through my body as I stared at the symbols. Ezra's warning popped in my head.

*Kill or protect.*

There was no way anyone could deny my theory now.

The marks on Jordin Cisco's back were not his harmony as he claimed.

They were his name.

Continue reading for a sneak peek of Zealot
Book two
Blood & Sacrifice Chronicles

Available: May 14, 2025
Pre-order your copy now!

A small package leaned against the wall just outside my apartment door. The sight of it had an icy chill running down my spine, stopping me dead in my tracks. Dirt and grime coated the brown wrapping paper along with several postage stamps. Cambodia this time. The fucking bastard didn't stay in one place too long. A tidal wave of anger flooded my body when I pictured the contents I knew were inside.

Pictures of his latest victim.

It was the third package I'd received from Doc—Ronald Stewart—in the past month.

I dropped my overnight bag on the floor and knelt beside it. My trembling hand hovered over the tainted thing, as if I could somehow destroy it with my magick.

The package must have arrived either Friday or Saturday. I hadn't been home since Thursday. Kara and I were taking turns staying with Marta and the kids. They were still suffering from the torture they had been subjected to.

Kara knelt beside me and picked up the parcel. I wanted to stop her, keep her from touching the putrid sickness inside, but I also understood that we'd eventually have to give it to Devlin. Silly as it sounded, to me, picking it up was a reminder that I'd failed. That if I had only figured out sooner what the Stewart family was up to, none of this would have happened.

The thought remained on a constant loop inside my head.

The first package from Doc arrived two weeks after we killed his sister and brother; a battle that took place on his family's land, hidden in the small marshland between Sandpoint and Alice. Doc, after murdering his nurse Emilia, had left a note for me, along with directions to the barn-like structure. There, his family was holding close to fifty people, including Marta, for their Harvest ritual. We'd won that fight. And I'd barely escaped with my life.

Like his first letter to me, he'd written in graphic detail about the torture he'd inflicted on Felicity Markum. Ronald had carved her up and eaten pieces of her. He'd even included photographs of his work. Unfortunately, he never signed the letter. It would have been proof of what he was doing—a confession written in his own hand. But he was too smart for that.

Mixed in with the gruesome photographs was a picture of him in Thailand, arms around a group of kids, while wearing a doctor's uniform. And while blending in with other physicians and treating the locals, he killed without the constraints his family had put on him. We'd scoured online news outlets in the locations he'd sent me boxes from: Thailand, Philippines, and Malaysia, and found articles on his victims. Local women who bore a passing resemblance to me. I still get nauseous thinking about those photographs and the fact that he, in his mind, was obviously killing me over and over again.

It was only when he left the area that he'd send me mementos with a bottle of Asbach Uralt—his favorite brandy—and photographs of his latest victim. Devlin sent copies of the first letter and set of pictures to the embassy in Thailand. Sadly, we never got a response.

After some debate, we'd sent the pictures and the note to the Markum family. I wanted to shield them from the horror, but Devlin argued since they'd hired him to find out about their daughter, he was obligated to share the information with them, no matter how much we wanted to protect them from the reminder of their daughter's death the pictures would surely invoke. And in the end, I understood why they needed to know, and it wasn't my decision to make.

A few days later, Devlin had received a letter—a check with an obscene amount of money along with a signed contract from the Markums. Regardless of their daughter not dying from the ritual, they hired him to investigate the other blood magick users on Tulare Island. The letter contained carefully worded instructions on what to do when we found them. While not direct, we all understood they wanted us to kill them all.

Despite their wishes, we simply couldn't do that. At least that's what Devlin said. I was firmly in the Markums' camp. We could, he said, investigate the five remaining families to determine if they were practicing blood magick. And if they were, we'd stop them. It seemed simple enough. Yet, I had a feeling it wouldn't be.

I stood up. My hand shook as I tried to ram my key into the lock—scratching at the polished brass. Pulling in a deep breath, I closed my eyes and pushed down the pain. Pushed down the images that were inside that dirty package. Pushed down the guilt and finally, hand steady, unlocked my door. Picking up my bag from the floor, I rushed inside and came to an abrupt stop in the middle of my living room.

A sudden kaleidoscope of memories cascaded through me, keeping me rooted in place. My bag thumped to the floor as I let the onslaught of them overtake me. The numerous instances clues had presented themselves—practically smacking me in the face. My chest heaved and blood rushed through my veins while black spots blocked my vision. I gripped my shirt, burying my knuckles between my breasts.

It all started with me walking into Tribec Insurance and smelling blood. Instead of running out of the building, I stayed.

When I spotted the magick wards and symbols peppered throughout, sure, I questioned it, but still, I didn't leave.

Then, when I was presented with the option to leave, I'd stayed.

And with Doc, I'd let hormones and anger at my having to

take a job I would hate fuel my decision making. Turning a blind eye when I sensed, deep down, something was off about him.

I couldn't change the past, no matter how much I wished I could. But accepting what had happened felt wrong too. Like giving up, somehow. Each time I was faced with it, my body, mind, and soul wanted to shut down. To block out the world and just forget. That was how I usually handled things. But lately, it hadn't been working. Alek advised me to use cleansing breaths and mantras to help.

Fuck mantras. I wanted blood.

But sadly, until we stopped Doc and all the other blood magick users on this damn island, I would probably keep having these episodes.

I could do one thing to help myself, though: I could stop referring to that sadistic monster by the pet name I'd given him.

I threw my keys on my brand-new coffee table. They skidded across the glass, most likely leaving little dips and grooves—permanently damaging the surface—and came to rest near the stack of self-help magazines I'd started accumulating. I had hoped the articles would help me deal with the panic attacks. But sadly, they, along with the book on surviving abuse I'd purchased, weren't working.

Figuring if I couldn't get my mind right, I could at least give my apartment a makeover. I'd bought a few items of furniture with the money Devlin gave me. Along with the coffee table, I found a small dinette set in pretty good condition at a yard sale. Eventually, I'd get some towels and a few pictures for the walls.

The only drawback of me making my apartment into a home was that I still pictured my previous neighbor, Wade, dead on the floor in the corner of my living room. And sadly, no amount of gussying up would ever wipe that gruesome apparition from my mind.

Kara walked up behind me. I could feel her eyes boring into my back and feel the weight of her concern hanging in the air.

"Why did you pick it up?" I asked, not turning around.

"You know why," she answered, her tone cautious.

I dug my fingernails into the palms of my hands.

"Devlin said we need to keep tracking him," she continued, her voice softening. "And if he's crazy enough to send us information on where he is, we shouldn't just throw it away."

I whipped around and snatched the package from her. "He sends these sick little mementos *after* he's left the area. How can that information help?" I was arguing with the wrong person. But my anger had to go somewhere. And sadly, Kara was the only person in the room. I threw the package on the ground; the *thump* was like nails on a chalkboard.

My damn fault. All of it.

She didn't move. Just stood there with love and patience in her eyes. She, like everyone else, had become used to my sudden outbursts. I hated that. I'd promised myself I would stop, but today, it really couldn't be helped.

I didn't understand why Devlin wanted to start with the church. It made more sense for us to focus on the Sinclair family since they were the ones who had hurt Marta's kids. But he pointed out the protection around them right now would pose a risk to us, so we'd begin with the Young family.

When I continued to argue with him, he must have picked up on my hesitancy and figured out there was more to my not wanting to deal with the Young family than what I was saying. He stopped insisting and had given me the opportunity to explain my reluctance. But true to form, I had declined to go into detail, leaving me with no way out of the situation.

Kara continued to stare at me as I cycled through my anger.

*Pull it together, Nicole.*

It was the love in her eyes that chipped away at my resolve.

Besides, our friendship was the one thing that kept me sane. I couldn't afford to lose her. Not now. Not ever. And more importantly, she didn't deserve my rage.

"Sorry," I said, reaching for her.

She smiled and wrapped her arm around me, pulling me close. "You know I will always have your back, Nicole."

"I know," I mumbled. "I just…"

She stepped back and looked at me. "We all, just… The key is to keep it together. Let the fury build." Her mouth stretched into a wicked grin. "And when the time is right, we strike. Letting all that rage feed our magick."

"And bathe in the blood of our enemies?" The last of my anger slowly seeped out of my pores. I could do this.

She laughed, her body also relaxing as she studied me. "That's right. We will bathe in their blood and let their screams be our soundtrack."

"Have I told you lately that I'm a little frightened of you?"

Her face took on a pensive look while she tapped her finger on the side of her cheek. "No. But I'm thinking I should get that printed on a t-shirt." She gestured across the spans of her chest. "Fear me."

I shook my head. "I've corrupted you."

She picked up the package off the ground. "Well, maybe I needed a little corrupting." She pointed toward my bedroom. "Now, why don't you go find something proper and decent to wear to church."

"Shit," I said and rushed out of the room. Despite not wanting to go, I still loathed the idea of being late. Hated having to rush in at the last minute. It made me feel as if I were missing something. Like in my haste to beat the clock, I'd left out a crucial task or step when getting ready. That's why I always left early. It gave me time to not only think, but also circle back if I had, in fact, forgotten something.

I opened my closet door and stared at the mounds of clothing crammed into the small space. I didn't have church clothes, at least not according to society's standards. But then again, I never much cared for the boxes the illusive "they" put people in in the first place. So, fuck them.

And it was that very attitude that had me staring at the many clothes in my closet, contemplating wearing a short red dress to church.

"He's in Cambodia," Kara said as she walked into the room. "And yes, there are pictures."

*Why the hell had she opened the package?*

"That's inconvenient," I said as I stared at a skintight green dress. I doubted I could blend in showing off my cleavage, and if I had to bend over for any reason, I was sure to cause an uproar. Might even get a few people offering to pray for me. I groaned and shoved it back in the closet. It landed on the floor with the rest of my clean clothes. I really needed to do something about my closet.

"The pictures?"

I glanced over at her. "No, Kara, the fact that he's in Cambodia. How the hell am I supposed to kill the sick bastard if he's not here?"

She set the pictures on my bed and joined me at the closet door. "Remember what Devlin said," she slanted her eyes toward me, "he'll return eventually."

Devlin believed Doc was obsessed with me. Even after he'd gotten away, he continued contacting me. Taunting me. And that level of fixation would not only make him careless but also force him to return to Tulare. So, he wanted us to keep the sick mementos Doc sent. That way we could keep an eye on his progression into madness. It would be the only signal we had when he inevitably returned to Tulare Island.

When I objected, he pointed out that I got away from him once and would do so again. This time, with the team backing me. Yes, it's true I did survive. Even if I hadn't known my life was in danger. But it didn't mean I liked the idea of waiting around patiently for him to come and finally finish the job.

The bastard had told me in one of his letters he wanted to kill me—that his desire to do so was so overpowering that he had to fight hard against it. So, instead of raping and killing me, he had turned me into a useful pawn in his scheme to get away from his family and free himself from the shackles they'd imposed. He'd wanted free rein to continue with his sick proclivities, and I was the useful idiot who helped him get away.

I shook my head. "Eventually? How many women will he kill between now and then?" My stomach flipped and bile rose, burning my throat. A wave of dizziness came over me. I stumbled toward the bed, shoved the pictures out of the way, and sat down. "I can't do this."

Kara turned and extended the dress to me. "This will work."

"Did you hear me?" I took the pale-yellow summer dress from her. "I can't do this."

"I heard you. And"—she smiled sarcastically—"I'm ignoring you."

"Fine. If I fuck up, I will blame you."

"That's the spirit," she said, and went over to my jewelry box. "Do you have earrings to match?"

Honestly, I couldn't recall when I'd bought the dress. So, there was no way I'd remember having earrings to match. While Kara rummaged inside my jewelry box, I slipped out of my clothes, pulled on the dress, and groaned. The damn thing was too tight.

Kara handed me a pair of gold hoops. I put them on and surveyed myself in the mirror. My hair stuck out all over the place, looking as if I'd stuck my finger in a light socket. Red splotches covered my cheeks, forehead, and chin. And the bags under my eyes made me look as if I'd been awake for the past thirty days. I could cover it all with make-up, but I refused to put any on in this heat. And doing my hair would take too much time. So, tight yellow dress and wild-woman-do, it was.

Kara took the box back into the living room and put it on the coffee table while I grabbed my purse. Before we left out, I debated briefly on whether or not we should take the damn thing with us. I didn't want it in my house. But I also didn't want to touch it again, either.

So, I left it where it was.

Wade's apartment sat next to mine near the entrance. As we

made our way to the front door, Kara stopped and stared at the for-rent sign affixed to the frame.

Mr. Wan still hadn't been able to find a renter, especially since he was required to disclose Wade had been found dead inside the apartment. We had moved him to his own place after our confrontation with the men sent to kill me by Andrew Snow, a former trainer at Tribec Insurance.

The other tenants had speculated about Wade's death for weeks. At first, they believed his murder had something to do with the previous tenant who used to live in my apartment. After-all, the man had started growing marijuana in the garden outside. Eventually, they started giving me accusing glances as if I was somehow responsible. It was my fault. I should have shut Wade down long before that night. I'd told him I wasn't interested, but obviously not in a way he understood. If I had, it would have stopped him from coming over every time he believed I was home.

"How much is the rent here?" Kara asked.

"Don't tell me you're giving up your house? I thought you said your grandmother left."

"No." She continued walking. "Paul is looking for a new place."

I stood there for a minute, watching her. She better not suggest Paul move next door to me.

"Kara?"

She turned. "Come on, Nicole. We need to get going."

I caught up to her. "If this is some weird attempt on your part to have Paul keep an eye on me, I will be pissed."

"You have got to stop being so paranoid." She pushed open the front door. "Now, come on. Let's go join a cult."

"You actually managed to put those two things together," I said, following behind her. "Paranoid and a cult." I turned away before she could see the fear in my eyes.

She unlocked the doors, and we climbed inside the stifling car. We rolled down all the windows, and Kara turned on the air-conditioning full blast. Humidity made it easier to cool off the car. But nowadays, despite the moisture in the air, it seemed to be taking longer for the air-conditioning to work. The lack of rain puzzled a lot of people on Tulare Island—especially the weatherman, who had grown increasingly agitated every time his prediction for rain wasn't fulfilled.

Once the car had cooled down, Kara faced me. "You don't have a problem with Paul moving in, do you?" she asked, looking as if she were bracing for the worst.

I shrugged. I'd gotten over my petty jealousy of Paul a few weeks ago. It was misplaced and stupid. Paul was a decent guy. Strange? Illusive? Yes. But also nice, and fun to go drinking with. The man could not hold his liquor.

"I hope you told him about what happened," I said. "I'd hate to have it slip out when he comes over for a night of drinking."

Kara smiled then reversed out of the parking spot. "See, you've already found the bright side." She slanted her eyes toward me. "I thought you gave up drinking."

"I'll probably be drinking again real soon. And it'll be nice to have someone to drink with."

Kara frowned and pulled out onto the street. She wouldn't say anything about me going back on my word. It was a song and dance we were used to, only speaking up when things got too bad. She gave me the space to decide if I wanted to talk to her when something was bothering me. My usual way of dealing with these uncomfortable situations was to make some sarcastic remark. Opening up and expressing my feelings just wasn't me.

My apartment was a few blocks south from our old stomping ground, Jordin Cisco's. I should have told her to take the long way around to avoid the place, but it was too late now.

Kara slowed as we came to the gray brick building with blacked-over windows and a single reddish steel door. The neon sign wasn't lit. The bushes were still thriving. Which meant someone was still pissing and pouring beer on them. In the daylight, the once-familiar spot had taken on a more sinister caste.

As if the light, finally showed me what had remained hidden for so long.

I'd learned weeks ago that Jordin Cisco was an Old One—a god created by blood magick a few thousand years ago. And I had taken to him like a moth to flame. He had been my lover. The one constant in my life that I could depend on never changing. Sure, he slept with many other women, but I never had an issue with it. I enjoyed his company when I could.

"I still think you should confront him," Kara said, stopping at the intersection.

Ezra, another Old One, had warned me about the pact he and his siblings had made regarding people with my strange type of magick, a power that allowed me to keep a dead person's soul tethered to their body. I'd learned about this rare ability during a battle with the employees at the Sinclairs' at-risk youth facility. During the attack, a man had died. And my hand on his body had kept him somewhat alive—his soul resting inside his long-dead flesh.

He'd told me they would either kill or protect me.

Ezra had chosen to protect me, marking me with an elaborately drawn brand that I was still trying to decipher. Unlike the shen ring on my wrist, his brand was engraved into my bottom lip and only showed when I was in danger. Yet, Jordin had only slept with me. He had to have known about my magick, which made me wonder why he decided not to brand me for protection as well? And since he hadn't, that left him with only one option.

To kill me.

Jordin was the true embodiment of Dionysus. The original basis for the mythical god of wine and madness. Often driving women insane. Turning them into Maenads. The raving ones. Women who were given to divine possession and frenzied, ravenous like behavior.

When I learned this, I thought of the women who had become fixtures at the bar, sitting on bar stools staring raptly at him, hoping to gain his attention.

I must have sensed the danger inside of him like a coiled snake ready to strike. His attentiveness was intoxicating and always left me in a drunken state. Could that have been the reason I'd been so drawn to him? Yes, I loved sex. And yes, Jordin was extremely good at it. I'd slept with many men but with Jordin, it had been different. My nights with him had always left me high, feeling as if my skin were on fire.

I never questioned it, though. Like I said, I enjoyed the ride.

But now, I worry what my time with him could have done to me, if seeing him again would have the same effect. Would I be able to refuse him? Or would I let him pull me back into his powerful embrace?

I turned away from the bar and Kara continued driving. I pushed the thoughts of him down deep, burying them in the vast basement of my painful past. I couldn't dwell on the *many* opportunities Jordin had to slaughter me while I'd lain naked and vulnerable in his bed. The many ways in which he could have killed me was too much to think about. And I already had the images of Ronald's victims in my head. I didn't need anything else to keep me up at night.

W e drove in silence—cutting across the island using the back roads instead of the main highway. I appreciated the detour; it gave me time to get my thoughts in order and review the plan the team had gone over this week.

A few years ago, most people on Tulare started referring to The Better Day Church as a cult. Including myself. Of course, this certainty was never anything anyone could prove. It was just rumors and conjecture based on the odd beliefs of its parishioners.

The lack of concrete details was why Devlin outlined that our objective today would be to determine if the church was in fact a cult, and if so, secure an invitation to join. If not, we would have to keep digging and find another way to verify if the Young family was using blood magick. We all doubted their true purpose would be revealed to those who attend church services occasionally—so we'd also have to show an interest in all their activities.

I was not looking forward to purchasing more useless clothes like I did when I got the job at Tribec Insurance. And I drew the line at elaborate hats and white gloves. There was no way in hell I would ever wear some extravagant hat. Especially in this heat.

I turned to Kara. "I can understand why Jonah is part of this recon mission. He is a faith mage." I paused. Maybe asking why she chose to come today would sound unappreciative. Fuck it. She knew me. "Why did you decide to join us today?" I sounded like a damn self-help guru. *Why did you decide to join us today? Seriously?*

She laughed. "Did you just say, 'recon mission'?"

"Devlin's words. Not mine," I said, smiling. "I think he's wearing off on me." *Was she stalling?*

Kara blew out a noisy breath and shrugged. "You..." She trailed off, then glanced at me. "I knew you were struggling. I saw it in the way you kept staring off into space, wringing your hands like you needed something to take the edge off. I'm surprised you didn't buy any cigars." I let out a bitter laugh. I had been entertaining the idea of buying a pack for a while. "And," Kara continued, "I wanted to be there in case you needed me."

I rubbed my temple and looked out the window. "Yeah, this is going to be hard." I stopped short of telling her why. No one knew about my past dealings with a religious cult and now was not the time to go into it. I needed to stay focused on the job at hand or I'd breakdown into a useless puddle of emotions. "Thanks. I appreciate it."

"And Nicole," she said, drawing my attention to her. "Try not to be cynical." She smiled. "Make it a mantra: *I will not by cynical.*"

"What about questions? Can I ask those?"

She laughed. "Of course. It would show interest. Just"—she gave me a look, her eyes dancing with humor—"try not to add any cynicism to them."

Her suggestion was eerily like the advice she had given me when I was applying for a job at Tribec Insurance. Kara knew I had a hard time not peppering people with questions. Truthfully, I'd been this way since I was a child. It used to drive my mother crazy. But the cynicism came later, when life had dealt me a shitty hand, and the only way I could cope with it was by using an unhealthy amount of sarcasm at the wrong time. I was working on it. Well, at least trying to work on it. But until I did manage to deal with the lemons I refused to make into lemonade, I had Kara to keep me grounded.

Kara crossed the border from Pleasanton into Alice, and I shifted my focus.

My limited abilities with magick disturbed me. It was a constant reminder of my parents and Luisah's betrayal of not teaching me the things I needed to know about my own abilities. Ones that had been locked away behind a black mass of energy that had been destroyed weeks ago. Now, my body had this thrum of power running through it—waiting to be used. Only, I had no idea how to use it. Sure, I understood all the rituals and even knew about the roots and herbs used in earth magick, but I didn't know how to wield my power to make a spell work.

When the team started teaching me, *the right way*, about magick, they gave me a strange analogy. They said to look at my magick like I had a green thumb. While two people could use the exact same methods to care for plants, it was always the person with a green thumb who managed to keep the plants alive and thriving—able to connect on a cellular level and assess the plant's needs. While the other person, time and time again, ended up with dead vegetation.

Magick was in the blood. In our very DNA. And surprisingly, everyone had it to some degree. However, like the green thumb analogy, only a few could access and wield its power.

Devlin considered those who couldn't use magick as having none. During his entire career in law enforcement, he had refused to use his own magick against those who didn't have any active magick of their own.

I had a strong suspicion this rigid belief would change eventually.

Given this, I decided to start off small by working on viewing the human aura or soul as some referred to it. It was where a person's magick resided. My first encounter with this was when we fought the people at the Sinclair at-risk youth facility. Alek had been bathed in a rich orange that looked like the sunset, Rachel a dark green, and Devlin a vibrant, lush blue. Using Jonah as a test subject, I was able to see his aura consisted of a white-goldish color tinged in black. My own had a green hue, representing earth, but it also had striations of red running through it. Which could possibly explain the anomaly in my magick. Kara, being an earth practitioner, had a dark green aura. But she also had blue ridges cutting into the green. The more vibrant the color, the stronger the magick. Only earth and mind practitioners had the ability to see the magick in others.

But unlike other earth practitioners, I had an additional power that they had never seen or heard of before.

I could keep a dead person's soul tethered to their body. Recently, I've practiced both seeing and feeling the small ball of energy pulsing in the center of an individual's aura. Alek had graciously volunteered for this experiment. When I touched his soul, it felt like a cold orb of energy, crackling in my palm. Alek said the sensation made his fight or flight response kick in, giving him a level of fear, he never thought he would feel.

It was going to take more practice, and understanding, before I could use my strange ability in battle. And while I would have loved to continue working on it, learning about the other principles was also important. Especially given what we were setting out to do. So last week, I switched gears.

According to Jonah, faith magick had never really been about religion. Its power was meant to create. But some thousands of years ago, after creating the first god using faith magick, the practitioners also formed religion. Using mankind's spirituality against them to garner control over the people. Today, it was the most common principle used across the world, which was why it was too easy for people to become fanatical in their beliefs and try and impose them on others—creating Zealots.

And in the wrong hands, faith magick could be the deadliest.

Given my own experience with religion, I had to agree.

* * *

Twenty minutes later, a little after eleven, we pulled into the packed parking lot of The Better Day Church, located in Alice, two miles North of Tribec Insurance. The service started at eleven thirty, so we had made it on time.

Kara circled the lot as I took in the garish structure: a towering white and gold cathedral with Roman columns and white marble statues of lions on either side of the walkway leading to the building.

One Sunday, when I was younger, my mother and I had ridden by the place on our way to Sandpoint. It was a year before David and Karen Young had been killed. A massive white tent had been erected in the parking lot. Scores of people roamed about, holding plates of food. My mother had called it a revival and said most churches held them. I had been curious and asked if we could go. She gave me a look I will never forget; one so laced with fear that I'd turned away and just stared at that tent as we continued to drive by.

Looking at the giant cathedral now, I wondered about that look. Did she know something about the family? Or was it just the aversion she and my father had to organized religion?

The original church had been modest—a small white and black building with a large lot. Once Gavina and Boyd took over the church after her parents' death, they'd turned it into a spectacle.

Kara pulled into a spot in the last aisle close to the exit and shut off the engine and, sadly, the air too. I sat there, staring, trying to build up the nerve to get out of the car.

"Are you ready?" Kara asked.

"Yeah, I just need a minute," I said, not looking at her.

She didn't push. I appreciated that. Instead, she turned the car back on and the air on full blast as I continued to gaze out at all the people making their way toward the large building.

The last time I'd been in church was four months after my best friend Steve's death. Two weeks after my boyfriend Frank had been killed. After pumping ten bullets into Frank's chest, his uncle had turned the gun on me while I lay there in a drugged-out state, unable to muster up enough willpower or concern to save myself. If not for him using all the bullets on Frank, I would have died that day.

I spent the next few weeks in so much pain, it felt as if my very soul was clawing away at me—hollowing me out until there was nothing left. My skin burned. My heart ached. And I just wanted everything and everyone to go the fuck away.

My parents tried. Especially my mother. But in the end, I climbed out of my window and ran away to stay in New Orleans with a woman who I had believed was my Aunt Delilah.

Her way of helping involved her church, a congregation whose roots came from twisted rituals and lust and power and subjugation. Pastor Jeremiah ran this small cult-like church with a zeal born from madness. Every once in a while, I still saw his dark, evil eyes staring down at me—willing me to believe in him.

Their place of worship was hidden in a deep, shadowy part of the bayou. Away from prying eyes and those who would question their beliefs. They had tried to convince me I only needed to have my soul cleansed to free myself of my pain.

Even now, all these years later, I can feel the rough, pitted texture of the concrete slab they had laid me on. Still feel the cold biting into my naked skin as the pastor stood over me praying while my aunt stood by watching. When the rest of the men surged forward and the pastor's wife handed him a knife, I yanked free of my loosely tied bindings, jumped off that slab, and ran.

When I'd returned home the next day, I didn't tell my father what happened. But somehow, he must have known. He told me Delilah was not really my aunt, but a family friend, one who they had long stopped talking to when they learned the depths of her beliefs. Only, no one ever told me this before. But then, why would they? We had left New Orleans and settled on Tulare Island when I was young. And while my father's brothers kept in contact, we never stepped foot in our old neighborhood again.

After all, my mother had buried the man who raped me when

I was six behind our house. To them, the land would forever be poisoned.

On a sigh, I pushed open the car door and stepped out into the sweltering heat.

Kara turned off the engine and got out of the car to join me. "Well, I hope we'll be able to find seats," she said as we started toward the church—mixing in with the other people making their way across the lot.

"The size of the building says we will. Besides—" The humidity made me gasp. *Please let them have air-conditioning.* "Jonah's probably already here. And he would have saved us one."

Kara made a non-committal noise that sounded suspiciously like a moan and continued walking.

The closer we got, the more my stomach turned. I had sworn to never set foot in another church again. But here I was, swarming to Enlightenment like the rest of these people.

Halfway to the building, my steps faltered. A man, leaning against a white Cadillac with dark tinted windows, caught my attention. Bald head, tanned skin that suggested he might be mixed with something, with a long, jagged scar tracing from his ear to the middle of his neck. He wore a pair of dark jeans and a tight gray shirt, molded to his massive physique. Even though his shaded gaze remained fixed on the church, I got the impression he was watching us. A chill ran down my spine and I reached out and stopped Kara.

She turned and gave me a questioning look. I pointed to the man. "Does he look..." I paused, unsure of what I wanted to say. All I knew was that his presence felt wrong.

"What?" she asked, glancing between me and him. "Do you know him?"

I shook my head and turned to her. "He just seems out of place," I said finally.

She studied him for a moment, her face going pensive. "Probably just some rich guy's driver," she said after a while. "We should keep walking. I feel like my skin is on fire in this heat."

I nodded. She was probably right. I was on-edge and most likely looking for danger when there wasn't any.

By the time we reached the front entrance, my entire back was covered in sweat. My hair was plastered to my head; strands lay across my face as if they had grown directly out of my pores. My sandaled feet slid forward on the verge of slipping completely out of my shoes. And my throat screamed for water.

"Fucking heat," I croaked. I should have brought a bottle of water with me.

"It's like the sun was trying to cook us as we walked." Kara wheezed, her breathing shallow.

"Please tell me you have a tissue or a bath towel in your purse."

"A bath towel?" Kara ran her hand over her forehead. "I might just go dive in that enormously large fountain they have over there."

I glanced over in the direction she was looking and found a marble statue of a woman wearing a toga in the center, holding an upturned jug in her hand. Mist smoked out as water cascaded down into the pooling water below. "You make the first move, and I promise I will follow."

She laughed. "No, I think that's more your speed."

"Don't tempt me." I ran my sticky arm across my forehead as if that would help. All it did was add to the already gritty, clammy sheen of sweat covering my face.

I spotted Jonah standing outside the large gold and white cathedral doors waiting. An immobile force of a man wearing a short-sleeved white button-down shirt and dark green pants. Parishioners gave him a wide berth. I didn't blame them. He was giving off this 'get the fuck away from me' vibe that was hard to ignore. I loved it.

He watched us as we made our way toward him. Correction, those brown eyes were *glued* to Kara as if she were just the spiritual healing he needed. I chuckled.

"What?" Kara asked, her eyes on Jonah as she straightened her cream-colored short dress.

I glanced at her. She had worn her long red hair down and had even curled the ends. Something she almost never did. I didn't have the heart to tell her what it looked like now.

"Oh, nothing," I said, smiling.

In the past few weeks, she and Jonah had been giving each other some extremely heated looks when they thought no one was watching. It was cute. And I really wished they would just go ahead and get down with it. Kara needed to have someone put a smile on her face.

"D, that man is sexy as hell," Kara said.

I turned to her. "Wow, you managed to curse. Well, your version of cursing, at least, and you said hell before we even got inside." I shook my head and linked my arm with hers. "You're such a heathen, Kara."

"Shut up, Nicole. And I'm serious. Give me some pointers."

"Outside of church?" I asked in mock outrage.

"Forget it." She turned to me. "Do you remember your mantra?"

"Yes, I will not be cynical."

She nodded. "Good."

"Welcome. Are you new?" a woman asked.

Kara and I whipped around and came face to face with three young girls. They stood behind us, wearing white lacy dresses that came to their ankles. Smiles stretched across their faces as they took us in. I was surprised they weren't covered in sweat. I mean seriously, how the hell did they manage to be covered from head to toe and not be affected by this heat?

The blonde-haired girl looked like she was the oldest: maybe early twenties. She kept her gaze steady as she continued to smile, waiting for our response. She gave off an air of authority, as though she commanded the space around her and everyone else were mere obstacles in her way. *Okay, yes, I was telegraphing.* Honestly, while she did give off this sort of, 'I'm in charge' vibe, she also had an openness about her. Like she wanted to invite you in.

The dark-haired girl looked no older than eighteen. Her dark green eyes held a well of inquisitiveness that gave me the impression she was trying to figure something out about us. Her slight build looked unassuming. But then again, the dress she wore was probably meant to give that impression. The younger girl, maybe no older than seventeen with similar features, stood by her side. Her dark brown hair was pulled up into a tight bun—stretching her face into a porcelain mask. She kept her green eyes averted, only stealing a few fleeting glances at us as she pressed into the other girl. Sisters?

I felt movement behind me but didn't look away from the girls. Jonah's familiar cool woodsy scent washed over me. The girls' eyes tracked up, taking him in.

Kara smiled and I worked my mouth into a facsimile of the gesture.

"Yes," Kara said to the girls. "We are most eager to hear the wisdom of Boyd."

*Most eager to hear the wisdom of Boyd?* When the hell did Kara start talking like that? I glanced at her. She was serious!

*Don't laugh, Nicole. Please, don't laugh. I will not be cynical. I will not be cynical.*

Kara turned to me. "Isn't that right, Nicole?"

"Yes," I said, and immediately went into a coughing fit. Me being here was a bad idea. I'd be surprised if I managed to hold it together for the entire service.

"I'm Sara," the blonde one said. "And this is Juliette and Bridgette. It's very nice to meet you. All are welcome to enjoy the word of Boyd. And we'd love for you to sit with us."

Jonah placed a hand on both our shoulders. "They're with me."

I smiled. Jonah sounded like our pimp.

"You're welcome as well," Juliette said, her voice small, as if speaking up wasn't what she was used to doing. Interesting. Especially since she had no problem making eye contact with us.

Sara turned to me, locking eyes. "Are you sure you won't sit with us?"

"Umm…"

Something in her eyes frightened me. It was a predatory look I'd seen before in a similar situation—the sinister hunger I received at my aunt's church from all the parishioners as they watched me walk toward the altar.

A breeze pushed at my back and suddenly I was back at the outdoor church hidden in the thickness of the bayou. The cloying smell of dead things filled my nose. Water lapped nearby, but I couldn't see it. All the men and women that surrounded me wore false smiles. "Welcome," they'd uttered. "We will heal you," they'd said as they led me to the middle of the clearing.

But I didn't look at them. I had become transfixed on the concrete altar in the middle of the clearing. The ground appeared to have given birth to it. All the vegetation caressed its sides, keeping it cocooned. Safe. The surface gleamed in the moonlight. And the leather straps nailed into the stone had been polished, laying wide. Waiting.

I'd gone so far beyond fear and hope that I never registered the tears streaming down my face until the scene became hazy. Or the fact that they had to carry me the last few steps until my feet no longer felt the ground beneath me.

"No thank you," Jonah said, the timbre of his voice pulling me out of the memory.

I shook myself and both Jonah and Kara looked at me. I turned away from them and swallowed the lump in my throat. "Yes, no thank you," I whispered.

I really didn't need to say it again. I was sure the women had gotten the message. But I needed to say something. They were all staring at me; their scrutiny made my skin itch. It was almost as if they were scratching away at the surface, digging into me. At any moment, they would see the fear building inside and the raw anguish that was taking all my strength to bury once again.

*I will never let anyone tie me to an altar again.*

"Yes, of course," Sara said finally and extended her arm toward the church. "The service will be starting soon."

Jonah's hand went to my back, urging me forward, and I took a step. Sweat had accumulated at the base of my neck. I pulled my hair up and a warm breeze blew across my nape. I glanced up at the sky. White clouds rolled overhead. Our frequent showers were no more. It was almost as if something was holding the water back with an invisible dam. The pressure could be felt in the air, and at any moment, it would become too much. The dam would break, releasing all that water. And with it, an enormous amount of power.

# Acknowledgments

I may have started off alone in a cave—pounding away on my keyboard, giving birth to the book you hold in your hands, but I didn't end up alone. Many people helped me on my journey to publication. So, it's an accomplishment of a dedicated tribe that "Lineage" is now out in the world for all to enjoy!

I thank God for blessing me with the awesome people who have touched my life in so many ways. And for the gift of storytelling. He always knew I would be a writer, he was just waiting for me to realize it and when that didn't work, he sent me a tribe!

To my husband, Bobby, your tough love gave me the gumption I needed to put my work out there. You believed in me and that has made a tremendous difference in my life. Not to mention your hard work to keep a roof over our head while I spent my days working away at my dream. You will always be my rock. I love you to the moon and back!

To my Mom, Gynda McCluskey, thank you for your belief in me. Your encouragement has made such a difference in my life. I love you tremendously.

To my Mother in law, Betty Lewis, thank you so much for your kind words and support with my writing. Your positivity has really helped me throughout this journey. I love you!

To my brother and sister, Carl and Tara, you two believed in me at the beginning. You have always pushed me to excel, and I love you both, always.

To Aunt Pearl Magee, thank you for all the time and hard work you put into making sure my novel shinned. Your wisdom and support has truly helped me. Your joy and belief in me has brought me to tears. I love you and am truly glad we are family.

To Nick Codignotto, my first critique partner. You saw potential in "Lineage" 5,235 drafts ago and was also able to see my characters and really help me keep them consistent. You are an amazing person, and I am so glad to have met you! I can't thank you enough for all the time and dedication you put into my book. And I truly hope I was able to help you as well.

To my awesome beta readers, Amanda Poole, Connie Martinez, Catherine Williams Phillips, Michelle Borne, and Krystal Campbell, all of you have read this book multiple times and have offered so much valuable feedback that I truly wouldn't have gotten to this point without you. Your support and belief in me is cherished.

And a special thanks to Amanda Poole, who is the best damn cheerleader a person can have hands down!!

To all the wonderful individuals in the "Writing Bootcamp Buds" group! OMG, you guys! Seriously, I can't even begin to touch on how much I value your support. Joining the group was definitely a positive step in my writing career. We will be each other's rocks FOREVER!

To my entire family and hosts of friends, your joy at me finally reaching my goal has really touched my heart. All of you have given me the support and encouragement I needed to succeed. I love you all!

To my early editor, Terry Valentine. You saw potential in my work and when you offered to help, I couldn't have been happier. Thank you for your feedback, your extensive notes, and your time.

To my early proofreader, Christine Pingleton, thank you for your kind words and help pointing out my grammar errors.

To my development editor, Loni Crittenden. Thank you for pushing me to dig deep and add those lovely scenes to my book. I really feel that it took my story to the next level. You are an amazing editor and I'm glad we were able to work so well together. And, "Nicoleism" still laughing about that today!

To my line editor, Erica Farner. Thank you so much for your careful attention to my story. I loved your feedback and notes. And I cried, too at **spoiler** scene. You are the best! And it was truly a pleasure working with you!

To Midnight Tide Publishing for giving my book baby another home!

And finally, to my readers, you are in for a journey. So, buckle up buttercup, and be sure to put the kids to bed and remove your pearls. This book will take you there. I hope you enjoy it as much as I enjoyed writing it!

# About the Author

C. Vonzale Lewis is the best-selling author of the Blood & Sacrifice Chronicles and various short fiction. She resides in Hesperia, CA where she spends her days plotting the demise of her enemies. All her stories tend to be dark with a little mystery thrown in and some love to round out the mix. When not writing, she enjoys reading, spending time with her husband, and binge-watching British crime fiction.

# More Books You'll Love

If you enjoyed this story, please consider leaving a review.

Then check out more books from Midnight Tide Publishing!

**The Hex Next Door by Lou Wilham**

What's a little necromancy between family?

For the Crow Witch, Icarus "Rus" Ashthorne, Moondale seemed the perfect hiding place. But like they always say, you can't go home again, and Rus finds out quickly that nothing is how she remembered, while at the same time very little has changed. Then she comes face to face with the only woman she's ever loved, Az Elwood, and... well, things get messier than she thought they ever could.

The Elwoods are a staple of Moondale, respected, feared, powerful, and Azure Elwood was always happy with her place amongst them. Happy to play the part of the good little witch, until Rus Ashthorne. Eleven years ago, Rus got on a bus and left Azure behind, but she's back, with two little girls trailing her like ducklings, and enough unspoken things between them to drown the town.

Now witch hunters are knocking at their proverbial door, the council of magic is being a real pain in the ass, and Rus wonders how much magic it'll take to protect the people she loves from herself and the danger following her.

*Available Now*

These Dangerous Fates by Whitney L. Spradling

**I live in a magical world. A world filled with vampires, shifters, and mages.**
**Mysteriously, I was born without powers.**

After living the past two years in a personal hell, enduring abuse from a fiance I didn't choose, I finally snapped. An act of self-defense against my fiance angers my father, and in retaliation for my actions, he creates the ultimate contest. One that only the most powerful magicals can compete in to win my hand in marriage.

It sounds bleak, but anything has to be better than my current situation. At least, I thought so, until *they* appeared in the middle of the night to whisk me away.

**A vampire prince.**
**A wolf without a pack.**
**A powerful mage.**

My three captors do everything they can to win the contest, and as the attraction between the four of us grows, so does their desire to keep me safe.

When the mystery of my birth comes into play, we begin to question everything I thought I knew about my life. Am I just a human with no magical powers? Or am I something else entirely? One thing is certain, if my captors cannot keep me safe, more than my heart is at stake: my life is on the line.

*Available Now*

**Dead Rockstar by Lillah Lawson**

Stormy Spooner is at her wits' end. Careening towards bitter after a nasty divorce, she sometimes wonders what her life is becoming.

After unearthing a cryptic set of lines from a dusty album cover, Stormy tries the impossible: to resurrect Phillip Deville, enigmatic former frontman of the Bloomer Demons. Stormy's love for her favorite dead rockstar knows no bounds...but it was all supposed to be a joke.

When she answers a knock on her door the next day and finds herself face to face with the dark-haired rock god of her every teenage fantasy, her entire world is turned upside down.

Turns out, she's awakened more than just Philip, and Stormy will have to do battle against a cast of strange characters to keep herself and her new undead boyfriend safe.

*Available Now*